TEMPLAR SECRETS

TEMPLAR SECRETS

Andreas Economou

Copyright © 2017 by Andreas Economou

All rights reserved. No part of this book may be reproduced, scanned, or distributed in any printed or electronic form without permission.

This is a work of fiction. Names, characters, places, and incidents, other than those clearly in the public domain, are either the product of the author's imagination or are used fictitiously, and any resemblance to actual persons, living or dead, business establishments, events, or locales is entirely coincidental.

First Edition: 10/2017
ISBN: 978-9963-2179-6-0

To the ancient Phoenician colonists of Larnaca.

And to those still carrying their genes forward into the future.

Table of Contents

Introduction ix

    PROLOGUE 1

PART ONE: BIRTH **7**
    CHAPTER 1 : BOAZ 11
    CHAPTER 2 : FUGITIVES 32
    CHAPTER 3 : BROTHERHOOD 76
    CHAPTER 4 : BUILDER 112

PART TWO: LIFE **135**
    CHAPTER 5 : JACHIN 139
    CHAPTER 6 : RESTRUCTURING 152
    CHAPTER 7 : TYLER 164
    CHAPTER 8 : ARK 189
    CHAPTER 9 : TORTOSA 207
    CHAPTER 10 : ASSASSINS 229
    CHAPTER 11 : CLOUD 256
    CHAPTER 12 : SHEBA 268

PART THREE: DEATH **283**
    CHAPTER 13 : TUBAL-CAIN 287
    CHAPTER 14 : GUNPOWDER 327
    CHAPTER 15 : FORMATION 350
    CHAPTER 16 : WELL 377
    CHAPTER 17 : THEFT 392
    CHAPTER 18 : PAPYRUS 412
    CHAPTER 19 : NORTH 418

APPENDIX **447**
    Chronology of Events *448*
    Historical Persons *455*

Introduction

> *"The lunatic is all idée fixe, and whatever he comes across confirms his lunacy. You can tell him [the lunatic] by the liberties he takes with common sense, by his flashes of inspiration, and by the fact that sooner or later he brings up the Templars."*
> Umberto Eco, *Foucault's Pendulum*, p. 67

I've also heard it whispered that anyone who is mentally unstable will never admit to it. So, for the record, allow me to state this: "I consider myself completely sane."

"All the same," you may ask, "what on earth compelled you to risk everyone's ridicule by writing a book about the Knights Templar?" Well, for starters, to set things straight. I believe too many authors and writers have disrespected the Templars in recent years, not to mention that they've taken the Templar name *'in vain.'* (Yes, I know: this last comment doesn't bode well for my sanity's case either.) But it's true. Over the past few decades, all sorts of ludicrous stories about the Templars have come out—with them forging evil conspiracies, popping up on every corner of the globe, or even practicing magic and time travel—stories, mind you, which have nothing to do with what they really were, or stood for, as a religious Order. So if you're reading this, hoping to find a Templar waving a wand about, uttering spells, or searching for the Holy Grail, you've bought the wrong book. (Yes, there is a sacred relic involved—we're talking about the Templars, after all—but it isn't the Holy Grail.)

My second reason for writing this was that throughout the 22 years I used to be a Mason I'd often felt something was amiss. While taking part in the meetings, I had a persistent nagging in the back of my mind that the institution's origins were not at all what the official history claimed: i.e. that Freemasonry was descended from the stonemasons of old. It's true, there *were* medieval elements involved—this was more than evident in the rituals—but I gradually became convinced it couldn't have originated from illiterate stone-working laborers. However, it was only *after* I left the Masons behind me that things became clearer. And when I started reading about the Order of the Knights Templar, many seemingly unrelated issues just clicked into place (see how the *'flashes of inspiration'* light up?)

This novel is divided into three Parts: *Birth*, *Life* and *Death*—with every stage being a powerful symbol for each of the three Degrees of Craft (or, Blue Lodge) Freemasonry: When an Entered Apprentice is initiated, he is considered much akin to a newborn who, on first sight, is unaccustomed to his new surroundings, fumbling about with no knowledge or abilities. Passing on to the Second, or Fellow Craft, Degree, he is now an adult who must familiarize himself with this world and make sense of it. And finally, upon being raised as a Master Mason, he is now at a wiser, more mature age, awaiting the inevitable destiny which binds us all: Death.

These three fundamental life-stages are useful for following our principal hero's Freemasonic path in Cyprus, but also the steps he takes in solving the puzzle this institution poses for him. At the same time, they provide a valuable framework for witnessing how the surviving Knights Templar could have morphed into modern-day Masons in England, and how a Phoenician ultimately developed into Hiram Abiff, the tragic protagonist of Masonic lore.

(In case anyone is wondering why I chose an obscure, insignificant location such as Cyprus for the main character, let me remind them that before the Templars were arrested that island was their last headquarters.)

Introduction

Just to clarify, this is a work of fiction—however much I'd like to claim otherwise. But, whereas the Templars may provide ample ground for crank stories and loony conspiracy theories, what I tried to achieve here is a narrative that's plausible. And I believe I've achieved this by taking advantage of gaps in the historical record, not by distorting it. To this end, feel free to peruse the **Appendix** which contains a list of actual events and persons relevant to the overall story. My aim isn't only to entertain, but to inform as well.

Today, 710 years later—to the day—when the arrests led to the Templar Order's annihilation, the fascination and mystique it provokes remain undiminished. Adding to the attraction (and credibility to the book's timing) is the fact that this year also marks the tercentenary since the official unveiling of Freemasonry, and the founding of its very first Grand Lodge.

If you persevere for a couple of chapters, I can guarantee you shall enjoy it.

Andreas Economou
Friday, October 13, 2017

PROLOGUE

Jerusalem
955 BCE *(Before Current Era)*

A FEVERISH CHILL was making its way down his spine. All the same, Hiram peeked out from behind the inwardly folding doors. *Someone is there. And whoever it is, he's not supposed to be inside the Temple*, the Master thought. A moment earlier, and while in the Holy of Holies, Hiram was certain he'd heard the distinct sound of a metal object crashing onto the floor outside. It was just before nightfall, so whomever caused that noise couldn't have been one of the priests. They had already left to start their observance of the Sabbath, and it was unlikely any of them would've returned. But he needed to make certain the operation, and his getaway, hadn't been jeopardized in any way. So, mustering his courage, the Master closed the lavishly decorated doorway behind him and descended the steps to the Temple's Holy Place to investigate.

Keeping his ears peeled for any sound, Hiram soon arrived on the Hekhal ground floor. Due to the hour, just a hint of light filtered through the clerestory windows up high, which meant he could only depend on his hearing and sense of touch to discover if there was an intruder. Coming up against the golden altar of incense, at the foot of the stairs, he stepped off to the right. And as he cautiously inched forward, in front of the southern row of the shewbread-bearing tables, the Master soon stumbled upon the source of the noise. One of the tall, menorah-like lamp stands was lying on the ground. *How did this get knocked over?* Hiram wondered, and was about to bend over to lift it up, but never got the chance to follow through. At that very instant both his arms were grabbed from behind and held onto tight.

A sinister voice breathed into his ear. "What are you doing here, builder?"

Hiram gasped, nevertheless replied decisively, "That is none of your concern." And heaving his arms forward he managed to free himself from the stranger's grasp. His assailant was definitely not a member of his crew—since Hiram didn't recognize the voice—so he knew that no loyalty, or sympathy, would be forthcoming. The Master did have the Ring, however, but somehow he doubted whether knowledge of the fact would make any difference to his attacker's violent intentions. So, the only sensible thing to do, it seemed to Hiram at that moment, was to try to get as far away as possible from this ruffian, and from the Holy of Holies. Turning left, the Master started running towards the Temple's exit, to the east. But in the dim light filtering through the doorway he saw the outlines of two more figures blocking his escape. They were brandishing weapons at their sides, a fact which forced Hiram to stop abruptly in his tracks.

"You *will* tell us what you are doing in here, Phoenician," Hiram heard the man on the right say. Then, as the previous thug came up from behind and grabbed hold of the Master's arms once again, the person who had spoken last ordered the one standing next to him, "Go look in the Debir." Wielding a sword, the third bearded ruffian made his way through the Hekhal, past Hiram, walked up the steps and cautiously opened the folding doors which concealed the Holy of Holies. The small candle that Hiram had left burning there was still alight. After taking a look inside, he turned, shouting out in alarm to the others, "It's not here!"

Prologue

The Master could feel his captor's grip tighten after hearing this, and the ruffian in front of him let out a growl. "Where is it?" the apparent arch-thug yelled, as he stepped forward. Hiram's reply was one of total silence. However, this only served to infuriate his interrogator even more. When the hoodlum got within reach, he used the metal rod in his hand to strike hard on Hiram's left shoulder. The Master let out a cry of pain, but was swift in his thinking: he brought his right foot all the way up and kicked the ruffian in the groin. Then, Hiram retracted his head back with force, butting the one holding him in the face. His captor momentarily eased his grip, freeing the Master to start running for the exit. However, the one who was in front of him quickly recoiled from holding his aching genitals and grabbed hold of Hiram's flapping robe as he passed by. This threw the Master off balance and he fell down, hitting his head on the wooden floor. By the time he managed to stand up, he was dazed and surrounded by all three hoodlums.

"How did you get in? Where is it?" asked the thug who'd been kicked, in an even more menacing tone. Hiram, once again, did not reply. So the ruffian in charge came forward with his metal rod and hit Hiram, even more forcefully, on the other shoulder—but withdrawing swiftly before Hiram could manage to kick him again. The Master did not give them the satisfaction of revealing how much more it hurt this time; he held his ground and noble silence. The unarmed, third goon, however, then came close, from behind, and punched Hiram on the back of the head. "Where *IS IT?*" the same ruffian asked in anger.

Hiram began to realize he was in grave danger. *I probably won't get out of here alive. Not unless I do something now*, he thought. So he pounced, attempting to grab the chief hoodlum's metal rod, as it was the nearest weapon available. While Hiram was struggling with him to get possession of the rod, he heard that ruffian's desperate cry to the others, "Stop him!"

He'd almost wrested the weapon from the arch-thug's

grasp, when the Master failed to notice one important detail: the whooshing sound the sword made, as it sliced through the air on its way to the side of his neck.

If it had been at all possible for him to see and think, within the next few seconds, Hiram would've been very confused as to why his head was rolling haphazardly around on the floor. And he would have been especially shocked to see all the blood spewing out from what used to be the base of his neck. But, the most curious thing of all would've been to notice that the rest of his body was still standing, a few feet away...

PART ONE

BIRTH

GEORGE

Chapter 1

BOAZ

Larnaca, Cyprus
2011 CE *(Current Era)*

THE ABRUPT OPENING of the door filled the near pitch-black chamber with an abundance of light. A silhouette of a man holding a sword in his hand stood in the doorway. "They are ready for you now," he announced.

It was what George had been waiting for all day.

TWO HOURS EARLIER, at home, George Makrides shut the book he'd unsuccessfully been trying to read. It was still a bit early, but being unable to concentrate he stood up and decided it was time to start getting ready. In fact, George had a good reason for feeling restless: that evening was when he'd finally become a Freemason.

So, after taking a shower, he carefully shaved off his three-day stubble, making certain that no stray facial hair remained. Then, as instructed, he put on his new dark suit over a white shirt, as well as the black tie his friend, Alex (the one who'd proposed him for membership), had given him as a gift. After getting dressed, Makrides looked into the mirror. He had a strong-limbed body of average height, a broad, but handsome-looking face with intelligent hazel eyes, and short dark hair that was just curly enough to always seem untidy. Nevertheless, the only thought to cross his mind, after seeing himself in those clothes, was: *I look like a penguin*—and it made him chuckle. Being a single, 28-year-old professor of mathematics at a local university, didn't often give him cause to dress so formally. But there was nothing he could do about it now, so he took a deep breath and stepped out of his apartment.

Arriving earlier than agreed at the specified address, George started to climb the broad, marble staircase, which was just inside the double door entrance. And while he glanced at some old group photos, which were displayed on the stairwell's walls—like windows into bygone years—the memories came flooding back: As a teen he'd attended the high school still across the street. Makrides remembered how sinister that white, two-storied building had seemed to his classmates at the time. Filled with fascination—and with every degree of conviction—the young boys used to whisper that, among other things, the Masons sacrificed live roosters in there, and that they would then drink the fowls' blood as part of their evil rituals. George chuckled, as he walked on up. *I guess I'll get to find out soon enough if there was any truth in those stories.*

When he reached the main floor, Makrides entered a large room and saw it was filled with men all dressed exactly like him: Many were huddled around a bar that was to his immediate left as he came through the wide doorway; others were scattered between the rows of long tables in the middle of the room; and a few more were gathered outside, on the balcony, talking and smoking. No one had noticed him come in, and he was still taking in his surroundings when he heard a familiar voice call out his name.

"George, you're early!" Alex said with a smile, as he stepped closer.

Alex was George's oldest and dearest friend. They had been close to each other ever since their very first day at a Greek primary school—a day which already seemed like a lifetime ago to both of them. Although they were born in different parts of England, chance, and their repatriated parents, had brought them together at the start of school in Cyprus. Their friendship continued throughout high school as well. And they were even in the same military unit when they enlisted for the compulsory, two-year service in the National Guard. Their paths separated, somewhat, during their university years—with George at Oxford and Alex in Canterbury—but they managed to keep in touch.

In Alex's final year at the University of Kent, he joined a local Masonic Lodge. And, on his return to the island, when a new English-speaking Lodge opened in Larnaca—under the auspices of the recently established Cypriot Grand Lodge—he transferred to it. Ever since, he'd been pestering George to join as well. But, Makrides resisted for quite some time, mainly because of the bad reaction he got from his parents when he told them he was thinking of doing it. In fact, their opinion wasn't the exception: a large percentage of the Greek-Cypriot community had strong negative feelings about Freemasonry. And this resulted in the circulation of many bizarre stories about the goings on in Masonic Lodges—as evidenced from George's high school memories. Nonetheless, Alex persisted and was finally able to convince George that all those silly rumors were just that: nothing but nonsense.

Alex towered over his friend with his tall, broad-shouldered frame and round shaped, pleasing face. Giving George his hand, his smile widened, displaying a full set of pearly teeth. "It's so nice to see you here at last," he said, and when another gentleman came near, Alex introduced them. "Worshipful Master, this is George, our candidate for tonight." The Worshipful Master also shook hands with George and welcomed him to the Lodge.

Alex asked his Masonic superior, "Since George arrived a bit early do you think we have time for a drink?"

"No, I believe it's best if he went straight in."

Go 'straight in' where? George wondered, but was soon to find out. The Worshipful Master gestured to another gentleman, and when he came near, the Master of the Lodge gave instructions. "Please take George to the Chamber of Reflection and tell him what he's supposed to do." Then, turning back to George, he said with an encouraging smile, "Good luck. We'll see you on the other side."

Unsure whether that was supposed to be a good thing, George, nevertheless, smiled back and thanked the Lodge Master. He then followed the other man (who introduced himself as Nicos) down to the end of the hall. And after going through a couple of doors, George found himself in a very small, dimly lit room. When Nicos shut the door behind them, George realized that the striking feature of this tiny room was that its walls, the back of the door, and its ceiling, were all painted black. Even the floor tiles were of a darkish hue. *The only things missing are a cauldron and a few hook-nosed witches to stir the boiling brew. But it's so small, none of them would fit in here,* he thought. He was desperately trying to cheer himself up.

On the ceiling there was a round, flat lamp (also painted black), upon which a white skull-and-crossbones design permitted a tiny amount of light to trickle down into the poorly lit room. Contributing also, somewhat, to its eerie illumination were a few backlit panels on the walls, with transparent phrases printed on their black surfaces.

Makrides did not have time to read what they said, however, because Nicos spoke. "You are to remain in here, George, until someone else comes to get you. When I leave, please take off your tie and jacket, any undershirt you may be wearing, your belt and your watch. Also, empty your pockets of everything, especially if it's made of metal. Then, remove your right shoe and fold the right leg of your trousers all the way up to your knee. Good luck," Nicos told him in an austere, military fashion. He then turned around and left. George was left standing there dazed.

Removing his jacket and placing it on the only chair available, he slowly started to follow Nicos's instructions. While doing so, he also read the sayings on the wall-mounted, backlit panels. The first one was the all familiar, *'Know thyself.'* The second advised: *'If you are afraid, leave.' That's not very reassuring*, George thought, but continued to read on. The third one cautioned: *'Withdraw, if you are here out of curiosity.'*

This last one gave him pause. Was that why he wanted to join? Sure, curiosity as to what went on in there was a factor, but it wasn't the only one—or even one of the major reasons, at that. *But come to think of it, what are my motives for joining?* George asked himself next. The first one to pop to mind, and which also made him chuckle a bit, was that he'd finally be able to get Alex off his back. *Then, there's the promised improvement of myself, isn't there?* A question which inevitably prompted a further one: *But how am I supposed to accomplish that?* The only answer he could give, however, at that point in time was: *Obviously, they must have very old, secret, and trusted methods.* All these thoughts reminded him again of the potent mystique surrounding this international institution in his mind. Everyone always seemed to be sure the Masons were in possession of ancient, mysterious, and powerful secrets; or, even maybe that they were all part of a clandestine religion. But, his train of thought was suddenly interrupted by the sound of three loud, consecutive bangs. They appeared to be coming from somewhere inside the building and it was as if someone was pounding a piece of hollow wood with something.

Taking off his tie and shirt, in order to remove his undershirt, he turned his attention next to the small desk up against one of the walls. Painted pitch black, as per usual, that table along with a solitary chair were the only pieces of furniture inside the miniature room. A number of unrelated objects were placed on it: There was a loaf of bread on a dish (which seemed to have been there for quite some time); a glass of water (that also didn't look fresh); a candlestick with a burnt, unlit candle on top; a minuscule hourglass; and a small, toy-like rooster. But the most striking object of them all was the human skull at the center of the desk.

I hope this isn't one of the previous candidates, George nervously joked to himself. Still smiling from this, he was startled when someone holding a sword suddenly burst into the Chamber of Reflection and announced that *'they'* were expecting him. In front of the man's trousers hung a white, rectangular apron, the thick sky-blue lines of which made it look a lot like the back of an envelope. He also wore a down-pointing triangular collar, of a similar color, on his shoulders, and white gloves on his hands.

"Take off your right shoe and fold the right leg of your trousers up to your knee," said the man, strictly, while offering no introduction as to who he was. Makrides had neglected to carry out those steps. *I just hope this doesn't mean I'll end up like the skull over there,* he thought uneasily. After he'd done as instructed, the Officer picked up a slipper from the floor and told George to place it on his shoeless foot. He then opened George's shirt, all the way down, and told him to turn around. Without another word, the Mason passed a piece of rope, shaped like a noose, loosely around George's neck and placed a blindfold over his eyes. Makrides couldn't see a thing.

Even though Alex had cautioned him not to, nevertheless, George had read about this part of the ceremony on a website. However, reading about it and experiencing it firsthand were two entirely different things. He felt unsettled. *What shall I do now? Should I make a run for it, or wait and see what this is all about?* George wondered. *The thing is, all these people have been through the same experience, and everyone seems to have survived it... I guess.* This last thought comforted him, somewhat, so he decided to let fate take its course.

Then the Officer instructed George to come with him and holding onto his arm he guided the blindfolded candidate out of the Chamber. After Makrides took a few cautious steps, the Mason stopped and knocked (on what George assumed was a door) three times. Indistinct voices could be heard from inside, and a moment later George sensed something opening (a small window perhaps?). A voice clearly asked, "Who goes there?"

The Mason beside him replied, "Mr. George Makrides, a poor, blind candidate who seeks to be admitted to the mysteries of Freemasonry."

The same voice spoke again. "How does he hope to achieve this privilege?" To which question the man assisting him instructed George to say aloud the following words, "By the help of God, being free and of good reputation." The Mason inside, obviously satisfied by the answer, replied, "Halt, while I report to the Lodge Master." And then shut whatever he'd opened up in the first place.

A few more moments of indistinct conversations followed from within until George heard the unmistakable sound of a door opening. The Mason holding him led George a few steps forward, let go and walked away. Standing there, all by himself, Makrides heard the door closing behind him. Although he was indeed in a state of total darkness, George's other senses told him he was in a room full of people. Aside from the slight telltale sounds, which he'd occasionally hear, the bodily heat radiating from everyone made the room he was in much warmer than outside. George tried to imagine how he looked to them. Blindfolded, with his shirt open all the way, his trouser's leg folded up, a slipper on his foot, and with a noose hanging around his neck: *I probably look like a disheveled bum being led to the gallows.*

Someone came close, interrupting his thoughts, and within the next instant, George felt the edge of something sharp (possibly a dagger) pressed up against his left breast. A new voice asked, "Do you feel something?" And Makrides replied meekly, "Yes." The object pressing against him was removed (to George's immense relief) and someone took hold of his left arm and guided him a few steps forward.

(He was later told that this part of the ritual—that of baring the candidate's breast—was introduced because a Lodge had initiated a female by mistake, a couple of centuries ago. Presumably being a woman who didn't look too much like one, legend has it she'd managed to deceive those early Masons into initiating her—which was, of course, an abomination. Freemasonry was supposed to be, and was, especially during those formative years, an all-male affair. Hence, the baring of the breast to make sure it wasn't a female one.)

Then a different person with a booming, raspy voice, which George recognized as that of the Worshipful Master's, began to speak. "Mr. Makrides, as no one can be made a Mason, unless he is free and of mature age, I demand of you, are you an adult, free man?"

The Mason standing next to him whispered into George's ear, prompting him to say, "I am." And the Master of the Lodge went on. "With this assurance, I will now ask you to kneel while the blessing of Heaven is invoked on our proceedings."

The person beside him helped George kneel on a stool that was apparently in front of him the whole time. Then, he heard three loud bangs—one coming from the front, one towards the back, and one to his right—and the sound of people rising to their feet.

The Lodge's chief Officer began the prayer. "Grant Thine aid, Almighty Father and Grand Governor of the Universe, to our present assembly, and allow…"

George had never been religious, mainly because he felt that organized religion wasn't beneficial to mankind (much to his mother's dismay). So, he sort of tuned out after the beginning of the prayer. On the other hand, he did believe in an abstract, overall guiding force in the universe; a belief which, as it seems, was an important prerequisite for joining the Brotherhood. He'd been pleasantly surprised to find out that Freemasonry also had a similarly vague belief system. However, it remained to be seen whether it wasn't an organized religion in itself... At that point, though, his thoughts were interrupted by the simultaneous chanting of, "So mote it be," by a number of Masons in the room, presumably following the end of the prayer. George didn't know if he'd missed something important in the prayer's wording, so he decided not to daydream anymore and to pay close attention from that moment on.

The Worshipful Master's booming voice rang out again. "In all cases of hardship and peril, in whom do you put your trust?" The man next to him leaned into George's ear and prompted him to reply, "In God." To which the Worshipful Master remarked, "Relying on such strong support you may safely rise. For where the name of God is invoked, we trust no danger can occur."

This was the cue for the one assisting him, to help George rise to his feet. Then, three loud bangs were heard once more, from the same locations, and the Worshipful Master said, "The Brethren at all cardinal points will take notice that Mr. Makrides is about to pass in view before them to show he is a fit and proper person to be made a Mason."

Still unable to see anything, George was next led around the room a few times, at which point the Worshipful Master posed another question. "Do you declare on your honor that you freely offer yourself a Candidate for the mysteries and privileges of Freemasonry?"

George, his right arm held by his attendant, was prompted by him to reply, "I do."

After an order by the Lodge Master, the assisting Mason (who'd been addressed as the Junior Deacon) whispered to Makrides they were about to go up a flight of four steps. Although George stumbled a bit on the first one, he kept his balance, and they shortly arrived on the higher level. Then, the Junior Deacon told him to take three steps forward.

George did as instructed even though on his third step he felt his left foot hit a piece of hollow furniture. He subsequently heard the Worshipful Master speak once again. This time George knew the Master of the Lodge was directly above him.

"Are you willing to take a Solemn Obligation, to keep the secrets and mysteries of the Order secure?"

George needed no prompting now. He immediately replied, "I am." *Finally! We're getting to the part with the secrets*, he thought excitedly.

"Then you will kneel on your left knee," the Worshipful Master commanded. After George had done so, the Master of the Lodge continued, "Give me your right hand which I place on the Volume of Sacred Law." Someone took hold of his hand and placed it on (what George thought must be) a book. He could also feel loose objects on its top, beneath his palm.

The Worshipful Master said, "State your name at length and repeat after me: I..." George did so, filling in his name. "... in the presence of the Great Architect of the Universe, and of this warranted Lodge of Free and Accepted Masons, of my own free will and accord, I hereby solemnly promise and swear, that I will always hele, conceal, and never reveal any part of the secrets or mysteries belonging to the Free and Accepted Masons..."

George dutifully repeated every sentence, as the Obligation went on to list all the ways Masons were not supposed to disclose whatever they heard or saw in the Lodge, and of the ensuing shame if one did. It concluded with the phrase, "So help me God, and keep me steadfast in this my Solemn Obligation as an Entered Apprentice Freemason."

The Worshipful Master spoke again. "What you have repeated is considered a Solemn Obligation. And to render it complete, you will now seal it with your lips on the Volume of Sacred Law."

With his right hand already resting upon the Book,

George bent over and lightly kissed it. He did not care for this part very much.

The Worshipful Master then asked him, "Having remained for some time in a state of total darkness, what, in your present situation, is the foremost wish of your heart?"

The Junior Deacon whispered into his ear, "Light," and George repeated it. So, the Master of the Lodge commanded, "Let that blessing be restored to the Candidate." And after striking his gavel loudly, and a single clap from everyone else in the room, George's blindfold was removed.

Makrides spent the next couple of seconds trying to get his eyes accustomed to the light. Standing directly in front and above him—behind a thin brown desk—was the Worshipful Master, also wearing an apron and a triangular collar. His regalia, though, were more elaborate than the previous ones George had seen: they had gold trimmings and designs on them. The other thing he initially noticed was an illuminated triangle on the wall, almost above the Worshipful Master's head. Inside it there was a depiction of a single human eye, reminding him of the one shown hovering above an unfinished pyramid on the back of the American dollar bill.

Interrupting George's thoughts, the Worshipful Master said, "Having been restored to the blessing of material light, let me point out what we consider the three great lights in Freemasonry. These are the Volume of Sacred Law, the Square, and the Compass." He then took George's right hand off the book and commanded him, "Rise, our newly obligated Brother among Masons."

As George was standing up, he noticed that the Book his hand had been placed upon was the Bible. And also that the loose objects he'd felt beneath his palm were a square and a compass, arranged in the all too familiar way: the square resting over the compass's legs. *Just like a couple of mirror-image triangles, both of which are missing their horizontal sides, one pointing up and the other down,* was George's spontaneous, geometrical observation.

The Junior Deacon, having received instructions from the Lodge Master, once again, took hold of George's arm and led him to the right of the now seated Master. As they went, George noticed there were other people sitting on that elevated part of the room. And they were all wearing much more ornately decorated aprons and collars; some even had ceremonial golden chains placed around their shoulders. On reaching their destination, the Worshipful Master turned, facing George. "Brother George, by your gentle and candid behavior this evening you have, symbolically, escaped two great perils. The dangers you have escaped are those of stabbing and strangling; for on entering the Lodge this poniard..." and he picked up an unsheathed dagger, "... was presented to your naked left breast, and if you had rashly attempted to rush forward, you would have been an accessory to your own murder." However, what impressed George the most, out of all this, was that everything the Worshipful Master had said was delivered by heart.

When the Master put the dagger down, the Junior Deacon removed the noose from around George's neck and handed it to his Masonic superior, who held it up. "Likewise, there was also this cable-tow, with a running noose about your neck, which would have made any attempt at retreat equally lethal."

The Worshipful Master handed the cable-tow to someone beside him, and went on, always from memory. "Having taken the Great and Solemn Obligation of a Mason, I am now permitted to inform you that there are several degrees in Freemasonry, with each having its own unique secrets. I shall therefore proceed to entrust you with the secrets of *this* Degree."

After George complied on how to stand, the Worshipful Master ordered him, "You will now take a short pace towards me. This is the first regular Step in Freemasonry, and it is in this position that the secrets of the Degree are communicated. They consist of a Sign, a Grip and a Word."

When George performed the Step, the Worshipful Master

stood, raised his leveled right hand and said, "Place your hand this way, with the thumb extended out in the form of a square, to the left of your windpipe. The Sign is then given by withdrawing the hand sharply across the throat and bringing it to the side."

Makrides copied him and the Lodge's chief Officer explained. "This is an ancient reference to the penalty of our Obligation. It implies that as men of honor we would rather have our throats cut across than disclose the secrets entrusted to us."

The Worshipful Master then proceeded by taking George's right hand into his. "The Grip is given by a distinct pressure of the thumb on the joint of the other's index finger. This Grip demands a word, a word highly valued amongst Masons as a guard to their privileges. Great care must therefore be observed in communicating it. However, to enable you to do so, I must first tell you what the word is: It is *BOAZ*."

After George and the Worshipful Master had enacted the secret handshake and went through a process of repeating the word *Boaz*, George was informed that, "This word originates from the left-hand pillar which stood at the entrance of King Solomon's Temple, in Jerusalem. It was so named after Boaz, the great-grandfather of David, who was a king of Israel. The meaning of the word is: *'In Strength.'*"

Following the Master's instructions, the Junior Deacon then led George down to the main level of the Lodge. Its floor resembled a giant chessboard, with large white and black sequentially placed tiles traversing its entire width and breadth. Arriving at the Senior Warden's pedestal, in the west, that Officer—the Lodge's second in command—stood up to speak. "Worshipful Master, I present to you Brother George, for whom I humbly solicit some mark of your approval." To which the Worshipful Master replied, "Brother Senior Warden, I entrust you to clothe him with the distinguishing badge of a Mason."

The Senior Warden descended from his pedestal, and

placed a white, unadorned lambskin apron around George's waist. He said, "Brother George, by the Lodge Master's command, I invest you with the distinctive apron of a Mason. It is more ancient than the Golden Fleece, more honorable than the Garter or any other Order in existence, being the badge of innocence and the bond of friendship."

The Senior Warden returned to his seat after which the Worshipful Master instructed the Junior Deacon to guide George to the North-Eastern part of the Lodge. Upon arrival, the Worshipful Master addressed George once again. "It is conventional, to lay the foundation stone at the North-East corner of each building. You, being newly initiated into Freemasonry, are placed at the North-East part of the Lodge to symbolically represent that very cornerstone. I shall now go on to put your principles to the test, by calling upon you to exercise that virtue which may justly be described as the distinguishing quality of a Freemason. And by that I mean, Charity."

The Junior Deacon, holding a blue velvet bag in his hands, came close to George and asked him, "Have you anything to give for Charity?"

But I left all my money, and everything else, in the Chamber of Reflection, was George's immediate thought. He remained silent.

As if he'd read his mind, the Junior Deacon posed a different question. "Were you deprived of all valuables before entering this Lodge?"

George nodded.

"And if you had not been so prevented would then you give freely?" the Junior Deacon asked again.

"Yes, I would," George replied.

The Junior Deacon turned to face his superior. "Worshipful Master, our new Brother assures me he was deprived of all valuables prior to entering the Lodge, or else he would give freely,"

"I congratulate you on your honorable sentiments," the Worshipful Master said to George. "This trial was not made in order to mock your feelings. It was done for three special reasons: First, to put your values to the test. Second, to show your Brothers that you had neither money, nor metallic objects on you—for if you did, it would have been necessary to repeat the ceremony of your initiation, thus far. And third, as a warning to your own heart, that should you ever meet a Brother in distressed circumstances, you will remember that you were received into Masonry poor and penniless and cheerfully embrace the opportunity to practice the virtue of charity."

The Lodge Master then instructed George, at length, on how to apply the working tools of an Entered Apprentice to hone his morals. And when that was finally over, he said, "You may now leave us in order to restore your attire."

Once outside the Temple, George was at a loss on where his clothes were. Fortunately, the Outer Guard—an Officer known as the Tyler—who sat there, showed him where the Chamber of Reflection was. He also gave George a plastic bag containing a pair of white gloves. "Alex asked me to give you these," he whispered. "You're supposed to put them on before you go back."

When George got dressed, he secured the lambskin apron around his waist, put the white gloves on, and dejectedly headed to the Lodge entrance to be readmitted. He felt disappointed because the ceremony was not at all what he'd expected. Still, he did harbor a smidgen of hope that something more interesting might happen when he went in again.

The Tyler knocked three times, and after he announced George's return, the door opened wide. Makrides entered and stood in the middle of the room for about five minutes, listening to a long-winded post-initiation Charge (filled with clichéd, unmoving principles) which the Worshipful Master delivered, as always, by heart. After it was over, George was led to sit in the northeastern-most seat on the row to his left. He remained there throughout the—also unremarkable—ceremony, which followed, for the Closing of the Lodge.

During all that time, George's only thoughts were: *That's it? No significant insights? Their legendary secrets are just a handshake and a meaningless word?*

He had expected so much more.

✢ ✢ ✢

ABOUT TWO WEEKS later, George and Alex found themselves once again in the same Masonic Temple. This time, though, they'd come to witness an initiation ceremony of a Lodge other than their own. Pavlos, a mutual friend, had invited them to see how his Greek-speaking Lodge received new members. It prided itself for staging the best ceremonies, out of all the Greek Lodges on the island, and Pavlos promised it would be an interesting and completely novel experience for them.

And it was. As soon as the candidate was brought in, disheveled and blindfolded, someone placed the tip of a sword against his naked breast. He was then told by the Lodge's Worshipful Master that the sword's edge symbolized the remorse he'd feel if he ever thought of betraying the Brotherhood he was about to enter. The use of archaic, non-modern Greek in the ceremony's wording made it difficult at times for George to understand what the Worshipful Master and the others were saying. Nevertheless, the first thing which needed no language to indicate its novelty was the absence of a cable-tow around the candidate's neck. Apparently, for some reason, the Greek Masons had done away with that detail.

The Lodge Master went on to reassure the candidate that Freemasonry is not a religion. At the same time, he stressed that Masons *do* believe in God—who is acknowledged by them as the Great Architect of the Universe—and in the immortality of the soul. The blindfolded candidate was then guided three times around the Lodge, making a stop each time, successively in front of the Junior Warden, the Senior Warden, and, finally, the Worshipful Master. After every round he'd be led to stand between the two tall, bronze-colored columns, which were just inside the Temple's entrance, and then subjected to a tedious moral lecture about what the last perambulation meant. These long-winded explanations were also difficult for George to understand, due to the old-fashioned language used, but also because they were not delivered from memory. None of the Officers seemed to know their *lines* by heart, and some even blundered a few times while reading them.

But, for George, what differentiated the whole process of the candidate's three rounds was that music, obstacles, and various sounds were employed in each one. As soon as the candidate began his first round, everyone sitting in the Temple unexpectedly started to stomp their feet, creating such a deafening racket that it must have startled the young man to death. Likewise, the loud classical music, which all of a sudden erupted in the room, also helped in generating a disturbing atmosphere. And the fact the blindfolded candidate was supposed to step over various objects—symbolizing barriers in life—with the guidance of the Officer next to him, must have been equally unsettling. During the second perambulation, though, the music was less harsh and the only other sound heard came from the rubbing of swords. The barrier objects the candidate had to overcome were less this time, making it a much easier task to reach the Senior Warden. Finally, when the candidate went on his third guided round, which terminated in front of the Worshipful Master, up in the East, no barriers existed, the music was mellow, and a few of the Masons made a light hissing sound—supposed to imitate that of a blowing wind.

Perhaps the most dramatically interesting part of the entire ceremony happened just after the candidate took his Masonic oath, still deprived of sight, and was led out of the Temple. Five Lodge members attached some sort of flammable material at the end of their swords and set them on fire. And when someone turned off all the lights in the room, they and a few candles still alight were the only sources of illumination. The young man was brought back in, to stand between the bronze-colored columns, and the Worshipful Master gave the command for the blindfold to be temporarily removed. Blinking his eyes, the candidate suddenly saw five Masons standing in front of him, with flaming swords in hand, all pointing menacingly in his direction. The Master declared, in a thundering voice, that this was what the candidate would face if he ever went back on the promises he'd given in his oath. After that, the blindfold was once again placed over his eyes, and the young man was led out. George felt certain that his soon-to-be brother had been quite unnerved by the sight of those menacing swords.

After the lights were switched on, and the flaming swords extinguished, the candidate was readmitted to stand between the columns. The Worshipful Master asked his Senior Warden what he most desired for the candidate. He replied "Light," and the Lodge Master gave the order for the permanent removal of the blindfold—which was unceremoniously thrown to the floor. The five sword-bearing Masons were still there, standing in front of the candidate, but this time their blades weren't ablaze, just amicably aimed at the floor. This new situation prompted the Worshipful Master to reassure the young man that those in front of him were no longer his adversaries, but on the contrary, that they were friends prepared to come to his assistance if he ever needed them to.

The candidate was then escorted up to the East where he confirmed his vows once again. What struck George as interesting, about this part, was that immediately after the new Mason reaffirmed his oath, the Worshipful Master placed his sword on the young man's shoulders and head. It was an action very much similar to the way medieval knights used to be dubbed. Makrides made a mental note to look into it.

When the meeting ended, Pavlos insisted the two friends stay for the Festive Board which was to follow in the adjacent large entrance hall. George and Alex accepted, so they dutifully took their seats at one of the long tables.

Alex looked over at George. "Well? What you think about this one?"

"It was certainly more theatrical than *my* initiation, that's for sure," George replied. "I mean... the racket, the loud music, the flaming swords... And all this while the poor chap was blindfolded and half naked? It's as if they *wanted* him to run out of there in fear for his life."

"Yes, the whole thing was rather intimidating, wasn't it?" Alex agreed with a chuckle.

"But what's the point? I still don't get it."

"The point of what?"

George lowered his voice so that those beside them couldn't overhear. "Here we have two vastly different ceremonies, but which both lead up to revealing some words and handshakes, as if they were *'secrets'* of the universe. It doesn't add up. What's it all about?"

Alex smiled. "You've been a Mason for... what? ...two weeks now? And all of a sudden you want to know what it's all about? I've been one for more than five years, and I still don't understand anything." But when he saw how troubled George looked, he added, "Maybe it *is* just a system of self-improvement, like they claim it is. Who knows?"

Raising his voice a bit now, so that Alex could hear him over the laughter and clamor others in the room were making, George asked, "And do you know many Masons who've achieved that?"

"Well, no. But how am I supposed to notice it? We're not exactly dealing with a criminal element here."

"Yes, I realize that. So we agree that whatever moral improvement Freemasonry can bring about, if any, it'll be extremely small—almost unnoticeable. And that's exactly my point. All these half-baked, done-to-death, Sunday-school principles they preach—without providing any tangible ways to achieve them—couldn't have been the starting point for such a successful and long-lasting institution."

George leaned in. "No one can persuade me that looking at a simple gavel is enough to make one think about his conscience and be convinced he shouldn't commit bad deeds. Or that seeing a chisel will seriously make him consider the advantages of a good education. No, there must've been other, completely different motives for creating Freemasonry in the first place."

"Perhaps it's just a glorified, buddy-system, social club—a chance for men to get away from their nagging wives, once in a while, and do a bit of business on the side, as well," Alex suggested with a smile. He was watching a few Masons around them as they joked and talked excitedly with one another.

"Then why lace it with such arcane rituals? No, that doesn't cut it either," George said, frowning. And then he added decisively, "But I will find out!"

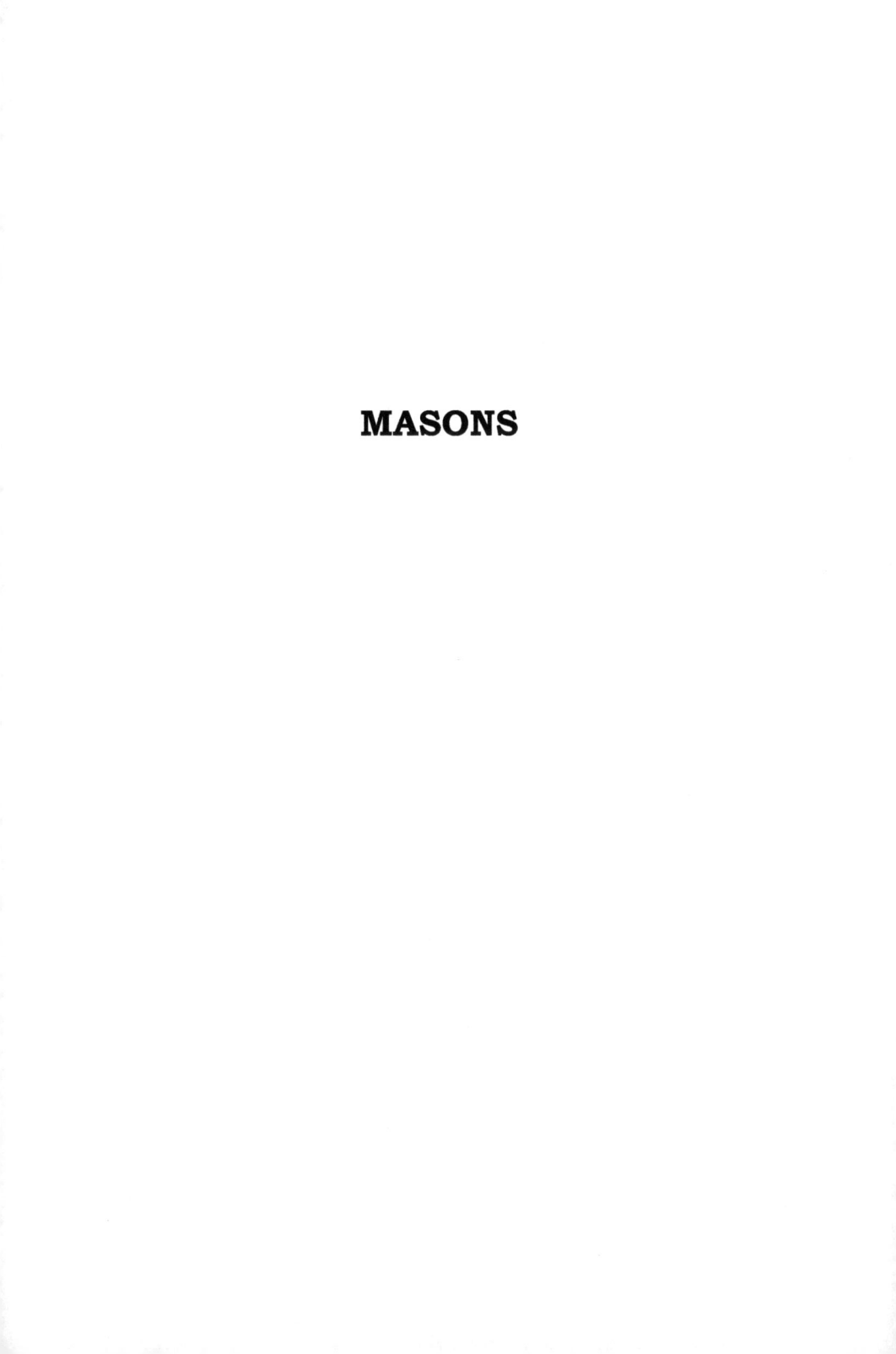

MASONS

CHAPTER 2

FUGITIVES

England
October 1310 CE

PIERRE DE BOLOGNA still wasn't comfortable with the bushy beard on his face. Having been clean-shaven his entire life, the facial hair he'd reluctantly been forced to grow over the past few months—ever since his escape—was often infuriating. It not only got itchy at times, but it also presented a problem whenever he ate soup, or each time he attempted to drink a bit of water—as he had done just now. And even though he did recognize the beard's necessity as a means to alter his appearance, looking down with dismay at the water dripping onto his woolen cloak and leather breeches didn't make him feel any better. Of course, the fact he'd tried to drink from within a shaking carriage, which was pounding its way from Great Yarmouth to Norwich, hadn't made the task easier.

After an almost three-hour journey the wagon finally reached the River Wensum, which cradled Norwich's east side. A sturdy wooden bridge traversed the flowing water, while a fortified gatehouse, evidently still under construction was on the other side. Crossing over into the city, the carriage driver expertly guided his horses past the Great

Hospital and stopped outside the inn Pierre had requested as his destination. After stepping down, he paid the driver and secured his woolen cap. Although hair had grown on the top of his head as well—something which helped conceal his former tonsure and the perimeter beneath that always used to be shaved—it still wasn't enough to make him feel confident he wouldn't be recognized. However, aside from the cap, de Bologna had also chosen the rest of his attire with care. Having done away with his priestly cassock forever, he'd started following the current trading-class fashion of clothes that allowed more yield, rather than the tight-fitting ones of the lower classes. Consequently, his brown cape, green doublet and black breeches indicated a much higher status than that of a serf, looking more akin to what a normal tradesman would wear. It was important no one would question his right to be there, and that the meeting he was about to have went without disruption.

It was just before noon when Pierre walked into the dimly lit and crowded inn. Squinting and looking around, he eventually located William sitting alone at a table by the wall, so he headed in that direction. It hadn't been easy recognizing him, however. In direct contrast to Pierre, William de Grafton had shaved off his once generous beard, and was now wearing his ginger hair much longer.

When he noticed de Bologna coming his way, William raised his hand up in greeting and began to say aloud, "Bro—." But he never got the chance to complete the word because Pierre's eyes opened wide advising caution. Then as de Bologna took a seat across him, William smiled, leaned in, and whispered in French, "It's so good to see you again, Father."

"You mustn't call me that either."

"Then how may I address you? Just call you Pierre?"

"Not even that," de Bologna whispered back in French. He looked around to see if anyone was looking at them and added in English, "You must call me Peter. After all, we are in England now."

"Yes, quite," William said, taking the hint and replying in English. "I apologize. I was so overjoyed to see a friendly face again that I wasn't thinking straight."

"It's good to see you again too," de Bologna told him and smiled for the first time.

Even though they'd only met twice before, and under vastly different circumstances, Peter had always liked William. Maybe the fact they were both in their early forties, or that de Grafton exhibited none of the haughty airs the other knights used to put on, while also being sensible, was what made him such a good choice to make contact with. *But the difference in William's clothes is even more striking than my own,* Peter thought, after he took a closer look at him. Seeing the burly, former knight out of his white mantle with the red cross across the chest, and all his other usual knightly apparel—only to be wearing the lowly, dusty garments of a workman—made de Bologna reflect once again on how dramatically their world had changed.

"Last I'd heard you were locked up in the Paris Temple compound, along with…" de Grafton whispered, his eyes implying the name of the person he meant.

Peter understood and nodded. "Yes, we were both there—for a time. But I wasn't able to meet or speak to him. And from what I gather the Grand Master has now been taken to the Château at Gisors, poor soul."

William lowered his voice even more. "But how did you manage to escape?"

Leaning in, Peter told him the whole story.

✚ ✚ ✚

THE DE BOLOGNA part of his name should have, under the prevailing practice of the times, indicated his place of birth, but this wasn't the case with Peter. He was often called *de Bologna* in jest by some of his brethren—to signify the city where he was to receive his formal education in Canon Law—instead of *de Tyre,* and it stuck.

Being born in the city of Tyre, in Outremer, before the Mameluk Turks conquered both in 1291 AD, he joined the Order of the Templars at a young age. In fact, over the nearly two hundred years of the Order's existence, he'd been only the latest in a steady stream of Tyrian boys to do so. At nineteen he started out as a humble scribe and remained as such even as Acre, and the entire Holy Land, fell to the Muslims. It was only after the Templars had by necessity relocated their headquarters to Cyprus that the current Grand Master, Jacques de Molay, was made aware of Peter's talents. His aptitude in mastering multiple languages, his dedication, intuitiveness, and the levels of knowledge he exhibited had impressed de Molay's advisors considerably. As a result, at the age of twenty-six he was ordained a chaplain of the Order and four years later promoted to a priest. And even though the Grand Master came to value Peter's counsel and was loath to part from him, he decided the young man needed a more formal education to fully develop his potential. So, Peter was sent to the university at Bologna to learn and train in Canon Law. After he graduated three years later, in 1301 AD, he was appointed as the Order's Ambassador to the Holy See in Rome; an appointment many of his Tyrian Brothers believed was most fitting for someone distantly related to the legendary Nicodemus.

The time Peter spent at the papal curia proved to be yet another valuable experience. And that was because as soon as he was posted verbal hostilities broke out between King Philip of France and Pope Boniface. It was a dispute, essentially, over who was to be considered the ultimate head of the French kingdom in the eyes of God; a role that the monarch, of course, could allow none other than himself to assume. So, the king's officials staged a trial which summarily condemned the pope of blasphemy, heresy, simony, and treason—by using the flimsiest of evidence to support the charges. Measures and countermeasures then took place between the two parties, all of which culminated in September 1303 AD. That was when Guillaume de

Nogaret, the king's chief minister, physically attacked and threatened the pope, in Boniface's residence at Anagni, just outside of Rome. Even though the ageing pontiff was saved by the local populace who rallied to his aid, he did not last long, succumbing to his injuries a month later. And the next one didn't last long either: Pope Benedict, the Eleventh, was also dead within a year—which gave rise to rumors that de Nogaret had his hand in this as well.

Consequently, Peter was already attached to his third pontiff when he reunited with his Grand Master, after so many years, in the summer of 1307 AD. Pope Clement, the Fifth of his name—who was whispered to have been King Philippe's personal choice—had summoned Jacques de Molay over from Cyprus to his new court in Poitiers to discuss matters of grave importance. One of those was the possibility of conducting a new campaign to liberate the Holy Land. But the other—and the one which troubled de Molay a great deal—was the merging of the Templars and the Hospitallers into a single military and religious Order.

The Templar Grand Master was smiling as he emerged from the pope's private chamber. His Hospitaller counterpart, Foulques de Villaret, still remained within, but de Molay found an excuse to step outside. He wanted to give Peter the good news.

"Pierre, I think we've done it."

"Done what, Master?" de Bologna asked, genuinely interested.

"I think the pope will go ahead with our plan for a full-scale assault to recapture Outremer. And with none of that limited, preliminary attack hogwash, either," Jacques de Molay said, looking quite pleased.

Peter smiled. "That's good."

"No, it's *very* good," the Grand Master emphasized, and went on. "Now here's what I want you to do. Send word to all of our preceptories in Christendom that they are to dispatch whatever revenue and supplies they have available now, to Cyprus. I also want you to go to Marseille and personally see to it that everything the French preceptories send is dispatched to the island immediately. We have to start preparing."

"Yes, of course. The summertime is a quiet period for the Curia, so it shouldn't be a problem if I'm away. And what about you, Master?"

"Well, as soon as His Holiness doesn't require my presence anymore, I will start a tour of France in search of new recruits—we'll certainly need all the able bodies we can get," de Molay said and made to turn back into the papal chambers.

"What about the other matter, Sir Jacques? What did the pope say about the unification?" Peter asked, interrupting his retreat.

"Interestingly enough, he hasn't mentioned it." De Molay turned to face de Bologna and spoke in a lower voice. "Now that a new campaign will be underway I don't expect it will figure very high in his priorities. Maybe the reasons I cited in my letter last year influenced him after all."

Jacques de Molay smiled with confidence and returned to his meeting, leaving Peter standing there. The priest was not convinced that the matter would be totally forgotten, but there were more important things to think about: he had to start following his Grand Master's instructions.

On October 13, 1307 AD, Peter de Bologna was still en route back to Marseille, after paying a short visit to a Templar farm in the Languedoc. He'd spent the past few months at the Mediterranean port writing to every preceptory and bailie, he knew of, throughout Christendom. And the results were gratifying. Almost every Preceptory Master had rallied to the cause, eagerly sending off whatever money, supplies, and horses were on hand, to the Order's headquarters in Cyprus. The priest was returning to Marseille that day to supervise, yet again, what would probably be among the last of the shipments to leave France.

Dusk had descended as he rode into the city's outskirts.

Passing by a solitary house there, he came upon an acquaintance of his who was sitting outside, tending to chores. Peter waved a greeting, but as soon as the elderly man saw him pass, he threw his hands up and started shouting something. De Bologna could not make it out, so he turned his horse around to listen to what the old-timer was saying in such an agitated tone.

"Father, you must leave at once!"

Peter smiled with bewilderment. "Why? I've only just got back."

"This morning, the king's men stormed the Temple House in the city and arrested all your brothers there. They took them away and from what I hear they're being detained in the Commandery of the Hospitallers," the bearded old man reported.

De Bologna couldn't believe what he was hearing. Afraid of falling off his horse, he dismounted. "But why would the king want to arrest the Templars of Marseille? It makes no sense," he wondered out loud.

"It's being said these arrests didn't take place only here, but that they've happened all over France," Peter's friend informed him. "Crazy accusations have also been rumored as being the cause, Father. But knowing you Templars, all these years, I don't believe a word of them."

"What sort of accusations?"

"Things like idol worship, spitting on the crucifix, denouncing Christ... Crazy things like that. I really don't know what this country is coming to anymore. That's why I'm telling you, Father. You have to flee before they grab you too."

Although the priest was starting to feel dizzy, he still possessed a degree of clear-headedness to realize his brethren back in Cyprus needed to be forewarned of this. If what he feared had come to pass, they would have to take precautions. Peter grabbed a blank parchment out of his side-satchel and swiftly scribbled a coded message. He gave it to his elderly friend, urging him to take it to the captain of the next ship sailing for Cyprus. Its ultimate recipient would be Aymon d'Oiselay, the Templar Marshal of the island. Peter then gave him a pouch of money to give to the ship's captain as well as a few coins for himself. The old-timer promised he'd do as asked, took the pouch, but declined to receive any personal compensation.

Not having the presence of mind, anymore, to even thank the old man for his warning and assistance, Peter merely mounted his horse again and galloped back out of Marseille. And he remained in that shocked and confused state for several days. Everywhere he went, as incognito as possible, he would hear news of the local Templars' arrest and the shocking deeds they were accused of. He also overheard someone say that surprisingly enough the Grand Master had been a pallbearer at the funeral of the king's sister-in-law, just one day before the Order was attacked. Peter could only imagine the anguish Jacques de Molay must have felt the very next morning.

At first, de Bologna was equally bewildered about where to seek shelter and assistance. Then, in an epiphany, he remembered his good friend, Gaston, a merchant who lived up in Burgundy, so he decided to head there. The priest was certain Gaston would not refuse him. But Peter had not discarded his brown priestly cassock, and neither did his beard and hair have a chance to grow, up till then. So, inevitably, he was spotted by a king's official and arrested in early November.

Everything in his mind was shrouded in a thick mist after that. For at least a couple of days, he was held in the local dungeon at Mâcon, where he'd been caught. Then, he was carted off to Paris and upon arrival at the Paris Temple—the former Templar headquarters in France—Peter realized the basement and ground floor of the structure had been converted into holding cells. Taken down from the cart, still bound in chains, he was then thrown into a large basement cell. In that poorly lit and stinking chamber there were already about forty other Templar prisoners, none of whom Peter knew from before.

Conditions were so appalling that each new day sort of blurred into the previous one. The only sustenance the prisoners received was the bread and water thrown to the floor, twice daily, by their guards. And sleep provided no comfort to anyone either. As soon as de Bologna would manage to drift off, the agonizing screams of whomever was currently being tortured would reach his ears, startling him back to the grim reality. All he could do, after being awakened so, was to tremble in fear that undoubtedly his turn would soon come.

The only new thing Peter had been able to find out, during that first week, or so, of his incarceration, was that even the Grand Master had confessed. He'd overheard two of his cellmates discussing what Jacques de Molay said in a letter he had addressed to all Templar prisoners. Apparently, in late October, the Grand Master admitted that the accusations the Order faced were true and urged all of his brothers to confess freely. After hearing that, Peter was stunned. He always knew de Molay was illiterate and that he possessed no great intellectual capacity, but he never doubted the Grand Master's courage. *How can he betray the Order this way and after just a bit of torture?* Peter de Bologna thought amazed. He was painfully to find out how, the very next day.

Four guards burst into the gloomy chamber and without uttering a word they grabbed Peter, along with Aymeric, another Templar sitting in his own feces nearby. Dragging them up the stairs, the prisoners were taken into a windowless room on the ground floor. With no natural light entering, its only source of illumination was the three burning torches perched up on wall sconces.

As soon as the priest was forced to sit in a chair, he saw a tall, frame-like object leaning against the opposite wall. It had several horizontal wooden planks connected to its long, vertical sides and large, metal rollers on either end. *So this is what the rack looks like*, the priest thought. He knew this was the Inquisition's favorite instrument of torture, simply because it kept them within their mandate: they were allowed to inflict pain as long as no blood was spilled, or no limbs were broken. Turning his head to the right he then noticed that two more men were in there, sitting behind a table by the wall. From their posture and what they wore, Peter assumed that one of them must be the scribe and the other the papal inquisitor.

A guard stood next to de Bologna, making sure he didn't move, while the other three grabbed Aymeric. Undoubtedly realizing what lay ahead the poor man resisted, but in his weakened state he was no match for their combined strength. The guards took hold of him and turned him upside down. Then, they pinned him to the rack, fastening his feet below the top roller and his down-stretched arms, by the wrists, slightly above the bottom one. His face, due to this unnatural inverted position, was already turning red.

The inquisitor asked the Templar his name, his place of birth, what his role was within the Order, and where he'd first been received. Aymeric gave the requested information, with as steady a voice as he could muster, and Peter noticed the scribe making note of the replies. The pope's representative then, using a tone overflowing with loathing and contempt, asked Aymeric whether at that reception he had denied Our Lord, Jesus Christ. When the knight replied he had not, the inquisitor nodded to the guard standing near the top roller to turn the wheel attached to it. When he turned it a notch and then another, Aymeric's feet were gradually wrenched away from the rest of his body, while a ratchet mechanism prohibited the roller from falling back. The Templar howled with pain, but the inquisitor merely repeated the question again in an icy manner. This happened two more times, until amid his screams of torment Aymeric was forced to shout, "Yes, yes... I did deny Him."

The sight and especially the sounds were unbearable, but whenever Peter tried to turn his head away, or avert his eyes, the guard standing next to him would punch him in the face and order him to keep watching. *So this is why they've brought me here*, de Bologna thought. *They want to terrorize me into saying whatever it is they need.*

The inquisitor went on with a new set of questions: Did Aymeric spit on a crucifix during that reception? Did he give or receive any obscene kisses? Had he ever engaged in homosexual activities? Given that the ratchet device would not give way and fully sustained his horrific pain, the Templar shouted affirmative answers to all questions except the last: he had not engaged in homosexual actions. The papal representative looked down at a parchment on the table and rephrased the question. Were, then, homosexual practices encouraged in the Order? Aymeric screamed out they were and that was when Peter understood this whole interrogation process was carefully scripted. Whatever the person under torture would reply, either more pain would be inflicted, or a less incriminating question—out of a set of questions, apparently available on the parchment—would be asked, in order to secure the desired reply.

The inquisitor made a hand gesture and the two guards took Aymeric off the rack. He was still whimpering with pain and unable to walk, so they dragged him to a wall and threw him down on the floor. The poor man started to weep and de Bologna's heart went out to him. *How is it possible for any man to condone such cruelty... such barbarism?* But Peter was unable to carry on with his thoughts because in the next instant the guards came and grabbed hold of him. They dragged the priest over to the rack and set him on it—although upright in his case. Stretching his arms above his head, they secured his wrists and then tied his unshod feet to the bottom roller. And just to make sure that de Bologna's body would be taut, and ready, the guard turned the top roller a couple of times.

"What is your name, priest?" the inquisitor asked—apparently recognizing Peter's station by his worn out, priestly cassock.

"Pierre de Bologna."

"And where were you born?"

"In Bologna," Peter replied, lying. He did not want to reveal he'd been born in Tyre. The Biblical connection to the two Hirams of Tyre was well known, and he did not want his place of birth to lead to questions which might expose his Phoenician ancestry, or anything else. After that he replied candidly that he was a priest of the Order and its ambassador attached to the Holy See. He'd been received at Bologna by the Preceptor of Lombardy, Peter then said—untruthfully once again.

"Did you deny Our Lord, Jesus Christ, at your reception?" the inquisitor asked him in a cool tone.

"No, I did not," Peter replied emphatically. "And that's because—"

But he didn't get to finish his reply. The guard posted at the top roller turned it, and Peter's arms began to be tugged away from his torso. The resulting pain, all over, was so intense that the only relief available was for him to howl.

"I am not interested in your reasons, priest. Did you, or did you not, deny Our Lord?" the interrogator persisted.

Even though the pain was unbearable, Peter managed to explain through panting breaths. "Yes, I did... But it was only part of a test... We were supposed to emulate St. Peter's denial... It didn't count."

The inquisitor turned to his young scribe and ordered, "You are not to take any of this down, except that he *did* deny Our Lord. This is just another one of their heretical attempts to deceive our Holy Mother Church." Then, as if Peter had said nothing new, the papal representative went on to the next question on his list. "Did you spit on the cross?"

"Yes, I did. But it was also—" de Bologna started to say, but was cut off by the added pain, as the roller turned another couple notches. Peter felt that his arms were about to leave their sockets.

"Did you spit on the cross?" the papal representative asked again, with determination, to which the priest could only scream, "Yes... I did."

Peter had painfully realized that his interrogator was not interested in finding out the truth; the official's purpose was to merely collect confessions to a set of accusations already believed to be true. So, to the next question of whether he had given or received any obscene kisses, de Bologna untruthfully answered that he did. However, for the last one, if he'd ever engaged in homosexual acts, he replied he hadn't, but was quick to add that they'd been allowed.

"With the priest having been an ambassador at Rome, the king will be especially pleased to hear we've secured his confession," the inquisitor told the scribe, with a smile. "You may take him down," he then indifferently ordered the guards.

So this is the king's representative, not the pope's, Peter realized as they released him from the rack. That would be his last memory of that day, however, because in the very next instant he blacked out.

After his ordeal, it took de Bologna's body about a week to recover fully and to stop hurting. Fortunately, by then, his living conditions had improved a great deal. Three days after he'd 'confessed' Peter was moved, along with two others, up to a small room on the second floor of the Parisian Temple; a living space which was much cleaner, airier and brighter. It even had a window for him to look out onto the city streets. And although the food provided was also more nourishing, it didn't alter the fact that he and his brothers were still held captive.

More than two years later, in late March 1310 AD, de Bologna, and almost six hundred of his brothers had stepped forward as potential defenders of the Order. They were to put their case in front of a papal commission that was to decide whether the Templars were guilty of the charges as a whole. The commission's conclusions were to be submitted to the Council of Vienne, which the pope had convened for October of that year.

As they stood around with the others, in the garden of the bishop of Paris, while waiting for the commissioners to arrive, Peter was talking with Reynaud de Provins, the former Preceptor of Orléans. Reynaud, about ten years younger than de Bologna, was someone who'd also been trained in Canon Law.

"While I was being tortured, I tried to tell my interrogator about the test which was part of our initiations, but he didn't seem to be interested. In fact, he ordered the scribe not to write anything down," Peter said in a low voice. "Maybe it would be a good idea to inform the papal commission about this?"

Reynaud took a long moment before replying. "No, I don't think it'd be very prudent. If we told them we'd denied Christ, spit on the cross, worshiped an idol, and then explained it had all been part of an elaborate test to demonstrate our complete obedience to our superiors, it would be perceived as just another admission of guilt."

"But the acts were highly symbolic. They're reminiscent of the three times St. Peter denied Our Lord. Surely the Church would accept the legitimacy of that," de Bologna persisted.

"Under normal circumstances it might, but our present predicament has none of those. First of all, don't forget it was the king who initiated this so-called exposé of ours and not the pope. Second, the commission may reason that our attempt to emulate St. Peter's denial is just another form of heresy. Third, our initiation test was kept a complete secret and is not reflected in the Rule given to us by Rome. And fourth, and most important, none of the depositions mention any sort of test connected to what we stand accused of."

Peter opened his eyes wide. "Of course they don't! That's because the scribes were forbidden to write anything down."

"Yes, this may be true in a few cases. But, I suspect the vast majority of our present brothers were never made aware of the test. I believe most receiving preceptors either did not go through with the test at all, or if they did, they left out the last part of the ritual where they had to explain to the candidate why he'd been coerced to commit those abominable actions. The part, I mean, where they were supposed to tell the new Templar that whatever he did was just to demonstrate his loyalty and obedience to the Order. And then to continue by stressing that even though a brother must obey his superiors in everything, this *cannot* apply to matters against the faith, or if it leads to sexual misconduct. Plus, finally, that no matter what happened during the reception, it could be absolved in Confession. In fact, I've heard stories that in some preceptories..." Reynaud de Provins said, and leaned in closer. "After a candidate kissed his receptor lightly on the mouth, as per usual practice, he was told he was lucky: In any other preceptory, he'd have been obliged to also kiss his initiator's penis."

When Peter raised his eyebrows with surprise, and curled his mouth in disgust, Reynaud went on. "Yes, I really can't say what they were thinking. Apparently, some of my fellow preceptors had a mean streak in them. Instead of educating our new brothers they preferred to instill dread and revulsion in them. And for what purpose only they knew."

"It's a foolish tradition, if you think about it. I still don't understand why Nicodemus started this tradition in the first place," de Bologna said.

"Back then, when almost all the Templars were in the Holy Land, fighting for their lives against the infidels, I suppose it was a good way to separate the wheat from the chaff. But now... Well, now it unfortunately gives those wishing to dismantle our Order too much ammunition. That's why I feel that telling the commission about it might further damage our case," de Provins concluded.

Peter was still pondering over the sensible points that Reynaud had raised when the commission finally made its appearance in the garden. To begin the proceedings, its president, the Archbishop of Narbonne, ordered that the charges against the Order be read out in Latin and then in French. But hearing those accusations caused a great cry of outrage among the assembled Templars, forcing de Bologna and de Provins to step forward in the Order's defense. The two litigators condemned the way the brothers had been treated by their captors, up to then: They had been denied their religious habits and the sacraments; they'd been kept in chains; and the food provided was extremely poor. Furthermore, they informed the commission that without consulting their Grand Master, and other leaders of the Order, it would be impossible for them to mount a viable defense. To this—the very first coherent reaction by any Templar, ever since the clampdown on the Order had happened—the commission coolly replied that the Templars were supposed to choose procurators among themselves and do so fast; such a meeting with everyone present would not take place again. The assembly was subsequently dismissed, reaching no definite conclusion, other than that Peter and Reynaud were, from that day on, the de facto defenders of the Order. Everyone was then transported back to where they were held.

For more than a month after that, the two lawmen were frequently called to appear before the commission. Their main strategy, aside from denouncing the actual accusations and questioning the legality of confessions obtained under torture, was one of gaining time. They claimed that no procurator could officially be chosen among the brothers without the direct consent of their Grand Master. The hearings continued, however, and by May 1310 AD, it was apparent that the Order's legal team was gaining some positive traction. But this did not please King Philip at all, so he found other, indirect, ways to deal with it. Philip de Marigny, the Archbishop of Sens, and brother of one of the king's chief ministers, took it upon himself to begin trials for Templars on a one-by-one basis. Even though the commission had been setup to investigate the Order as an entity, local prelates still had the authority to try Templars individually. And it was the archbishop's intention to do exactly that.

Since the beginning of May 1310 AD, the members of the commission, along with the Order's defenders, had been relocated to the monastery of St. Genevieve, in Paris, so that they could carry on with their deliberations in a healthier environment. Being able to move about without chains fastened to his limbs, and sharing a cell with a single monk, Peter found his new living conditions much more bearable, compared to what they'd been before. But, when he and the others heard about the archbishop's decision to start individual trials, fear resurfaced once again. If the archbishop went ahead with his intentions every Templar who'd recanted his confession faced the possibility of being executed as a relapsed heretic. Although both de Bologna and Reynaud begged the commission to prevent the archbishop from proceeding, the only answer they received was that nothing could be done: Archbishop de Marigny was within his prerogatives. Consequently, two days later, on May 12, fifty-four Templars were taken to a field outside of Paris and burned at the stake.

The next day, Peter took part, as usual, in the commission's proceedings, but the event of the mass execution weighed heavily upon everyone's mood. As a result, the commission agreed to suspend hearings for a few days. That was when de Bologna decided he wasn't going to wait around to be burned alive. He had to escape. Fortunately, security at the monastery was much more lax than at the Parisian Temple: there were only a couple of guards posted at the entry gate. So, he formulated a plan.

It was late afternoon, on May 13, when Peter headed back to the cell he was assigned to. Antoine, the monastery's monk with whom he shared it, was already there. Peter asked Antoine if he had a spare hooded cassock he could borrow: the chill was seeping into his bones and the thin coat he wore offered little protection against it. (Peter's priestly garment had been ruined and replaced with civilian rags for some time now.) The young monk gladly gave de Bologna his extra cassock. He admired the Templar for his knowledge and training and was happy to be of assistance.

Peter's reason for the request wasn't just because of the cold—although the extra layer of clothing would be a bonus. The actual reason he needed it was so that he might blend in with a group of monks. He'd noticed that each morning after the service of Prime, and the Mass which followed, several monks always left the monastery compound to buy provisions at the local market. If he could join them, undetected, he just might be able to escape.

That night, de Bologna barely slept a wink. He was aware that if caught it would mean his immediate return to the Paris Temple and after that most probably the stake. So his movements and actions, on the morrow, would have to be both calculated and precise.

When the bell tolled at six, inviting everyone to the Office of Prime, Peter delayed a bit, allowing Antoine to go on ahead of him. He used the monk's blade to swiftly shave off his scant beard and then put on the long, hooded cassock. Pulling the hood so that it covered his entire head and most of his face, he headed towards the Chapel of St. Eloi. This would be the first test. If no one took notice of him in there, his plan stood a good chance of success. As a precaution, though, he stood near the back of the chapel and due to his unease he barely heard a word delivered in the service. When it was over and people started to leave, de Bologna turned around and went outside. The day was gray and overcast, which helped in no one noticing his features. The hood concealed his eyes and nose, and after a little while he cautiously lifted it up to see a group of monks gathering near the exit gate. Taking short, steady steps he made his way over to them. But, apparently, they were still waiting for someone else to join them, so Peter stopped a short distance away and bent over, pretending to be tying his bootlaces. When the monk they were waiting for joined the group, de Bologna took larger strides and followed them towards the gate, at their rear. As they passed through, the monks wished the guard on duty a good morning and Peter also mumbled something as he walked by him. The hood was drawn so far down that only Peter's mouth was visible. However, the priest's heart was pounding at such a frantic rate, as he passed under the gate, that he was sure the guard would hear it. Fortunately, though, the sentry noticed nothing suspicious, and the Templar was finally free.

After that, Peter left Paris as fast as he could and headed for Antwerp, in Flanders. By the time he'd reached the Flemish port the few deniers he had on him were already spent, so de Bologna had to work at the local docks in order to pay for his room and board. He'd decided that England would be the safest place for him to go. Although King Edward, the Second of his name, had begun proceedings against the Templars there by now, Peter knew that conditions were vastly different from those in France. And in any case, he had no intention of getting caught again. So, he let his beard and hair grow and wrote coded messages to various brothers in England. He was not concerned whether anyone might intercept those letters, for only a true Templar would be able to decipher and read them. The single one to reply, however, was William de Grafton, so they arranged to meet when Peter would arrive on the island.

✛ ✛ ✛

Norwich, England
October 1310 CE

WILLIAM'S HEAD WAS bowed when de Bologna finished with his recounting of the events. The former Templar preceptor of Ribston and Yorkshire had been especially shocked while hearing the details of the priest's torture. Bringing his eyes up to meet Peter's, he whispered with anguish, "How can anyone treat another human being like that?"

It was already 3:00 p.m., and the two of them were still

sitting in the dining area of the 'Bull and Bush' Inn. They'd each ordered a portion of the establishment's famous lamb stew and a pint of brown ale to wash it down with. By the time it took them to eat their meal most of the other customers had left, so both Templars were forced to continue their conversation in even more hushed tones.

Peter's eyebrows went all the way up. "Well, apparently, the King of France has no reservations in making certain his men do apply such barbarous methods."

"But why has he done this to us, in the first place?"

"I can't say, for sure. One possible explanation could be the large sum of money he owes to our Order. If we Templars disappear so does his debt. Or, it might have something to do with the notion of merging us with the Hospitallers, and him becoming the new Grand Master. As you know that was an idea Jacques de Molay strongly resisted. In any case, I don't think we'll ever find out for certain." What de Bologna purposefully neglected to mention was that there was a third possible reason: the French king being after the Templar treasure. But, Peter did not want to get into a discussion about where it was and what had been done with it; the fewer people to know about that the better. So, he said nothing.

"And the pope? How can he stay silent in all of this? After all, we're supposed to be answerable only to him, aren't we?" de Grafton wondered.

"We are. But I don't believe Clement has said his final word on the subject. I'm sure that at the Council of Vienne, which has been postponed again for next year, he will come to understand that the charges are false and that he'll find the courage to reinstate our Order."

William had a hopeful smile on his face. "Do you really think so?"

"Yes, I do. He's already moved his court to Avignon, which is out of the French king's domain. This can only mean he doesn't want to be under Philip's thumb anymore. And furthermore, when he sees the evidence before him, he'll realize for certain that none of it makes any sense. Even if our brothers—including myself, I daresay—have 'confessed' to the denial of Christ and spitting on the cross, etc, etc, it's all completely baseless. If every Templar is a heretic, what do we ultimately believe in? No alternative has ever been presented, or proposed, about our Order believing in anything else other than Christianity—just like all God-fearing people. Nor has it been stated anywhere that our offences continued after the initiation ceremonies were over. And besides, would so many thousands of valiant and pious men, over the past two centuries, have committed theirselves to such a shameful institution and not instantly cry out its trespasses to the world? It's just not possible," Peter said with conviction. He took a deep breath before concluding. "I'm confident the Good Lord will guide His Holiness to consider all these points properly and liberate us from this horrible injustice. And even though yet another power struggle is going on between him and the king, I feel certain Clement will prevail."

"I do hope you're correct," William de Grafton sighed.

"I believe I am, and that is why we must make ready."

"What do you mean?"

Peter de Bologna felt energized. "As you are aware, aside from Cyprus and France, England has the highest concentration of Templars on its soil. We must get in contact with as many of our brethren as we can, so that when the pope frees us from this yoke, everyone will finally be able to resume their duties."

"It may not be as easy as you think, Peter," William said, shaking his head. He then gave details about what he meant. "Many brothers have already taken wives and started families, ever since the clampdown happened, while several others committed themselves to monasteries. Also, following King Edward's writ, a few are now facing trial. Up in York and Lincoln, specifically, proceedings began in the spring, but have been postponed for next year."

"Yes, but many others may still be out there searching

for their brethren—especially now that trials are underway. We must set up a few of the safe-houses, here in England, to provide aid for them," de Bologna suggested.

The safe-houses Peter referred to were remote buildings, all over Christendom, that the Order had its couriers use as stop-over points. No one knew the Templars owned them, so they were the ideal places for each courier to stop and rest. This method of concealment had been necessary, since these riders would often be ferrying gold or silver, and naturally needed to avoid any bandits lurking along their way. The funds they transported were then shipped off to the east—initially to Outremer, and then to Cyprus—to fund the increasing needs of the Templar contingents stationed there.

"Some of the safe-houses *were* set up, after the events in France. But with inadequate organization and funding they inevitably dwindled and shut down. In fact, one brother in charge of a safe-house, up in York, even referred to it as his Templar Lodge," William said with a chuckle.

Peter's eyes lit up. "That's a very good name for them, actually. We must establish a few of these Lodges, again, in key areas of England and Scotland, as secret locations for providing room and board. I fear many of our brothers, who are still free and possibly on the run, will have great need of them in the months to come."

When de Grafton nodded, agreeing with the notion, Peter smiled at him. "I must apologize, William. I'm afraid I've been monopolizing our conversation. I never asked about what *you* have been doing these past three years."

William de Grafton sighed deeply and started to recount his story. "As soon as news reached us about the arrests in France, I decided I wasn't going to hang around and get captured. So, I left the Chief Preceptory of Yorkshire and after a couple of months spent wandering, I ended up here in Norwich. I'd heard that Gerald, a Templar brother stonemason, had also come here, so I sought him out. When I finally found him, he put me up at the cottage he'd been renting, and arranged employment for me with the local stonemasons' guild as well. By then I was penniless, so finding any means to earn some money was more than welcome. I became Gerald's apprentice and have been learning the masons' craft ever since." William smiled. "I've spent my entire adult life being a knight, so you can imagine how good a man, such as I, can be at this. But it's an interesting, God-blessed profession so I persist in trying to learn its secrets. The good thing is that there'll be no shortage of this kind of work in the years to come. The city of Norwich has been constructing its fortification walls for about thirty years now, and it should take as many more to complete them."

"What about your family? Did you not try to make contact with them?" Peter asked with interest.

"When I left the preceptory only my elder brother, Lord Grafton, and my mother remained of my family. My father had died a few years earlier, and I didn't want to get them into any trouble by seeking their help. Especially not after hearing that Brother Ralph de Bulford—in order to protect my escape—selflessly identified himself as me when he was arrested. But unfortunately, last year, I learned that my mother passed away as well." William bowed his head in sorrow.

Peter had also been a widow's son and knew how the loss of one's mother felt: his own mother died just a few months before the dreadful events of October 1307 AD. But in contrast to William, de Bologna had never met his father. He'd been a baby when his father got sick and eventually passed away. And even though his mother was a handsome woman, in her day, she decided never to remarry. Instead, she chose to concentrate on bringing up her children with the ancient Phoenician traditions.

"I'm very sorry for your loss," Peter said, offering his sympathy. And then in an attempt to lighten the mood, he asked, "What about a wife? Did you not also succumb to the temptation for female companionship?"

This question, however, only served in clouding William's expression even further. "I will not lie and say I didn't consider it. In fact, I was courting a fair maiden for a time, but regrettably it went no further. Her father did not think a mason's apprentice would be good enough for his daughter. And since I could not reveal to them who I truly was, it inevitably ended."

They both sat in silence, for a long moment after that.

"Maybe it is for the best. After all, God does work in mysterious ways, does He not?" Peter said. And when William nodded, de Bologna decided it was about time they stopped dwelling on the past, and carried on with planning the future. "Do you think we could gather each region's leading brothers, those who are still free, for a meeting?"

"I don't see why not—if we give them ample warning and take precautions, that is," de Grafton replied. "But what would be the purpose of such an assembly?"

"We have to start organizing these so called '*Lodges,*' so that everyone will be able to be in close, local contact with everybody else. And when the pope finally liberates our Order from these obscene charges, this system will enable us to quickly get in touch with every brother—even those who are already married, or in monasteries. Do you know of a place that might be suitable for this meeting?"

William de Grafton took a moment to think before replying. "Although the Faxfleet Preceptory is now deserted, it's best if we don't go there. However, there's a large, deserted barn to the south of Winteringham, on the River Humber, that no one knows about. I'm sure we could use it; it's big and remote enough to suit our needs."

"Good thinking, William," Peter congratulated him. "Now, make a note of the directions and the time of our meeting. Would three months from now be ample warning for everyone?"

"Yes, I believe the end of January would be a good time for all," de Grafton agreed. Even though most knights were still illiterate in those days, William, fortuitously, was not.

So, after saying that he started rummaging around in his work satchel, which was on the floor, trying to find a pencil and a piece of parchment to write. During the momentary silence that followed, de Bologna's eyes happened to glance at some of the stonemason tools which were in de Grafton's satchel. And the way two of them accidentally landed on top of each other, due to William's searching hands, gave Peter an interesting idea.

"William, what are those tools called in English?" the priest asked, as he pointed to the two he'd noticed.

Looking down into the contents of his satchel, the slightly puzzled knight asked, "Which ones? Do you mean the square and the compass?"

"Yes, precisely: the square and the compass. I think it would be a good idea if in your letter you instructed our brothers to bring either one with them as they come to the meeting."

William knit his brow in bafflement. "For what reason, Peter?"

"It will be an excellent way to make sure everyone present is a genuine Templar and not a spy," de Bologna explained. But when he saw that de Grafton still didn't understand, he pointed at the two items. "Look at them. What do they remind you of, especially this way where one lays over the other?"

William kept staring at the two tools, but couldn't see what Peter was driving at. It was only when he turned his head around—to view them from de Bologna's angle—that he exclaimed, "Of course!" Then, fearing the Inn's keeper might overhear him, de Grafton looked deep into the priest's brown eyes and announced his deduction in a barely audible whisper. "The Grand Master's Ring!"

"I knew you'd spot it, eventually," Peter said with a smile. "That's why I believe it's such a foolproof and safe way of guaranteeing everyone at the meeting is indeed a Templar. None other than a true brother would know how to place them together so that they give an approximation of the Ring's engraving. And even if some are apprehended and searched, along the way, carrying a simple tool on one's person is neither suspicious, nor incriminating."

William was also smiling as he made an additional note on his parchment. They were all supposed to bring along either one of those tools.

Peter then looked determined. "Also, please stress that after deciphering and memorizing the letter's contents everyone must burn it. We cannot risk them falling into the wrong hands."

✚ ✚ ✚

North Lincolnshire, England
January 1311 CE

ALL WAS READY. For the previous three months, Peter de Bologna and William de Grafton had dedicated themselves to getting everything prepared for this seminal assembly of the Templars in England. Fortunately, almost everyone contacted had pledged their attendance, and overall almost thirty brothers were expected. They were to be the caretakers; the ones who'd set things up and see to it that every other brother, throughout the British Isles, was informed about the meeting's deliberations and decisions.

Although a chapel could not be used—as in all past Templar chapter meetings—the secluded barn William selected as the venue, by lucky chance, had its own west to east orientation. With an entrance on its western wall, the two Templars placed facing rows of benches for the attending brothers to sit, along the empty structure's north and south sides. They also put a table at the east end, set on a dais, from where they would both co-chair the meeting. And since the invitation pointed out that the assembly would begin at sundown, lit torches were perched all along the barn walls.

It was already dusk, and Peter had just finished placing

the two wooden columns a few feet in from the entrance, when the first participants arrived outside. To make sure everyone attending was indeed a Templar, William had enlisted the help of Gerald and Arthur—another fugitive brother who'd also been working with them as a stonemason in Norwich. Both were armed with swords, just in case an imposter showed up seeking entry.

It was snowing again and the howling wind chilled everyone to the bone. Nonetheless, Arthur managed to keep the group at a distance from the barn's entrance before allowing the first one to proceed. Gerald, who was posted in front of the barn's door, held a square and a compass in each of his hands. After greeting the man who'd stepped forward, and who was unfamiliar, Gerald asked him his name.

"My name is Sir John de Poyonton, Brother," the man replied.

"Sir John, to prove you are a true Templar, please place the square you are holding onto one of the tools in my hands," Gerald told him next.

Poyonton frowned, perplexed, for a moment, looking closely at both tools in Gerald's hands. But when he saw the slightly opened compass, which Gerald held down by its hinge point, for a second time, John realized what he must do. He held his square by its corner and bringing it up he placed it, pointing down, over the compass. John was so proud of himself that he cracked a smile. He'd been able to figure out that the test was to create an approximation of the well-known engraving depicted on the Grand Master's Ring. The compass and square when brought together, with their joints in opposite directions, only missed two horizontal lines to form a complete Star of David—which was exactly what was engraved on the Ring.

Gerald smiled back, also happy—and relieved—that John had worked it out. "Welcome, Brother de Poyonton. Please enter," he said to him. And so, one by one, each new attendee would come up to Gerald and when he let him pass, Arthur would send the next one forward.

Inside, William would greet each brother with the customary triple Templar kiss: first on the right cheek, then the left, and again on the right. If he was unknown to him, de Grafton would introduce himself and ask the brother to place any weapons he had on a table by the door. Then, William invited them all to sit on the benches. And when everyone was in attendance—leaving only Gerald outside in the cold, with his sword drawn to guard against unwelcome intruders—William rose from his seat at the table to address the assembled Templars.

"Brethren, I would like to welcome you; but also to extend my gratitude since many of you have travelled great distances to be here. As you know, our Master in England, Brother William de la More is unfortunately still incarcerated, so Father Peter de Bologna and I took it upon ourselves to convene this meeting. These past three years have been a difficult time for us all. Our Order has gone from being celebrated and admired for its bravery and sacrifice, to accused of vile charges and persecuted. But before we begin, I would like to call upon Brother Peter to say a short blessing and may the Good Lord hearken to his words. Brethren, please be upstanding."

They rose, bowing their heads in reverence.

"O God, author of all life and portal to all wisdom, guide Your humble servants, in the paths we take this day, that trusting in Your defense, we will not fear our adversaries, no matter how powerful they might be, and that through our actions Christ shall be honored and Thy will be done, through Jesus Christ our Lord. Amen."

And when de Bologna had finished delivering the short prayer they all chanted, *"Amen,"* in unison, crossed themselves thrice, and sat back down.

"I would like to thank Father Peter," William said, as he glanced at de Bologna next to him before continuing. "As you realize, our assembly tonight does not take place in the familiar surroundings of a chapel, as did most of our chapter meetings in the past. And I'm sure you may be puzzled by a few, unfamiliar objects in here as well. So allow me to explain them to you by beginning with the two columns standing by the door."

Everyone turned their heads to gaze at the two wooden pillars, which Peter had positioned a short distance from the entrance. They were no more than three feet in height and, other than a coat of bronze paint, they were completely plain and unadorned. But with them placed at a distance of about six feet apart, they created an implied gateway—a gateway through which all of them had passed.

William allowed them all to have a good look before he proceeded to explain the columns' presence. "Our official name is the *Poor Fellow-Soldiers of Jesus Christ and of the Temple of Solomon.* So what better tribute to our Order's ongoing existence than to have representations here of the two remarkable pillars that once adorned Solomon's original House of God? Boaz and Jachin, as those magnificent columns were called, were renowned icons of that famous structure, and one had to pass between them to gain entry into the ancient Temple. Therefore, Brother Peter and I thought it would be fitting if all of us were to enter our assembly area in the same way.

"Allow me to direct your attention now to the tapestry in the middle of the floor," de Grafton said. He then gestured to the large carpet-like canvas, made up of many large, black and white squares, which had been placed in the barn's center between the two rows of benches. "It consists of multiple Beauseants—as they were originally, before the blood-red cross was added—all sewn together, sequentially, to create its checkered black and white appearance."

When a chorus of loud objections broke out among the Templars after this, William was forced to throw up his hands and raise his voice over the commotion. "It is not meant to disrespect our war banner, my Brothers, I assure you," he stated loudly. And when they calmed down, giving him a chance to explain, he did. "It has been constructed like this for two main reasons. The first one is concealment.

If we had been discovered transporting a single Beauseant here, by agents of the Crown or the Church, this meeting would never have happened. We therefore had to combine many of them together, to create this design—a design, which incidentally looks quite similar to a giant chess board.

"The second reason, however, is symbolic. In those glorious days when our brothers were still fighting the infidels in Outremer, they did so by rallying around the half-black, half-white Beauseant. But on certain disastrous occasions it happened to fall to the ground, defeated. Except that it never remained there for long. Circumstances would change and our banner would yet again be lifted and waved proudly in the air. That is what this tapestry symbolizes, my Brothers: That even though our Order may be down at the moment, it will surely rise again! And then we shall once more cry out the words of the Psalm: 'Not unto us, O Lord, not unto us, but unto Thy Name give Glory.' "

William's rallying last words resulted in an outbreak of cheers and applause from the rest of the Templars. Peter looked up at him proudly. He'd never imagined that de Grafton would've been capable of such eloquence. Even though it was he who'd explained to William the symbolic significance of the columns and the checkered canvas, de Bologna was convinced he couldn't have expressed it better himself.

"Allow me to come back to that in a moment, Brethren," William went on, after the cheering had died down. "For now, I would like you all to notice the illustration of an eye which is behind me."

Fixed on the eastern barn wall, behind both him and de Bologna, was a drawing of a large human eye, enclosed within a triangle. Aside from the connotations he was hoping it would create for the Templars, Peter decided to draw and include it as a tribute to his own heritage as well. The ancient Phoenicians used to have an all-seeing eye depicted on the prow of every boat, to protect them on their trade journeys. In fact, his mother had told him that before embarking on a new voyage each Phoenician mariner was supposed to touch it for good luck. *So what better symbol to be included in a new endeavor such as this?* Peter had thought.

"The ever-watchful eye represents that of Almighty God, Who is looking over us at this very moment," de Grafton informed the assembly next. "Yes, I grant you, a crucifix would have been more traditional, but yet again security reasons cautioned against transporting one here. At the same time, none of us need a crucifix to remind us of the suffering Our Lord Jesus Christ endured for us. This symbol of the all-seeing eye, however, suggests even more. It implies that the Good Lord acknowledges our cause to be a just one and that He will keep an eye out for us to prevail. Furthermore, the fact that it is placed on the eastern wall is also significant. It obliges us to always turn our attention to the east, which is where our ultimate duty lies: the liberation of the Holy Land from the infidels, once and for all.

"Finally, Brethren, the fact you see Father Peter and me wearing white gloves is not because of the cold weather—although, I must admit they do help. On the contrary, they are suggestive of the fact that the nature of our work has changed, for the time being, as an Order. Whereas before we would have concentrated all our efforts in waging battles for the true faith, this phase—which has been forced upon us against our will—calls for reflection and preparation. But, I remain convinced that one day, very soon, we shall be removing these gloves to carry on again with what we do best. And to elaborate on this certainty, I'd like to call upon Brother Peter de Bologna to address you. Before I do, though, let me inform you that the good Father has recently arrived from France, where he'd been jailed and tortured by agents of the French kingdom. Fortunately, he managed to escape and brought along with him our Grand Master's instructions about what we need to do."

They had spent some time debating whether to include

this part about Jacques de Molay issuing orders. Obviously, Peter had never seen, or spoken with the Grand Master, during their joint imprisonment, but de Grafton had managed to convince the priest that saying he did wouldn't hurt anyone. It was just a white lie, as William put it, and was to be used merely as an added incentive for the brothers to go ahead with what was needed of them. Besides, de Grafton reasoned, who could say that de Molay *wouldn't* have sanctioned their plan if he knew about it?

"Brethren, I too would like to welcome you to this meeting, and believe I would be remiss if I did not congratulate Brother William for his eloquence," Peter said as he rose. "Yes, I was a 'guest' of the French monarchy for more than two years, and it is true I was severely tortured once. But after the King of France saw to it that fifty-four of our brothers were brutally burned at the stake I decided to escape. When I informed the Grand Master of my intentions, he bade me to come to England. As he was in no physical condition to risk an escape and travel, he gave me a broad outline of what he wants us to do.

"The Grand Master and I both share the certainty that Pope Clement will reinstate our Order—despite King Philip's wishes—at the Council of Vienne, when it finally convenes this October. Therefore, we must prepare ourselves for that eventuality. All of you are key figures at your respective locations. The first thing you must do is to reorganize the safe-houses in your areas. Aside from providing room and board for brothers on the run, these Lodges will also serve as your secret meeting places. Using the symbols you've seen here tonight, you must instill confidence into all the brothers of your region that better days are coming—including those who have already created families, or committed themselves to monasteries. Everyone needs to be informed, so they may be able to make their choice when the time comes. Gather them around you and keep them close so that at a moment's notice you may give them any instructions necessary."

Peter glanced at all the hopeful faces staring back at him before going on. "The early Christians had formed an underground movement to avoid persecution. Therefore, we shall have to emulate that for a year, or so, and establish our own Secret Society. And when the call from our Grand Master to assemble around him is heard, we in England shall emerge triumphant and prepared. Until then, though, trust no one outside the Order with any of this. You have all passed the test to gain entry here. Use it, whenever you are unsure if anyone is a true brother. Or, additionally, you may employ a more inconspicuous method of identification in the form of a handshake. As you take another man's hand in yours and apply pressure with your thumb on the joint of his index finger, he will realize you are a brother. And if he *is* a true Templar, he will utter the first letter of the word *'Boaz.'* To this you will reply with the second one, he'll proceed with the third, and then you with the last, after which both of you shall utter the whole word aloud, at the same time. Naturally, all this should be performed if no one around can overhear you. I shall demonstrate this to everyone, separately, at the end of our meeting, so don't worry if you haven't grasped it yet. Then, you'll be able to pass it along to all the brethren in your region.

"Before we proceed to the next item on tonight's agenda, let me address two final points. First, if you are concerned with funds for setting up your Lodges, I'm happy to inform you we will be able to assist you with that. Fortunately, not all revenue managed to get shipped off to Cyprus, as per our Grand Master's instructions, before the arrests. By lucky chance, a good amount stayed behind and is now in Brother William's and my possession. So you will not have to concern yourselves with that. And second, I would suggest you always carry a square and compass on your person, when going from place to place. Aside from them being objects with which you can easily test if someone is a Templar, carrying such tools can afford a certain degree of freedom in your movements. Stonemasons are allowed to travel freely from project to project, all around the realm, and at times posing as if you are masons will make things much easier for you, especially if you're ever stopped and questioned. So my advice is that you adopt this additional identity of a stonemason, for your own protection—and for the Order's, as well."

This last piece of guidance served as William's cue to get up and address the assembly once again. "In the years to come, Brethren, after we have been vindicated, we'll need all the able-bodied men we can find. To illustrate how new members must be received into our Order, from now on, we have arranged for a young man to be initiated as an Entrant Sergeant. Our Brother-to-be, Stephen de Beverley, currently works as an apprentice stonemason, alongside Father Peter and me, in Norwich. When vetted, he displayed a genuine eagerness to join our fraternity and to keep its secrets. But the final approval shall be yours, my Brethren, after you've seen him for yourselves. Brother Arthur, would you be so kind as to bring our candidate in?"

Arthur got up, bowed, and exited through the barn door.

William de Grafton continued. "Allow me to inform you on a few issues until they arrive. For obvious reasons, we will have none of the tests that some of us went through when *we* were received—they have caused us enough trouble. No, from now on initiations shall be dealt with in a rather more practical manner. From Whitton, where he stayed at an inn overnight, Stephen was moved to a nearby shed this afternoon. For the entire duration of the journey here he was blindfolded so he wouldn't know where he was being taken. The young man has stayed in that shed for a few hours now and was told to reflect on his reasons for wanting to join our Order. We shall soon see how firm his resolve still is.

"At the moment, Brother Arthur is preparing the candidate. He will be instructing Stephen to remove any coins, weapons, or other metal objects he may be carrying on his person. Then, he will be asked to take off some of his upper clothes and for his right foot to be shod only with a slipper. Both are necessary as protective measures, should he decide to flee before taking his solemn oath: The lack of clothes in this weather will not enable him to get far, and the slipper on his foot will also hinder him from running off with speed. When he is brought inside, he will have a loose cable placed around his neck so that Arthur can tow him if necessary—another protective measure. Stephen, still blindfolded, will then be led three times around the checkerboard tapestry so that you may ascertain his physical fitness, and I suggest that we all be observant but completely silent during those rounds. At the end of each I shall ask him a question. These will enable us to determine whether he has anyone in his life to whom he may betray our names, our location, or anything else we entrust to him. After he has taken his oath, and his blindfold is removed, he shall be given a white lambskin apron to place in front of his genitals. This is in lieu of the sheepskin girdle our first brothers in Outremer had to wear around their waist, at all times, to remind them of their vows of chastity. Given our current circumstances, Brothers, one cannot expect any of us to apply that tradition, literally, anymore. However, soon, we shall all be required to wear such symbolic aprons around our waists during our meetings. Finally, our candidate will also be given a set of white gloves, and then Father Peter will teach him our new secret handshake."

The timing could not have been better, for as soon as William uttered his last words they all heard three loud knocks on the barn door.

"Enter," de Grafton called out, in an imposing tone.

The door opened and Arthur guided the blindfolded candidate in. Around Stephen's neck was a cable, fashioned like a noose, the end of which was in Arthur's hand. Without an overcoat, the initiate's tunic was open and loosely hanging out of his breeches, as if he had just awoken from a fitful sleep. On his left foot he wore a leather boot, but his right one was shod only with a flimsy slipper. Disheveled like this—and without a doubt feeling very cold—Stephen was led to stand between the two bronze-colored pillars.

"Candidate, state your name," William de Grafton ordered.

"Stephen de Beverley," he replied in a fairly vigorous voice, even though it was apparent he felt quite uneasy.

"And for what purpose do you appear before us tonight?"

"I wish to become a member of the glorious Order of the Templars, as an Entrant Sergeant," Stephen answered. This had been the only thing he had been coached on how to respond.

"Then put your trust in God and the hand guiding you," William told him and nodded to Arthur to proceed.

Arthur took him by the arm and led him around the checkerboard tapestry so that all the Templars present would be able to ascertain that Stephen was of sound body.

When they arrived between the columns again, de Grafton's voice rang out once more. "Are you a serf, or otherwise tied to any such allegiance of curtailed freedom?"

"No, sir, I am a free man," de Beverley replied.

William nodded and Arthur with the initiate went around the tapestry again, subsequently taking their position at the pillars.

"Are you married, have you ever been married, or are associated with a female in such a way so as to compel you to reveal our secrets to her?" William de Grafton inquired.

"No, sir, I am not and never have been."

After the last round was finished, de Grafton asked his final question. "Do you owe money, or are otherwise indebted to anyone who may coerce you to tell him about your membership in our Order?"

Stephen shook his head. "No, sir, I do not."

William looked at everyone assembled. "Brethren, our decision needs to be unanimous. What say you of Stephen de Beverley? Do you give your consent for him to join our Order, aye or nay?"

To which question everyone in the barn shouted back, "Aye."

"If no one disagrees, we shall proceed with the oath," de Grafton announced. Then turning to the young man, he added, "Stephen de Beverley, due to our Order's present situation we will not require any vows of chastity and poverty from you; those shall be pledged at a later date when our brotherhood has been reinstated. But, you will take a solemn oath of obedience now. Father de Bologna, would you please attend to it? Brethren, be upstanding."

Everyone stood, while Peter de Bologna got up from his seat on the dais and walked over to the candidate. In his right hand he held the bulky tome of the Holy Bible he'd borrowed from the stonemasons' guild master, and in his left a square and compass. When he arrived in front of Stephen, Peter arranged the two tools, in the way approximating the Star of David, on the Bible's closed top. Then, he instructed the young man to kneel and place his right hand on the Holy Book. Arthur assisted the blindfolded Stephen to do so.

"Please repeat after me," de Bologna told the initiate. "I... state your name... with my hand placed on this Holy Bible, solemnly promise to be a perpetual servant of the Grand Master and of the Order of the *Poor Fellow-Soldiers of Jesus Christ and of the Temple of Solomon*. My only purpose in life shall be from now on the recapture and defense of the Holy Land. I furthermore pledge my complete obedience to everything my superiors will order me to perform in achieving this noble objective. If I fail to keep my promises may my throat be cut across, and may I be known as a dishonest man for all eternity. So help me God and keep me steadfast in this my great and solemn obligation as an Entrant Sergeant Templar."

After Stephen had dutifully repeated each word, de Bologna instructed him to rise and nodded to Arthur to remove the blindfold and noose. When they were removed, William allowed everyone to resume their seats and Peter gave Stephen his first triple kiss on the cheeks.

"Welcome, *Frère* Stephen to our Order," Peter said, using the French word for *Brother*. "I shall now present you with two objects and an instruction. The first object is an apron, much akin to what we both use when laboring as stonemason apprentices in Norwich," he told him, and with Arthur's assistance fastened a small, white lambskin apron around the new brother's waist. "However, this is meant as an allusion to what the earliest Templars were obliged to cover their loins with, at all times, to ensure their chastity. You have not taken such vows yet, so let this serve as a reminder that you shall do so when our Order is restored. Another object which will also remind you of our present state is this pair of white gloves I present to you. These shall be discarded when we are reinstated and proceed to fight for the recapture of the Holy Land. Finally, the instruction I'm about to give you, is a method for distinguishing if someone is a true brother and it is something you must always apply."

Peter then went on to teach Stephen how to perform the secret handshake, using the word *'Boaz.'* When the new Templar had mastered the process, de Bologna led him to sit alongside himself and William, on the dais, in honor of his initiation that day.

William de Grafton rose to address the assembly. "Brothers, this concludes our formal business tonight. I hope Father Peter and I were successful in conveying our enthusiasm about the better days to come. When you return to your respective areas, please prepare the meeting places in your Lodges like this one. It will impart all the right messages and shouldn't get you into any trouble if seen by strangers. Also—and this is most important—aside from informing our existing brothers about our deliberations here, you must get busy seeking new members for our fraternity. From within your communities single out and secretly evaluate suitable candidates who could potentially become new Templar knights, or sergeants. And after you feel certain they would never betray our secrets, proceed to initiate them in the way you have witnessed. I trust you'll remember the wording used, because nothing from this ceremony will ever be written down. It's up to you to pass it on word for word. Finally, in a short while—after we've set the tables—we shall hold a Festive Board here, to celebrate and answer any questions you may still have."

Everyone rose from their seats feeling very optimistic and exuberant.

✛ ✛ ✛

York, England
April 3, 1312 CE

FOURTEEN MONTHS LATER, William de Grafton and Peter de Bologna were in York Minster Cathedral attending the early Sunday Mass. Their stonemason guild had recently acquired a contract of restoring the York city walls and they, along with other co-workers, were relocated there. The service was almost over when the archbishop announced he was going to read the latest Papal Bull called *Vox in Excelso*. It concerned the findings of the Council of Vienne, which every Templar was looking forward to, so both of them decided to pay extra attention.

When the prelate read out the words of the pope, *"For all these reasons we were unwilling to lend our ears to insinuation and accusations against the Templars",* William and Peter glanced at each other with hopeful smiles. They were feeling confident this was what they'd been waiting for: at long last, their beloved Order's acquittal and reinstatement. Those, however, were the only favorable words they would hear. After several paragraphs of merely recounting events, the pontiff's edict concluded that, *"Therefore, with a sad heart... we suppress, with the approval of the sacred council, the order of Templars, and its rule, habit and name, by an inviolable and perpetual decree, and we entirely forbid that anyone from now on enter the order, or receive or wear its habit, or presume to behave as a Templar. If anyone acts otherwise, he incurs automatic excommunication".* Both their faces turned instantly pale. They simply couldn't believe that their worst nightmare had just become a terrifying reality.

After the service ended, the two Templar brothers headed back to their lodgings in a stunned silence. In fact, de Bologna was so wrapped up in his thoughts that he did not hear even a single word of what William had been saying.

"I said, what are we to do now, Peter?" de Grafton repeated, when the priest indicated he hadn't heard the first time.

"I really don't know."

"But everything we've worked for, this past year, depended on the Order being exonerated. And now this happens... I can't believe it," William stated with a sigh.

However, Peter was feeling much worse. After swiftly wiping away an escaped tear with the back of his hand, so that de Grafton wouldn't see it, his rage started to surface. "This is all my fault," he said in a self-accusing tone. "I'm the one who convinced you, and everybody else, that the pope would acquit us for sure. But it was just wishful thinking, wasn't it? I should have realized that Clement is just Philip's talking puppet. What did the pope call him? Ah, yes... '...*our dear son in Christ, Philip, the illustrious king of France.*'" De Bologna scoffed. "Precisely the words a serf would use when paying homage to his master. And I'm sure those bastards, the Hospitallers, were behind this as well. Mark my words, William: they'll be the ones who'll be getting all our properties. Of that I cannot be wrong."

With them still on their way back to their lodgings, de Grafton became concerned someone in the street might overhear. So, he attempted to quiet his friend down. "Calm yourself, Peter. All of your arguments made perfect sense. In an ideal world the pope would've judged our case exactly as you said he would. And this world is far from ideal! Yet to be honest with you, I'm glad you convinced me as you did. Nursing that hope, however flimsy it turned out to be, gave true meaning to my life this past year."

Just as de Grafton finished speaking they arrived at the inn where they stayed. "I'll go check on Elias and come to your room in a bit," de Bologna told him and hurried up the stairs.

Elias was Peter's twelve-year-old nephew, who'd arrived in England two months earlier. The boy was the youngest son of de Bologna's widowed sister, who decided to remain in Tyre and raise her family there even after the city had been sacked by the Mameluks. Although Peter had never met Elias before, his sister's letters convinced him the young boy was insightful and intelligent. He'd been home-schooled in all the old Phoenician principles and know-how, so de Bologna arranged passage for him to come to England. Peter wasn't getting any younger and therefore needed someone he could trust to take over. He'd hoped that, one day, Elias would be ordained a priest of their reinstated Order—something which, alas, would never happen now.

"He's still asleep. The little rascal must have been very tired yesterday. It's just as well I didn't wake him to come to church with us," de Bologna told William, with a chuckle, as he stepped in the room. Witnessing his young nephew sleep had apparently stirred a new level of confidence in Peter.

"Hmm?" was de Grafton's response, as he raised his head, evidently not having heard a word. He then added, "I've been thinking. We need to convene a general council of the Lodge Masters, as soon as possible, to discuss this development with them."

"Yes, you're right. They are bound to find out about this edict, sooner or later, so it's best if they hear it from us first," de Bologna agreed.

"My God! And what do we tell the hundreds of young knights and sergeants who've joined our Order, with such enthusiasm, this past year? That we have no other choice but to disband now? This whole situation is unconscionable," William burst out, bowing his head. *His* miserable mood had not improved in the least.

Peter sat down as he felt his newly-found level of optimism take over. "Let me ask you something, William." And when de Grafton nodded, he went on. "Do you feel the Papal Council's conclusions are correct? Are we heretics who deserve such a fate? Is this a fair decision?"

"No, of course not," he replied emphatically, to all three questions.

"Then I suggest we do not take this lying down."

"What do you mean?"

De Bologna looked into William's eyes. "I mean that we carry on what we've created and not give it up. Obviously, we'll have to give our Secret Society a new perspective, a new direction, now. We cannot continue to hope for the Order's reinstatement, but we *can* strive to keep its ideals alive. Originally, it was founded on the chivalrous idea of protecting the defenseless from those of another faith. So maybe we ought to carry on doing that, but for people of all religions and all denominations—in the name of true justice. And instead of reconquering the land where the Temple was located, perhaps we should now focus on erecting a new, internal Temple of virtue within ourselves." To allow everything to sink in, the priest paused momentarily before he added, "You could lead this effort, William."

But when de Grafton frowned, indicating he didn't understand, Peter explained. "As you know, William de la More died in the Tower of London two months ago, and Jacques de Molay will definitely not be allowed to survive this turn of events. The poor soul will either be burned at the stake, or incarcerated for life. So that leaves just you to be our new Society's Grand Master."

A glimmer of hope finally lit in William's eyes. "Aye, you're right. We *can* carry on our Order's legacy, but under a different guise. And if we are to construct, as you say, internal Temples of virtue from now on, our experience as stonemasons could be an invaluable source for symbols and allegory."

"Yes, we could all become *frère* masons. And everyone, whether of noble or common birth, would be on equal footing," de Bologna suggested with emphasis. "Although nobody else will know it exists, this Secret Society of ours will be the first, indirect, way of getting back at the Church—for now." Peter then paused momentarily while he turned something over in his mind. "I realize that *'Secret Society'* isn't much of a name for a newly fledged covert organization. But it's generic enough to keep us out of trouble if anyone ever reveals it by mistake."

What he'd intentionally neglected to reveal, however, was an additional, private, reason he had for wanting the brotherhood to carry on. It would provide the means for the knowledge of what the Templar Order had hid, and where, to remain alive.

By then, it was obvious that both former Templars had overcome their earlier feelings of despair. So, they went on bouncing ideas off each other as to how the Secret Society could be transformed.

TEMPLARS

Chapter 3

BROTHERHOOD

Outremer
March 29, 1119 CE

THE HORSE STOPPED and reared on its hind legs, neighing loudly. The sand viper, which had slithered onto the dirt road all of a sudden, also seemed to have been startled, and it responded by coiling its body in defense. Hissing threats, at first, the snake soon realized that the huge rearing beast could very well trample on it. So it sensibly decided to slide away to the safety of the nearby bushes instead.

With the danger having passed, the destrier returned itself to the ground, and Hugh de Payns patted on its neck to calm it down. His broad-shouldered, well-proportioned frame, clad in a light-grey surcoat that day, was seated firmly and once again in complete command of the mount. He had a full head of long, auburn hair, framing a pleasant, round-shaped face, and his thick mustache and beard—now starting to turn gray at places—only drew attention to his penetrating green eyes even more. Although initially caught off guard by his destrier's abrupt reaction to the snake, Hugh was now more concerned with the sounds of metal clanging upon metal echoing in the distance. De

Payns lost no time: pressing his roweled spurs into the horse's flanks he urged it forward again.

After a brief, high-speed gallop, on the rough dirt road to Joppa, Hugh arrived behind a short hill and was able to see who were creating the commotion. Just off the path a few paces, a man, with his back to Hugh, was lying injured on the ground of a dry wadi—a small pool of blood next to his left leg bearing witness to this. He was propped up on his elbow, however, desperately using the sword in his right hand to counter the attacks from a bearded man standing above him. The attacker—by all indications a Saracen—repeatedly brought down his curved scimitar sword in an attempt to finish off his wounded opponent. Since both were wearing similar loose, Arabian burnoose robes, Hugh assumed them to be infidels and pondered for an instant whether he shouldn't get involved in their scuffle. But when the attacking heathen saw de Payns appear, he stopped, cursed in his own tongue, turned about-face, and started to run away. Then, the wounded man—surprisingly—shouted out in perfect French, "Please stop him. He's got my scrip."

As Hugh got closer and was able to get a good look at the man's youthful, clean-shaven face, he realized that he wasn't a Saracen after all, but a native Levantine. His brown eyes were clear and bright, the chin firm; and when the young man removed his cap, the distinction from his attacker could not have been more obvious: the top of his head had the characteristic shaved tonsure of a Christian clergyman. This was all Hugh needed to see, so he immediately prompted his destrier to charge after the escaping thief.

The Saracen was running to retrieve his own horse, which was standing nearby, when he heard de Payns's mount galloping behind him and closing in. He'd almost arrived at where his mare was waiting, but the bandit's luck had run out. Hugh's already unsheathed steel-hilted broadsword, in one mighty downward swing, split the heathen's skull in two. Blood spewed out and an instant later the lifeless body fell limply to the ground.

The infidel's steed, witnessing its master's fate, bolted in fear and galloped away. Under normal circumstances, de Payns would have chased it, since horses were very valuable in Outremer, but an internal voice convinced him that tending to the injured native was much more important at that point. As a result, Hugh dismounted and snatched the stolen pouch from the dead Saracen's grasp. Then holding his horse's reins in hand he walked back to the stranger who was still lying wounded on the ground. As he got closer, de Payns got a better look at the growing pool of blood next to the man's leg.

"You have literally saved my life. Thank you," the Levantine said, once again in perfect French—the only language that de Payns knew.

Happy to find a native fluent in his own tongue, the knight replied, "My name is Sir Hugh de Payns, and I'm glad I could be of service. But, what's happened here? Who are you?"

"I am Priest Nicodemus, and I have been dispatched on a secret mission to Jerusalem by the Bishop of Caesarea. I've been on the road for three days now. This morning, though, after leaving Joppa, I was attacked by him..." Nicodemus said, glancing over to where his assailant's dead body lay.

This puzzled Hugh. "But your clothes... If you hadn't spoken to me, I would've mistaken you for yet another Saracen." As he spoke he handed the retrieved scrip back to its owner.

"Yes, I altered my dress in the thought that I'd be able to travel more safely. Alas, I was unable to deceive my attacker," the cleric said with a self-mocking, half smile, yet winced in pain as he extended his hand to take possession of the pouch. "Thank you again, good Sir."

Kneeling over Nicodemus's left side and after lifting the young man's robe, Hugh saw the ugly wound the thief had dealt him. The gash was just above the knee, but it was quite deep and bleeding profusely. It needed immediate tending to. In his nearly fifty years of age, Hugh had enough experience with wounds to know that if the blood loss was not curtailed soon, then the priest would die for sure.

"Do you have anything I can use to tie your leg with?" he asked.

Nicodemus pointed to a horse to his left that was lying dead there. "You might find something inside my saddlebag."

The knight stood up and headed over to the unlucky animal. It was already being besieged by swarms of flies, and he could see the two arrows responsible for its death sticking out from its neck and breast. Hugh looked in the saddlebag and found a linen tunic which he proceeded to tear up into strips. Then, walking back to Nicodemus, he tied and bandaged the priest's leg, amid cries of pain. After he'd finished, blood was still flowing, but it was to a much lesser degree now. The knight felt sorry for the young man, who was clearly more than twenty years his junior.

"Can you stand?" Hugh asked and when the priest nodded, de Payns helped him get up. They slowly started walking towards Hugh's mount, Nicodemus wincing with every limping step he took. "I have to take you back to the monks of Saint John's Hospital in Jerusalem, Father" de Payns said. "Only they will be able to treat your wound properly." Hugh, with a great deal of effort, helped Nicodemus to sit on the destrier, just in front of his saddle's pommel, then rose and sat in the saddle himself.

A moment later, the two men, astride a single horse, began their journey to the capital of the Kingdom of Jerusalem. In fact, a few years later that very image would be used as the official seal of the Order they were destined to create. The only difference would be (at Nicodemus's insistence) that both riders shown on the seal would be depicted as knights, instead of how it truly was that day.

✚ ✚ ✚

Hugh de Payns had been in Outremer—the land beyond the sea—for nearly three years now, having arrived there accompanying his suzerain, Count Hugues de Champagne, in 1116 AD. Originally the lord of the town of Payns, in the French County of Champagne, Hugh decided he wanted nothing to do with that life anymore. So when his liege lord was ready to return home, a year later, Hugh requested to be released from the Count's service.

The reality was that de Payns had nothing to go back home to. His wife, Elizabeth, had died two years earlier and although they did have a son together Hugh was never really convinced the boy was his. Throughout their marriage he'd loved Elizabeth passionately. However, her constant indifference towards him made Hugh seek love and sexual favors elsewhere. And with him being the local lord, and also rather handsome in his youth, he'd no trouble finding such favors. His two illegitimate children were a testament to this. But, after his wife died he became convinced this was God's way of punishing him for his indiscretions. Penance in the Holy Land was beginning to feel like the only appropriate remedy for his sins, hence his request of release to Hugues. The Count reluctantly agreed and Hugh stayed behind, travelling from pilgrim site to pilgrim site ever since.

"Where were you going when my plight interfered with your journey?" Nicodemus asked, cutting into Hugh's thoughts, as they trotted along the road to Jerusalem.

"I was on my way to Joppa, to celebrate our Lord's Resurrection there on the morrow. And then I was going to proceed to Nazareth," Hugh informed his injured travelling companion.

"I am sorry to have interrupted your plans."

"As I said, I'm glad I could be of service. It's not often I get the chance to put my knightly training into actual use anymore—I was starting to feel a bit rusty." Hugh smiled at that, but a moment later he frowned, puzzled. "What is this secret mission of yours, if I may ask?"

Nicodemus seemed reluctant to answer straight away and took a moment considering his options before doing so. "I might as well tell you, given that I may not be able to follow through with it. I'm starting to feel quite weak," the priest replied. Hugh could see that blood was still dripping down from Nicodemus's wound. The bandaging had been good, under the circumstances, but not good enough to stop the bleeding altogether. And the fact the injured leg was placed vertically on a trotting horse did not help the situation either.

The priest began. "Two days after Palm Sunday, the Bishop of Caesarea was informed that a band of Saracen marauders from Ascalon is planning to ambush a large party of Christian pilgrims on Easter. The pilgrims are organizing a walk from Jerusalem to the site of Jesus's baptism on the River Jordan, in celebration of His Resurrection. It seems that this pilgrimage has been so widely publicized that the infidels heard of it. But the Bishop's network of local spies also got wind of these evil plans and told him about them. So the Bishop decided something must be done. Obviously he couldn't make the trip to Jerusalem himself—what with Easter coming up and all the time he'd have to spend attending services—so, instead, he asked *me* to go warn the authorities. Apparently he reasoned that with me being a native it would bode well for the mission," Nicodemus said, again in a self-mocking manner.

"But how are you to warn them?" de Payns asked again.

"I was told to give this to Patriarch Warmund, and that he's supposed to take care of the rest," Nicodemus said, as he took out a scroll of parchment from within his pouch. He held it up for Hugh to see.

"What does it say?"

"Read it for yourself. That way you'll be better prepared if His Excellency has any questions to ask."

Hugh knit his brow. "What are you saying, Father? Am I to take on your mission?"

"No, not at all. It's only in case I'm unable to go meet

him myself... because of my injury," Nicodemus replied, still holding up the scroll. What the priest could not see, though, due to the fact Hugh sat behind him, was that the knight had bowed his head in shame.

"I'm afraid I cannot read. In truth, I can barely write my own name. I was never interested in letters, when I was young, just in fighting," de Payns informed him, in a quiet, embarrassed manner.

Nicodemus remained silent again for a moment. But when he next spoke his tone was a cheerful one. "Well, we must try to remedy that mustn't we? For the time being, let me read to you what it says."

The learned priest proceeded to read the Latin text inscribed on the parchment and then translated each sentence into French so that Hugh could understand. The content of the scroll was a detailed account of everything the Bishop of Caesarea had heard about the planned attack on the Christian pilgrims. It ended with a sincere plea to the Patriarch to do whatever was in his power to prevent such a dire event from occurring. After Nicodemus finished reading, he rolled up the parchment and placed it back in his scrip.

The two riders then continued their journey towards Jerusalem in silence. Fortunately, the weather on that antepenultimate day in March was mild and in their favor. It had neither the stifling heat one felt in the summer, nor its mind-numbing humidity.

✛ ✛ ✛

IT WAS WAY past noon before Hugh could catch his first glimpse of the Holy City from afar. The priest was unable to see it, though, as he'd been unconscious for some time now. From the moment the weak Nicodemus began to lose consciousness, de Payns had been forced to prop his slender body upright to keep him from falling off the horse. And although their mount was trotting at a leisurely pace, it didn't take them long to pass through David's Gate: the western portal in Jerusalem's thick defense walls.

Twenty years had already gone by since the Holy City was reclaimed by the Christians, in 1099 AD. The massacre and bloodbath which followed its conquest was excessive, but it'd helped forge the Kingdom of Jerusalem into existence. Arm in arm with the Principality of Antioch and the Counties of Tripoli and Edessa, these four Christian states held onto a narrow sliver of land, by the skin of their teeth, all along the Mediterranean's easternmost shores. And with infidel armies threatening it on all sides that strip was what everyone in faraway Christendom longingly referred to as *Outremer*.

Once in the city, Hugh directed his destrier to head for the lodgings of the monks of Saint John's Hospital—Nicodemus's condition was in urgent need of attention. When they got near the Hospital, Paulus, a black-clad Saint John's monk standing outside saw them, noticed that one of the riders was injured, and rushed over. Paulus opened his arms and the knight gently passed Nicodemus down to him. Hugh knew the monk well as he and his attendants had resided there ever since staying behind in the Holy Land.

"Take good care of Father Nicodemus, Paulus. I have an errand to run, but I shall be back to check on him soon," Hugh told the monk. Then spurring his horse on, de Payns galloped through the city toward the Temple platform. Warmund de Picquigny, the Patriarch Archbishop of Jerusalem, had his residence up there at the *Templum Domini Church*—or, as the infidels once called it, the *Dome of the Rock*. Hugh had to reach the patriarch before he started with Holy Saturday's Easter Vigil Service at sundown.

Galloping at a frenzied speed, through the cobblestoned streets, de Payns soon arrived up on the Temple Mount and headed towards the Holy City's most distinct landmark: the golden dome of the newly consecrated church. There was only about an hour left till sunset, so Hugh dismounted swiftly on arrival. As he clutched the manuscript he'd retrieved from Nicodemus's scrip, the knight entered the northern side of the octagonal structure, where the Latin Patriarchs had established their residence. Passing under an archway, he then saw a solitary wooden door in front of him, in between two lean columns, and realized this must be where the prelate's chambers were.

A priest who sat by the door, noticed Hugh step in and remarked, "The church's entrance is on the other side, Sir Knight."

"Yes, I know, Father," de Payns replied. "I urgently need to speak with His Excellency, the patriarch. Where can I find him?"

The priest looked at him with indifference and crossed his hands over his protruding belly. "I doubt if His Excellency has time to see anyone now. He is getting ready for the Vigil."

Hugh realized the priest would most probably not let him pass, so he spoke in a pleading tone. "Father, it is of the utmost importance that I speak with him now. Many Christian lives may be at stake. Please, take me to him. I will only take a moment of his time."

The urgency in Hugh's voice must have been able to convince the priest because he got up, walked over to the door, half opened it, and spoke to the patriarch within. "Your Excellency, there is a knight outside wishing to speak to you on a matter of some importance. Shall I let him pass?" A voice from inside the room told the priest to allow the man in, so the priest kept the door ajar, permitting de Payns to enter. As Hugh passed by, he thanked the priest and closed the door behind him.

The patriarchal chambers had been cordoned off from the rest of the building by a series of tall, clay brick walls, which traversed four of the lavishly decorated, thick pillars of the original structure. Other than them, and the equally impressive leaner columns on the opposite wall, the room was frugal in its contents and decor. A single feather mattress with skin covers could be seen on a corner carpet as well as a plain wooden table surrounded by chairs. The only other object in there was a large chest, up against yet another brick wall, out of which de Picquigny was currently removing his vestments. He was a tall, impressive man, of a similar age to Hugh, but one who had sustained the slender figure so often found in those able to avoid all physical toil in their lives.

"You will excuse us if we continue to get ready for tonight's service, Sir...?" the patriarch said, using the majestic plural, while probingly asking for the knight to introduce himself.

"I am Hugh de Payns, Your Excellency, and I beg your pardon for interrupting you. But I do believe the matter at hand justifies such an intrusion."

"And what pray *is* the matter at hand?"

"I think this will explain things much better than I ever could," Hugh told the prelate and handed over the parchment.

Warmund de Picquigny took the scroll, walked over to the table and sat down next to the lit candle to read; he did not bother inviting de Payns to also take a seat. The patriarch spent the next couple of minutes reading the parchment's contents intently. Then, he set it on the table and looked up into Hugh's eyes.

"We do not remember you being in the employ of our Brother, the Bishop of Caesarea. How did this come to be in your possession, Sir Hugh?" de Picquigny asked, while momentarily glancing at the parchment.

"A priest from that bishopric, Father Nicodemus, was bringing it to you, but was attacked by a Saracen on the way here. Fortunately, I came upon them and was able to save him by killing the infidel. I then brought the priest to Jerusalem to receive treatment for his wound. And with this being such an urgent matter, I thought it best to bring the parchment to you myself, as Father Nicodemus is incapacitated."

The patriarch arched an eyebrow. "And you know what it contains? You have read it?"

"Yes, Your Excellency," Hugh lied. He did not wish to admit his ignorance twice in the same day. "If it's not too impertinent to ask, what will Your Excellency do about this?"

The prelate was lost in thought for a long moment before he gave de Payns his reply. "Actually, we are not fully convinced that our Brother Bishop's information is all that solid." De Picquigny looked up at Hugh again. "Is it not curious that this valuable piece of intelligence managed to find its way up to Caesarea, while much closer—here in Jerusalem—nothing to this effect has been heard? No, we can only say that this information is highly suspect. We believe it to be yet another example of the many attempts the infidels make to disrupt our ways of worship—in this instance, the right of the pilgrims to visit the site of Our Lord's Baptism."

Hugh was confused. "So Your Excellency plans to do nothing then?"

"Listen, Sir Hugh," the patriarch said, as a smile appeared on his thin lips. "Even if we did have similar, corroborative intelligence about an imminent ambush plan, there is little we *could* do about it. This pilgrimage, like all others taking place in the realm, is under the king's auspices. And the king desperately needs pilgrims to come here to visit the various Holy Sites. The pilgrims bring much needed revenue as well as being potential candidates in further populating the kingdom—both very important issues. So you see, my good Sir Knight, we could not singlehandedly cancel the event, even if we wanted to. Especially not with such flimsy evidence such as this."

"Well, maybe Your Excellency could warn them to be on their guard at least?" Hugh suggested.

"Yes... We could do that," the prelate said with hesitation. "But we must not forget the pilgrims will ultimately be in God's hands. Surely, He would not let any harm come to them." De Picquigny smiled reassuringly and stood up. "Thank you, Sir Hugh, for bringing it to our attention and do not mention this to anyone else. It would do no one any good if unfounded rumors start to circulate. Now, please excuse us, we *do* have to get ready."

Hugh de Payns bowed respectfully to the prelate and walked to the door. As an afterthought the patriarch called out, "Please relay to Father Nicodemus our sincerest wishes for a speedy recovery."

The knight turned and bowed once more. "I will, Your Excellency. Thank you."

Hugh mounted his horse and rode back to his chambers at Saint John's Hospital. In truth, he was not entirely happy with the results of his meeting with the patriarch. He felt the prelate should have taken the threat extended against the pilgrims more seriously. Still, in light of the fact that he didn't possess all the facts, de Payns believed he'd done everything possible. And as de Picquigny had said, the matter was indeed in God's hands.

As soon as de Payns arrived at the rooms he'd been renting from the monks of the Hospital, Philippe rushed out the building and took hold of the horse's reins. Its coat was splattered with sweat. Philippe was Hugh's squire and companion at arms, and had been in the knight's service for many years, ever since their youth. In fact, Philippe, along with a cook and a page boy, were the only ones, out of all of de Payns's attendants, who'd willingly stayed behind with him in the Holy Land. The rest he had released from his service and even provided them with travel funds to get back home.

"Decided to stay in the city for Easter after all, Sir Hugh?" Philippe asked, as de Payns dismounted.

"It was not of my own choosing, Philippe. I will tell you about it later," Hugh replied as he started walking over to the Hospital; he wanted to find out how Nicodemus was doing. The squire was leading the horse towards the stables, when he heard his master shout out, "Give him a good rubdown, Philippe. I'm afraid I have exhausted him today."

Hugh soon saw Paulus coming out of one of the mud-brick buildings and called out, "How is our patient?"

"His wound has been cleaned and dressed. Although he's lost a lot of blood he looks strong, so I am confident he'll recover. He fell asleep, as soon as we finished bandaging him, and will probably sleep throughout the day," Paulus reported when de Payns got near. Then, after another monk called out to him, Paulus left hastily, adding, "I will keep you informed of his condition, Sir Hugh."

The knight offered his thanks, just as the monk was rushing off to deal with what was apparently a new emergency. Hugh had nothing else to do but to go find his good friend, Godfrey de St. Omer. He needed to tell him he was back in Jerusalem and, in light of this, for them to make plans on where to observe the Easter services.

✢ ✢ ✢

By late afternoon, the following day, the whole city was abuzz with the grim details of the pilgrim massacre.

On Easter morning, just after receiving the Sacrament of Holy Communion at Mass, a group of about seven hundred devout pilgrims began their planned journey towards the site on the River Jordan where Jesus was believed to have been baptized. En route, they were attacked by a large band of infidels who proceeded to murder, pillage, and rape the joyful Christians. Nearly three hundred of them perished and a further sixty were taken to be sold into slavery. When the king heard of this, from the returning survivors, he sent out a contingent of his guards to punish the culprits and rescue the captives. But, regrettably, none could be found.

Hugh was alone in his room that evening, feeling quite depressed, when Philippe tapped lightly on the door. After being given permission to enter, the squire informed his master that word had come of Father Nicodemus asking for him. The knight had tried to visit Nicodemus, several times throughout the day, but the recuperating priest had always been asleep when he got there. Having to face him now, though, and especially after hearing about those dreadful events, made Hugh uneasy. Nevertheless, he thanked Philippe and told him to inform the messenger that he'd go straight away.

It was a short walk over to the patients' quarters, and de Payns soon walked into the candlelit Hospital room where the priest lay, along with others. Dragging a stool next to the pallet bed, the knight attempted a bright, confident grin as he sat down. "How are you feeling, Father?"

"Well, it doesn't hurt so much anymore, and Paulus says the wound has started to heal. But other than that, I feel miserable. Have you not heard the news, Sir?" Nicodemus asked.

Hugh de Payns bowed his head before replying. "I'm afraid I have. It's a most dreadful business. Everything your Bishop warned about has come to pass."

"But did you not go and warn the patriarch about this? Did you not show him the parchment?" the priest persisted. "I was sure you did, because when I heard the news I looked for it in my pouch and it was gone."

"I *did* show it to him!" Hugh blurted out, but then lowered his voice so that the others around could not overhear. "He was confident that it was just some ploy on the part of the infidels, to disrupt our ways of worship. He did, however, promise to warn the pilgrim leaders of the threat."

"I don't know if any such warning was given. Yet, even if it had, how were the pilgrims supposed to defend themselves?" Nicodemus wondered. But, realizing how distressed and self-accusing the knight looked, he added more soothingly, "I'm sure you did your best, Sir Hugh."

"Alas, it was not enough," de Payns said and remorsefully bowed his head, once more.

They both spent a few moments in silence before Nicodemus decided to express his thoughts out loud. "If only there had been a detachment to safely escort the pilgrims on their way."

Hugh lifted his head and looked into the priest's eyes. "Do you mean some sort of army unit?"

"I don't mean an official army unit, as such, but... a kind of militia... composed of knights, perhaps?"

"That might've been useful, except the King has forbidden knights to form any private groups, unless they are all under his authority," Hugh countered.

"Yes, that's true..." Nicodemus agreed, and remained lost in thought for a while. He then snapped out of his trance to suggest, "What if this militia to protect the pilgrims was not under the authority of the King, but under that of the Patriarch Archbishop instead? I mean, pilgrimage is a purely religious activity, is it not?"

Hugh de Payns lowered his voice further before replying. "But the Patriarch was against doing anything for the pilgrims today."

"And I'm sure he's regretting his decision even more than we are. He probably reacted so because he could do nothing worthwhile."

"Aye, he did say something to that effect."

"See?" Nicodemus said, as a bright smile emerged on his face.

"This group of knights that you speak of, though... how can they be under the patriarch's jurisdiction and not that of the king's?"

Just as Hugh was uttering the question, Paulus the monk stepped through the door to check on another patient in the room. Seeing him gave Nicodemus a subsequently famous idea.

"They could be warrior monks," he suggested with enthusiasm.

"But that's absurd!" Hugh shouted out. And because everyone turned their heads in their direction, he lowered his voice again. "How can a knight ever become a monk, Father? Monks aren't allowed to kill anyone."

The priest took another moment before replying. "Think of it this way. These are extraordinary times and our circumstances here in Outremer are equally unusual. In fact, the whole essence of the Pope's War to free the Holy Land, was based on the teachings of St. Augustine who justified the use of force when it's in the service of God. The patriarch archbishop is the representative of the pope here, and as such his authority is unchallenged—especially on matters concerning the Church. If he wished to establish a group of knightly monks, with the sole purpose of protecting pilgrims, who can say he can't do so? I'm sure King Baldwin wouldn't have any objections to it," Nicodemus said excitedly. In truth, the priest felt so thrilled that a little color became visible on his pale face.

Hugh had to admit he was impressed by Nicodemus's knowledge and arguments. However, he still had reservations. "But this will mean that any knight eager enough to join this new force will have to spend the rest of his life as a monk, will it not?"

"Permit me to ask you something, Sir Hugh," the priest said and when the knight nodded, he went on. "What is the reason you are still here in Outremer?"

"I stayed behind to do penance for my sins."

"Then what greater atonement is there than fighting to protect Christian lives and perhaps even dying for our faith?" Nicodemus asked again, clinching the argument.

The priest correctly deduced that the long silence, which followed, meant Hugh was considering the idea in a favorable way. So, Nicodemus lost no more time in taking it a step further. "How many knights do you think might be interested in such a venture?"

Hugh looked deep into Nicodemus's eyes and realized that what they were actually talking about was the creation of this force by *them*! Nonetheless, it only took an instant for him to decide whether he wanted to be a part of it. So he replied, "Off the top of my head I can think of about a dozen, or so. And I'm sure my friend, Godfrey de St. Omer, can come up with as many more. But it will not be easy convincing them to give up their current worldly lives and to live henceforth as monks."

"I have great faith in your powers of persuasion, Sir

Hugh. This being an undoubtedly justified and noble cause, I'm sure your fellow knights will view it exactly so. As for my part, when I am able to walk again, I shall visit the Patriarch and present the idea to him. I'm certain he'll be very pleased," Nicodemus said.

"If Godfrey and I are able to muster the necessary volunteers, what do you think we should call ourselves?"

"I think you should call yourselves precisely what you'll be," the priest replied in matter-of-fact manner.

"And what's that?"

"The *Poor Fellow-Soldiers of Jesus Christ*."

For the first time since stepping into the room, a genuine smile appeared on Hugh's face. "I like that." He was pleased.

✢ ✢ ✢

OVER THE NEXT few days, and while Nicodemus was still recuperating, Hugh and Godfrey de St. Omer were busy drumming up support from fellow knights for this new endeavor of theirs. Godfrey had needed little convincing when de Payns put the idea to him as he'd also done things in his life which desperately needed atonement. In fact, this was the very tactic the two friends decided to use as they approached the other knights: Do you not feel your soul is in need of salvation? How are you going about to redeem your shameful deeds? What if you were offered a noble way to atone for all of your sins?

All in all, Hugh and Godfrey were able to receive almost thirty pledges from knights willing to enlist in the new militia force. The only snag was that many of them were still under obligation to their feudal lords and couldn't see how they'd be able to get out of it. Hugh reassured them he'd think of something, but in the meantime they were to wait for his summons and reveal their conversation to no one. Everyone readily agreed.

As far as Nicodemus's meeting with the patriarch was

concerned, amazingly enough, the one to initiate it was the prelate himself. On the Thursday after Easter, Warmund de Picquigny surprised the priest—and quite a few of the others in that Hospital room—by casually stepping in. Apparently, he'd already been informed which bed Nicodemus was on because he walked straight over.

The patriarch stood over him. "Are you Father Nicodemus?"

"Yes, I am," the priest replied, and made an effort to sit upright. He was supposed to kiss the patriarch's hand, as was the custom, but Warmund cut him short.

"Please do not inconvenience yourself, Father. How are you feeling?" the prelate asked again, as he took the chair one of the monks brought in for him to sit.

"I'm much better, although I do feel a bit weak at times. Thank you for your concern, My Lord Patriarch."

Warmund looked somewhat surprised. "You have recognized us?" He was wearing a simple black robe that day and not his usual patriarchal attire.

"Yes, Your Excellency, I remember you, from when you visited our Bishopric last year."

"You have quite the memory," the patriarch complimented him. "At any rate, we have been visiting the wounded victims of that cowardly Saracen attack to wish them well. And seeing you are also an indirect casualty of it, we thought it proper to extend our best wishes to you as well."

"That is most kind of you, My Lord. Thank you," Nicodemus said.

De Picquigny spoke in a quieter tone now, revealing a sense of guilt. "Although it clearly isn't enough, given it was our inactivity which caused it all to happen in the first place." And then drawing closer, he added, "As you most certainly are aware."

"I'm sure you did what you thought best at the time, Your Excellency," Nicodemus said, also in a low voice.

After a long moment of silence passed between them, the Patriarch scrutinized him with interest. "Where are you from, Father?"

"I am originally from Tyre. My family has lived there for countless generations, and—"

"Maybe even from the time of the Phoenicians, eh?" the prelate cut in, in jest, and chuckled.

Nicodemus grinned as well, but lowered his eyes as he replied. "Perhaps... I couldn't say for sure, Excellency."

"And how did you get involved in the Church?" Warmund went on to ask.

"By the time I was fifteen years of age, my father's commercial affairs were not doing very well and so my parents thought that perhaps a life in the Church—and away from the Saracen rule of Tyre—might be better suited for me. As a result, I was sent to a monastery, up on Mount Lebanon, where I became a monk. I spent five years there furthering my education, particularly in the French language, after which the Bishop of Caesarea happened to visit the monastery. For some reason he singled me out and asked whether I wanted to become a member of his retinue. I replied that I did, so within a year I was ordained a priest and have been one of the Bishop's advisors, ever since."

"Very good..." de Picquigny said while nodding several times, apparently deep in thought. He was considering his next question carefully. "How would you like to be a member of *our* staff, instead, here in Jerusalem?"

"Excellency, that would be quite an honor!" Nicodemus blurted out. And then checking himself he said more somberly, "But, I wouldn't want to create any problems with my bishop. He *is* expecting me to return to Caesarea, eventually."

"You just leave it up to us, Father. I'm sure our brother the bishop will not oppose our wishes," the patriarch reassured him and was about to rise from his chair.

Thinking fast, the priest realized this was the right moment to put his idea forward. "There is one other matter, however, Your Excellency, that I was considering giving my assistance to, before I returned to the bishopric."

"Oh? And what is that?" Warmund asked, returning to his seat.

"In light of recent events, Sir Hugh de Payns—with whom you have met—has come up with a plan of creating a fighting force consisting of knights, with the sole purpose of protecting pilgrims in the future. This force would be under your authority since the knights will be required to take monastic vows. In essence, the concept is that they'd be warrior monks answerable only to you, My Lord." Nicodemus then looked deep into the patriarch's eyes for any reaction. He had chosen to credit Hugh with the idea, instead of himself, feeling it stood a better chance of acceptance if it originated from a knight.

The prelate spent a long moment considering what he'd just heard before speaking. "We believe it's an excellent idea—a novel one, to be sure—but excellent all the same. And what would your involvement be in all this? How were you thinking of assisting this new force?"

"As you know, Your Excellency, most, if not all of these knights are illiterate. And since such an endeavor would need schedules, planning, provisions, as well as correspondence with various parties, I was considering providing my services, for a short time, in those areas... If the plan met with your approval, of course." Nicodemus was feeling very excited the Patriarch was favorably predisposed.

"Yes, well, this definitely puts matters in a different perspective. Although we had other plans for you, you shall just have to spearhead this new venture, instead, Father. We shall speak more about this when you have recovered," Warmund said.

And just before the prelate got up to leave again, Nicodemus saw a clear chance of putting Hugh's problem to him, as well. "There is one drawback, though, Excellency," the priest said. And when the patriarch frowned questioningly, Nicodemus elaborated. "Many of the knights already willing to take part in this are still bound to their feudal lords. Unless they are released from their obligations they can neither participate, nor take the necessary monastic vows."

"A difficulty easily solved," Warmund de Picquigny replied with conviction. "A force like this would be very favorably viewed on by the king, as it will solve his most vexing problem concerning the pilgrims. We are certain *he* can find a way to convince the lords in question to release their vassals in aid of this noble cause... We shall speak to him."

Then, the patriarch finally rose from the chair, wished the priest a speedy recovery and left the room.

Nicodemus was overjoyed.

✝ ✝ ✝

A FULL YEAR passed since the dreadful affair of the pilgrim massacre. And it was a year filled with events and activities intended to ensure such an incident never happened again:

King Baldwin, the Second of his name, having readily endorsed the creation of the *Poor Fellow-Soldiers of Jesus Christ*, decreed that if any knight wished to join this new force, then his liege lord was expected to release him from his vows of fealty. Naturally, this decree created a flurry of excitement amongst the knights who'd already pledged themselves to Hugh, and as a result, one by one, they started to enlist. In addition to that, the king even knighted a few squires who had expressed a wish in becoming members of this new enterprise as well. All in all, by the fall of 1119 AD, the Poor Fellow-Soldiers numbered more than thirty knights and almost twice as many sergeants—as the knights' squires and men-at-arms were now called.

At first, they all started by sharing rooms with their fellow monks of St. John's Hospital; but as new recruits kept coming in, the conditions there soon became crowded. To alleviate the problem, the king initially gave them new accommodations in a wing of his palace up on Temple Mount—following an idea put to him by the patriarch who in turn had been counseled in that direction by Nicodemus. Later on, in February 1120 AD, when King Baldwin moved to a new palace, he was again convinced that his former home should be handed over entirely to the new contingent of knights. This structure, formerly known as the al-Aqsa Mosque, was on the southern edge of the Mount's platform and was believed to be situated above the site of the original Temple of Solomon. The inevitable association of the knights with their living quarters soon resulted in them becoming known as the *Poor Fellow-Soldiers of Jesus Christ and of the Temple of Solomon,* or in short, the *Knights Templar*—or even shorter still, the *Templars.*

The Templars, slowly but surely, began assimilating themselves into a dedicated monastic Order from the very moment the idea took form—this being achieved under the overall spiritual guidance of the patriarch, Warmund de Picquigny, but especially under the direct supervision of Father Nicodemus and Hugh de Payns. Observing the ascetic Benedictine Rule at first, and later the stricter Cistercian one, the knights, sergeants and other confrères, started living an austere communal life. Among other things, they were obliged to attend six church services, throughout the day and night, as well as to eat meals of a strict diet at designated times, while listening to Bible passages in complete silence. And all this aside from the many hours spent in taking care of their numerous other duties, such as combat training, patrolling the pilgrim roads, and looking after their horses.

Christmas day of 1119 AD had been a very special one for the Order. In the crowded Church of the Holy Sepulcher, Hugh de Payns, Godfrey de St. Omer, and all the other Templars took their solemn vows of poverty, chastity, and obedience, in the presence of the patriarch. After that, Warmund de Picquigny gifted each one of them a mantle that was to be worn over their clothes and armor—a white one for the knights and a black one for the sergeants. These two conflicting mantle colors were what gave rise, a few years later, to the *Beauseant*: the Templars' standard and battle flag.

Another seminal event for the Order, during its first year

of existence, was the Council held at Nablus (a town about 30 miles north of Jerusalem), in January 1120 AD. Although the Council's deliberations were mainly concerned with the locusts and crop failures, which had plagued Outremer in recent years, it did take time to justify the Order's mandate, indirectly, with one of its canons which stated: *'If a cleric takes up arms in the cause of defense, he is not held to be guilty.'* However, a more direct way in which the Templars got involved with the Council was that they safely escorted the many high ranking lay and spiritual dignitaries to Nablus. By doing so, their existence was made known to everyone of importance within the Holy Land.

Their reputation, unbeknownst to them, was even starting to spread to Christendom. Some of their patrol missions, which had resulted in clashes with Saracens and the subsequent rescuing of pilgrim lives, had created quite an impression back in France, England and other countries the stories had reached. So great an impression, in fact, that when Fulk, the powerful Fifth Count of Anjou, decided to come to Outremer, after the Council of Nablus, he chose to stay with the Order, in its newly acquired palace up on Temple Mount. On his return home, the count expressed his admiration and gratitude by providing the Templars with a very generous annual income.

✢ ✢ ✢

Jerusalem
1120 CE

WHEN HE SAW Nicodemus walking in the distance, Hugh de Payns called out, but the priest didn't hear him and kept going. The knight quickly dismounted and threw his horse's reins over to Philippe for him to take charge. They'd both just returned from an uneventful patrol of the Jerusalem-Bethlehem road.

Attempting to make large strides, within the confines

of his white mantle, in order to reach the priest, was not an easy proposition for Hugh. He was weighed down by his chain-mail coat, his sword, the shield on his back, as well as with the many hours he'd spent in the saddle that day. Nevertheless, he pressed on and after covering some distance he called out the priest's name again. This time Nicodemus heard him, just before starting down the steps, so he stopped and turned in Hugh's direction.

"Father, I need to speak with you," the out-of-breath knight managed to say, after he got closer and took his helmet off.

"Very well, Sir Hugh. Let's go down to my room, shall we?" Nicodemus suggested, and they both started descending.

The priest's living quarters were a level below that of the main palace—where all the knights and sergeants lived— and to the east of it. When the former mosque was assigned to the Templar Order, a vast, underground chamber had been handed over as well. Consisting of countless thick pillars, which supported its tall vaulted arches, this massive, cavernous space below the Temple Mount's surface was still, naively, referred to as the *'Stables of Solomon.'* The truth was, it had nothing to do with the ancient Hebrew king, but had been used as a stable by King Baldwin while he used to live there, and now by the Templars, who also utilized parts of it to shelter their horses. Nicodemus—at his suggestion, and after receiving the patriarch's approval—had used up a small area near the south-east corner of the Stables to construct his chambers. At the same time, a few rudimentary cubicles were also built to house the scribes he'd recruited from around his hometown of Tyre. In fact, Hugh often lightheartedly spoke of those subterranean rooms as the *Brains of the Order*, since it was there where all correspondence, patrol schedules and other planning activities took place.

Nicodemus gestured to a chair after they'd stepped inside. "Please have a seat, Sir Hugh. What can I do for you? Do you wish to continue our reading lessons?"

"No, not today, Father," de Payns replied, as he unburdened himself of his sword and pointed shield. "I will come straight to the point. Godfrey has been told that, lately, strange sounds can be heard from down here, especially during the night—sounds resembling those one hears when someone is digging. Do you know anything about this, Father? Has anyone been excavating?"

The priest remained silent and lost in thought for a moment. Then, he said, "I shall not lie to you, Sir Hugh. But whatever is mentioned in this room must remain our secret. Agreed?"

"Yes, of course."

"In fact, I am glad you are raising this. However, please allow me to start my reply by first asking *you* a question. What do you know of the Phoenicians?"

The knight, although puzzled by this, nevertheless shook his head and replied just as candidly, "Nothing really. Why? What's so important about them?"

"Well, to begin with, they had a civilization that spanned almost three millennia—maybe more—and about which very little is widely known."

When Hugh raised his eyebrows as far up as they could go, signifying he was duly impressed and interested, this encouraged Nicodemus to continue. "It all started with a small fishing village on the Mediterranean coast, north of here, named Byblos—or Gibelet, as it is now called. Using the legendary cedar trees found only on nearby Mount Lebanon, these fishermen little by little transformed themselves into master shipbuilders, but also, in time, into expert mariners and successful traders. As they began to expand, the ancient Phoenicians of Byblos established two more ports to the south of their city. And these settlements eventually grew into thriving city-states in their own right, the names of which I'm sure you will not fail to recognize: Sidon and Tyre."

When de Payns nodded he knew them, the priest carried on. "These ports, however, were not the only ones the ancient Phoenicians founded. They went on to establish several colonies in and around the Mediterranean Sea. Kition of Cyprus, Palermo in Sicily, and Carthage in North Africa, are just a few examples of their—"

"Carthage was a Phoenician colony?" Hugh cut in with enthusiasm. As a boy he'd always been interested in stories about the Punic Wars and especially those concerning the great General Hannibal of Carthage.

"Yes, it was. And apparently the most well-known, among several others," Nicodemus replied, with a chuckle. After taking a moment, though, to collect his thoughts, the priest continued with his narration. "Over the many centuries that followed, the Phoenicians not only maintained their status as renowned shipbuilders and merchants, but they also evolved into masters of masonry and construction. In fact, their most famous building project took place very near from where we are sitting."

"What do you mean?" a once more puzzled Hugh de Payns asked.

"What I mean is that the Phoenicians built King Solomon's Temple."

Realizing the knight was ignorant of this as well, Nicodemus decided to tell the story from the beginning. "These events are well documented in the Bible's Old Testament. When King Solomon wanted to start building the Temple, he sought help from King Hiram of Tyre. And he did so for two reasons: The first was because the king used to be a friend of his father, David. But the second, and most important reason, was because the Phoenicians of Tyre were by then expert builders—as opposed to the Hebrews who had no skills in that area. King Hiram not only chose to grant Solomon's wish, but in addition, he even provided him with the services of his master builder, a Tyrian also named Hiram.

"Master Hiram proceeded to work on the construction of the Temple for over seven years and after it was completed, he was then entrusted with building King Solomon's palace, as well. At some point, for reasons I shall not go into now, Master Hiram hid the Hebrews' Ark of the Covenant, along with other treasures. And Solomon had him killed for that."

"This is all very interesting, Father, but how can you possibly know what happened so long ago?" Hugh asked. He looked quite puzzled, yet at the same time highly intrigued.

"First of all, there are indications in the Old Testament that something untoward happened between the two kings, and which threatened to sour their relationship."

"What sort of indications?"

"Well, after all construction had ended..." Nicodemus started to say, and then reached for his bulky, handwritten copy of the Bible, which was on a shelf behind him. Opening it up and finding the relevant passage in the Old Testament, he continued. "In the First Book of Kings, chapter 9, it says: *'(Now Hiram the king of Tyre had furnished Solomon with cedar trees and fir trees, and with gold, according to all his desire,) that then King Solomon gave Hiram twenty cities in the land of Galilee. And Hiram came out from Tyre to see the cities which Solomon had given him; and they pleased him not. And he said, What cities are these which thou hast given me, my brother? And he called them the land of Cabul unto this day. And Hiram sent to the king sixscore talents of gold.'* Now why would he do that, Sir Hugh?" the priest asked emphatically as he slammed the Holy Book shut.

"Why would he do what?"

"Why would King Hiram send Solomon all that gold after receiving twenty cities which did not please him? Cities that were given, mind you, as payment for everything King Hiram had supplied for the building of the Temple and palace. Obviously the Tyrian king did not consider those cities as adequate payment for what he'd provided Solomon. So why give him so much gold, on top of everything else?"

"Yes, it is strange," Hugh agreed and frowned. "How do you interpret it, Father?"

"Knowing how the actual events unfolded, I'd say the

only logical explanation for this passage is that something happened, *before* Solomon decided to give Hiram those worthless cities. An event which probably convinced the Phoenician King to reimburse his Hebrew counterpart if they were to maintain a good trading relationship in the future—which they did—and despite the murder of his trusted architect. Maybe for a prized possession that had been taken from Solomon, perhaps?"

"Aye, that does sound logical. But does the Bible speak of the Ark being stolen?" de Payns asked once again.

"No, of course not, how could they ever admit such an event? The Ark of the Covenant was the single most precious object the Hebrews ever possessed. The stone tablets of the Ten Commandments, said to be concealed inside the Ark, were their direct connection to God and the sole reason for them building the Temple in the first place. I have done extensive research of all the Old Testament Books, and after they speak of Solomon placing the Ark in the Temple, it is hardly mentioned again. The only exception to that is when another Hebrew King, named Josiah, called on the priests to transfer the Ark back into the Temple, many decades after Solomon. But obviously this was a much later, made-up story of political necessity. Since most Hebrews blamed Solomon, and his turning away from God, for their nation's misfortunes, the chroniclers probably wanted to reassure everyone that the Ark hadn't been lost during the Babylonian Captivity and that it was still in their possession—which it certainly was *not*. Or, perhaps a duplicate Ark existed by then—who knows? Other than that, it seems to vanish into thin air and is never spoken of again. Isn't it strange?" asked Nicodemus.

"Yes, it is." De Payns frowned. "But this still doesn't solve the mystery of how you know about the theft and the murder which followed."

"Well, Sir Hugh, that's no mystery because there were men who witnessed the whole thing, first hand."

Hugh's eyes opened up wide. "There were witnesses?"

"Of course there were. While Hiram was being murdered in the Temple, his two assistants were hiding in an underground crypt, unaware of what happened. After some time passed, they wondered where Hiram had gone off to so they crept out of their hiding place, only to discover that their master was dead. They secreted his remains away, and then escaped from the Temple Mount, via a series of subterranean tunnels and passageways, which had been constructed earlier. Leaving Jerusalem behind them, the two Phoenicians arrived at a small settlement, several miles north of the capital, and stayed there incognito for a few months. When they felt sufficient time had passed, and thought it safe, they broke with my ancestors' tradition of not leaving written records and sent a full report to King Hiram, so that he—"

"Wait a minute, Father," de Payns interrupted, once again. "Did you just say *'my ancestors'*?"

"Yes, I did. I'm proud to reveal to you, in confidence of course, that I am a direct descendant of ancient Phoenicians. In fact, my lineage traces all the way back to Hiram, himself—on my mother's side. You see, Sir Hugh, even though the Greeks and Romans conquered Tyre, as well as all the other Phoenician cities, our civilization never truly vanished. An intact Phoenician state may not have existed anymore, but the things we knew as a people, and which made our civilization last for so long, did not disappear overnight. We still knew how to expertly build ships; we still possessed our trading skills; we could still build marvelous structures; and we still had our thirst for learning other people's languages and customs—among many other useful qualities. Generation after generation, our history and knowhow has been secretly passed down in the homeschooling parents and grandparents provide, to safeguard it wouldn't be forgotten."

"I must say I'm quite impressed, Father. I have never heard anything about this before," Hugh said, after he had a moment to take it all in. "But why did you say that Hiram's assistants broke with the tradition of not making records and decided to write a report to the king?"

"Because, although the ancient Phoenicians were the first to create an alphabet—an innovation later adopted by the Greeks, the Romans, and everyone else—they were very secretive about the way they lived and handled their affairs. They believed that written records of how things were done could be very dangerous if they fell into the wrong hands. So, the Phoenicians kept their writing to a minimum. That is why so very little about them has survived—for the rest of the world."

And after he stayed silent for a moment, Nicodemus had a spark of creativity—an idea which would plant the seed for one of the Templar's most distinguishing features. "In fact, I propose that secrecy should become our Order's fourth pillar."

"What do you mean?"

"Well, you and the rest of our Brotherhood have all taken vows of poverty, chastity and obedience. But a solid structure always needs four pillars to stand securely. So, let us make secrecy that fourth pillar for us. Our affairs must never be made public, and even then, some of those should be known only to a select few within the Order."

"And why is that, Father?"

"My suggestion has to do with how I will conclude my answer to your original question: The one about the sounds of digging coming from down here, remember?" Nicodemus asked.

"Ah, yes. With all the stories you've told me, I'm afraid I lost track of what I asked you in the first place. So why *is* digging taking place?"

"Master Hiram's two assistants did manage to return to Tyre. And their verbal accounts, as well as the written report they'd sent earlier, all give us a good idea about where the crypt, that Hiram hid the treasure in, is located. So, my scribes and I have been busy, these past few nights, trying to find it," the priest replied, all the while looking intently at Hugh for his reaction.

The knight did not respond for a while. Although he was intrigued by the whole subject, he did not like the idea of being kept in the dark by Nicodemus like this. When he next spoke he openly expressed those exact sentiments. The priest countered by telling Sir Hugh he would have told him, eventually, but that they shouldn't dwell on it now. What was more important was that they should join forces on this, and that the potential discovery could be bigger than any of them.

"So you've been digging down to find this crypt?" Hugh de Payns asked after another long moment. The question clearly indicated he acquiesced to what Nicodemus was suggesting.

The priest was relieved. "No, we have been tunneling through the north wall, trying to reach the crypt Hiram's assistants talked about."

"But surely one must dig down. We are sitting on top of the old Temple, are we not?" the knight protested.

"No, no. This part of the Temple Mount was an extension to it, constructed at first by King Herod when he erected the Second Temple, and then expanded by Emperor Justinian when he built the church that was to become the al-Aqsa Mosque. It did not exist in Solomon's time. No, the First Temple was situated north of here. Exactly where the Templum Domini Church stands now," Nicodemus said and pointed in that direction.

"Then what do you propose we do, Father?" de Payns asked.

"I propose that you choose a small, but discreet group from among your knights. Together with my scribes we shall all continue tunneling north to discover the crypt. However, everything must be conducted in absolute secrecy and discretion. If anyone else finds out what we're doing, we shall be compromised for sure. So no one, apart from our group, must know anything about this. Agreed?"

"Agreed," was Hugh's eager reply. The promise of an imminent adventure had got the better of him.

✝ ✝ ✝

AFTER LEAVING THE priest, Hugh went straight to his second in command, Godfrey de St. Omer, to share what Nicodemus had revealed. Godfrey, being also intrigued by the prospect of them searching for treasure, helped Hugh come up with a list of seven other knights whom they both felt were the most trustworthy for a task like this. Along with four others, those who were approached included Payns de Montdidier, Archambaud de St. Agnan and Geoffrey Bison.

The following evening, the nine knights met with Nicodemus and his three scribes, down in the priest's room. They were all there to discuss how this undertaking would proceed. The small chamber soon became very hot and crowded, and everybody struggled to find a place to sit or stand. But regardless of this, the prevailing mood—especially among the knights—was that they were in considerably high spirits; the sense of an exciting quest in the offing had helped stimulate them.

When everyone settled down, Hugh de Payns stood up and began to speak. "Sirs, Father, Brethren, you all know the reason why we have gathered here tonight. We are about to embark on a pursuit that, if it proves successful, I believe will help define our Order even further. Although I would love to give you more details on how we are to proceed, alas, I do not possess them. So, I think it is best if we heard from Father Nicodemus who does. Father?" de Payns said and gestured for the priest to carry on.

"Thank you, Grand Master," Nicodemus said to Hugh, as he started to address those assembled. "Yes, I also believe this venture has the power to further define our Order—if we succeed. Even though there are many more Templar knights than the ones in attendance tonight, and no sergeants are here, nevertheless, I feel this quest will instill an additional sense of purpose in all whom are present. One which will be strengthened by the shared, and necessary, secrecy of what we are about to embark upon. Allow me then to share with you what has been done so far and what is needed from this point forward.

"For the past week, or so, the scribe brothers and I have been excavating at the northernmost location of the Stable walls. Aside from the fact that this spot is not near the stabled horses, it also has the advantage of being the one closest to our objective. Now, from everything Hiram's assistants had revealed, and by my calculations, the crypt in question should be located just below the northern side of the Templum Domini Church, and at roughly this depth beneath the surface."

Nicodemus stopped talking when the knights started whispering amongst themselves. "Forgive me Father, but isn't that a distance of over a thousand feet from here?" Godfrey de St. Omer asked, voicing everyone's concern.

"Yes it is, and probably more if we do not arrive there in a straight line. That is why I was glad when the Grand Master questioned me about what was going on down here. As soon as we had dug just beyond the bricks covering the Stable wall's surface, we discovered that what lay ahead was virtually solid rock. It would've been impossible for us to continue on our own, since we are not miners, nor did we have the appropriate tools." The priest then looked around the room for any reactions.

Archambaud de St. Agnan spoke out next. "Now that you mention mining, Father, I remember when I was a child, some of the old folk spoke about how the Romans used to mine, when they were trying to discover minerals in the nearby Ardennes Mountains. Instead of going in, with only pickaxes and shovels, they used to break up the rock by first soaking it in vinegar, igniting it, and then abruptly cooling down the rock with water."

Nicodemus smiled. "That is a most excellent suggestion, Sir Archambaud. Although vinegar is in short supply here, we may have to use our own concoction of 'Greek Fire' made up of cedar resin and sulfur."

This comment brought about an outbreak of simultaneous conversations between the knights as everyone seemed to have an idea to express about something or other. The resulting cacophony compelled Hugh de Payns to stand up and demand everyone's attention.

"Brothers, please! I'm sure all of us have thoughts on the matter and we are all very excited, but if everyone speaks at once little progress can be made," the Grand Master roared. He then proceeded to ask Nicodemus a question of his own. "Father, you've told us that by your reckoning this crypt should be beneath the northern side of the church. What I'd like to know is whether we will have to tunnel all the way there. Are there no tunnels, or passageways, in-between, which might reduce the distance we must dig?"

"That is a good question, Sir Hugh. From what Hiram's assistants had revealed, they used a series of tunnels on the northern side of the crypt in order to escape. Unfortunately, they never spoke of any tunnels on the south side. There may be some, but I don't know of any. At any rate, finding underground passageways would not be very helpful, I think," Nicodemus said, as he looked around at everyone.

"And why is that?" de Payns asked again.

"Because reaching the crypt is another problem which has been puzzling me considerably. Tunneling underground, with no sun or landmarks to help guide us, will be quite difficult since we'll never be able to be absolutely sure that our course is correct. So, even if we do find some ancient tunnels, we'll never be certain whether they lead in the right direction, or not. They will probably only serve to confuse us."

After a moment of everyone being silent and lost in thoughtful reflection, someone spoke up. "I think I may have a solution to the problem of us straying from the right track, Father." Geoffrey Bison was the one who'd spoken, and when he had everyone's attention he went on. "If we attempt to dig from here directly to the north of the Church, we may soon find ourselves tunneling out of the Temple

Mount's walls—something which none of us would want. And that's because we can never be sure the angle we'll be taking is the correct one. Now, to remedy that, what I propose is to first determine the exact spot, up on the surface, which corresponds to where the starting point of our excavation is down here. From that location up there someone can plot a route to the north of the church by walking towards it in straight lines and only making sharp turns where necessary—carefully noting the number of paces and turns he makes along the way. Then, all we have to do while tunneling is to replicate that same route. I know it will take longer, but I feel it's the only certain way for us not to go astray—or to tunnel accidentally into that other, known cave, which is beneath the church."

Geoffrey's suggestion was followed by a long silence. Then, when he saw his brothers starting to smile and nod their heads, he knew they approved.

"That's brilliant, Sir Geoffrey," the Grand Master congratulated him and to stop everyone from talking all at once, yet again, he added quickly, "This idea solves another problem. What else do we need, Father?"

"Other than for all of us to keep this undertaking a safely guarded secret, I think the only minor issue left is to obtain the necessary digging tools and supplies," Nicodemus replied.

"That shouldn't be difficult," Hugh said.

And after looking at all the eager faces around the room, the Grand Master stated energetically, "Right, let's get to work!"

HIRAM

Chapter 4

BUILDER

Tyre
966 BCE

Hiram Binne had just finished placing the goat's entrails in the ceremonial copper dish when a man stormed into the temple. "Master, you must come at once... The king requires your presence urgently," the breathless messenger blurted out.

Without responding, Hiram stood up and passed the dish over to the nearest priest. After that, he used a piece of cloth to remove the animal blood from his hands, and proceeded to dust off the parts of his long, green linen robe where he'd been kneeling. Only then did Hiram turn around to address the courier. "Inform my namesake the king that I shall be there in a short while." On hearing that the messenger lost no time; he ran out of the temple to deliver the reply, with the same urgency as he'd entered it. Hiram Binne walked over to the High Priest and handed him a small pouch filled with coins.

"I am confident our god will do his utmost to grant you your wish, Master," the High Priest said, bowing his purple-robed figure with respect as he received the payment.

"Let us just hope this little interruption will not upset

his eagerness to do so," Hiram commented with a smile. "If you'll excuse me, though, I must see what the king needs of me." Then, after nodding politely to the High Priest, he donned his cap and stepped out the temple of Melqart—just as the smell of burning entrails began to fill it.

The Master had every reason to be cheerful that morning. The previous evening, his wife, Mirha, had revealed she was once again with child. And after a sequence of three girls, Hiram had high hopes for a son this time around. Even though he doted on his daughters, he nevertheless longed for a boy who could carry on his name and craft. So, during the night, he'd decided to enlist the help of Melqart, the male patron god of Tyre, in order to secure this outcome. Knowing a goat sacrifice was always considered an effective way for getting into the deity's good graces, his first task of the day had been to do exactly that.

Just three years shy of forty, Hiram was a relatively good-looking man, with sharp, dark eyes, and already the city's most celebrated architect and town planner. In fact, even his surname reflected that profession: *Binne* meant builder in Phoenician. It was a last name he'd inherited from his father, who'd also been one. But, alas, Hiram's father died while he was very young—a tragic circumstance which left his mother, Elisa, all alone to raise him by herself. In fact, she was the one who'd instilled in him the desire to surpass his father's reputation. And he did. Over the years that followed, the widow's son came to be regarded as the most astute master builder and planner the city of Tyre had ever known. And an important reason for securing that reputation was his idea to create a narrow canal connecting the kingdom's two seaports, which were located at opposite ends of the main island.

For centuries, Tyre had thrived on two nearby, oval-shaped, rocky islands—both of which had a north to south orientation—about a half mile from the mainland. Inevitably, though, as its population kept growing, land became increasingly scarce. So when King Hiram assumed office he decided to increase his realm's terrain by landfilling the narrow strip of sea, which separated the two neighboring islands, thus creating a larger one. It'd been a monumental undertaking and one which took years to complete. During the early stages of that project, though, Hiram Binne had suggested that there was a way for Tyre's two harbors not to remain isolated and for ships in one to be able to securely pass over to the other. His proposal was for the landfill to continue up to a point where a narrow inland waterway was created, and which would connect the north seaport with the southern one. By using this canal, Tyrian ships could then pass safely from one end of the unified island and from one harbor to the other, regardless of sea conditions. Hiram's namesake king thought it to be a brilliant idea and not only endorsed it, but he even charged Binne with carrying it to fruition. As a result, over the next decade, or so, the Master had been busy with developing that waterway, along with the many bridges necessary to keep the new island's two segments connected.

Hiram had already taken several steps, on his way south to the palace, when he turned back to look at the temple of Melqart. For some reason, he felt so optimistic at that moment that he made a solemn promise to himself, right on the spot: *If the god grants me my wish for a son, then I will see to it he receives something of value in return as well.* Hiram couldn't think exactly what, just then, but he was confident he'd inevitably come up with something.

Also, during that fleeting glance, the Master did not fail to note the wonderful, and ancient, columns, which adorned the temple's entrance. Ever since he was a boy, he'd been in awe of those huge pillars standing there. When one witnessed them for the first time, in the light of day, they created the impression that the first column was made up of solid gold and the other entirely by emeralds. But the fact that they both shone at night should have dissuaded a perceptive observer from thinking they were solid. The reality was that the pillars were actually hollow. Although much gold and many emeralds had indeed been used in their exterior construction, a great deal of their circumferences was just made up of skillfully positioned gold- and green-colored glass plates. Thus, whenever night descended, the burning torches placed inside them would produce the gold and emerald radiance which made those pillars look so spectacular—especially in the dark.

The Master had begun ascending the steps of the palace when he became aware of two unknown men exiting and making their way down: Their clothes were made up of rough, non-Phoenician material; the facial hair covering their cheeks and even their upper lip (a place no self-respecting Tyrian male would allow hair to grow) was bushy and unkept; and Hiram also noticed that their feet and sandals were dusty. *They must have been traveling non-stop for quite a while,* he thought. An observation which was swiftly confirmed when he happened to catch a whiff of them as they passed by him: the two strangers stank.

"Ah, Hiram, welcome!" the king exclaimed, as he saw his namesake enter the Council Room. "I do apologize for dragging you here on such short notice, but a rather pressing matter has just come up."

When King Hiram spoke he'd been standing, stooped over a long table in the center of the room, apparently going over some papyri documents spread out on it. He then straightened up and walked over to the Master, offering his hand in greeting. The king was four years Hiram's junior, nevertheless he yielded a striking presence. He was lean, tall, and handsome, with a graceful cast of features, but what singled him out the most were his black, brilliantly piercing eyes. He was clad in his usual dual-colored linen robes, and that day's choice had been the one with the green and gold vertical stripes. They shook hands and Hiram was invited to take a chair opposite the king.

"I'm sure you noticed two strangers leaving the palace, as you came in," King Hiram said.

"Yes, I did. Who are they?"

"They are envoys of the Hebrew King, Solomon. And they were sent to bring me a message from him about a project he's about to begin. He plans on building a Temple in Jerusalem for his God, Yahweh."

Hiram chuckled. "Do they even know *how* to build a temple?"

"Of course not. They only know about goat herding and farming. That's why they came. They want *us* to build it for them," the king said. He then eyed the Master intently while stroking his immaculately trimmed beard.

In the brief silence that followed, Hiram realized why he'd been summoned. "Oh no, not me... Please don't make me do this," he said and attempted to rise from his chair.

"Please sit, Master, and at least hear me out. Then you can decide," King Hiram urged. And after his namesake was seated again, the sovereign continued with what seemed like a casual question. "How large is our army?"

The Master frowned at first, but then sighed. He realized where this was going. "We haven't got one," he replied with resign.

"Exactly. And we've never had an army! That's why we have always used a policy of appeasing our mightier neighbors by offering them lavish gifts, or partnerships in our business ventures—or even both, sometimes. And also, occasionally, by just going along with something they want done. All these approaches were designed to make them realize their interests are better served by keeping us intact rather than by obliterating us. My father used such methods, while I also granted a similar favor to King David, years ago. And now we must do it again for his son, Solomon."

The king looked deep into the Master's eyes before speaking again. "They may be sheep herders, Hiram, but the truth is they possess the military capability to destroy us at any moment—if they wish to. So, we don't really have a choice."

"But why must *I* be the one to go? There are so many

other good architects. A job like this might take years to complete," the Master said, fretfully. He bowed his head in frustration.

Nevertheless, the king appeared determined. "For two main reasons: First, you are our top builder. Solomon will be much more inclined to accept our intentions are sincere if we send him our best. And the second one is because of your mother."

The Master looked up. "My mother...? What has my mother to do with all this?"

"Actually, she has a lot to do with the matter. Don't forget that her parents... your grandparents, belonged to one of the Israelite tribes—a fact which makes you half a Jew. You will be much more acceptable to them than anyone else: they are very fussy when dealing with complete strangers to their heritage. But, the most important reason is that you speak their language. Elisa taught it to you when you were a boy, did she not? And you still speak it with her sometimes?"

"Yes, we do, but—"

"Don't misunderstand me, Hiram," the king cut in. "I'm not saying that you, or your mother, are not loyal to Tyre. Quite to the contrary, both of you have proved your loyalty and love for our city-state, many times over. In all honesty, I must admit I'm counting on those feelings for you to agree."

"And what about the city's defense walls? I was supposed to start work on them next week. Who will take care of that while I am gone?"

"I'm certain that whoever takes your place will remain true to your designs. I won't let anyone stray away from those. But, to be frank with you, the fact we don't have any defense walls yet worth mentioning weighed heavily in my decision to grant Solomon his request."

One of the words the king used made Hiram wonder, so he expressed his thoughts aloud. "Shouldn't the Council be the one to decide on such an important matter?"

The Master's question was relevant, given that the King of Tyre did not exercise absolute power—unlike all the other, non-Phoenician kingdoms in the vicinity. On the contrary, whoever occupied the Tyrian throne, at any given moment, did so under the direct authority of the City Council: A body made up of elected representatives from the most important families in the realm. And although the kingship inevitably evolved into a hereditary institution in Tyre, it was not always so. In the beginning, every 'king' had been chosen from among the Council members, while that body retained the discretionary power to relieve him of his duties, if his performance was not deemed sufficient. This was a capacity the City Council still possessed, and one which it hadn't failed to exercise in the past.

"In fact, the Council has already decided on this," the king replied.

Hiram frowned. "When did that happen? I thought you mentioned these envoys have just arrived."

"They have," the monarch said, with a smile. "But I'd been anticipating this request, ever since I heard that King David died about four years ago. As a result, last fall, I presented my proposal to the Council. We needed to have a decision ready, in case Solomon should ask us to do this. And the result was unanimous—even Mirha voted in favor."

Hiram Binne's wife was a member of the Tyrian Council, while he was not. Such was the egalitarian nature of every Phoenician kingdom: women were freely allowed, encouraged even, to contribute to public affairs—unlike in all the other non-Phoenician states around them.

"She never mentioned anything about this..." Hiram mumbled, as if to himself, although he knew the answer.

"My dear friend..." the king said with a heartfelt smile. "You are well aware the Council's deliberations are always kept a secret. Naturally, she *couldn't* say anything."

"I'm not so sure she would've voted the same if a decision were to be made today."

"And why is that?"

"Because last night Mirha told me she's pregnant."

The king's face lit up with a smile. "Congratulations! Maybe now you'll have the son you've always wanted."

"That's what I'm hoping for. I even sacrificed a goat to Melqart this morning to gain his support."

"That should do it!" the smiling king said with conviction. But after a moment or so, he took on a more somber tone. "Irrespective of this happy development, I'm certain Mirha would have still voted in favor. Being a good Tyrian she knows how important it is for our city-state to grant this request. Aside from warding off the dangers Solomon's armies pose, this arrangement could also be quite lucrative. The king's letter promises large quantities of grain, oil, and wine, in exchange for us providing construction expertise and cedar timber from Mount Lebanon. He has even promised to hand over a number of cities belonging to his domain once the project is complete."

The Master sighed. "So I guess King Solomon must get whatever his heart desires."

"No, not whatever he wants," the king objected. "The fact we are doing business with him doesn't mean we should trust him blindly as well. He must never learn our building secrets. Those you must guard with your life. We're dealing with a young man who's spent all of his life living under his father's shadow, and now that David is finally gone he is desperate to surpass him. Aside from ruthlessly eliminating anyone who stands in his way, Solomon has also been busy cultivating a reputation that he's the wisest man alive. Although he's not as clever as he thinks he is, you shouldn't underestimate him either. So be very careful in your dealings with him."

"I will."

"And one last thing," King Hiram added. "Solomon's letter mentions he wants a crypt to be constructed beneath this new Temple, as well, in order to secure valuable documents and other effects in there. Do it for him, but also build another one he won't know about."

This made Hiram Binne frown. "Why should I do that?"

"It might come in handy... You never know," the king said with a devious smile. "It's always good to possess a secret advantage when dealing with someone who's more powerful than you."

"But, they might see me building it."

"The Jews have no experience in large project construction, so they will not understand what you're doing. Especially, if you do most of the secret crypt's work on days they won't be around, like their Sabbath for instance."

Hiram was still nodding to this when his namesake stood up. "At first light tomorrow the two envoys will wait for you at the Egyptian Harbor," the king said. "From there you will take a boat over to the mainland where an armed escort is waiting to accompany you to Jerusalem. Your assistants and equipment will follow in a few days time. Good luck, my friend." The king then embraced him, and they gave each other the customary triple kiss on the cheeks, which all Phoenicians exchanged in greeting, or whenever parting.

The Master exited the palace, taking a northern route, in a daze. Everything happened so quickly that he felt his whole life had been overturned in a matter of minutes. In fact, Hiram was so wrapped up in thought he even failed to notice the pillars of Melqart he so admired when he passed by them. Proceeding north, past the temple, Hiram soon arrived at Tyre's residential area—an area that, surprisingly for those times, consisted almost entirely of multistoried buildings. Being on an island where land was always at a premium, the Tyrians had innovated, once again: they constructed their homes on multiple levels, instead of adopting the single ground-floor abodes, which were the norm everyplace else. That way, several families could share the same plot of land, instead of only one.

Just as Hiram climbed the steps to his residence on the second floor, the sound of his wife's voice drifted down to him. On arriving at the door, the Master decided to linger there a bit before stepping in. He watched with affection as Mirha unfolded the final part of the Europa myth to their two younger daughters. That story was always a good way of introducing homeschooled children to the fact that the Minoan civilization had been established by Phoenicians, many centuries earlier.

"And then Europa, the Tyrian princess, gave birth to a lovely baby boy, whom she called Minos. With him being the son of a god, the boy eventually grew up to be a powerful man, and he became the King of Crete who—" Mirha was saying, but never got to complete her phrase.

As he relished that tender family moment, the Master had inadvertently let out a soft sigh, while thinking, *Will I ever be able to witness something like this again?* But the two young girls had heard the sorrowful sound their father made and shrieked as they turned to see him standing there. Without any delay, they ran over to Hiram and started hugging and kissing him; it was a rare occasion for him to be home with them at that time of day. Sitting nearby, Hiram's eldest daughter considered herself too old, at sixteen, for such childish displays. So, she just smiled at him lovingly, but remained by the window and continued reading the papyrus in her hands.

"What are you doing here?" Mirha said, as if scolding him, but then smiled brightly.

"I've just come from the palace. The king asked to see me," he replied. After he kissed both little girls, and they let go of him, Hiram started walking towards his and Mirha's private chamber.

She followed him into their room. "Oh? And what did he want? Was it about the defense walls project?"

Hiram turned and looked into his wife's eyes. "No. He told me I have to leave for Jerusalem tomorrow."

"Oh… So, it's finally happened," Mirha said with dismay, and plumped herself down on their feather bed. "It seemed like such a remote possibility when the king informed us of his thoughts several months ago."

The Master could have asked her why she didn't tell him anything about it, but he knew she'd only start defending herself. Instead, Hiram sat down next to her, took her into his arms, and began mentioning events which he would regrettably miss while being away.

"I'll probably be gone for many years, my love. And this means I will not be around when he's born, or watch him take his first steps, or even listen to his first words. But in my heart, I shall always be here with all five of you."

When she turned to look at him tears were already streaming down her face. Yet, she put on a brave smile and asked, "So you're certain it's a boy then?"

He hugged her tighter and said with conviction, "Melqart won't let me down. Not after this."

✛ ✛ ✛

AFTER THEY ATE their midday meal, Hiram decided he should go tell his mother the news, and say his goodbyes. So, he walked over to her building, which was nearby, and entered his mother's ground-floor abode. She greeted him with a hug, and when he announced he was going away and for what reason, she beckoned him to sit by her side. Even though not yet sixty-years old, she'd already begun to look frail.

"You must be extremely cautious while you're around this new king, Solomon," Elisa stressed in Hebrew. It was the only part of her ancestral culture she still clung to. "I hear he's a very devious and deceitful young man."

"So I've been told."

"And you must convince them you believe in Yahweh—they won't respect you otherwise, if you don't. As for myself, I cast away that vengeful and jealous God, years ago, but *you* must persuade them you sincerely worship Him. Do you hear me?"

"I will, Mother, don't you worry," the Master reassured her.

And after a few more minutes of listening to her sound motherly advice, on various matters, Hiram got up to leave. She blessed him, and they kissed each other's cheeks, in sequence, three times. The widow's son started walking back to his own house wondering if he would ever see his mother again.

That night he and Mirha made love, with such passion and intensity, that it was as if it might make up for all the years they'd be apart. And when the new day's light broke, he gave everyone a tender triple kiss, assured them he loved them all, and left.

✝ ✝ ✝

THE JOURNEY TO Jerusalem took more than five full days and nights to complete. It should have taken only three, but on the second day their party was unexpectedly attacked by bandits, and in the skirmish which followed a few of the guards were wounded. One of them, in fact, was so seriously injured they had to drag him behind a horse on a makeshift stretcher—a turn of events which slowed everybody down. Just after the attack was quashed, Hiram came to realize why an armed escort had been so necessary. If he and Solomon's envoys were alone, they would've been slaughtered for sure. So he was thankful to whomever made that decision.

Early on the morning of the sixth day, they'd just climbed a short ridge when one of the two envoys exclaimed, "Jerusalem!" all of a sudden. The Master looked over and saw him pointing excitedly at something in the distance. Hiram put his hand up to block the rising sun's glare and saw Jerusalem in front of him for the first time. The city was sprawled down the right side of a hill, to the south, shaped like a tear escaping on a cheek. The very summit of the bedrock outcrop, interestingly enough from that great distance, looked barren and empty to Hiram; nothing had been built on it. The Master later found out that the hill, on the side of which Jerusalem was built, was called Mount Moriah, and that its peak had been the site of an ancient Hebrew drama: Abraham, one of the Jews' first and foremost patriarchs, had been ordered by Yahweh to sacrifice his son, Isaac, there, to prove his fidelity. Just before he went through with it, though, an angel appeared to Abraham, staying his hand, and told him that his loyalty to God was already confirmed. So the patriarch sacrificed a ram instead, but the location remained one of the most sacred and revered for all Israelites.

As they got closer, the Master was better able to observe the defense walls that enclosed the simple, sun-dried brick houses of the city. The fortifications were built high but with single-row masonry, and he knew they were the first of two favors King Hiram had granted David—the Hebrew king at the time—many years earlier. The second one, he could also see at the very top of the fortified enclosure, just below Mount Moriah's peak, and in an area called the Ophel: It was David's Palace, and it had been constructed exclusively with cedar timbers brought all the way from Mount Lebanon.

They were passing into the city, through its western gate, when Hiram, still looking up at the palace, caught a glimpse of something fluttering higher up on the Mount's summit. *So its top is not completely empty, after all,* he thought. The Master then turned to ask one of the envoys what was up there, and the Hebrew replied, "It's the tent of the Ark."

Hiram frowned, indicating he didn't follow, so the envoy elaborated. "When King David brought the Ark of the Covenant to Jerusalem, he did not bring the Tabernacle along with him. So, he pitched a tent up there for the Ark, until a proper home was built for it. That is where you will build the House of the Lord, Master Hiram." The envoy then went on to add that the tent wasn't guarded because the Ark didn't need protection. "It can take care of itself," he said.

However, after being informed of his objective, the Master

didn't pay much attention to anything the envoy added about the Ark. His engineering mind immediately started thinking about how he was going to erect a large temple at the top of such a barren, rocky outcrop. In fact, he was so immersed in thought that he hardly noticed much else as their horses trotted up towards the palace. Only once they'd arrived there did he snap out of his reverie. Hiram dismounted and before following the others inside, he smiled and patted one of the sturdy cedar beams of the entrance. He was happy to be able to touch something reminding him of home.

The Phoenician stepped into a large, long chamber, the walls and ceiling of which were adorned with fragrant cedar planks. At the end of that grand hall stood an equally remarkable gold-plated platform, elevated by four steps, upon which the king was about to take his seat on the throne. Apparently, news of their arrival had travelled fast. Although not more than twenty-five years old, Solomon already projected a striking presence. He wore a honey-colored robe on the inside, a purple mantle to cover that, and a yellow sash, to bind them both around his slim waist; his beard and mustache, though kept bushy, were carefully trimmed; and his dark hair was worn long, with curls forming midway down. Standing close to the king, just behind him, was Solomon's considerably older aide, dressed in a simple green-colored robe, and who at the moment was busy reading a papyrus he'd been handed. The only other person up on the platform was a scantily clad young woman, lying at the king's feet. But she wasn't the only female in the room. As Hiram walked in, he'd noticed several other young women there, on both sides, sitting upon pillows and leaning against the wooden walls. *They must be a few of the three hundred wives and concubines Solomon is rumored to have*, he thought.

The Master, flanked by the two envoys, arrived within a few feet from the golden dais, and following their example, he stopped and bowed to the king. Solomon's sole reaction to this display of respect was to simply remove his sandals and place his bare feet onto the young woman's buttocks in front of him. The aide then bent over and whispered something into the king's ear.

"You are the Phoenician who is supposed to build our Temple for me?" Solomon asked Hiram.

"I am, sire," he replied, in perfect Hebrew.

"And what is your name?" the king asked again, unsurprised that the Tyrian spoke his language.

"Hiram Binne."

This prompted Solomon's advisor to lean in and whisper something further into his sovereign's ear.

The king steepled his long fingers together. "I understand your mother comes from one of our tribes. Which one is it, that of Naphtali, or that of Dan?"

"The tribe of Naphtali, sire."

Solomon was looking at Hiram intently with his hazel-colored eyes. "And did your mother invest you with love for the one, true God?"

"She did, Your Majesty." The Master had put on the widest and most persuasive smile he could muster, hoping it would be enough to convince the king.

"Good," said Solomon, after taking a moment to evaluate the truthfulness of Hiram's reply. "God has spoken to me, you know. Hasn't He, Zabud?"

"He most definitely has, sire," the aide responded, now standing behind the throne.

"Yes. He came to me in a dream one night and asked me what I desired most. I could have replied I wanted a long life, or riches, or glory, but instead I shrewdly requested for wisdom. It seems, He liked my answer so much that aside from that, the Lord decided to grant me all the other things I didn't ask for, anyway. Hasn't He, Zabud?"

"He most certainly has, Your Majesty," the advisor answered, with no hesitation, once again.

Apparently, Solomon was feeling so exuberant that he kicked the young girl curled up at his feet, causing her to tumble over a few times. Without displaying any annoyance, though, she stood up and ran down the platform to sit with the others by the wall. At the same time, another equally attractive female stepped up to place her buttocks beneath the king's feet.

Although Hiram was deeply appalled by the way Solomon treated his women, the Master's expression betrayed nothing. He just stood there as if he'd witnessed the most ordinary thing in the world.

"How will my Temple look, Binne?" the king asked, after he'd settled his feet on the new female's behind.

"It will be most impressive, sire, I assure you. I have a preliminary plan of it in my head, and in a few days I'll be able to show you some designs."

"And how long will it take to complete?"

"That is difficult to say, Your Majesty. But a rough estimate, for a project this size, would be about six to seven years, at least.

Solomon arched his left eyebrow up and spoke in an austere tone. "You'll have more than a hundred thousand men and slaves at your disposal, Phoenician, so you'd better not take any more time than that."

"I'll certainly try my best, sire," the Master stated.

"Ah, and one last thing. After you've moved that silly excuse of a tent my father pitched to house the Ark of the Covenant in, I would like you to construct a hidden chamber beneath the spot where the Temple will be built. And then you must carve out a narrow shaft in its ceiling until it reaches the future floor of the Temple."

When Hiram's face registered bewilderment, Solomon rolled his eyes and scoffed in frustration. "So that people in the chamber can breathe! My goodness, Binne, I thought you were an engineer."

"A thousand apologies, sire. I did not realize what you meant. Of course, you are right. And I shall strive to do exactly as you bid," the Master said, bowing low.

"Good. Now go, and start building me my Temple," the king then said, with a dismissive flick of the wrist to send everyone away. He had given enough of his exalted presence to this peasant Tyrian builder.

Unsure about what to do next, Hiram followed the envoys' example once again. Each one bowed, climbed the four steps to kiss the king's hand, and left. When the Master stepped up and was about to kiss Solomon's hand, Hiram saw the Ring on his middle finger for the first time. It was just a fleeting glance, since he didn't dare linger, but the Ring's six-pointed-star engraving made quite an impression on him.

✚ ✚ ✚

Jerusalem
965 BCE

WORD HAD FINALLY arrived from Tyre. After thanking the courier, Hiram quickly unfolded the papyrus and began to read Mirha's message:

"Dear husband, I greet you. All is well, as I gave birth to a beautiful, healthy boy a few weeks ago. In accordance with what we've discussed, I shall name him Ithobal, in honor of your father. The girls send their love, as do I, and asked me to stress that we all miss you terribly." After a few more paragraphs about news of their city, she concluded with a declaration of her undying love and that she hoped everything was also well with him.

The Master was ecstatic. *At long last I have a son*, he kept thinking with joy, over and over again. After calming down, somewhat, he decided it was time Melqart was repaid for making his wish come true. And, fortunately, Hiram had been prepared for this happy turn of events. So, he called out to his assistant, Madal, that he was going down to see the king.

Hiram had not been idle in the ten months that passed. After moving the tent housing the Ark of the Covenant temporarily down to the Kidron Valley, the Master was able to survey the bare summit of Mount Moriah unobstructed. By chance, he stumbled upon a natural cavity, a few feet east from the Mount's peak, and which with a little extra digging would do nicely for the concealed chamber Solomon wanted. At the same time, he also selected the site for the other, secret, underground crypt: the one his king had suggested he build.

With those two matters out of the way, he then outlined a square area surrounding the summit, of about five hundred feet on each side. Using those sides, he'd be creating the elevated enclosure necessary for the initial Temple platform to take shape. And to make that platform's walls as robust as possible, Hiram Binne decided to bury a sequence of huge, expertly hewed ashlar blocks halfway into the ground. It would be an incredible amount of work, but fortunately, he had been provided with an entire army of workers and slaves to do his bidding. Nevertheless, to keep the secret Phoenician method of creating the square-cut, perfectly sided ashlar stones away from Solomon's prying eyes, the Master sent his Tyrian assistants—with about eighty thousand men—far into the mountains to prepare the blocks there. When they would be brought back and set halfway in the ground, a massive amount of soil would then be dumped within the enclosure to create the preliminary Temple platform.

But all that was still months ahead in the future. So, Hiram wrapped his cloak tight around himself, to fend off one of winter's last morning chills, and began walking down to the palace. He needed to put his idea to the king. The Master had decided that the best way to repay his debt to Melqart was to recreate the two majestic pillars which stood outside the god's temple in Tyre. Hiram only hoped the king didn't know about them and reject the suggestion.

He walked into the crowded Throne Room just as Solomon was about to start arbitrating a dispute. This time it was between two prostitutes. Seated up high on the golden dais, with Zabud at his side as usual, the king heard them, as each one argued her case. Both prostitutes were standing down below, a few feet away from the platform.

"Sire, this woman and I live alone in the same house, and we both gave birth to baby boys a few weeks ago," the first one said, while cradling a sleeping infant in her arms. "Last night, she smothered her son in her slumber and exchanged them while I was asleep. When I woke up to nurse my boy, I discovered he was dead. But after I took a closer look at the baby, I realized he wasn't mine and that she had taken him."

This remark provoked the second one to exclaim aloud, "That is a lie, sire. She's the one who's stolen my child. My son is alive and I want him back!"

These two conflicting viewpoints caused quite a stir among those present in the great hall. So much so, in fact, that Solomon was compelled to intervene. He stood up from his throne and in a commanding voice ordered everyone to quiet down. Then, he addressed the prostitutes. "Each one of you claims to be the mother of this child, and you both insist the other stole it." Solomon paused and looked closely at them. "So I see no other solution. Fetch me a sword," the king commanded the chief of his guard. "I'll cut this bastard in two, so that both of you can have an equal share of him."

The ominous silence that fell in the room terrified Hiram that Solomon would actually go through with what he threatened. But the first woman was wailing. "Please, sire, I'd rather give my son to her. Please, don't kill him," she said as tears streamed down her face, and her arms flew up, extending the baby in the king's direction. Startled by the sudden movement, it started to cry. At the same time, the other prostitute was shrieking, "Cut it in two, Your Majesty, yes. If I can't have him, neither should she."

At the exact moment when the chief guard was handing Solomon a sword, Hiram noticed Zabud's eyes light up all of a sudden. The advisor stepped over to the king and whispered something at length into his ear. Solomon listened intently to what Zabud was saying and then, somewhat reluctantly, turned to face the prostitute holding up the child. "Keep your son, for you are his true mother."

The king, ignoring the woman's sobbing displays of gratitude and still wielding his weapon, slowly walked down the platform. "As for you..." he said addressing the second prostitute, "You should have thought twice about trying to deceive your king." She did not have a chance to respond, however, because in the very next instant he plunged the sword deep into her heart. Everyone gasped.

After his initial shock, Hiram tried to get closer to Solomon. It wasn't easy, though, since the king was already surrounded by court flatterers congratulating him on his insight and good judgment.

"Your Majesty, how did you realize she was lying?" asked one.

"Sire, you are truly blessed by God," said another.

A third chimed in. "Without possessing your wisdom no one could have solved this puzzle."

Solomon, with a smug grin on his face, even though he was clearly enjoying their praise, did not respond to any of them. He kept wiping the blood off his sword with a piece of cloth. Glancing up at the platform, however, Hiram noticed Zabud, as his usually expressionless features cracked a thin contented smile. *So he's the source of Solomon's so-called wisdom*, the Master realized at last.

It was only after the king's guards came to take the dead woman's body away that the people gathered around Solomon began to disperse. Hiram saw his chance to get closer, just as the king was heading up the platform. The Master followed.

"Ah, Binne, did you see what I did?" Solomon asked full of pride, as he noticed the Master climbing the steps. "I solved an impossible puzzle, gave that lying bitch what was coming to her, and the people now know God definitely favors me."

"Yes, sire. It certainly was a powerful display of your wisdom," Hiram replied, while glancing fleetingly at Zabud.

"And what can I do for *you* today? Do we have any problems at the site that need solving?"

"No, no problems. I just had an idea I thought I should put to you."

"What idea is that?"

Hiram swiftly unfolded the blueprints he'd submitted months earlier and placed them in front of Solomon. "I've thought of placing two large columns at the Temple's portico. I feel they'll enhance the splendor of the entire structure a great deal," the Master said with excitement. He then drew two big columns on the plans so the king could visualize his proposal.

"Yes, they would be majestic," Solomon agreed, as he looked at the drawings and nodded. "But we mustn't make them out of solid gold, or emeralds. That would remind you too much of Melqart's temple, wouldn't it?"

Damn! So he has heard about the pillars, Hiram thought. Even though he'd been startled by this unexpected response at first, the Master recovered and replied, "Naturally, I wouldn't propose anything like that, sire. I was going to suggest we construct them out of bronze."

"Solid bronze?" the king asked.

"No, not solid bronze, sire, that would require enormous amounts of copper, making them too expensive. I can make them hollow and none would be the wiser."

"Except for me," Solomon added, with a chuckle.

"Of course, sire. None could ever be wiser than you," Hiram said, with a slight touch of sarcasm, while glancing at Zabud again. But neither the mockery, nor the glance, was spotted, and all three laughed.

As he was leaving the palace, the Master felt that under the circumstances, he'd been successful. Columns would be constructed for the Temple, and they'd be hollow. So even if they were to be the wrong color, with two out of three elements in place, his debt to Melqart would be considered repaid.

Hiram was very pleased.

PART TWO

LIFE

GEORGE

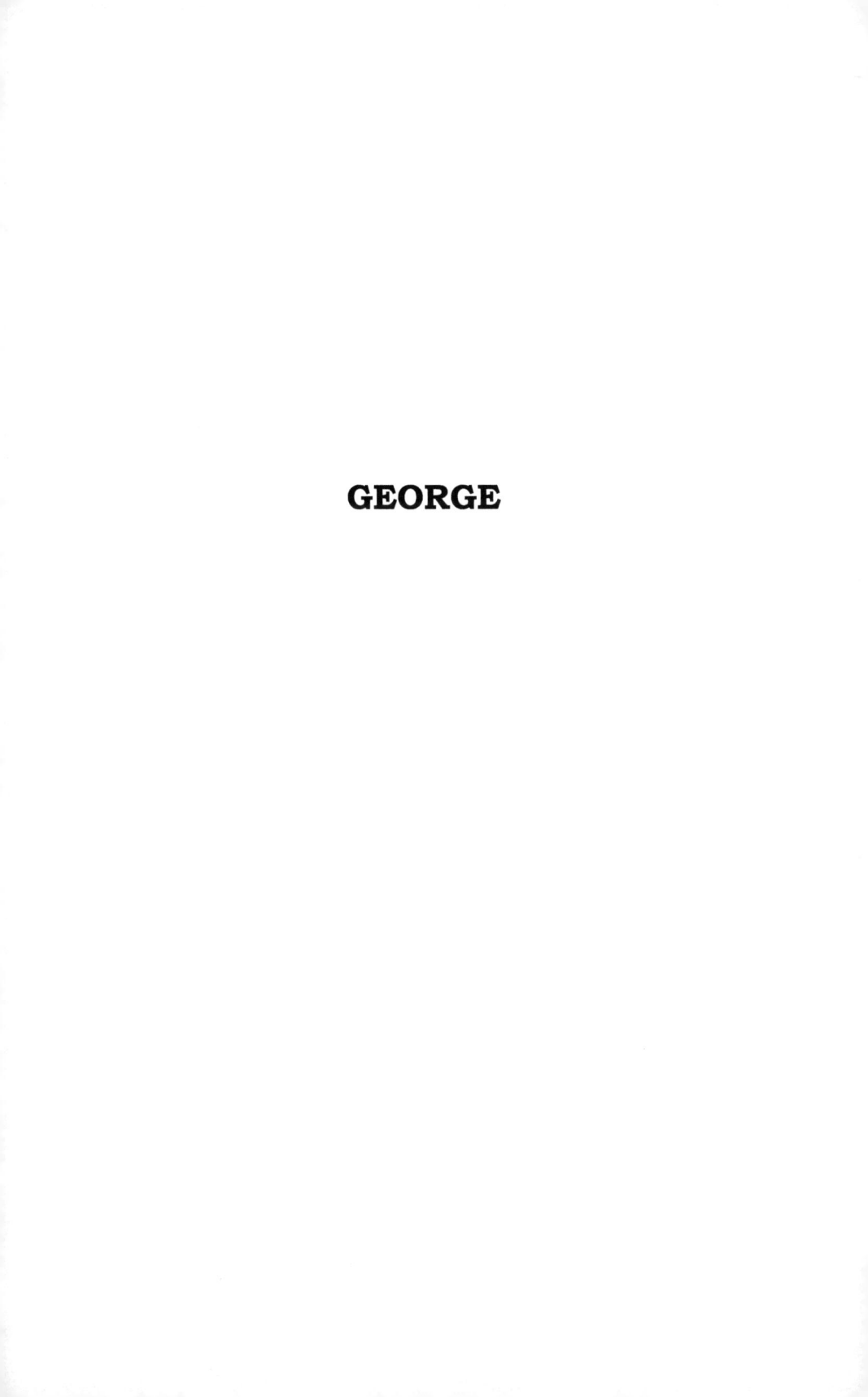

CHAPTER 5

JACHIN

Larnaca, Cyprus
2012 CE

ALTHOUGH GEORGE MAKRIDES did seem determined to figure out Freemasonry's origin, at the time, he didn't follow through with it straight away. Not only that, but even his attendance of Lodge meetings began to suffer for a while. And the reason for both of those turn of events had been Joanna, a 23-year-old nurse he'd started seeing. Having met a few weeks after his initiation, they began spending so much time together that he felt reluctant to sacrifice being with her for anything else. Of course, the fact that Lodge meetings took place on Mondays did not help the situation either: Joanna worked at a local clinic in Larnaca, and Monday was usually when she didn't have to work the night shift.

But after a year into the relationship, and once they'd somewhat satisfied their constant hunger for each other's company, George decided—with a great deal of coaxing on Alex's part—that it was time to reconnect with his Lodge in earnest. Although he hadn't been completely absent during this entire period, nevertheless, his attendance record was inconsistent. So much so, that he'd missed his chance for a swift promotion to the Second, or Fellow Craft Degree—something which would've normally happened a few months later. As a result, it was only after he was present at a fourth consecutive meeting—in late spring of 2012 AD—when the new Worshipful Master asked George if he felt ready to be promoted. Makrides replied that he did, so the Lodge Master promised to get the wheels turning: the Passing Ceremony would take place after the Lodge reconvened from its long summer recess. George later asked Alex why the upcoming ceremony hadn't been referred to as an initiation, like last time, and his friend explained that in Masonic parlance only an Entered Apprentice is *initiated*. After that, Alex went on, it's customary to say someone is *passed* to the Fellow Craft Degree, and, finally, that he's *raised* as a Master Mason in the Third.

George's reconnection with the Lodge had served not only in him getting promoted, but it also rekindled his curiosity on how, and why, this institution had begun in the first place. And being a perpetual optimist, he'd hoped his Passing Ceremony might shed light on those questions. But, alas, he was only to be disappointed, yet again.

When they all took their seats—on that hot, and humid, early October evening—the Meeting began with the First Degree Opening. It was the usual, drearily repetitive, starting ritual which consisted of four main parts: First, they made sure the Lodge was properly *tyled*, that is to say, protected—something which was always guaranteed by a sword-wielding Officer called a Tyler, who sat outside the Temple at all times. Then, everybody had to take the Step and perform the Entered Apprentice Sign, to prove that only Masons were present. The third part which followed was the most boring one of all: it involved a tedious Q & A session, whereby the Worshipful Master asked numerous questions about what each Officer's duty was, and how they were all supposed to carry out their particular functions. The fourth, and final, part concerned itself with invoking the assistance of the Great Architect of the Universe so that proceedings would run smoothly. It ended with them all chanting, "So mote it be."

While everyone else concentrated on the Opening Ceremony, George decided to pass the time more constructively by, once again, taking in his surroundings. He had realized that this Temple's layout—which was built and owned by the Greek-speaking Lodge—differed from others he'd seen on the Internet. Although certain similar features did exist, such as: The rows of seats, facing each other on the north and south walls; the black and white chessboard floor in between them; and, the Worshipful Master's pedestal in the east—those were essentially as far as the similarities went. Just about four feet inside the Temple, stood a pair of very tall, bronze-colored columns, straddling the wide doorway. The one on the left, as George looked at the exit, was labeled with the letter *J*, and the one to the right with a *B*—which made him assume: *That's probably the 'Boaz' pillar*. On the opposite side of the Temple, the east was situated on a higher, stage-like platform, about ten feet deep, accessible by four steps. But its most striking feature was that it was shaped like a semi dome, and its curved walls were painted crimson—in contrast to the sky blue of the rest of the room. Above the Worshipful Master's chair was the illuminated 'All Seeing Eye' that George had first noticed at his initiation. And behind the chair was a painting of a door, while an identical one also stood at the back of the Junior Warden's pedestal, to the south. Makrides wondered about the significance of those door images, when his thoughts were interrupted by everyone chanting, "*So mote it be*," signifying the end of the prayer.

After the minutes of the last meeting were read and approved, the Passing Ceremony began. At first, George gave replies to a number of questions put to him by the Master of the Lodge, concerning his First Degree initiation. When those were adequately answered he was led up to the Worshipful Master to be given a pre-grip and a pass word—both of which he was supposed to use on re-entering the

Fellow Craft Lodge. The pre-grip moved the pressure of the thumb from the joint of the index finger, as it was in the First Degree, to that of the adjacent empty space. And he was also informed that the pass word was *Shibboleth.*

Makrides was then guided out of the Temple to be prepared by the Tyler. After George took off his coat and tie, the Officer instructed him to bare his left breast, place a slipper on his left foot—while also baring the corresponding knee—and to put on his Entered Apprentice apron with the triangular flap pointing up. When a few minutes passed, the Tyler knocked on the Temple door three times and George was readmitted, in the charge of the Junior Deacon.

What happened next had always been a bit of a blur in George's mind—that's how tedious it was. He was first led around the room a few times, giving the pass word and performing the pre-grip with various Officers. Then, he took another Solemn Obligation never to reveal anything (as if there was anything worth revealing) and was subsequently informed of the so-called *secrets* of the new Degree. As usual, they consisted of another grip, a sign, and a different word.

The Second Degree handshake was now given by a pressure of the thumb on the other person's middle finger joint. The Degree's official word was *Jachin,* and as the Worshipful Master informed him, "This word originates from the right-hand column, as it stood outside King Solomon's Temple. It was so named after Jachin, the Assistant High Priest who presided over its dedication."

When George heard that, a couple of questions immediately popped into his head: *Why did the Assistant High Priest preside? Wasn't the actual High Priest available?* But, his thoughts got interrupted as the Junior Deacon took hold of his arm and led him down from the east.

Subsequently guided to both Wardens, George demonstrated his mastering of the new Degree's sign, grip, and word. Then, after being instructed by the Worshipful Master on how to apply the Seven Liberal Arts and Sciences

(Grammar, Rhetoric, Logic, Arithmetic, Geometry, Music, and Astronomy), in order to further improve his education, he was led out of the Temple to get dressed. Only when he was readmitted for the second time, and took a seat, did things start to get somewhat interesting.

The Lodge Master began to speak—as usual by heart. "When King Solomon's Temple was complete its magnificence became an object of admiration for all nations. However, the objects which particularly attracted everyone's attention were the two large brass pillars standing on its outer porch. The one on the left was called *Boaz* and that on the right, *Jachin*. They were cast hollow and are said to have contained the archives of Masonry. The man supervising that casting was none other than Hiram Abiff."

Who the hell is Hiram Abiff? And why does this imply I should know him? George wondered. He refrained from thinking any further, though, as the Lodge Master continued. "Many of our ancient brethren labored to erect the Temple in Jerusalem, and their large numbers comprised of both Entered Apprentices and Fellow Crafts. Whenever the Fellow Crafts were to be paid their wages, they were required to go to the middle chamber of the Temple. There, they had to prove they were truly members of that Degree by demonstrating its grip, as well as its pass word, which I am sure you all remember is *Shibboleth*."

The Lodge's Chief Officer then explained why 'Shibboleth' was selected as the Degree's pass word. In an ancient battle between two Old Testament tribes, he said, one of those had used the word to identify and subsequently slaughter forty thousand members of the other. Since it had been so successful, the Worshipful Master continued, Solomon adopted 'Shibboleth' as the pass word for the Fellow Craft's Lodge, in order to prevent any unauthorized access.

How utterly appropriate, George thought sarcastically, as soon as he heard this. And he was so disgusted that he sort of tuned out from hearing anything else afterward. But, when the Worshipful Master said, "During the building of the Temple in Jerusalem there were three Grand Masters: Solomon, King of Israel; Hiram, King of Tyre; and Hiram Abiff..." Makrides snapped out of his daydream. And that attracted George's attention because he'd never heard of King Hiram before. Makrides decided he would have to find out more about him, and his namesake Abiff—who was apparently an important figure after all.

✛ ✛ ✛

REGRETTABLY, GEORGE'S CEREMONY of Passing to the Second Degree had been as disappointing as that of his Initiation, in terms of what it revealed. Nevertheless, at the same time, it once more strengthened his resolve to figure out what this institution was all about. So, from that day on he started reading, and scouring the Internet, for anything which might be relevant to the question of Freemasonry's origin.

In a break from all that, a few days before Christmas, he and Joanna arranged to meet Alex and his new girlfriend, Maria, for coffee one afternoon. The two girls were longtime friends, and it had actually been Joanna who'd introduced Maria to Alex a month earlier. Their agreed upon rendezvous point was a popular café on Larnaca's Phinikoudes seafront—so called because of all the rows of tall palm trees gracing its beautiful promenade.

The few drops of rain abruptly turned into a downpour as Alex and Maria stepped out of the car, forcing them to huddle under an umbrella and scurry to the coffee shop. Alex's work in the IT department of a large Cypriot bank had caused him to be away on business for an entire week. So, when he and Maria stepped in to find the other couple already there waiting for them they all greeted each other with friendly pecks on the cheek. Maria, however, noticed the triple Masonic kiss the two men exchanged. And after everyone sat down, and ordered, she commented on it. "That's a very unusual way to kiss a friend." Her attractive face, with its small, upturned nose, prominent cheekbones, and bright green eyes, had a slight frown on it.

Joanna cracked a smile. "Freemasons always greet each other like that."

Both girls were similarly dressed: they wore knee-high black boots, distressed jeans, and dark-colored turtle neck jumpers under their overcoats. But other than that, their features couldn't have been more dissimilar. Whereas Maria was tall, with black hair and an olive complexion, Joanna was a shorter, blue-eyed blond, with alabaster-like skin.

Maria looked surprised and whirled around to face Alex. "You're a Mason?"

"Yes, I am... And so is George." He was swift to share the blame for something that sounded like an accusation.

She frowned again. "You haven't mentioned this."

"I was going to tell you two weeks ago, when we went to Pafos for the weekend. But, we got so caught up doing other things I never had the chance," Alex said with a mischievous little grin. "Why? Is there a problem?" he asked in a more serious tone.

Maria seemed hesitant now. "No... I don't think so. It's just that I've heard so many bad stories about you... about them, I mean."

"Well, I can assure you everything you've been told is utter nonsense. In fact, if I have one complaint it's that we've never had any of those orgies with virgins everybody promised me before joining." Alex started to chuckle.

"That's probably because they couldn't find any," George blurted out and joined in laughing.

But, Alex could see Maria still looked troubled, so he wiped the smile off his face and asked, "Exactly what have you heard?"

"Possibly the worst accusation, from my perspective, is that they say you don't believe in God." Being a member of the small Latin minority of Cyprus, Maria was also a devout Roman Catholic.

"Of course we do. Every one of us has to believe in Him,

as well as in the immortality of the soul, before we become members. It's a prerequisite," Alex stated with conviction.

"But do you mean *our* God… our *Christian* God?" Maria probed.

"Yes! Well… obviously, we don't call Him that inside the Lodge. But *He's* the one everyone means."

She was still frowning. "What name do you use then?"

"We acknowledge Him as the Great Architect of the Universe," Alex replied.

"And why is that?"

"Freemasonry embraces men from all religions. So for everybody to coexist in harmony a neutral name had to be applied. Don't you see?"

Maria was beginning to look angry. "All I see is that you equate the one true God with a Muslim's Allah, or someone else's Buddha… or whatever."

Alex could sense she was upset, so it was a good thing the waiter brought them their coffees when he did. The four of them then spent the next few moments awkwardly sipping their cappuccinos and espressos. The one who decided to break the uneasy silence was George.

"Maria, I understand how you feel. But, Alex's point is based on exactly the way you reacted," he said in a soothing tone. When he saw, however, she didn't quite grasp what he was driving at, he elaborated. "I've recently watched a movie called '*Agora.*' It was set in Alexandria, in the late fourth century AD, and it showed how pagans, Jews, and Christians had been able to coexist in peace with one another for a long time. But when every group started to leave their religious fanaticism unchecked, they began slaughtering each other… literally. What I'm trying to say is that it's natural for everybody to think his or her faith is the only true one. However, if you are an institution, like Freemasonry, which brings together men from many diverse religions, you have to find a neutral name for God. One which can encompass all beliefs, so its members won't be at each other's throats all the time. But what everyone believes in his heart is no one else's business. And that's what really matters."

Maria had calmed down a little—though it was evident she still had questions. "So what is Freemasonry, anyway?" she asked after a moment.

Alex gave her the official definition. "It's a peculiar system of morality, veiled in allegory, and illustrated by symbols."

She chuckled nervously. "That sounds a lot like a religion to me."

"Except that it's not! I've been a Mason for five years now and I've never seen anything in there to suggest that," Alex countered. "If Freemasonry was a religion wouldn't it have set up and promoted its own belief system, instead of allowing its members to believe in any god they choose?"

"I don't know. But, if it hasn't such a system in place why does the Church hold such a negative position against it?"

George cut into their argument at that point, hoping to defuse the situation once again. "No church is without its faults, Maria. Remember Galileo and how he died under house arrest for insisting the sun didn't revolve around Earth? But more to the point, do you know which other organization the Catholic Church accused of severe trespasses, yet never revealed what they actually believed in?" It was a question he did not wait around for anyone to give a reply. George felt energized, so he went on. "The Knights Templar, that's who! I've been reading a great deal about this matter these past few weeks. For almost two centuries the Templars fought Christianity's battles against the Muslims. But in the end, the Church's way of thanking the Templars for all their sacrifices was to accuse them of worshiping idols, spitting on the cross and other equally sacrilegious acts. Accusations, mind you, which resulted in a lot of them getting burned at the stake. And even though the Catholic Church never found out what, or in whom, the Templars actually believed in, it abolished their Order, almost overnight, in the early fourteenth century. So the Church certainly *does* make unfounded allegations. Maybe this is just another one of them."

Maria nodded, as if she agreed, but what she was in fact doing was buying time to come up with a reply. George took a sip of coffee and then his eyes widened, all of a sudden, as if he'd experienced an epiphany.

"Now that I think of it, the first condemnation of Freemasonry by a pope *did* come just a year after Chevalier Ramsay's Oration. Yes, that's it!" George exclaimed excitedly. But they all stared back at him blankly, not knowing what on earth he was on about. He explained. "The other day, I read that in 1737 a Mason named Andrew Ramsay gave a famous speech at a Lodge in Paris, about how Freemasonry was descended from the Templars. He didn't mention them explicitly, of course—he just called them *'our ancestors, the crusaders'*—but everyone knew who he was talking about. And then, about a year later, the pope issued the first papal Bull condemning Freemasonry, which forbade all Catholics from joining its ranks, under pain of excommunication. Don't you see? For twenty whole years after 1717, when the first Grand Lodge was formed in England, the popes had nothing to say on the matter. But the moment someone linked that institution to the Templars, the papacy lost no time in attacking it with everything it had."

"What are you getting at, George? That it's the Knights Templars who founded the Craft?" Alex asked, looking puzzled.

Makrides paused for a long moment. "Yes... I believe I am. This makes much more sense, if you think of it, rather than that myth about the stonemasons we've been fed, doesn't it?"

"Ah, my romantic love..." Joanna cut in, as she reached over and kissed him tenderly on the cheek. "Always thinking of knights and their shining armor. Am I your damsel in distress?"

"You will be... if you don't let me finish," George replied, with a twinkle in his eye. He then grinned, making it clear he was teasing, and she chuckled, enjoying the humor. So, he continued. "All I'm saying, Alex, is that it's too much of a coincidence to be ignored."

"But how could this be? From 1717, when the Grand Lodge of England was established, down to... When were the Templars arrested?"

"1307."

"Yes, 1307... well, down to there, that's a gap of over four centuries. How is it possible the Templars set up an institution four hundred years *after* they'd been abolished? It's a bit of a stretch, don't you think?"

"Yes, I know," Makrides said, nodding. "But the more I think of this, the more sense it makes, in spite of that big gap in time. For instance, the fact that only men are allowed in as members has been something women have constantly held against Freemasonry. The standard excuse is that it's a tradition—that it's always been this way. But if you think of it as an institution the Templars started, how could it have been otherwise? There were no women in their Order, so anything they created would've necessarily been an all-male concern. And another point: what's with all this Masonic obsession with the Temple of Solomon? If the medieval stonemasons were involved in setting this up wouldn't they have used a contemporary structure... for example, a prominent cathedral, or castle—something they actually worked on—as a reference point, instead of a three-thousand-year-old Temple no one knew anything about?" George anxiously looked at his friend for a reaction.

Alex accepted the challenge. "Don't forget the stonemasons were very devout Christians. And that the Catholic Church—in fact, the only church around then, before the Reformation—was probably their biggest customer. Therefore, it wouldn't be inconceivable for them to use something straight out of the Bible."

"Yes, but if what you say is true, why did they make this

new institution of theirs a religion-neutral one? Why would the devout—and largely illiterate, I'm sure—medieval stonemasons risk antagonizing the Church to accommodate any other faith? It just doesn't add up," George countered. "On the other hand, if the Knight Templars did start Freemasonry the neutrality thing makes perfect sense, given what they'd suffered at the hands of the Church. And furthermore, the fixation with Solomon's Temple—from their perspective—also makes perfect sense: it's from where they got their bloody name, for crying out loud!"

Unable to come up with a response, Alex chose to remain silent. Maria, however, who hadn't spoken in a while, saw her chance to voice something she'd been mulling over for the past few minutes. "Perhaps the two of you haven't advanced high enough in the Brotherhood to be informed that it is indeed a secret religion." Both looked at her blankly. "There are a total of thirty-three Degrees, aren't there?"

"Yes, but not in the Craft Freemasonry *we* belong to," Alex told her. "The so-called 'higher' Degrees exist in appendant systems, as optional add-ons, and are regulated by separate governing bodies."

Maria went on, unperturbed by the explanation. "And from what I gather, I doubt either of you has reached those top levels. So, maybe the ultimate truth about this institution hasn't been revealed to you yet."

George chuckled. "Well, if all thirty-three are anything like the two Degrees I know of it's definitely the most boring system ever invented." He paused, shaking his head. "No, I don't believe a secret religion lies at the top of the ladder. What I am starting to see, though, is that regardless of how the Templars started this whole thing, it somehow got lost along the way. And I'm pretty sure that remnants of their original intentions are hidden deep in today's rituals... somewhere."

MASONS

Chapter 6

RESTRUCTURING

England
1333 CE

W HEN ELIAS RECEIVED his uncle's urgent message, he thanked the person who delivered it, and sought his crew master's permission to travel up to York straight away. The stonemason's guild he worked for in Norwich had policies in place which made it necessary he should have such consent before travelling, otherwise his job might be at risk. Fortunately, the crew master, albeit grudgingly, did agree—as long as the trip was kept short—and Elias de Norwich was therefore free to go visit his ailing relative.

Interestingly enough, his last name hadn't always been that. At first it was *de Tyre*, but his uncle changed it to *de Norwich* as soon as Elias arrived in England. Peter had feared the boy's true surname might bring too much unwanted attention on them, and on their city of origin.

At thirty-three years of age now, Elias was already a skilled stonemason. His bronze, Mediterranean complexion was usually in stark contrast to the light-colored one of most people around him. That feature, in addition to his perceptive black eyes, wavy dark-brown hair, full beard, and large hooked nose, was what often made him stand out of any crowd.

Dashing back to his house, Elias quickly packed a few things in a satchel. He kissed his wife and children goodbye—giving special attention to his son, seven-year-old Anthony, who was also his favorite—and then guided his horse up the road toward the city of York. Even though the entire north was still in turmoil over the Scottish attempts at independence that year, by happy coincidence, a few of the Secret Society's Lodges were along his way, which meant he could seek shelter at a new one every night. Aside from the refuge they'd afford, visiting them would also provide him with a rare opportunity to see how they fared up close.

The entire journey took three days to complete and when Elias finally arrived, and was shown into his uncle's room, he found him lying on a straw bed with his eyes closed. Peter de Bologna, well into his sixty-seventh year by then, was looking very frail. Although a properly trained advocate and former priest, Peter decided that neither calling was relevant for him anymore. Instead, he chose to carry on with the safety and anonymity that being a common stonemason provided. But being ill for the past few months and unable to work, his treatment and daily needs had been fully funded by the Brotherhood.

Elias fought off tears when he saw how helpless his uncle looked. The beard Peter had been compelled to grow ever since his escape was already completely white, and after having lost a lot of weight, his ragged, ashen face now appeared tired and spent. Sensing someone had stepped close, de Bologna opened his watery eyes and smiled at his nephew. He beckoned him to sit by his side.

Peter's voice was weak. "I am so glad you could make it, my dear boy. I fear I have little time left and there is a great deal to discuss."

"Do not say that, Uncle. You'll get better and be up and about again very soon. Of that I'm certain," Elias told him, in the most cheerful tone he could muster. In reality, though, he was gravely worried—he'd never seen his normally strong and resilient uncle in such a weakened state.

"Ah, the optimism of youth... What I wouldn't give to feel like that, one last time," Peter said, smiling faintly. "I've been bedridden for the past three months, from whatever's ailing me, Elias, and I sense my strength being sapped away bit by bit every day. So we must be realists, I'm afraid. Nonetheless, I do appreciate your effort to cheer me up, my boy."

Elias's only response to this was to bow his head in sorrow. But then Peter de Bologna, impatient to move on, tapped his nephew's hand and said, "Let us speak about more important matters. How are our Lodges doing?"

Relieved to be able to think of something else, Elias started his report. "Surprisingly well, under the circumstances. Other than a few of them, further up north, which have been disrupted by the Scottish uprising, all the rest seem to hold meetings at regular intervals. Fortunately, they keep me informed of their activities."

A wide, proud smile appeared on his uncle's face. "And of course they should inform you! You are their Grand Secretary after all."

"And you their Grand Master, Uncle. Everyone I've seen these past few days is very troubled by the news of your illness. They all send their best wishes."

"I am grateful for their concern, but let's not go back to that subject again. Listen, the reason I summoned you here, is that I want you to take over when I'm gone."

Elias had feared this all along, but having to actually hear it spoken aloud sent cold shivers down his spine. "Let's just hope that what you want won't be necessary for a long time to come," he said in a soft tone.

"Yes, yes," Peter responded impatiently, while tapping on his nephew's hand once again. "When I'm gone, however soon or late that may be, you have to take charge of the Brotherhood as its Grand Master. I shall write a coded letter informing the Council members of my decision. But this ought to be the last time someone takes over like this. You must see to it that all Grand Masters, after you, get *elected* to the office. If he so wishes, you may groom your son, Anthony, to become Grand Master one day, but he will occupy the position only after he has won an election. You and I have got to be the last to be appointed to it."

Peter de Bologna had been the Secret Society's Grand Master for the past ten years. Just before William de Grafton died he chose Peter as his successor, something which all the brothers recognized as the most sensible solution. But the Brotherhood's early days were behind it—twenty-two years had already passed since its formation—and de Bologna felt it was time for it to move up a phase.

An issue which reminded him of what he wanted to ask next. "You've mentioned that most Lodges meet regularly, but what of new members?"

"The truth is that the inflow of new blood has been slowing down as of late. In fact, I'd say that our membership is currently d—...decreasing," Elias said, checking himself just before he used the word *dying.*

"Yes, I had a feeling it's dying out," Peter remarked, astutely as ever. "This is another reason why I wished to speak to you in person. We have to take measures to stop this trend."

"What do you have in mind?"

"When William and I founded the Society, in 1311, we did so with an expectation that our Order was about to be restored very soon. And as you know that's why I brought you to England in the first place: I wanted you to be a Templar priest one day. But when the Holy Mother Church..." de Bologna said, his face hardening with anger, "decided to stab us in the back by abolishing the Order, by giving all our properties and privileges over to those Hospitaller bastards, and by finally burning Jacques de Molay at the stake, we had no alternative but to change course. While we were exchanging ideas about this, one day, I suggested to William that our brothers could alternatively concentrate their efforts on something new. Instead of reconquering the actual Temple in Jerusalem they might endeavor, from then on, to erect a new personal and spiritual one within themselves. He liked the idea and added that our experiences with stonemasonry might be helpful in setting up allegories and symbols to be used."

"Aye, and that's exactly what we've been doing all these years."

"Except it's not working as it should. Apparently, this new direction has failed to capture the hearts and minds of young men—especially those coming to us from the gentry. In the beginning, when we were recruiting people to join the Templars, the sense of adventure it projected made hundreds of them want to enlist. But when we changed our focus, as you've seen, new members are very hard to come by anymore."

"Then what do you propose?" Elias asked his uncle.

"I propose we must now adopt the *second* idea I had put forward that day: to protect the defenseless and persecuted people of all religions and creeds, in the name of true justice. William did not want us to go into a rebellious mode at that point, and so we didn't go ahead with it. He felt it might be too dangerous, and maybe he was right under those circumstances. Recognizing that Man's imperfections arise from within himself, and not Satan, was rebellious enough. But things have changed. And if my gut feeling is correct, they are about to change even more. The fact our Society's existence has never been betrayed and that we continue to survive, up to now, may mean God favors us in some way. Yet it is imperative we give our brethren a new purpose. We can keep the 'Internal Temple Building' aspect in place. Nevertheless, it's necessary to enrich it with newer and more exciting features."

"Don't misunderstand me, Uncle Peter, but what's the point anymore?" Elias asked, all of a sudden.

"The point? You will soon be leading this institution, young man, and you ask me 'what's the point'?" Peter exclaimed in anger; so much so that he even attempted to sit up in his bed.

"I'm just saying aloud what others are probably thinking, Uncle. The Order has been abolished—that's a painful, but irreversible fact. Every original Templar remaining, like you, will regrettably, but inevitably, be gone one day. So, yes, what's the point in trying to keep our Secret Society from drifting off into oblivion as well?"

Peter de Bologna calmed down and settled back into bed. He realized that what his nephew said didn't arise from bad intentions. But, at the same time, he also understood that Elias needed to be thoroughly convinced, if he was going to be able to lead one day.

"You've never had the good fortune of seeing the Templars in action, my boy—before the infidels took the Holy Land, that is—but I have. And I'm not talking only about the white-mantled knights charging fearlessly at the enemy with their steeds, but of the common men, the sergeants and the turcopoles as well. They were all something truly remarkable, believe me. The bravery with which everyone fought was always a sight to behold. No one would leave the battle field, unless they all did—that was the sense of true camaraderie and brotherhood which had been cultivated: it was either all who'd get to survive, or none. In fact, this was exactly what inspired the Order's famous seal of the two knights riding astride a single horse. No one would desert his brother, alone and in distress," de Bologna said. His last argument was a white lie, of course, told simply as a means to illustrate his point. He'd known of the seal's true origin ever since he read Nicodemus's report in the Templar Archives.

Elias's thoughtful silence encouraged Peter to continue. "If we become dispirited and abandon our Secret Society, it will mean we are abandoning all the thousands of brothers who came before us. It will mean all their sacrifices and labors were for naught; that they left nothing behind. This is why the Society must go on, my boy: for their memory and for the few of us left who are the very last of those Templars. I'm convinced I'd die a happy man if I knew it would continue to exist, and by doing so that it would keep our Order's memory alive."

"But our ritual, as it stands now, only mentions the Templars a few times. Are you suggesting we should include more references to them?"

"No, I do not mean that. This might surprise you—especially after everything I've said—but what I am proposing is that even those few instances, where the Templars are mentioned at all, should be removed."

Elias frowned. He did not understand any of this, so his uncle explained. "It's not by mentioning the Templar Order more that its memory will be served, but with what our Society's future actions will be. Most of the young men we want to bring into the fold know nothing about the Templars anyway, and they certainly don't know the reasons why the Society was formed. However, if we agree to make our Brotherhood's purpose, from now on, to fight for all those who are oppressed and victimized, then I am sure new potential members will be intrigued by this. And not only that, but all of our dead Templar brothers would rest in peace since in essence that's what they fought for themselves. Leaving any direct mention of the Order in our rituals, though, would not only be unhelpful it could also be highly dangerous."

"What do you mean?" Elias asked, puzzled, once again.

"As things stand at the moment, any surviving Templar is a person constantly running away from an appointment with death at the stake. And if the Church ever gets wind that the Order has anything to do with our Society you can be sure it will not take it lightly. Mark my words, my boy, as long as the Catholic Church remains as powerful as it is, our future brothers will definitely feel its wrath if it ever finds out. That's why all direct references to the Templar Order must be removed from the ritual. Only indirect allusions may be left in. See to it."

"I will. But how do you think this will help in the matter of attracting new recruits? I mean, since the original appeal was for young men to gain entry into the exciting world of the Templars, wouldn't this bring about a negative result?"

Peter became thirsty from all the talking, so he asked Elias to hand him his flask of water. Although tired, de Bologna was also feeling highly energized by their conversation, so he took a sip of water before replying. "Not if we enrich it with other topics youth always finds fascinating, such as myths, mysticism, and... magic."

"Did you say magic?" Elias exclaimed. Then lowering his voice, he added, "May I remind you, Uncle, that what you suggest is just another guaranteed way of getting us burned at the stake?"

"Well, not real magic, obviously—we know nothing about it. But rumors *could* circulate that something mystical or magical takes place in our Lodges. And we could also provide vague hints that those secrets can be found higher up."

"What do you mean *'higher up'*? We only have one kind of initiation ceremony. The one you and William de Grafton came up with, back then," de Norwich said, confused about what his aged relative had in mind.

"Which is why we must now include more levels, or... Degrees... Yes, that's a much better word. We should have additional Degrees, with each one sending subtle hints that the next one up has even more secrets to reveal. There are few things more powerful, in capturing someone's attention, my boy, than if he's convinced he is being denied a secret. This mystique will attract new recruits to us, like moths to a flame, and it will keep them there."

Elias remained silent, for quite some time, pondering over his uncle's words. "Yes, I see what you mean," he said with a satisfied smile, as it was finally becoming clear. "Since there were three classes of Templars (the sergeants, the priests, and the knights), we can create three Degrees to begin with—and maybe even more in the future—so that we don't give it all away at once. This will always keep them wondering about what's up ahead. Naturally, when they reach the top Degree, they might be a bit disappointed by the lack of any genuine revelations, but by then they'd be hooked."

Peter de Bologna was pleased to see his nephew coming around to his way of thinking, at last. "Exactly! Except, they would be hooked to perform valiant and chivalrous deeds in the world. Very soon, people will start to see the oppression and excesses of the Catholic Church for what they truly are, and they'll begin objecting. And when the papacy inevitably lashes out against them, our Brotherhood shall be there to provide succor and support to those suffering. But, in the meantime, many injustices are already happening around us, even as we speak. The Society can begin honing its skills by aiding those victims first."

"And I know just the story that should be included in our rituals to illustrate the injustices people in power hand out," Elias announced. But when his uncle's look indicated he didn't follow, de Norwich hinted, "It's a story we both keep close to our hearts… About a man who got cut down in his prime by a jealous and ruthless king?"

Peter's expression remained puzzled for a while, when all of a sudden his face lit up with understanding. "Yes, of course! You mean the widow's son, our ancestor Hiram à biffe," he said, using the French phrase for *'who was eliminated.'* "I believe it would be a very appropriate addition. But you must be careful to disguise the true story. Solomon's true motives and especially what Hiram hid should never be revealed."

"Of course, they won't. The story will be dressed up in so much stonemasonry garb that the only thing visible will be that three of Hiram's workers wanted him to reveal something to them—I'll think about precisely what, later—which he did not, and so they killed him. And this way, he, as a personality, will get to appear in our rituals, not his mummified head."

Peter realized his nephew's mind was still turning things over, so he allowed him to go on. A moment later, de Norwich expressed his subsequent thoughts. "Perhaps this story could also be embellished with one who discovers a scroll... or a parchment relevant to the crime. And further still, perhaps another Degree might show how retribution was enacted for this abominable act. I'm not quite sure how, yet, though. I shall have to think more on this."

"You are on the right track, my boy," de Bologna told him with enthusiasm. "But bear in mind that the Brotherhood's membership doesn't consist solely of stonemasons, such as we are. In fact, unless I'm very much mistaken, actual stonemasons make up a small percentage of our membership. Besides a few nobles there are many other free professionals, such as merchants, legal practitioners and artificers. So try to pay homage to as many of them as possible. For instance, the fact that Hiram created the bronze Temple columns hollow could be a chance for you to showcase the metal artificers' profession. But whatever you do come up with, it has to be religion neutral."

Elias was surprised by this last remark. "What do you mean?"

"What I mean has to do with what I told you earlier: about people rebelling against the Church. When this happens—and you can be certain it will happen many times over—they'll want to find shelter in an organization which isn't against their beliefs, even if it doesn't exactly cater to them. So in terms of religion, our Brotherhood must only invite candidates who possess a sincere belief in God and the immortality of the soul—otherwise their oaths about keeping our secrets would be meaningless. But other than that, the Society must not only be religion-neutral, it should even prohibit religious discussion altogether... In fact, now that I think of it, prayers could be directed to the Supreme Architect of the Universe—yes, that's a good neutral name for all deities and creeds. And they should end with *'So mote it be,'* instead of the Christian *Amen.*"

Peter de Bologna took another sip of water, before adding, "You must summon all the Lodge Masters to an assembly, as soon as possible, and present these issues to them. With everyone contributing you might even come up with better ideas than these."

Elias nodded. "I will. But we shall also have to discuss ways to get more members from the nobility. Our funds are beginning to run dry and we'll need new patrons and benefactors to support us, if we are to succeed with this new mission. The problem is that being men of the professional classes, we don't move in the same exalted circles as those of the gentry."

"You could always use our existing noble brethren to screen other possible high-born candidates for you. There are many lesser sons of the aristocracy constantly looking for a gallant cause to devote themselves to. And when suitable candidates are found, and you're satisfied they are sound, our knighted brothers will discretely introduce them to you," Peter proposed.

Elias agreed once more that this was solid advice. But they had been talking for quite some time now, and his uncle looked tired. So he decided to let him rest for a bit; they could always speak some more later on. Even though he was indeed exhausted, de Bologna still had the energy for one last afterthought.

Peter eyed his nephew intently. "You know what was found up on the Temple Mount, and where it is hidden now," he said in a whisper, as if asking. When Elias nodded he did, de Bologna went on. "The decision to hide it from the world was a very conscious one. Ever since Hugh de Payns, Nicodemus, and the others found this item, it was kept out of sight for fear the Order might be accused of heresy." He chuckled before saying, "I guess we weren't able to avoid that after all." Then, in a more serious tone, he added, "And it needs to remain hidden—especially now, after everything that's happened to our Order. If the papacy were to get its greedy little hands on it, the Church's hold over Christendom would become even more powerful. So, although I agree that what it is must not be revealed in the new rituals, nevertheless, I feel its whereabouts can be hinted at. As things stand now, in that part of the world, neither you, nor I could ever hope of going there to retrieve it. But it would be a comforting thought to hope that someday, if circumstances were to change, a brother of ours might be able to do so. And that he'd also be able to uncover the true story. So, my advice would be to insert *'breadcrumbs'* within your new rituals, in the hope that a discerning Frère-Mason might be able to decipher them in future."

Elias de Norwich nodded his agreement. "By the way, Uncle, did you know many of our members have started calling themselves Free-Masons now, instead of *Frère*-Masons?"

"No, I didn't... Well, I suppose it's only natural they'd anglicize the French word for *'Brother'* like that, so we mustn't discourage it. Now, where was I? Ah, yes, from what Father Stephen de Safed wrote to me in code, twenty years ago, the treasure is so well hidden no one can find it, under normal circumstances. That is, not unless someone got ahold of the parchment he put away and was able to decipher it."

Peter de Bologna then went on to give his nephew details about the location of both the treasure and the parchment. "So leave a few clues along the way," was de Bologna's final comment on the matter.

"I will, Uncle, don't you worry. I'll take care of everything. But you must rest now. We'll speak again later."

The next day, before de Norwich started on his return journey, Peter kissed his forehead and blessed him. It would be the last time Elias would ever see his uncle again.

CHAPTER 7

TYLER

England
14th Century CE

A FTER PETER DE BOLOGNA passed away, Elias convened a meeting of the Grand Council, later that month, as promised. Aside from himself and the Grand Treasurer, the Council also included eleven of the Society's most prominent Lodge Past Masters—thus honoring the old Templar tradition of governing bodies consisting of thirteen men. But this was the last time it would have such a number of members. All direct references and indirect allusions to the Templars were to be removed from the Society after that day.

The most senior of all Past Masters presided over starting the meeting, and their first order of business was to choose who would be Peter's successor as Grand Master. Naturally, since everybody already knew that de Bologna's wish was for his nephew to replace him, none in the Council objected and Elias was unanimously appointed to the position. Taking possession of the Grand Master's gavel he thanked everyone for their confidence and proceeded to inform them of his uncle's suggestions. And after much discussion they reached a number of unanimous decisions:

First, it was agreed that all future Council positions—including that of Grand Master—were to be determined by elections; no appointments would be made from then on. Second, so as to attract new members, the Society would subsequently steer its primary goal towards aiding the unjustly persecuted, while at the same time keeping the original 'Internal Temple Building' aspect intact. Third, everyone concurred that a sense of mystery, as well as a religion-neutral policy would better serve the Brotherhood's future objectives. And fourth, all references to the Templar Order were subsequently stripped from its existing ritual.

However, when the issue of creating new Degrees and ceremonies was raised, they decided to compromise. The existing Degree—that of Entrant, meaning newcomer, Apprentice, and later anglicized to Entered Apprentice—was supplemented with just one more: the aptly named Fellow of the Craft. Elias had proposed the adoption of an additional, third, Degree—that of the Master Mason—but the Council seemed reluctant to accept any more. Nevertheless, it was agreed that its proposed ritual could be used whenever the Past Masters installed a new Worshipful Master in their Lodge. This was where the Hiramic Legend would be introduced—albeit with a different storyline than the actual events, as well as with clues to the hidden treasure's location—the phrasing of which, Elias alone undertook to formulate.

After this seminal assembly of 1333 AD, the Council members began screening for new potential candidates, particularly among the gentry. Using their existing network of high-born members they evaluated each proposed nominee with care, giving permission for an initial approach only after they were completely satisfied it was a sound possibility. At the same time, however, one of Elias's first initiatives was to implement another of his uncle's ideas: targeting influential townspeople, from all over the country, irrespective of whether they were high-born or not. Aldermen, local council members, bailiffs, and others—especially in the London boroughs—were all valued prospects for membership, so he started looking into them.

The Secret Society, armed with its new sense of purpose, did well in the next fifteen years, as far as finding new members was concerned. Local village priests—disillusioned by the poverty in which the Church abandoned them; soldiers—weary from the constant wars the crown subjected them to; councilmen—disappointed by the lack of power to create better living conditions for their people; and young noblemen—always seeking valiant and noble causes to dedicate themselves to: Every one of these groups found what the Society promised to be relevant and worthy. And accordingly many of them started to swell its ranks.

That is, until the Black Death began to rear its hideous head.

Rampant superstition in those times, actively inflamed by the Catholic Church's pulpit rhetoric, caused most of the household cats to be exterminated—not only on the British Isles but throughout most of Christendom as well. Foolishly believed to be the physical form Lucifer's evil minions transformed themselves into, the peaceful felines started getting slaughtered by the thousands. So much so that when rodents, infested with Plague-carrying fleas, began spreading the gruesome disease, their natural predators were nowhere to be found. As a result, the Black Death was so widespread that at least four out of every ten people suffered a horrific death, and in some areas the toll was even higher. Very few families were spared and, unfortunately, Elias's was not an exception. The Bubonic Plague claimed the lives of his wife and two daughters in mid-1349 AD, leaving him and his son, Anthony, alive, but devastated.

After those tragic events, Elias decided he couldn't keep on living in the same house, or in Norwich for that matter; there were too many beautiful, but painful, memories everywhere. So he decided, along with Anthony, to relocate to Oxford. Changing their surname from *de Norwich* to *Norridge*, to be in better tune with the times, Elias accepted employment as crew-master with the local stonemason's guild there. His choice of Oxford for relocation, however, was influenced not only by the job he found. It was also based on the fact that he now wished his son to receive a proper education at the town's university. Up to then, Anthony had worked as a stonemason's apprentice in Norwich. And although home-schooled when he was younger, his father had always harbored a guilty feeling that this wasn't enough for such a gifted boy. So after his family's tragedy hit him, Elias finally realized their Phoenician heritage cried out for his son to get a better education, and that Anthony deserved a more promising future.

Sponsored by Sir Roger Bacon, a noble fellow-member of the Brotherhood, Anthony Norridge was accepted into Oxford's Merton College, where he began reading for an Arts degree. While being exposed, for the first time, to the seven liberal arts—arithmetic, geometry, astronomy, music, grammar, logic, and rhetoric—at the same time, he also developed a close friendship with John Wycliffe, a classmate of his. Although a bit older than John, Norridge had been quite impressed by his younger friend's novel views on the Church of Rome. Wycliffe's opinions about how the popes lived and ruled—as if they were latter-day Caesars—and how they relentlessly kept all those uneducated in the dark by maintaining every service and the Bible in Latin, instead of the vernacular, made a lasting impression on Anthony. And as things turned out, the group of dissenters who were to follow Wycliffe demanding religious reform—later on mockingly called the Lollards—were to provide a consistent source of new members for the Secret Society.

+ + +

Chelmsford, England
May 31, 1381 CE

SOMEONE SCURRIED INTO Walter Tailer's weaving workshop

and instead of introducing himself, or stating his business, merely stuck out his hand to be shaken. Although puzzled by this, nevertheless, Walter limped over to him and took the stranger's hand into his own. But when he felt the distinct pressure the other's thumb started to exert on his index knuckle, and noted the determined look on the newcomer's face, this compelled Walter to ask, "Are you a traveling man?"

"Yes, I am."

"In which direction do you travel?" Tailer asked again.

"From west to east," replied the stranger, his eyes never abandoning Walter's.

"And what is it you seek to find?"

"That which is lost."

Since the man had fully demonstrated his knowledge of the identification catechism, Walter now felt confident he was indeed a brother Free-Mason. So, Tailer invited him to take a seat and start talking.

"Grand Master, all your predictions have come true. Trouble has started down in Brentwood," the, as yet, unidentified visitor blurted out.

"State your name, man! Who are you?" Walter snapped.

"I'm so sorry, sir. I got carried away. My name is John Geoffrey, bailiff, and I was sent here to inform you of the events by Thomas Baker, the Master of the Lodge at Fobbing. I was received at our own Brentwood Lodge barely a fortnight ago so that is why you don't know me."

Tailer was certain Brother Thomas wouldn't have dispatched this young man without good cause, so he prompted the Entered Apprentice to tell him everything.

"As you anticipated, the crown finally sent an envoy to Essex to collect the poll tax we've declined to pay. Yesterday, Brother Baker organized a group of about a hundred men from his home village of Fobbing. They marched to Brentwood and confronted the crown's commissioner, a man called John Bampton. Brother Thomas told him we'd paid our taxes already and that we would give no more.

Bampton didn't like that so he ordered his attendants to arrest Brother Baker. Then, all hell broke loose. The crowd started attacking *them*, and Bampton barely escaped alive. That was when Brother Baker, with my own Master's consent, bid me to come tell you the news. I've been riding through the night to get here, and I'm to take back with me any orders you issue."

"So it's begun," Walter murmured to himself. And after remaining lost in thought for a long moment, he asked, "How large was Bampton's party?"

"He only brought along two sergeants," Geoffrey replied.

"But more will come—if they haven't already. All right, here's what I want you to do, Brother John. Go back to Brentwood and tell Brother Baker to expect more of the King's envoys. When they come, his group must deal with them just as decisively. Even kill a few, if necessary, this time. That will send a clear message to the crown they're not dealing with people who are afraid to fight. Also, inform Baker, your own Worshipful Master, and any other brothers you can find, that there'll be a general meeting up at Bocking in four days. When you've had sufficient rest, I need for you to ride on down to Kent. Tell all the local brethren you can locate to start notifying and organizing the populace for an uprising as well. And also tell those in Canterbury, that when I arrive there in about a week's time, I'll expect to find the city gates open."

"You will be leading this effort yourself then, sir?" John asked. He was puzzled because from the little he'd heard no Grand Master had ever got himself personally involved in previous disturbances the Society took advantage of.

"I feel this situation has the potential to turn into something much bigger than the Great Rumor, from four years ago, or any other insurgency which happened earlier. And I do have the military experience to lead," Walter said with confidence, as he smiled and tapped on his lame leg.

Years before, he'd been an archer in the ongoing wars

against the French, but after his left leg got injured, he was discharged. Unfortunately, though, the injury left him with a noticeable limp.

"Now go, Brother John. There isn't a moment to lose," Tailer ordered.

✛ ✛ ✛

THE DAYS THAT led up to the gathering at Bocking were filled with events, many of which were unprecedented. As expected, the crown reacted to Bampton's ousting by dispatching an even higher representative: Sir Robert Bealknap, the chief justice of common pleas. But, alas, his mission was not successful either. Although the angry mob he came up against allowed him to flee as well, his party's reception was not as merciful: three of Bealknap's clerks and an equal number of his jurors were beheaded. The crowd, clearly taken over by a fit of wild frenzy, mounted the severed heads on poles and paraded them through the streets of Brentwood. At the same time, in Canterbury, Kent, another royal envoy—the Franciscan sergeant-at-arms, John Legge—also attempted to set up an inquiry there. He was ousted as well, albeit with much less brutal results.

Walter Tailer had not been idle either. He sent riders all over Sussex, in order to incite and prepare its population for the march on London he was planning. Tailer also summoned brethren from neighboring Suffolk and Hertfordshire to be present at Bocking, as well as notifying Society members at Northampton, Leicester, Worcester, Beverley, York, and London—among others—about what to do.

Being the Secret Society's Grand Master for fourteen years now, Walter strongly believed this uprising could be the greatest opportunity the Society might ever have for realizing its raison d'être. Not only that, but he also hoped it would help him a great deal. After Elias Norridge died in 1361 AD, the brethren elected the last surviving, original

Templar as their Grand Master, unopposed; but he died just six years into his tenure. So, in 1367 AD the Society's first true elections were held. The two main opponents, for the new fifteen-year term of the Grand Mastership, were Walter Tailer and Anthony Norridge, Elias's son. Although Tailer prevailed, it was by a weak margin of just three votes, and it was an outcome he always brooded over. Consequently, in Walter's mind, this unrest wouldn't only be useful in achieving the Society's objectives, but it could also help him secure a more solid re-election the following year. He'd make sure it did.

✝ ✝ ✝

Bocking, England
June 4, 1381 CE

A CROWD OF over a thousand common people, many armed with axes, scythes and clubs had gathered in a field just outside the village of Bocking. Secret Society member John Wrawe, a former chaplain, whom Walter had appointed as the gathering's speaker, stepped up on a large boulder to address them.

"Friends, these are the days everyone will remember," he began. "When the Black Death ravaged our families, we endured our losses and grieved. When the kingdom decided to start a never-ending war with the French, we obeyed and we fought. And when parliament fixed wages to pre-Plague levels, even though the manpower was severely reduced, we swallowed our rage and complied. But enough is enough! We shall not submit to a poll tax so unjust, and so evil, that its very name brings to mind an abhorrent disease. Will *you* agree to a levy which encourages the king's collectors to lift up your daughters' dresses to see if they're old enough to pay?"

The crowd shouted, "No!" and everyone waved their weapons menacingly in the air.

"No, we will not! That is why we need to rid our beloved king of those evil vultures who surround him: John of Gaunt, Archbishop Sudbury, and especially that leach of a Treasurer, Robert Hales. So we'll march en masse to London and present our demands to His Majesty: We will urge him to hand over those hated officials to us; we shall demand immediate elimination of serfdom and unfree tenure; and we shall require a general pardon for whatever has happened these past few days. What say you?"

Every one of the butchers, bakers, peasants, and other common folk, who were gathered there, shouted out at the top of their lungs, "Aye!"

"When the order for the march is issued, you must be prepared. And get as many more people you know to come along with you as well. But remember, whatever we strive for cannot take priority over our love for England. So we mustn't abandon our country's defenses. None within twenty leagues of the shores must follow, lest the French decide to take advantage of their absence. And to prove we're not brigands and thieves, but rather righteous men in pursuit of justice, everyone must refrain from stealing. Any such incident would only put a stain on our just endeavor. May God bless you, and may He also bless His Majesty, King Richard the Second."

The crowd was still cheering when John Wrawe's burly figure stepped down the makeshift podium. Walter walked over and shook his hand. "That was a very inspired speech," he congratulated him, only to add swiftly, "But it's time we got down to business." Backing away from the throng, Tailer invited John, as well as Jack Straw, Thomas Baker, and several other select Society members, to draw near. Walter knew he needed to get his lieutenants wound up as well.

"The reason we are doing this, Brethren, is freedom: To liberate England from those traitors that bind the king to their evil ways; to release good, common folk from serfdom and unfree tenure; and especially to free us all from yet another unfair taxation. You must never forget that. But in order for us to be successful we will have to fight and do things we would never do under normal circumstances. So we must stand united."

He paused and looked at all the eager, nodding faces around him. Satisfied his message was getting through, Tailer went on. "I will make my way down to Kent on the morrow. And when I arrive at Maidstone, in about three days from now, I shall release our preacher brother, John Ball, from the Church's prison there, so that he can join our struggle. Then, all together we'll head to Canterbury to see if that worm of an archbishop is hiding out there. If not, we will surely settle our score with him in the capital. Now, I feel obliged to inform you that this insurgency, aside from allowing us to pursue the noble cause of freedom, will also give us a chance for some personal satisfaction." He knew he shouldn't be mentioning this subject in public, in case someone overheard, yet Walter couldn't help himself. It was too good an opportunity to miss.

Thomas Baker was first to voice the question. "What do you mean, Grand Master?"

"I mean that this uprising provides us with the perfect cover to finally serve those Hospitaller bastards their just deserts. They have never paid for conspiring with the French king and the pope to bring down our ancestors, the Templars, or for taking the Order's holdings. So, they will have to pay now. We shall inflict such a level of destruction on their properties that it'll be unprecedented, yet nobody will understand why. Everyone will think it's because the people hate Robert Hales, the King's treasurer, so much. But no one will know it's actually because he's also the Lord Prior of the Hospitaller Order in England—none besides us, that is. So before you start leading the rebels from Essex down to London, Brother Straw, I want you to gather a sizeable group and sack the Hospitaller manor at Cressing Temple. Take away anything you can carry and burn all the documents you find."

Jack Straw smiled and said, "Yes, Grand Master," acknowledging the command. But every younger brother there merely nodded blankly as if they knew what Tailer was talking about. The elimination of all Templar references in the Society's rituals meant that those under a certain age had never heard of the connection.

Walter turned to face John Wrawe. "Brother John, I want you to go up to Suffolk and organize the people there. Gather as many as possible and coordinate with Brother Straw about the march to London. Then, wreak as much havoc as you can on the way." And after giving various other, individual instructions, he turned to them all and said, "Remember why we are doing this, my Brothers. Discourage theft by anyone with you, but if you catch a brother doing the thieving then kill him on the spot, so that you set an example. I hope to see you all in London. Farewell, and may the Supreme Architect of the Universe watch over you."

+ + +

London, England
June 13, 1381 CE

MIDSUMMER'S DAY, THE longest one of the year, was less than a fortnight away. So, even though it was already past eight in the evening the sun still hadn't set. Sitting at his table by the window, Anthony Norridge was desperately trying to concentrate. He wanted to put the finishing touches to the pleading in front of him, but with his mind unsettled by that day's events it wasn't an easy task. Even so, Norridge decided he needed to soldier on and take advantage of the continuing daylight. The document was supposed to be submitted in court the next morning. And although the courts in Westminster most probably wouldn't sit—with the city being in so much chaos—nevertheless, he wanted to have it ready even if that proved to be the case.

Anthony was a barrister now, associated with the Middle Temple—one of the most prominent Inns of Court. After he'd received his Arts Degree from Oxford, in 1355 AD, Sir Roger Bacon helped him in pursuing a legal career too. It was a field which had always interested Norridge, but it was also an important profession his father felt the Brotherhood should be represented in as well. So, Anthony studied hard, and five years later he was given the privilege of 'passing the bar,' as it'd been called. In those times, the Inns of Court were quite near the Temple Barrier—a gate which separated them from the legal courts of Westminster—and to pass through the checkpoint each person had to pay a toll. But when an agreement was reached later on, whereby each accredited lawyer was allowed to pass the gate's 'bar' without payment, that concession resulted in them becoming known as barristers.

He was just starting to get the document's wording exactly as he wanted it, when Anthony heard someone step into his outer chambers. A moment later the door creaked open, revealing two men standing there.

Norridge looked up and asked the man on the right, "Have you come to kill me as well?"

Walter Tailer was smiling. "Now why would I want to do that?"

"Oh, I don't know… So many lawyers and scribes were murdered today that it made me think my turn may have come," Anthony replied dryly.

"No, I stopped by to show our neophyte brother here your chambers. He is to make sure no one disturbs you. Brother John Geoffrey, this is Brother Anthony Norridge, our Grand Secretary."

Both men shook hands, using the Entered Apprentice's grip, and Geoffrey expressed his joy in finally getting to meet Anthony; he had heard so much about him. Then, Tailer asked John to leave them, as he and Norridge had matters to discuss in private.

When Geoffrey closed the door behind him, Anthony

looked deep into Walter's eyes and spoke in a reprimanding tone. "This is a very foolhardy thing you're doing."

"You mean the rebellion?"

"No, of course I don't mean the rebellion," Norridge snapped. "The fact you are leading it, that's what I mean. It's not how we do things, and you know it. We should be pulling the strings from the shadows."

"Well, what was I expected to do? When everybody started chanting my name in Maidstone, about a week ago, and proclaimed me their leader, was I supposed to decline?"

Anthony was scowling. "Yes, you should have. What if someone arrests and tortures you, what then? No one knows we exist yet, but if they put you to the rack, you'll probably tell them everything. You've placed the entire Brotherhood in jeopardy, Walter."

"You mean, Wat," he replied. And when Norridge frowned, indicating he didn't understand, Tailer chuckled before explaining. "When I arrived in Maidstone, a few of the men saw fit to shorten my Christian name, while others started mispronouncing my surname. So, from that day on everyone knows me as *Wat Tyler*. Which conveniently disguises my true identity, don't you think?"

His original family name of 'Tailer' was the final vestige he had of his French grandfather. As a tailor, Wat's paternal granddad used to be the Templar Order's last Draper in France. But after successfully escaping arrest in 1307 AD, he travelled to England and became a professional weaver. His son and grandson followed his footsteps in that vocation as well as in becoming members of the newly hatched Secret Society.

"Whatever they call you now, your actions have been reckless," Anthony responded, still feeling very annoyed.

"As always, you're entitled to your opinion. But despite that, what I really want to know is whether you support this rebellion," Wat Tyler then said.

"Support it?" Norridge exploded. "Who do you think arranged for your mob to find the gates of London Bridge and

Aldgate open today? How else do you think you might have made such a swift entry into the city if I hadn't helped?"

Wat was nodding, his head bowed. "Yes, well... thank you for that." Realizing he had to help Anthony calm down, he added with a weak smile, "You'll be happy to know that with your aid we've dealt a severe blow to those traitorous Hospitaller bastards. After we sacked John of Gaunt's Savoy Palace, we turned our sights to their properties in Fleet Street. We freed the prisoners from the gaol there and destroyed everything belonging to their Order we could find in the vicinity. The two forges they stole from our ancestors, the Templars? Well, I can guarantee they will never be operational again. Then, we moved toward Temple Church and—"

"You damaged the main church of the Knights Templar in England?" Norridge cut in, alarmed.

"No, of course not. You know I would never allow that. No, what we did was to take all the records, and other artifacts, out into the street to be burned there. I also sent a group of men up to the Hospitaller headquarters in Clerkenwell with orders to tear down the Priory—which they did. Their Order all over Christendom will be reeling from these attacks for many years to come," Tyler added with a satisfied snicker.

"But there's been so much unnecessary loss of life, especially among my colleagues," Anthony then said. "Even a hint of ink-stained hands was enough to send a man to his doom today." He was referring to all the scribes and lawyers who'd been killed by the rebels that day.

"That was unavoidable, I'm afraid. The men felt they had to do away with as many of those who would be able to draft cases against them later on."

"And what of the scores of dead Flemish weavers? What justification could you possibly have for *their* murders? Maybe it was on your orders, to get rid of some major competitors?" Norridge asked accusingly.

Wat lowered his head again. "Aye, those were unfortunate events, and I was afraid you'd look at them that way—even if I had nothing to do with it. When a member of our Brotherhood stole a silver goblet from the Savoy Palace, and I heard about it, I had him executed on the spot. But I can't control everyone's actions. Apparently, the local members of the weavers' guild have their own agenda."

Anthony was almost about to counter that this was why Tyler should've never placed himself in the limelight. However, he decided it was best to defuse their conversation, so instead he took a deep breath before speaking again. "The king has sent out town criers announcing he'll meet with you on the morrow, and that he's willing to satisfy your demands. What do you plan to do?"

"Actually, this is one of the reasons why I came by here tonight. I need you to take care of a few matters for me," Wat said, after raising his eyes. "You must make sure the Tower of London's drawbridge is down tomorrow morning, and that its gate is left open."

"Why? Are you not planning to go meet with the king?"

"No, not tomorrow. I have better things to do: like killing Archbishop Sudbury and Robert Hales, for example."

Anthony frowned. "But how do you know they'll not be in the king's party?"

"Because that's the second thing you need to take care of. Tell Brother Robert de Vere to convince the king not to take those two officials with him on the morrow. As the Earl of Oxford, and a person who has the king's ear, it shouldn't be too difficult for him to persuade Richard that taking them along might be more dangerous than beneficial."

"And killing those two, even if they are scum, is what this whole rebellion is about?" Norridge asked in a dry tone again.

"Of course it isn't, that's much bigger. Killing them, however, affords us some satisfaction that we finally get to exact revenge on two out of the three major parties which caused the Templars' downfall: the Church and the Hospitallers. I believe a reason like that should be sufficient enough to miss a meeting with the king, don't you think?"

"Then what is the bigger picture? What are you ultimately trying to achieve here?"

"In one word: freedom," Tyler replied. But he continued before Norridge had a chance to add anything. "Let me put it to you this way, Anthony. When I got to Maidstone, one of the first things I did was to free Brother John Ball from the Church prison there. This morning, our roaming priest gave us a very eloquent and inspired sermon. If I remember his words correctly, it went something like this: 'When Adam dug and Eve span, who was then the gentleman? From the beginning all men by nature were created equal, and our bondage came in by the unjust oppression of wicked men, and contrary to God's will. For if God would've wanted any bondsmen from the beginning He would have appointed who would be a serf and who a lord. And, therefore, I exhort you to consider that now the time has come, appointed to us by God, in which we may cast off the yoke of bondage, and recover liberty. It is our duty to uproot and make away with them all—evil lords, unjust judges, lawyers—every man who is dangerous to the common good. Then we would have peace for the present and security for the future; for when the great ones have been cut off, all men will enjoy equal freedom. And all will have the same nobility, rank, and power.' ...They were quite stimulating words, I can tell you," Wat said with a smile.

"And extremely dangerous ones too—words which go way beyond our Society's mission of aiding simple folk from the wrath of evil lords and the Church. You are not seeking the mere elimination of serfdom here, Walter. You and John Ball are preaching outright revolution—an extermination of the aristocracy and... and the monarchy!" Anthony exclaimed in alarm.

"To be frank with you, although I personally wouldn't find either outcome displeasing, it will never come to that," Tyler replied. "The men are devoted to the king. They only want to do away with all the parasites surrounding him, and to secure a fair way to make an honest living."

A long moment of silence passed between them. Wat Tyler was the first to break it. "So you'll help me with what needs to be done at the Tower tomorrow?"

Norridge nodded dejectedly. "Yes."

"Do I have your brotherly word?"

"Aye, you have it."

"Good. Thank you," Wat said as he stood up to leave. He headed toward the door, but before going out, as if in an afterthought, he turned around and said, "When I came in you asked me if I had come here to kill you. Remember?"

"Yes, I do."

"I would just like to add that I'd never want to do that. I need you to be very much alive when I beat you again in next year's elections. And for certain the rebellion will help me achieve a much larger margin this time," Tyler said with a spiteful chuckle.

"You are such a vain man," Anthony countered, as he looked at him with disdain.

"That may be so. But everyone will remember who Wat Tyler was. Unfortunately, though, history will never even *whisper* your name."

After saying that, he walked out of the room, laughing.

✝ ✝ ✝

THE FOLLOWING MORNING, on June 14, King Richard and his entourage travelled a short distance outside the city walls to Mile's End, to meet with the rebels as agreed. Although Tyler wasn't amongst them, the insurgents appointed by him put two requests to the king: he was to surrender a number of traitorous officials over to them, and serfdom was to be abolished. As far as the first demand was concerned, the young monarch countered that *he* should be the one to mete out any necessary judgement, and only after fair trials were conducted. But as to the second one, he was more accommodating: Richard instantly declared that serfdom was hereby abolished. And to prove the sincerity of his intentions, he had his scribes begin issuing charters of universal freedom.

While the meeting of the king with the rebels was in progress, a force of about four hundred insurgents made its way to the Tower of London. Led by Wat Tyler, John Ball and Jack Straw, they soon found out that Anthony Norridge was a man of his word: the drawbridge was down and the gate was open. Not only that, but their two principal targets were also there, cowering inside. Tyler and his men soon grabbed ahold of Archbishop Sudbury and Hospitaller Prior Robert Hales and swiftly decapitated them. Their heads were then proudly displayed by mounting them on London Bridge. After it was all over, Tyler dispatched Jack Straw over to Highbury. It seems the district there had a particularly luxurious Hospitaller Manor which needed sacking.

Looking back on those events it appears that almost every objective of the rebellion had been achieved that day. Which makes it all the more curious why Tyler agreed to meet with the king again the following afternoon, on June 15: a meeting that was to go down in history as an absolute disaster for the rebels.

+ + +

Birmingham, England
July 20, 1381 CE

"I HEREBY DECLARE this special gathering of the Grand Council now open," Anthony Norridge said and banged his gavel on the table. "Please note, Brethren, that even though only eight of us are in attendance, out of the regular fifteen members, we do have a quorum."

After the previous month's events, Norridge, as the Society's Grand Secretary and second in command, felt the Council should meet to discuss them and chart its future course. London was still in turmoil, which made it dangerous to gather there, so he decided Birmingham might provide a more convenient central location for everyone. Not only that, but it was at a safe distance from every other place the spark of rebellion had also ignited: cities like York, Leicester and Bridgwater, as well as the entire shires of Kent and Essex. Seven of the Council members sat around the table in the first-floor room of the local Golden Goose Inn, which Anthony had rented for the occasion, while another member was just outside the door with his sword drawn. The matters they had to discuss were sensitive and too dangerous not to take precautions.

"As you are all well aware, one of those absent today is our late Grand Master, may the Lord grant him peace, and his permanent absence from now on is one of the reasons why I summoned this meeting. But before we go any further, I believe it would be best for us all to hear just *how* Brother Walter died that day at Smithfield. Fortunately, we do have an eyewitness among us. Brother Thomas, would you please tell us exactly what transpired?" Norridge asked and turned to face Thomas Farndon, who sat next to him.

"Early in the afternoon of June 15, we gathered at Smithfield, while the king's party had already assembled in front of St. Bartholomew's Priory, far away from us," Farndon began. "A messenger rode out and called for Walter to join King Richard. Before going, however, Brother Tyler turned to address us. He said that if he raised his right arm straight up, with its fist clenched, it would mean he was in trouble and that we were to dash out to his aid. Wat demonstrated it, and everyone there who is a Free-Mason knew that what he showed us was the Brotherly Sign of Distress. Then, he rode off, carrying a St. George's Cross banner with him, to go meet with—"

"What I'd like to know, before we hear the rest of the events, is why Tyler agreed to speak with the king in the first place," Bertrand Wilmington, another Council member, cut in. "Did he suspect Richard had already decided to go back on his word about abolishing serfdom and unfree tenure?"

Farndon shook his head. "No, I don't think he did. From

what the Grand Master told me earlier, he was planning to pressure the king for more concessions."

"What sort of concessions?" Norridge asked, with a frown.

"Apparently, Walter wanted to achieve what he called 'the separation of State and Church.' And the first way to realize that, according to him, was to demand the seizure of all land belonging to the Church, by the crown, and then its equal distribution to the people who worked it."

Norridge looked around at the others, and they all had the same astonished expression he did. It appeared no one else had been made aware of Tyler's intentions. "Very well, we'll come back to this matter later. What happened after he rode out to parley with the king?" Anthony asked, inviting Thomas to continue.

"They were far away from where I was standing, so I don't know whether Wat put this demand to King Richard, or not, but they were speaking. What I did make out, though, a short while later, was the Mayor of London sneaking up and stabbing Wat in the back. Then another member of the king's party attacked Tyler with a sword, causing him to fall off his horse. He fell, without having a chance to give us the Distress Sign, along with St George's white banner with the red cross on it. It was as if he was a latter-day Templar," Thomas added sorrowfully. "All hell broke loose after that. Everyone wanted to attack and take revenge, but reinforcements on the king's side had already arrived on the field. Any further action would have been futile, so along with John Ball and John Geoffrey, I decided to leave. What's funny is that days later the king's side started circulating a lie that Richard rode out to speak to us all after Wat fell. The king supposedly told us that henceforth *he* would be our new captain and that he would meet with us again at Clerkenwell later. Pure fiction, of course—none of that ever happened. What did happen, though, was that later in the day the mayor went looking for Wat. And when he found him half dead in the Priory, he beheaded him."

For several moments, everyone sat around in a gloomy silence after hearing those words.

Anthony decided to break the silence. "Thank you, Brother Thomas. After hearing your account of the events, I believe there are a few issues we need to address. And the first is our revealed Brotherly Sign of Distress. Since so many people saw it, even if they don't know where it comes from, or what it means, I nevertheless feel we'd be more prudent if we changed it."

They spent the next several minutes discussing which Sign to adopt as its replacement. The one the majority finally agreed upon was to extend both arms outward on both sides, with palms open and fingers joined, while the upper arms and forearms created straight angles. The motion was passed and everyone received instructions on how to notify their Lodges of the change.

"A second issue I feel we must discuss is that which our late Grand Master deemed unnecessary to share with the rest of us. And I'm referring to his idea about the separation of church and state," Norridge then said. "Although I disagreed with him for accepting the role of leader in the revolt—something which I told him to his face—I believe Walter's heart was in the right place with this. As long as the Church has the power to intervene in the affairs of any sovereign nation no real progress can ever be made. Maybe we should—"

James Clarkwell, another Council member, abruptly cut in. "I agree, Brother Norridge. We Wycliffites believe the Church of Rome has too much power as it is. The papacy is too corrupt to be left in charge of people's souls, so its power must be curtailed."

The Wycliffites were the followers of Professor John Wycliffe, the nonconformist priest, and classmate of Anthony Norridge. Also derogatorily called the Lollards, they constituted a permanent thorn in the Church's side for decrying the sale of indulgences and dismissing the doctrine of transubstantiation. The vehemence with which the Church hunted them down would provide a steady source of new Secret Society members, over the next couple of centuries, even if John Wycliffe himself had chosen not to join.

"You know better than to bring up any kind of religious subject here, Brother James," Anthony scolded him. "We must always keep our meetings—in Lodge, or in Council—religion neutral, and you know that. And when I speak about the separation of church from state, I mean *any* church and *any* state."

Norridge was still eyeing the remorseful James Clarkwell severely when Bertrand Wilmington spoke out. "King Richard has proven himself untrustworthy, now that he's decided to repeal the abolition of serfdom. So, I don't think he's the best candidate to put this idea to. In fact, we don't even know whether Wat already suggested it to him in the first place."

"No, we don't," Anthony said. "And these are probably not the best of times for anyone in power to agree to this notion. So, I propose that we make it a very longterm goal for our Society. Agreed?"

Everyone nodded their agreement, and so the Council went on to discuss other matters. One issue was the need to organize aid for those still hiding out after the revolt's suppression. Another was the stern ban against Council members assuming a limelight role in similar, future insurgencies—it was determined that any such involvement would have to be kept in the safety of shadows. They also discussed about the Grand Mastership and decided that Anthony Norridge should continue as Acting Grand Master until elections were held the following year; the circumstances were still too dangerous to risk gathering all Master Masons in one place. Finally, Thomas Farndon expressed an idea on how the Council could honor their late Grand Master. He proposed that 'Tyler' should be the title for the second-in-command officer of every Lodge. After much discussion, though, an alternative proposal was ratified: the brother who sat on guard outside each Lodge's meeting room would be the one called a Tyler.

Anthony looked around the table. "If no one has anything else to add, and before we adjourn our meeting, I'd like to show you all something." Bending over he produced a thick batch of vellum pages from within his satchel. And after passing the bundle off first to Farndon next to him, he began to explain. "I commissioned this work from a brother of ours, a priest, whom I know from my Oxford days. And since he has a way with rhymes, he decided to write it as a poem. As you'll notice when you read it, it's a subtle call for the lesser sons of the nobility to become Free-Masons. And the good thing is it's absolutely safe—even if the authorities happen to stumble on to it—because the entire poem is written as if it were addressing potential stonemasons. The poem touches upon numerous issues: A basic mythology on how our Craft was created, thus concealing its true story; a good number of the moral lessons we expound in our Lodges; simple rules of etiquette for our less noble brothers; plus many more."

"And what are you proposing?" Thomas Farndon asked, after he glanced at them and passed the pages over to a brother near him.

"When you've all had a chance to look it over, I would like your consent to make copies and send them off to the Lodge Masters. Then, they can copy and give it out to whichever candidate they see fit," Anthony suggested. And when everyone looked at the text thoroughly, the Council agreed with the proposal.

That manuscript would be later known, further on down in history, as the Regius Poem. And it would constitute the oldest of Freemasonry's Old Charges. What Norridge purposefully neglected to mention, however, was that it also contained a few vital clues—clues which could be potentially useful to anyone who'd seek to find the hidden Templar Treasure. He had recognized that the Society's rituals, which also contained hints to its location, were vulnerable in that they were oral and could be changed on a whim. But a written collection of veiled clues might just possibly have a better chance of withstanding the ravages of time.

Aside from this, Anthony had also neglected to reveal something of equal importance. He had already taken steps for young men of Phoenician descent to be on hand so that in future they might take charge of the Secret Society.

Someone as reckless as Wat Tyler would never again be allowed to assume control.

TEMPLARS

CHAPTER 8

ARK

Jerusalem
1122 CE

THE ENDEAVOR THAT the nine Templar knights, along with Nicodemus and his three Tyrian scribes, had embarked upon hadn't been easy. Yet, over the next two years, every one of those present on that evening, in March 1120 AD, contributed equally hard to the grueling process of tunneling under the Temple Mount. And even though their daily schedules were filled with hours of attending to other duties—especially the knights, who were supposed to patrol the pilgrim roads, take care of the horses, and carry on with their training—nevertheless, they all still found the energy and some spare time each day, or night, to dig.

By command of the Grand Master the area in the Stables, from which the tunnel began, was cordoned off and only those directly involved were allowed to approach. Guards were even posted there, around the clock, to ensure against unauthorized access. This, of course, did nothing to dispel the rumors already circulating among the rest of the knights and sergeants about what happened down there. Quite the opposite, this tight veil of secrecy only served to encourage those left out to concoct even wilder theories in their minds. But, whatever was imagined by them, either some sort of sexual deviance or any other kind of irregularity, they dutifully kept it to themselves and nothing was heard outside the Order.

One night, and while Hugh de Payns was still in his dreams, someone started shaking his shoulder, all of a sudden, and calling out his name. Hugh felt instinctively certain it was far too soon to attend the Office of Lauds—a service which wasn't supposed to start before sunrise—nevertheless, he groggily opened his eyes. Godfrey de St. Omer stood over him, with a candle in hand. The bearded knight began to whisper in an excited tone. "Wake up, Sir Hugh. We've done it. The wall has been breached."

While still trying to recover his bearings, the Grand Master sat up in his straw bed and yawned. Then it all came back to him. Following Geoffrey Bison's suggestion, the dedicated knights and scribe-monks had tunneled, using calculated straight lines and sharp turns, for nearly two years. The solid rock the Temple Mount was made of gave them all a hard time and even though they did make progress, it was not without mishaps along the way: A miscounting of paces, at one time, had cost them the better part of six months, forcing them to retrace their route. And then there was also that unfortunate incident when Payns de Montdidier burned his left hand while igniting a boulder drenched in Greek Fire. But despite those, and a few other minor incidents, the brothers did manage to press forward. And the previous day they had come up against something that could only have been a man-made wall, and which was situated, by all indications, directly under the Templum Domini Church. They were confident they'd finally reached their objective, so Hugh issued strict instructions that no one was to enter the crypt unless he did so first.

The Grand Master got dressed in a hurry and lit a lamp. He then led Godfrey down to the Stables, past the guard on duty, through the tunnel opening, and all the way along the winding path the Templars had carved into the Mount. Although the underground passages barely allowed them to walk upright, their excitement about the discovery at hand soon dispelled the claustrophobic feeling they usually experienced whenever they were in those cramped, rocky corridors. After trudging along for almost fifteen minutes, Hugh noticed light penetrating the darkness at about twenty feet up ahead. A small group was standing there, evidently waiting for him: two of his bearded knights, along with the clean-shaven Nicodemus, who must have been notified as well. When he got even closer, de Payns could see a hole, of more than two feet in diameter, which had already been opened, inches above the base of the slab.

Since discovering that marble barrier in their path, the previous day, Nicodemus had suggested clearing the soil surrounding it. That way, he said, they would know exactly what they were up against before proceeding to break through. As a result, a team dug further on all sides of the wall. And after doing so, it was apparent that what they were dealing with was not just some big, random, square slab, which somehow got misplaced in the ground. On the contrary, it proved to be one side of a huge, boxed chamber of about six feet in height and equal width—a chamber most probably set underground before the Temple's construction had even begun. The only thing they could not make out yet was how far back into the Mount this crypt extended.

Nicodemus was the first to greet him. "Ah, Grand Master, welcome." His normally dark brown cassock and the jet-black hair surrounding his tonsure were almost white from all the dust that had settled on them.

"Father... Brothers..." de Payns said, as he nodded to them in greeting. Then, glancing momentarily at the hole, he asked the priest, "Has anyone gone in yet, Father?"

"No, Sir Hugh, no one has. We've just finished enlarging the entry point and have been waiting for you."

Hugh de Payns looked at all the eager faces around him. "This is a very special moment, for every one of us. I only hope that what's inside is worth all our hard work and sacrifices." He then crossed himself thrice, before adding, "May the Good Lord protect us from any evil lurking within."

After he ordered the three knights to stand guard outside and to allow no one else to enter, he invited only Nicodemus to follow him in. The Grand Master crouched down and slowly wormed his way into the crypt through the narrow opening.

The first thing to strike Hugh, as he entered through the hole, was how stale and putrid the inside of the chamber smelled. *But this is hardly surprising, given that it's been sealed underground for almost two thousand years,* he thought. As he stood up, the Grand Master discovered he could stand up comfortably. His stocky build of just over five and a half feet was a neat fit within the six-foot-tall crypt. Hugh de Payns held his lamp up against the darkness and what he saw in front of him next made him gasp.

Taking up a good part of the elongated chamber was a large chest, completely made out of gold! Its height and width, according to Hugh's reckoning, were both more than two feet, and its length extended to almost four. On opposite sides of the chest's rectangular cover were two golden figurines of kneeling angels, facing each other, their open wings stretched inward until they almost touched. Looking down, de Payns also noticed two long, golden poles, placed through double rings on either side of the chest. Presumably they were its means of transportation.

This is the Ark of the Covenant. The Ark commanded by the Lord, Hugh thought with fascination, as he reverently dropped to his knees and bowed his head. The Grand Master was still busy crossing himself when Nicodemus clambered into the crypt behind him.

"This is it, Father! It's just as you had described it. You were absolutely correct about everything," Hugh told him excitedly, as he started to stand up.

"Yes, it is impressive, isn't it?" Nicodemus said in a dry tone while looking at the Ark.

Hugh's eyes were wide open with enthusiasm. "Impressive? It's much more than that, Father! It's the find of an era, I would say."

"That it is, Grand Master. That it is. But let's see what else this chamber holds for us, shall we?" As he spoke the priest started walking to the left of the Ark and towards the back of the vault. The crypt had at last revealed itself to be about fifteen feet long.

Although Hugh was a bit puzzled by Nicodemus's nonchalant attitude, he followed him round all the same, only to confirm that pleasant surprises were not in short supply that day. When they arrived, after a few steps, at the far left corner of the crypt they saw five chests neatly stacked there, almost up to the ceiling. They were overflowing with all kinds of treasure: gold and silver coins, small golden bars and numerous precious gems—among many other valuable items.

But even this sight did not seem to impress the priest much. He walked on, holding his candle at arm's length to illuminate the other side of the chamber. Apparently, Nicodemus was looking for something else in there. Only when he stopped moving and stood perfectly still, did Hugh realize the priest had found what he'd been searching for. The Templar Grand Master stepped beside him, and following Nicodemus's downward gaze, de Payns saw a skeleton lying on the marble floor, mere inches from their feet. And the strange thing about it was not that a skeleton should be in there, nor that what used to be the person's clothes had been reduced to mere fragments, hanging from the bones at places. No, what really struck the Grand Master as bizarre was that the skull was missing!

Hugh looked at Nicodemus who stood completely still and silent, almost as if in a trance, his gaze undeviatingly fixed on the skeleton. "Do you know who this was?" he asked the priest in a whisper.

"Yes, I do," Nicodemus replied in a soft tone of voice, after taking a moment. "This used to be my great, great ancestor, Master Hiram."

Hugh de Payns looked surprised. "But I thought you said you were descended from *King* Hiram."

"No, what I said was that I could trace my lineage back to *Hiram*. I meant *Master* Hiram: him!" Nicodemus replied, while his eyes pointed to the skeletal remains.

"Now how could he be your ancestor given that he died here, so far away from his home?" de Payns persisted.

The priest was still looking intently at what remained of his forefather. "He was, because before coming here to work on the Temple project he'd left a wife and children behind him in Tyre. But, after his family was informed of his murder, and having no body to commit to a tomb, they chose to keep his memory alive by transmitting to all future generations his knowledge and life's story." Nicodemus looked at the Templar Grand Master and cracked a weak smile. "I'd heard so much about Hiram during my childhood that he was an absolute hero of mine. In fact, getting near his remains was one of the reasons why I accepted the mission to come warn about the pilgrims' massacre in the first place. And discovering them was definitely the reason why I decided to build my chambers down in the Stables. For so many centuries none of my fellow Phoenicians had got this close; I was not going to squander such a God-sent opportunity. I must confess, though, Sir Hugh, that finding him here today—exactly as described—almost brings tears to my eyes."

The dim candlelight within the chamber confirmed that Nicodemus's eyes were starting to well up, except that Hugh just had to point it out. "I don't know if you've noticed it, Father, but apparently Hiram's skull seems to be missing."

"Yes, I have. I never expected to find his head in here."

"And why is that?"

"Because, I already have it with me," Nicodemus replied. And while de Payns was still struggling to find words to respond to that, the priest reached into the satchel he'd been carrying on his shoulder all along and pulled out a large, egg-shaped, silver object. When he turned it over, it made Hugh gasp. Enclosed within a silver shell, was the head of a man long dead, but whose glazed, lifeless eyes were still wide open. There were remnants of a beard clinging onto the leathery skin at places while many parts of the forehead and cheeks had already turned dark.

"My Lord, you are full of surprises aren't you, Father?" the Grand Master blurted out after a moment of stunned silence.

"I'm sorry if I have shocked you, Sir Hugh, but allow me to make amends by telling you the whole story this time," Nicodemus said. "While Hiram was being murdered in the Temple, his assistants were in here, oblivious to what had happened. But when some time passed and their Master didn't return, they became worried, so they decided to sneak back into the Temple. Night had already descended, and after looking around for him in the dark, and whispering his name, they eventually stumbled upon their Master's remains. You can imagine their horror when they discovered the murderers had decapitated him."

"That's a very unusual way to kill someone. Was this how the ancient Hebrews used to execute people?" Hugh asked.

Nicodemus shook his head. "Not that I know of, no." He frowned. "To be honest, this has always puzzled me as well. Maybe it wasn't the murderers' intention to kill him like that and it just happened by accident... During the heat of a scuffle, perhaps? Who can say? At any rate, after they spent a few moments mourning their Master, his assistants took the head and body, and brought them here to this crypt. They also took care that no signs of its location, or any bloodstains in the Temple, were left behind. Then, they released a substantial amount of soil to fill the shaft connecting the crypt to the Temple. And before the soil could enter this chamber as well, they sealed the opening in the crypt's wall. Probably with that marble slab," Nicodemus said, as he pointed to a large, noticeable square block protruding from the wall behind Hugh's left shoulder. It had handgrip handles on both sides.

The Grand Master glanced at it and then turned back to face Nicodemus. "What happened next?" Although de Payns was shocked by everything he'd heard he was intrigued all the same.

"Hiram's assistants were dazed, but knew they needed to get out of here in a hurry, so they only took their Master's head with them. They wanted their king to see it as evidence of everything that happened. Then, they escaped by using a tunnel to the north." The priest turned and pointed to an outline of yet another slab, which was visible on the wall behind the Ark. "Through there, most likely," he said. The slab had a small hole at its center, probably as a means for allowing air into the chamber. Nothing was visible beyond it, however, since the underground passageway behind had also been filled with soil by the fleeing assistants, Nicodemus explained. "It was night, so no one saw them as they emerged from the Mount's hidden tunnel. Then, as I've already told you, they left Jerusalem behind them and arrived at a small village north of the capital. There, Madal, one of the two Phoenicians, was able to embalm Hiram's head. He'd been to Egypt several years earlier and had learned the art of mummification from the Egyptian masters. The silver casing you see was prepared a few years later after Hiram's wife received her husband's head back from the king. It has been my family's heirloom ever since, and in time I was hoping to pass it on to my younger sister's son."

Just as the priest was finishing his account of those ancient events, de Payns noticed a glint of light reflecting off the skeleton. Looking more closely, he saw there was a ring on one of the bony fingers. "What's this?" Hugh wondered, as he bent over to get a better look. Nicodemus also stooped down. On what used to be Hiram's right index finger there was a large silver ring, with a design engraved on it: two intertwined equilateral triangles, one pointing up, and the other down.

The priest gasped, and exclaimed in a whisper, "Solomon's Ring!"

The Grand Master, not paying attention to what Nicodemus had just said, kneeled and started removing it from the long-dead Master's finger. Although he tried to do so without damaging the hand, nevertheless the brittle bones soon disconnected and fell apart at his touch. When he had the Ring in the palm of his hand, he turned around to ask, "What did you say, Father?"

"I said this is the Ring of Solomon. It's engraved with the Star of David, his father's symbol, and it is shrouded in legend," the priest said with awe. "Although I'd heard many stories about this Ring, over the years, I never actually believed them to be true."

Hugh was puzzled. "Then what's it doing on his finger?"

The priest started shaking his head. "I really cannot answer that. I don't know," he said softly, as if talking to himself. "Hiram's assistants never mentioned anything about a ring. They might have been too shocked to notice it when they brought his body in here."

The knight turned the Ring around in his palm and looked at it intently. "You mentioned that it's shrouded in legend. What sort of legends?"

"It is said that whoever wears it can summon and command all kinds of spirits, whether for good, or for evil."

"Well, there's only one way to find out if that's true," the Grand Master said. So, after he placed the Ring on his middle finger he grabbed Nicodemus by the arm, and spoke to the spirits in a loud, commanding voice, "I order you to take us back to my chambers!"

Both fell silent and looked anxiously around the crypt. They were waiting for the spirits' response to the command, and their possible transportation to the Grand Master's room. But nothing happened, and after a few moments de Payns released the priest's arm. In fact, the only thing Hugh's loud order provoked was that one of the knights standing outside stuck his head through the entrance hole and asked, "Is everything all right, Grand Master?"

"Yes, Sir Roland, everything's fine, thank you," Hugh said. And after the young knight left them, de Payns was smiling when he looked at Nicodemus. "I think we can safely say these legends of yours are groundless, Father."

"It would appear so," the priest agreed, still lost in thought.

"Now that we've seen everything in here, what should be next?" de Payns asked.

"I believe we must hold a meeting later today, with everyone involved in this venture. When we tell them what's been found we can all decide about what to do together."

"That's a capital idea. Please see to it everybody's informed."

"I will, Grand Master. However, there is one favor I would ask of you," Nicodemus said.

"What is that?"

"That you allow me to remove my ancestor's bones from here. I wish to give them a proper burial, someday, hopefully in Tyre—if it is ever freed from the Saracens."

"I don't see why not. But what about Hiram's head, will you be burying that as well?" Hugh de Payns asked as he looked at the encased head Nicodemus still held in his hands.

"No. And I shan't be giving it to my nephew either. I'm now thinking it could be put to better use in our initiation ceremony—that is, if and when we ever get new recruits," the priest replied. While stating this decision aloud, Nicodemus had a mischievous smile on his face.

✝ ✝ ✝

AT NOON THAT day, everyone who'd taken part in the digging endeavor was present in the palace chapel. All in all—

knights, scribe-monks and priest—there were thirteen of them. And with thirteen being such a symbolic number, as it alludes to Jesus and His twelve Apostles, it would figure prominently in subsequent Templar history as well: To begin with, it would be the number of knights, including the Grand Master, of whom the Grand Chapter—the Order's supreme governing body—would eventually consist. Second, it would be the number of Templars (headed by a chaplain) who would make up the College charged with electing a new Grand Master—whenever the position became vacant. And finally, thirteen would also be, by a devilish coincidence, the infamous date on which the Order's destruction would begin, in October 1307 AD.

But all this was still far ahead in the future. So, on that day, the Brotherhood's first Grand Master rose from his seat and informed the rest what had been discovered inside the crypt. He told them about the treasure, Hiram's remains, and left the Ark of the Covenant for last. Naturally, mentioning this final item brought about such an additional wave of enthusiasm from the men, that it became necessary for Hugh to raise his voice above the commotion.

"Brethren, please! The object of this meeting is for you to be aware what was discovered and for all of us to arrive at mutual decisions about how to proceed. But nothing useful can be heard if we all speak at the same time," de Payns scolded them. At Nicodemus's suggestion Hugh was wearing Solomon's Ring. And he'd shown it to everybody when he told them about Hiram's skeleton and why it was in the vault.

Roland—the youngest of the knights—spoke out, after everyone else had quieted down. "From what you've told us, Grand Master, there's still that northern tunnel connected to the crypt, and about which we know nothing. What if someone stumbles on to it and gains access to the chamber from there? I feel we should move everything out—and as soon as possible."

"But if the Ark is as large as Sir Hugh says, we couldn't

possibly pass it through our tunnels. They're much too narrow," Geoffrey Bison objected.

"Then we should enlarge them," Roland countered, as he looked to the Grand Master for his response.

Hugh de Payns pondered over both concerns for a moment before reaching a decision. "Yes, I see your point, Sir Roland. All our finds should be retrieved and brought here, for now, where we can keep a close eye on them. And if that means a few extra months of digging, so be it. At least this time we'll know it's definitely worth the effort."

"Do you mean we should continue to keep everything a secret and tell no one of our discoveries? Not even about the Ark, Grand Master?" Godfrey de St. Omer asked, in a concerned tone.

Hugh was about to reply when the priest stuck out his gloved hand. "Allow me to answer that, Sir Hugh," he suggested. For some time now, Nicodemus had often worn gloves, because he felt they provided a more proper way to conduct his priestly duties. In due course, this was incorporated into the Templar Rule, whereby the Order's clerics, as well as its scribes, wore gloves at all times.

After de Payns gave permission, Nicodemus spoke, addressing them all. "Sir Godfrey's question is a valid one, but I think what we should really be asking ourselves is what would happen if we did reveal everything to the world. Wouldn't the king want a share of the treasure—if not all of it? Wouldn't the patriarch archbishop demand we hand over the Ark and perhaps even ship it off to Rome later on?" He paused and studied all the somber faces around the room for a moment. "No, I'm sure none of us would readily agree to either outcome. As relevant as secrecy was two years ago, for us to carry out our project without obstruction, it is even more relevant today. We have come this far by banding together, and it has yielded wonderful results. However, if we reveal our findings now, we'd be abandoning any future advantages they might bring. And not only that, but we could also be accused of heresy, or idolatry, at the same time."

"How so, Father?" Godfrey de St. Omer asked again.

"Do not think for one moment, Sir Godfrey, that there is no one out there who speaks ill of us. On the contrary, there are many who still disagree with our mandate of protecting the pilgrim roads, even by force if necessary. And as time goes by, and we become more established and powerful, these negative voices I dare say will increase. So imagine if someone like that was to find out we've spent two years digging—in secret—trying to find the Ark of the Covenant. Wouldn't that give him enough ammunition to suggest we had ulterior, maybe even heretical, motives for finding it?"

"Not if we produce the Tablets of the Lord's Commandments, which are in the Ark, and present them to the world," Sir Godfrey countered with a hopeful grin.

Hugh de Payns and Nicodemus looked into each other's eyes. This was going to be difficult, so the Grand Master took it upon himself to utter the words. He sighed. "I am sad to inform you that there is nothing inside the Ark."

As was to be expected, after a brief moment of stunned silence, this revelation brought about a new round of simultaneous comments, forcing Hugh to raise his hands once more so that order could be restored. "Yes, my Brothers, the Ark is empty. And from what Father Nicodemus tells me about those ancient events, there was nothing in there when Hiram took it down to the crypt either. So, I'm afraid he is correct. If we do reveal the discovery of the Ark to the world, we open ourselves up to all sorts of accusations."

"And regrettably the same applies for the treasure as well, Grand Master," Nicodemus added. "We are the Poor Fellow-Soldiers of Christ, with clothes and equipment donated by the Patriarch, living in this decrepit former mosque. If we begin to exhibit wealth that is well beyond our current means all of a sudden, this will also create suspicions. So, I'm afraid the only option available to us, for the time being, is to keep all items under lock and key, and maintain our existing level of silence—at least, as concerns the outside world. Now, obviously we cannot keep something like this from our fellow brothers, forever, so they ought to be informed of it in time. But, none except members of the Order must ever hear of this."

Hugh de Payns looked around at everyone. Their faces were solemn, but evidently convinced. "Then, I believe we should seal our accord with an oath of secrecy," he suggested. "I shall see to it that the rest of our brethren swear to this as well, before they are told."

✢ ✢ ✢

Jerusalem
October 1129 CE

FATHER NICODEMUS WAS all alone, on that grey autumn day, as he sat at one of the long tables in the Templar dining hall. He had been patiently waiting for the Grand Master, and the rest of the returning party, to arrive from the port of Joppa for some time now. But it was already getting past noon and even though Nicodemus did want to wait, so that he and Sir Hugh could eat together, he began to feel hungry. So the priest decided to pass the time by nibbling on the freshly baked bread, goat cheese and olives, which were set on the table. It was a Friday and therefore no sausages or other meat dishes were allowed.

Sir Hugh de Payns had been away from Outremer for two years now. He, along with Godfrey de St. Omer, Payns de Montdidier, Geoffrey Bison, Archambaud de St. Agnan, Roland, and two Templar scribes, had accompanied Gautier de Bure, the Constable of Jerusalem, to Christendom. The Constable's objective was to offer the hand of King Baldwin's eldest daughter in marriage to Count Fulk of Anjou. But aside from assisting with that, the Grand Master and his brethren had three additional reasons for going: First, it was crucial to recruit as many new knights for the Order as possible; second, he needed to raise necessary funds and donations, so that operations could continue running smoothly; and third, and most important, de Payns wanted his Templar Order to be ratified and blessed by the Church of Rome.

"Ah, Grand Master, welcome back," Nicodemus greeted him joyfully, as he saw Hugh enter the dining hall. The priest put down the piece of bread he was about to bite into and walked over to de Payns. They both kissed each other in greeting thrice, on alternate cheeks—as was the Phoenician and now the Templar custom—and smiled amicably. Sir Hugh looked exhausted.

"How was your return journey?" Nicodemus asked with concern after they sat down.

"We had stormy weather while sailing around Cyprus, but other than that it wasn't too bad. It has been a long trip and I must say I'm glad to be back," de Payns replied, only to add with a smile, "Although I can't say I've missed the climate here. I'm afraid I find the nice, dry and cool weather back in Christendom much more to my liking."

"Nevertheless, you have returned and I believe congratulations are in order. Your journey has accomplished some amazing results. In fact, you've fulfilled all three of the desired objectives," Nicodemus said, praising him. "But before we go into other matters, please tell me all about what happened at the Council of Troyes."

"Well, as you know from the Council Minutes you've received, the Church has fully endorsed the existence and mandate of our Order. And it has even given us a Rule, by which to regulate our daily activities. Nothing radical, of course—all the rules are based on practices already in place. But I can tell you, Father, it wasn't easy. There were many participants who were not favorably predisposed towards us. If Father Bernard, the abbot of Clairvaux, had not attended—as indeed it was feared he might not—I don't think we would have achieved much. I must remember to thank Brother Hugues for his help in bringing the abbot to our side."

The Grand Master was referring, of course, to Hugues,

the ex Count of Champagne and his former liege lord. Hugues had resigned his title, renounced all worldly possessions, and had become a humble Templar knight ever since 1125 AD. Even so, he'd been the only one who could have convinced Bernard to secure the pope's support for the Order. The venerable abbot owed a huge debt of gratitude to Hugues for all the aid and donations the ex count had given him, back when Bernard was setting up his new monastery at Clairvaux.

Nicodemus was smiling. "Yes, I'm so glad I was able to persuade him to dictate those letters to me. It seems they made all the difference."

"You cannot imagine how much, Father. If Father Bernard had been hostile, or even indifferent to our cause, we would never have been ratified. He controlled the Council's deliberations, singlehandedly. Nothing could go forward without his approval. And fortunately he *did* want us to be endorsed."

"Well, the fact that his uncle, Andre de Montbard, is also a brother Templar now, didn't hurt us either," the priest added.

"Indeed. The abbot is, without a shadow of a doubt, the most influential cleric in Christendom at the moment. More so even than the pope, I dare say."

"I'm glad you feel that way, because this will lift your spirits up even higher," Nicodemus said, as he passed a thick batch of parchments over to Hugh.

"What is this?"

"It's a letter to you from Father Bernard. It arrived here a few weeks ago while you were still in transit from Christendom."

Hugh opened the pages, but lost no time in handing them back to the priest. "You had better read it to me, Father. Although I'm getting better in French now, I still struggle with Latin."

Obligingly, Nicodemus took the bundle and began reading aloud, and translating whenever necessary. The letter contained everything Hugh had asked Bernard to say about what the Order of the Knights Templar was, and how significant its existence was to the faith—and more. In fact, it was a letter of such praise and encouragement that Sir Hugh's mouth was agape when Nicodemus finished reading.

"It's astonishing," was the only comment the Grand Master managed to utter.

"Yes, it is," the priest agreed. "This letter is such a powerful weapon for us that I believe we should send out copies of it to everyone of importance, and especially to Patriarch de La Ferté. If nothing else will, this should definitely shut him up."

Nicodemus was speaking of Stephen de La Ferté, who'd become the Patriarch Archbishop of Jerusalem after Warmund de Picquigny died the previous year. The new prelate was not as favorably predisposed towards the Order and had even tried to get the Council of Troyes cancelled. But, he relented after realizing how determined the pope was for the Council to go on as planned.

"Yes, I agree," Hugh said. "And also send copies to our preceptories. This will help lift their spirits."

After the Order's acceptance by the Council in January, Hugh de Payns had stayed behind for a short while. He used that time to organize the land and estates, which had been donated to the Templars, from all over Christendom, into regional administrative communities. Payns de Montdidier was put in charge of Northern France and other brothers headed preceptories in Carcassonne, Provence, Barcelona, and England—among others. Their mission was to convert whatever the estates would be producing into hard currency and then to dispatch it to the Templar headquarters in Jerusalem.

"Certainly. I will send it along with guidelines on how to make sure the funds they raise arrive here safely," the priest added. These guidelines were eventually to result in the setting up of safe-houses: the remote abodes unknown to everyone but the Templars.

"Aye, you do that," Hugh said, and came closer so that no one lingering outside could overhear him. "Now that you've mentioned money, what have you done with the... *treasure*?"

The priest also leaned in and whispered, "As soon as Stephen de La Ferté took over as patriarch, I thought it best if the Ark and the rest were all sent away from Jerusalem. So, about six months ago, I had everything secretly transported to a secure location of ours in Tyre. They're quite safe there."

Nicodemus's home city of Tyre had finally been wrested from Saracen hold in 1124 AD. In fact, the supreme commander of the winning siege had been none other than the late patriarch, Warmund de Picquigny.

"Good," de Payns exclaimed. "I must also give you all the gold and silver King Henry of England gifted us, for you to take care of as well. But first I must see to our new recruits and if they've been assigned their living quarters. I'm afraid that for many of them our sea voyage proved to be quite an ordeal."

An impish grin appeared on Nicodemus's face, as they both rose from their seats. "But not as great as their initiation ceremony will be tonight, I'm sure."

CHAPTER 9

TORTOSA

Jerusalem
1152 CE

SAVE FOR A few lit candles, here and there, the Templar chapel was otherwise shrouded in near total darkness. Not that this setting could make the least bit of difference to the three candidates, mind you: their eyes had been secured beneath thick blindfolds. Being confined in separate rooms, as of midday, they'd been prepared and then guided into the chapel after sunset. Deprived of sight, barefoot, and with their tunics open and unceremoniously pulled out of their breeches, they were left to stand there alone, without a doubt feeling quite vulnerable and disoriented. One initiate even had a hangman's noose around his neck. The Templars already inside grinned when they saw the disheveled state their soon-to-be brothers were brought in—probably because it reminded them of their own initiations—but none made a sound.

The only one to speak was the receiving officiator—the Order's Grand Master himself—Bernard de Tremelay. Standing in the chancel, in front of the altar, and facing the initiates in the west, de Tremelay ordered in a thunderous voice, "Candidates, state your names."

When the new recruits didn't respond fast enough, as they were still in a state of confusion, a Templar standing behind them whispered roughly into the first one's ear, "Say your name!"

After mustering the necessary courage, the candidate said aloud, "I am Sir Hugues de Quilioco."

This prompted the one next to him to also respond. "My name is Sir Albert d'Estaing."

Finally, the initiate with a noose around his neck, nervously uttered, "I am Ruben from Turenne, in the province of Limousin."

"Candidates, will you solemnly promise, upon peril of your immortal soul, to live henceforth as serfs of our Order, to follow through with the required trials, and to take the three monastic vows—of poverty, chastity and obedience—so that God's gift of sight may be restored to you?"

To that question all three answered at once, "I will."

The Grand Master nodded to his second in command, Andre de Montbard, the Templar Seneschal—who was standing next to the initiates—to proceed. Andre instructed the postulants to join hands, and after grabbing hold of Sir Hugues' arm, he began to lead the candidates in a series of perambulations within the nave's wide corridor. When the initiates started their circular processions, this served as a cue for the rest of the Templars in the Chapel to begin stomping their feet, banging on the pews, and in general to make any other loud, intimidating noise they saw fit. It was obviously an effort designed to unnerve the initiates—and it did. By the time they'd finished with their third perambulation, around the corridor's imaginary center, the candidates were visibly shaken. Left standing in front of the Chapel's western entrance after this, once again in their blindfolded darkness, the Grand Master walked over to them. Holding a bulky tome in front of him, de Tremelay said, "Place your right hands on the Holy Bible and repeat after me."

As soon as all three managed to place their hands on the

Bible, with some assistance from de Montbard, the Grand Master began reciting the oath, by heart. "I... repeat your names... solemnly swear to God and the Holy Virgin that as a member of the Holy Order of the *Poor Fellow-Soldiers of Christ and of the Temple of Solomon*, shall live, henceforth, for the salvation of my soul according to canonical law and the custom of my masters in the Holy City of Jerusalem. That following the example of our Lord Jesus Christ, I shall henceforth abandon every worldly possession, in the knowledge that all personal wealth can only distract me from what is essential and meaningful. That I shall hereafter remain chaste and celibate, seeking no carnal relations with either man, or woman. That my only purpose in life shall be from now on the protection of faithful Christians and of the Kingdom of Jerusalem; to which end I furthermore pledge my complete obedience to every deed my superiors will see fit for me to perform so that whatever has been acquired for this Kingdom may be preserved and what has not yet been obtained to be conquered. I also solemnly swear that whatever I am told, and everything I happen to hear, pertaining to our Order, shall be kept in absolute secrecy by me, never to be discussed with anyone outside it. So help me God and keep me steadfast in this my great and formal obligation."

After every initiate had obediently repeated the oath, Bernard de Tremelay passed the Bible over to a nearby Templar and took off Hugues de Quilioco's blindfold.

"Welcome to our Order, Sir Hugues. You are now an Entrant Knight Templar," the Grand Master told him, and they exchanged their first triple kiss, on the cheeks, as brothers.

When he said and did the same with Sir Albert d'Estaing, de Tremelay turned to the last new member, Ruben from Turenne. Untying his blindfold first, he then removed the noose from around Ruben's neck. (That piece of rope had always been placed on whomever was to become a Templar Sergeant, and it was a tradition obviously intended to highlight that unit's lesser status.) Bernard also welcomed him into the Order with the triple kiss, as an Entrant Sergeant, and then walked back to his previous position in front of the altar. New members for the third, non-fighting, class of Templars, that of the priests, were never received by a group made up of knights and sergeants, such as this one. In contrast, they were always initiated in an assembly consisting solely of other priests, chaplains, and scribes.

Picking up a different book from the altar, the Grand Master showed it to the new Templars and said, "Newly received brethren, this is the Rule of our Order, written by none other than Abbot Bernard of Clairvaux himself. It contains the way your lives shall be lived from now on, and its stipulations are not to be taken lightly. You may see that we are all well dressed and equipped, but no one in the outside world really grasps what our souls and bodies endure on a daily basis. As Templars you will have to withstand tremendous difficulties and even obey outrageous commands. But obey them you must. Are you ready to prove your loyalty with deeds?"

The three new brothers, albeit with varying degrees of conviction, all stated, "I am."

"Good. Now come closer," de Tremelay ordered them, as he put the Rule book back on the altar and picked up a golden crucifix.

When the novices stepped up to within a couple of feet from Bernard, along with a group of five knights who followed and stood behind them, the Grand Master spoke again. "I command you to spit on this cross and repeat the words: *'Jesus Christ is not a god.'*"

All three new Templars opened up their eyes wide in utter disbelief. Did they hear correctly?

"You have just sworn an oath to obey every order your superiors see fit to give you, yet you refuse to do so mere moments later?" de Tremelay shouted.

The group of knights standing behind the novices started to punch them repeatedly all over, until Hugues de Quilioco decided to bow over the crucifix and pretend to spit, without expelling any saliva. Seeing him do so, and without suffering any consequences for not being convincing, d'Estaing and Ruben reluctantly imitated their fellow neophyte.

"Now repeat after me, *'Jesus Christ is not a god,'*" the Grand Master persisted.

The constant blows the new Templars were receiving from the knights behind them intensified, causing Hugues to once again go first and repeat the words, albeit with great reluctance. When de Tremelay turned to face Albert, though, he saw that the young man was shaking his head vigorously. "I'm sorry, but I cannot utter such a heinous and untrue statement, Sir Bernard. I shall not risk condemning my soul to eternal damnation, however much I wish to become a member of your Order. Please excuse me," d'Estaing said with conviction and attempted to move away.

The knights at his back clustered together trying to block the young man's retreat, but the Grand Master ordered them to move aside. "Let him pass. Gather your things, Sir Albert and begone with you," Bernard snapped at him, just as d'Estaing was exiting the Chapel, looking decidedly disgusted. Then turning his gaze upon Ruben, the Grand Master lifted his bushy eyebrows all the way up as if asking him if he wished to do the same. The Entrant Sergeant, however, although visibly dejected, started whispering the words which denied Jesus's divinity, and de Tremelay smiled.

"Very good," he said, and placed the crucifix back on the wooden altar. He then picked up a large egg-like object from there. And when de Tremelay turned around the two remaining novices could see he was holding a bearded man's mummified head, enclosed in a silver casing. "This is your new god, now, and I order you to demonstrate the appropriate reverence by kissing it," the Grand Master said, while moving the object closer to them.

The jabbing and punching, from the knights at their rear, began again in earnest until both new Templars capitulated and lightly pressed their lips on the idol's silver shell. Bernard de Tremelay was pleased. He returned the idol to the altar and faced them.

"As a final act, and for you to prove your readiness never to leave any brother's carnal needs unsatisfied, I order you to kiss my behind." The Grand Master turned after saying that and bent over a bit, drawing attention to his white-mantle-covered posterior.

Not really sure about what was required of them the two novices hesitated once more. But when the Templars at the back began hitting them yet again and persistently urged them to, "Kiss the Master's behind," Hugues de Quilioco bent over and reluctantly placed his lips on the white mantle covering de Tremelay's buttocks. Just after Ruben followed suit, Bernard straightened up, turned around and said to his Seneschal, "Brother Andre, please bring me our new brethrens' girdles and mantles."

Andre de Montbard picked up the requested items from a pew, and walked over to where the Grand Master and the novices were standing, just as the bullying knights returned to their seats. The Seneschal handed Bernard a stretched-out piece of white lambskin, about a foot high and four feet long. De Tremelay held it up for the new Templars to see, and said, "This white girdle is a symbol of the chastity with which you shall live from now on. It must be worn beneath your clothes and armor, at all times, as an undergarment—never to be taken off, even on the rare occasion when you are to bathe. After you return to the privacy of your dormitory, you may put it on."

He gave a girdle to each novice and asked de Montbard to hand him the white mantle. Bernard then helped Sir Hugues de Quilioco wear the sleeveless garment—which had a prominent red cross on its left breast—over his clothes. After doing the same for Ruben, albeit with a black mantle which similarly displayed a red cross, de Tremelay gave them both the brotherly triple kiss on the cheeks. He then invited the neophytes to go stand at the chapel's entrance, in the west.

While Bernard was assisting his new brothers to put on their mantles, they saw the big silver ring he wore on his middle finger. And they also did not fail to notice the engraving on the ring's top, either. The depiction, that is, of two intertwined equilateral triangles, one pointing up and the other down, of which the Star of David consists.

The Grand Master addressed the new Templars. "Although we've had the privilege of displaying the red cross on our mantles for only five years now—ever since His Holiness, Pope Eugenius granted it to us—nevertheless, it has already become a powerful symbol for our Brotherhood. It represents the willingness to shed our blood to its last drop if need be, in order to achieve our Order's objectives. It is a badge symbolizing our bond of brotherhood, and I urge you to wear and consider it as such." Bernard then clenched his right fist and placed it over the red cross on his mantle. When the rest of the knights and sergeants rose to their feet and imitated him, he continued, "And bear in mind, Brethren: if you never disgrace it, it will never disgrace you." Then, all Templars lightly thumped their fists on their left breasts, and blood-red crosses, three times. After that everyone else returned to their seats.

"I'm sure both of you must still be wondering about the despicable acts you were forced to commit, just a few moments ago," de Tremelay said next. And after cracking a thin smile, he explained. "They were all simply part of a test, and I am pleased to say you've passed it. If Sir Albert had persevered, and stayed with us for the duration, he would have also learned that every action we asked of you was an ordeal merely intended to evaluate your readiness to follow orders. Blind obedience to commands from superiors is of paramount importance in our calling. We therefore had to test that before allowing you to take up your positions on the battle field. Knowing that your courage could never be in any doubt, your levels of obedience had to be assessed using a different method—one which we humbly compare to the three acts of denial by St. Peter."

As he gazed at the novices, Bernard noticed that their expressions had mellowed and started to show a sense of relief; something which made it easier for him to go on. "This ordeal was not a test of your faith, which I'm certain is very much unshaken. Nor was it a trial of your resolve to live henceforth in poverty and chastity. It was merely to see whether you had the courage to obey any given command—however seemingly dangerous, detestable, or absurd. But, having said that, you must bear in mind that in future no command, intended to lead you to actions against the faith, or to sexual misconduct, is ever to be obeyed. However, if you still believe your actions tonight may have endangered your souls, feel free to confess everything to a priest of the Order, so you may receive absolution. Brother Seneschal, please escort our new brothers to the North-Eastern part of the Chancel."

Andre de Montbard led the novices to stand a few feet from the Grand Master, who turned to face them and continued explaining. "Our Lord and Savior is Jesus Christ, and our devotion to the Holy Trinity is everlasting and resolute," he told the new Templars with fervor. "Consequently, the mummified head you were presented with, as if it was your new god, is not a deity at all. Yet, although not a god, it still deserves our undying respect and admiration. And that is because it used to belong to the very man who built the Temple of Solomon—from which the most distinctive part of our Order's name is derived. His name was Hiram..." Bernard de Tremelay said and proceeded to relate the entire story: He explained the way Hiram decided to build Solomon's Temple; how and *why* the Phoenician had taken the Ark of the Covenant; and by which means the nine knights of the Order, along with the others, had discovered it, thirty years earlier.

"So for you to be standing here tonight, at this North-Eastern corner of the chapel, is an important symbolic act," the Grand Master continued. "Not only does it represent the location of the foundation stone Hiram laid, before starting to build the Temple, but it also alludes to where the flagstone, inside the Holy of Holies, under which the passageway to his secret crypt was situated."

He let them both have a moment to digest all the new information before proceeding. "Whatever's been revealed to you this evening has been done so in accordance with our Brotherhood's fourth main pillar: that of Secrecy. You are never to discuss what you have heard tonight—or might hear in the future—with anyone who is not a member of our Order. Doing so will be considered an act of high treason and is punishable by death."

✟ ✟ ✟

BERNARD DE TREMELAY was the Templars' fourth Grand Master. When Hugh de Payns died, in 1136 AD, the baton passed to Robert de Craon. His Grand Mastership, spanning thirteen years, was deemed very successful, especially for all the ways in which he helped improve the Order's organization, but also because the Brotherhood saw unique privileges bestowed on it by the papacy: The Order was now exempt from all local tithes and taxes; independent of any religious or civil authorities except the pope; and its members could travel throughout Christendom freely. After de Craon's death in January 1149 AD, Everard des Barres was elected to lead the Order, but his was a rather short tenure. Following the pointless and failed siege of Damascus, Everard travelled with the French King Louis the Seventh back to France. Once there, though, he decided to enter the monastery of Clairvaux and officially abdicated his post in 1152 AD. With Bernard de Tramelay in effect leading the Order, ever since the spring of 1149 AD, he believed that to be chosen as its Grand Master would be a straightforward task for the Electoral College. But it was not. Other candidacies threatened to complicate the College's decision, forcing Nicodemus, who presided over it, to use his unchallenged authority to tip the scale in favor of

Bernard. The Tyrian priest, and co-founder of the Brotherhood—unknown and unsung by all those outside it, at his insistence—was revered by every Templar, and had already attained a legendary status by brothers stationed in faraway Christendom. So, it was not easy for someone to go against his wishes, on any issue.

Bernard was thinking about how much he owed Nicodemus—not only for getting him elected Grand Master, but also for all the sound advice the old man had given him over the years—as he continued walking down to the priest's room in the Stables. He was about to put his hand on the door when it suddenly opened, as if by itself, and Michel stepped out.

"I am sorry if I've startled you, Grand Master," the young man said. "I was just going to fetch my uncle some water."

"That's quite all right, Father. How is he feeling?" de Tremelay asked with concern.

"The fever from his cold has subsided, but it's his hands which are the real problem now. They are swollen and cause him a lot of pain. It has even come to the point where he can't handle a quill anymore, so he summoned me to write a few letters for him," the priest said in a sad tone. "Please excuse me, Sir Bernard. He's thirsty and I must get him something to drink." After saying that, he walked away.

Michel—a well-featured man of medium height and darkish complexion—was the son of Nicodemus's sister. After being recruited in his teens, he was, in due course, ordained a priest of the Brotherhood. Now, at 34, he was slowly but surely exhibiting all the signs of being able to carry on his uncle's considerable legacy.

The Grand Master walked into Nicodemus's room to find the priest lying on a straw mattress with no covers drawn over him. As usual, though, he was clad in his brown cassock, which also displayed the red cross of the Order. With whatever hair remained on his head, beneath the tonsure, by now all white, and with him fast approaching his life's sixth decade, the old Tyrian appeared spent and tired; the vigor of his youth long gone. The contorted, arthritis-afflicted fingers of his right hand were clumsily using a rag to wipe his nose clean, following a violent sneeze, just as Bernard stepped in. Nicodemus looked up and asked in a gravelly voice, "How was the ceremony?"

"Nothing out of the ordinary, except that another one stormed out again," de Tremelay replied. He walked over to a table by the wall and set down the silver-encased, mummified head of Hiram Binne. "Tell Michel to put this away for you, Father."

"Which one did we lose?" Nicodemus asked.

"Albert d'Estaing."

"And at what point did he leave?"

"After taking the Brotherhood's triple oath, he refused to repeat the words denying Christ. But don't trouble yourself, Father—once a Templar, always a Templar. Andre is taking care of it as we speak. No one will ever learn the secrets of our initiation from d'Estaing, or find his body, I can assure you. And a few weeks from now, I shall write the usual letter to Albert's parents informing them that their son died like a hero: While escorting a group of devout pilgrims, all of a sudden they were attacked by vicious infidel bandits. However, not willing to allow the Saracens to stop him from carrying out his sacred duty, the young knight fought them valiantly. Alas, only to be ultimately and tragically slain," de Tremelay said, concluding his fictitious scenario with a chuckle. An instant later, though, he added in a more serious tone, "This is becoming all too common now, Father. We are losing too many good men this way."

"Men who may compromise all of you out on the real battle field, however—don't you forget that," Nicodemus responded in a husky voice. "How else can you be sure that someone under your command will obey anything you ask of him? No, only by passing the Test can one be trusted to be completely obedient. And besides, doesn't our Rule state we should never consent to receive an applicant straight away? Didn't St. Paul say, *'Test the soul to see if it comes from God'?* You are only obeying the Lord's commands, Grand Master."

Bernard de Tremelay was still nodding in agreement when the door opened and Michel stepped in holding an earthen jug filled with water. After Nicodemus had a sip to quench his thirst, he noticed that Bernard was still lingering about, somewhat restless. So the old priest asked, "Is there something else you wish to speak to me about?"

"Yes, Father, there is," de Tremelay replied and his eyes darted over to Michel, wondering whether it was wise to speak in front of him.

Nicodemus intercepted Bernard's brief glance and stated with confidence, "Whatever this is, you may speak freely in front of Michel. I have no secrets from him."

"Very well," de Tremelay acquiesced. "Father Jean, from our Preceptory in Tripoli, sent an encoded letter addressed to us both. It was written yesterday and arrived by messenger this afternoon. The scribe who deciphered it, however, wouldn't tell me what the letter contains. Instead, he advised that it should be read out when you were also present. So I assume it must be something important."

Belonging to the overwhelming majority of knights and nobles who were still unable to read during those times, Bernard then gave a folded piece of parchment to Nicodemus, who in turn handed it over to Michel. The young man began reading the Latin contents of the letter aloud and subsequently translated them for Bernard's benefit:

"Brother Jean, Priest of the Order in Tripoli, to Brother Sir Bernard de Tremelay, Templar Grand Master, and to our reverend Brother in Christ, Nicodemus, health and good wishes.

"It is with great trepidation and sense of shame that I put quill to parchment this day. Not the least because I feel I must violate one of the most sacred duties entrusted to my office: that of the seal of confession. My only hope and consolation is that the Good Lord, and you, shall ultimately judge my trespass to be the lesser of two evils.

"Pierre de Mallay, our Preceptory Master, met with me in the confessional this morning and what he revealed shocked me to my very core. It seems he and the Lord of Tripoli, Count Raymond, the Second of his name, have been cultivating a close, personal friendship for quite some time now. Last night, and after a rather heavy drinking binge, Lord Raymond confided to Brother Pierre that he is considering leaving everything behind to join the Order of Saint John. It is common knowledge here in Tripoli that the count is obsessively jealous of his wife, the fair Countess Hodierna, and it is even rumored he suspects their daughter was not sired by him. Therefore, Lord Raymond's reasoning was that if he joined the Hospitallers, then this torment of his could be alleviated. On hearing that—and within his thick cloud of intoxication—apparently our Master thought it prudent to try to lure the count into joining our Order instead. So after introducing the alternative, he suggested to Lord Raymond that surely his final decision should rest upon which of the two Holy Orders God Himself favors the most. To this the count countered by asking how on earth was he supposed to answer such a question. And Sir Pierre replied it was easy: Wouldn't God be in favor of the Order which had the Ark of His Covenant in its possession, rather than the one which did not?"

Michel put the parchment down and looked over at his uncle and the Grand Master. They both had the same dumbfounded expression on their faces as he did.

"This is incredible!" de Tremelay exclaimed. "Unbelievable! Of all the stupid things to—"

"Let us see what else our good Brother Jean has to report," Nicodemus cut in, calmly. "Please carry on, my boy."

The young priest continued to read and translate:

"When the count heard this, he asked whether it really meant what he thought it did. And de Mallay replied that it did, even proceeding to boast about how the Ark of the Covenant was found all those years ago. But this disclosure did not bring about the result Sir Pierre was counting on. It merely provoked Lord Raymond into launching a tirade of abuse

against our Order, claiming in the end that this definitely confirmed he'd been correct all along for showing favor to the Hospitallers over us. The count added that he would be investigating the matter, and if it proved to be true, then he would be forced to inform the pope.

"Our Master was in no condition last night to realize the extent of his folly, but when he finally awoke this morning, free from his drunken stupor, he was distraught. So, the very first thing Brother Pierre did was to come to the confessional where he told me all I've already reported. When I suggested he should tell you about this, Grand Master, he refused vehemently and assured me he'd find a way to correct the situation. After that de Mallay would add nothing further, even refusing to tell me whether he had also disclosed the current location of the Ark. The only thing he kept repeating was to warn me that if I divulged his confession to anyone else, it would be a mortal sin—as if I needed to be reminded of that.

"I just hope you will not judge me too harshly when you read this, but I felt there was no choice other than to inform you in full. I'm certain you will take all the precautionary measures necessary.

"Farewell. I humbly remain yours in Christ, Jean."

A stunned silence followed for a few moments between them. When Nicodemus decided to break it, he said in a husky voice, "I believe we owe a huge debt of gratitude to Brother Jean. He may have broken one of his most sacred vows, but as he says it is beyond doubt the lesser evil."

"What are you thinking, Uncle?" Michel asked him.

"I'm thinking that this information could not have come at a more opportune moment. In truth, it ties in nicely with an additional report I've received recently," he said and paused. The fact Nicodemus was confined to his chambers and to the Temple Mount, most of the time, did not mean he was uninformed of what happened elsewhere. On the contrary, the vast network of spies he maintained kept him abreast of important matters throughout Outremer.

When Bernard and Michel looked at him inquiringly, Nicodemus explained. "Two days ago, I learned that Count Raymond was considering handing the town of Tortosa, and its neighboring island of Arwad, over to the Hospitallers. Now we know he is thinking of joining their ranks, it can only mean that these properties are supposed to be his gifts for receiving him..." The old priest glanced at both of them before going on. "The Order of St. John should have just continued doing what they do best: treating the sick and wounded—like me, all those years ago. But no... they had to copy us and create a fighting division of knights too." He then raised his raspy voice in anger to add, "Raymond gave them the castle of Crac de l'Ospital ten years ago, but I'll be damned if those buggers get that ancient Phoenician kingdom as well."

After putting too much strain on his vocal chords, Nicodemus began to cough. Michel handed him a cup of water and said, "Calm yourself, Uncle. They certainly don't deserve your getting upset over them."

"Your uncle is right, though, Father Michel. If the Hospitallers also get their hands on Tortosa, their influence within the County of Tripoli will be much greater than ours. Which is why an additional piece of intelligence, that happened to come *my* way, is not all that comforting," the Grand Master said. When he had the attention of them both, he went on. "Queen Melisende—who's visiting Tripoli at the moment—in an effort to resolve the marital problems between her sister and the count, urged Hodierna to return with her to Jerusalem for a while to rest. The countess agreed, and an armed delegation is to escort them back to the capital in two days time. An outcome that would inevitably leave Lord Raymond free to pursue his inquiry into Brother Pierre's disclosure... and perhaps even to hand Tortosa over to those lowlifes of the Hospital."

Once the old priest had another sip of water, he cleared his throat and said, "Not unless we can kill two birds with one stone. How good is your relationship with the Nizari?"

Bernard was surprised by this, so he replied by asking a further question, "Do you mean the Assassins?"

"Yes. Could you get word to their leaders up at Masyaf?"

Masyaf was the Syrian headquarters of the Nizari Ismailis, a sect of Shi'a Muslims, better known as the Hashashin, or Assassins. Although living in exile there, from their former stronghold in Alamut, Persia, strangely enough they did not pose a problem for the neighboring Christian states. Instead, they were notorious for the clandestine methods they used in eliminating key figures of their Muslim Sunni rivals.

"A word to what effect?" de Tremelay asked.

"Obviously, Count Raymond needs to be silenced—once and for all," the priest replied while his features hardened with hatred. "Our Order cannot be seen to be implicated in something like this, though. That would be inexcusable. So, someone else has to perform the deed for us."

Apparently all the long decades spent in seclusion, without experiencing any form of true affection, or the feel of a woman's touch, had turned Nicodemus into a bitter, spiteful, and ruthless old man. The only thing he truly cared about anymore was the Brotherhood he'd co-founded, making him willing to go to any lengths for its survival and growth.

"But, Uncle, that's a bit extreme, isn't it?" Michel objected. "Is taking a man's life worth it, just to keep our secret of the Ark safe from the papacy?"

"It's too late to debate that now," Nicodemus replied in a sharp tone, as he looked up at him. "After we had found it, Hugh de Payns and I, along with everyone else involved, took a solemn oath never to reveal this to anyone outside the Order. And with good cause. If we had disclosed our findings we would've lost them, and might even have been accused of heresy, or worse. That's why we never talk of what we found openly to anyone, apart from sworn-in Templars, or why the Grand Master only wears his Ring when he's among brothers. No one else must know anything about the items discovered. But think of it this way: The Ark of the Covenant is what you might call our Order's *lucky charm*. As long as we have it in our possession nothing bad can happen to us. If, however, Raymond were to tell the pope that we found it, wouldn't the next logical step be for Rome to take the Ark away from us? Is that what you want?"

"No, obviously not," Michel replied. "I was only wondering whether there might be another way to reason with the count."

"You've heard Father Jean's words. Do you believe a headstrong man, like Raymond, can be reasoned into changing his decisions just to accommodate an Order he doesn't even respect?" the old priest asked again.

"I guess not."

"Well, there's only one real option open then, isn't there? He has to be eliminated."

Bernard had stayed silent during the relatives' brief dispute, so now it was over, he voiced his own concern. "This is not a task the Assassins usually undertake, Brother Nicodemus. To go through with this, they'll definitely want something from us in return."

"And we *will* give them something: peace. We'll tell their leaders that if they don't do this for us, their strongholds will feel the unrestrained wrath of our Brotherhood on them, and that none of their Assassins will ever be safe again. Yet, if they do, their lives can continue untroubled. Not only that, but we might even provide them with assistance in any future attempts they make to eliminate infidel rivals," the Tyrian stated. He then asked the Grand Master, "Whom do you trust in the Tripoli Temple?"

"I thought I trusted Brother Pierre de Mallay..." de Tremelay replied in a mumble.

"I know you did," Nicodemus countered. "I hate to say it, but I did warn you he was unfit for the position of Preceptory Master. He is clearly too gullible and naïve—not to mention he's much too fond of the drink. However, what's done is done. You haven't answered my question though. Is there someone else at Tripoli we can trust?"

"His second in command, Brother Baudouin de Foucher."

"Aye, Baudouin is a good man," the old priest said, nodding. "Send word then, informing him of our predicament. Tell him to urgently get in touch with the Assassin leaders and give instructions on how he's supposed to handle their objections. But, all this must be in place before the armed delegation leaves Tripoli to escort the countess here. If all goes well, we might not have to worry ourselves about relocating the Ark."

The Grand Master nodded, and Nicodemus, in an afterthought, added, "Oh, and after Count Raymond is slain, authorize de Foucher to take care of Pierre de Mallay also, along with anyone else who may have heard what was spoken that evening—except Brother Jean, of course. We mustn't leave *any* loose ends."

✢ ✢ ✢

IT WAS EARLY in the afternoon, four days later, when Brother Baudouin de Foucher stood on the ramparts of the Tripoli walls, looking out onto the southern road leading to Jerusalem. Count Raymond had left that morning with two of his knights, to escort his wife, Hodierna, part of the way to the capital and was expected back at any moment. So, de Foucher had been keeping a keen eye on the road, ever since midday, in an effort not to miss what would happen.

From the moment he'd received his Grand Master's encoded instructions, three days earlier, Baudouin had been quite busy. After revealing de Tremelay's orders to a trusted group of Preceptory brothers, they secretly proceeded to place their master, Pierre de Mallay, under house arrest. Then, de Foucher and two of those loyal Templars rode up to the Nizari stronghold at Masyaf to speak with their leaders. The Assassins (an offensive name given to them by their Sunni rivals, as if they were all hashish-addled addicts) were not against dealing with the Christian states surrounding them. On the contrary, both parties found that the ancient proverb, *'The enemy of my enemy is my friend,'* had suited their living in proximity perfectly up to then. Except that what Baudouin was about to ask of them wasn't something they could easily agree to. So, it took quite a bit of convincing on his part, mainly with the use of explicit and unveiled threats, to get the Nizari leaders to accept.

When de Foucher saw a faint puff of dust rising above a hill, at about seven hundred yards away, he knew Raymond's party was getting near. A short while later, three horses trotting next to each other made their way around the short hill that blocked them from Baudouin's view earlier. Four figures emerged from nearby thick bushes and stealthily came up behind the mounts—unnoticed by any of the riders. Without making a sound, the Assassins crept up close and used their razor-sharp daggers to sever the animals' hind leg tendons, with lightning-fast precision. Inevitably, this brought all three of the neighing horses to the ground, along with their startled riders. Then, the Nizari pounced on Count Raymond and the two knights, stabbing them over and over again. By the time the Assassins were through, every one of their victims was lying dead within a large pool of blood. After the infidels rushed off to collect their own horses to flee, Baudouin nodded to a Templar brother, who was standing further down on the ramparts. He was to start shouting what they'd agreed.

"Count Raymond... The Assassins have attacked our beloved Count Raymond," the Templar yelled, repeatedly, while pointing in make-believe horror over to where the bodies were.

Townspeople who heard the shouts rushed to the city gates to see what was going on. This prompted de Foucher to hurry down the walls, his white mantle flapping about in the warm afternoon breeze. After jumping up onto his horse, he instructed his contingent of faithful brothers, who had been waiting nearby, to mount up as well. Ordering the guards at the gate to open it at once, they all galloped at full speed to where the slain count and his party lay. They did this for three reasons: First, to give the impression that they were rushing out in aid of possible survivors; second, if inadvertently someone *did* survive, to finish him off swiftly; and third, to have the advantage of dashing off to find and 'punish' the perpetrators first, before anyone else could think of it.

When they arrived at the scene, de Foucher and his men found out that, as hoped, none of the three riders was alive. In fact, the attack against Count Raymond in particular had been so brutal that parts of his face were missing! Baudouin gave instructions to one of his brothers to return to Tripoli. He was to inform everyone about what happened and fetch a cart for transporting the bodies back into the city. To another, de Foucher gave orders to ride ahead, towards Jerusalem, at maximum speed. He was to catch up with the countess's party and give her the news. Baudouin wanted Hodierna to return and take charge of the County. In the emotional state she'd be in, the countess would probably reward the Order's 'assistance' much more generously than anyone else.

Then, de Foucher led the remaining Templars north, at full gallop, towards the Assassins' stronghold of Masyaf. At the same time, he took extra care that everyone up on the city walls would notice this 'revenge seeking' charge by leading it right past them.

+ + +

A WEEK AFTER they'd hatched their plan, all three of them were back in Nicodemus's room. The old priest's cold had passed, but, sadly, his arthritis affliction took another turn for the worse. He could no longer hold on to anything for long.

"You'll be very pleased to hear that Tortosa, and its neighboring island of Arwad, are now in our Order's possession," Bernard de Tremelay proudly announced to Nicodemus.

"Yes, I know," he replied in a matter-of-fact manner. The old Tyrian, as always, had his own, independent sources of information. "Baudouin de Foucher did well."

The Grand Master wondered how Nicodemus could've heard this already, especially since de Foucher's message arrived just a few minutes earlier. Nonetheless, he shrugged it off as unimportant and went on. "Yes, well, when Countess Hodierna hurried back to Tripoli, she was told a contingent of Templars was at that very moment pursuing the culprits of her husband's vicious murder. And after de Foucher and his men returned to the city, from their so-called *successful revenge mission*, she asked him what she might do to reward their bravery and sacrifice. Holding up the dead body of Preceptor Pierre de Mallay—who was supposedly killed while finishing off the last of the Assassin murderers—Baudouin replied he truly wished none of this had happened. However, de Foucher then added shrewdly that he knew his late preceptor had always wanted the town of Tortosa to be one of their Order's holdings. Was this something her Ladyship could grant? The beautiful countess replied that it was—provided King Baldwin, or Bishop William of Tortosa, had no objections, which she was certain they would not. So, she signed an order giving us the town and castle of Tortosa, on the spot, along with the island of Arwad. Then, Hodierna asked Baudouin whether he'd uncovered the reasons behind this unprecedented attack. He told her that after they'd killed all the murderers en route, he and his band of brothers rode on to Masyaf. There, they allegedly confronted the Nizari leadership and asked them about their motives for sanctioning such an abominable act. The Assassins' reply was that they did so in response to Raymond's establishing the Hospitallers as a major force in the County."

Bernard chuckled. "It was sheer genius! Not only did Brother de Foucher manage to acquire Tortosa for us, but he also succeeded in casting the Hospital in a negative light. That wasn't all, however. Baudouin went on to announce that they had secured the Assassins' pledge to pay us a sum of two thousand bezants every year, as retribution. We will never see any of that money, of course, but I believe it was a nice touch."

"Yes, it was," Nicodemus agreed, nodding. "And I'm sure Brother Baudouin is delighted to be appointed to the post of Preceptory Master for all his efforts. But what about others who may have heard what the count and de Mallay discussed that night?"

"The only other one present, while those two talked about the Ark, was the tavern keeper. But even if he hadn't heard anything, de Foucher wasn't going to take any chances. On the same evening Raymond was murdered, Baudouin sent one of his knights over to that tavern. After he'd had enough to drink, the knight got into a brawl with the owner—about the bill being too excessive—and our brother killed him. So there are no loose ends."

"None, except the Nizari," the old priest countered. "They are the only ones who know we coerced them into killing the count. And it must stay that way. If our true role in this is ever revealed, we will lose any credibility we have as an Order." Nicodemus was looking at the Grand Master and Michel with a stern expression of warning on his face.

Chapter 10

ASSASSINS

Jerusalem
March 20, 1173 CE

Someone pushed the chapel door open and asked, "Pardon me, but I was told to come here to recover my funds. Am I in the correct place?" The man inquiring was lavishly attired. Under his sleeveless red silk surcoat he wore a long black woolen robe with a thick silvery belt fastened around his slender waist, while a brown velvet cap rested firmly on his head. A way of dress which made Father Michel assume the stranger must be a travelling noble. But when the newcomer stepped inside the Templar chapel and reverently removed his cap, the priest realized he'd been mistaken. The man's tonsured scalp could only mean he was a visiting high-ranking member of the clergy.

"Yes, you are in the right place, brother..." Michel replied, his voice trailing off so the visitor would take the hint and identify himself.

"I am Villano Gaetani, Archbishop of Pisa, Father," he said in perfect French, but with a distinct Italian accent. "And you are?"

"My name is Michel, Your Excellency, and this is Stephen, my scribe," he replied, gesturing to the person sitting at the table behind him. "We are pleased to make your acquaintance."

Without returning the sentiment, or responding in any other way, Villano walked past Michel and down the chapel's aisle toward the altar. A few feet from it he stopped, kneeled on one leg and crossed himself three times. When he retraced his steps west, where the priest was waiting for him, Michel bent over, kissed the prelate's gloved hand and offered him a seat. Then the Templar priest took his own place at the table, next to Stephen, and asked, "What brings you to Outremer, My Lord Archbishop?"

Gaetani sighed. "I came here on a personal pilgrimage, Father. I'm not getting any younger, so I decided that I should visit the holy sites blessed by our Savior's corporal presence at least once before I die. But, as you are well aware, in order to do so one requires funds. I am therefore here to collect part of the capital I deposited with your Order in Pisa."

For quite a number of years now, the Templars, aside from their other duties of protecting the lives of devout pilgrims and taking part in battles, had also become active in banking as a way to supplement their income. The escalating expenses of maintaining each knight, as well as the contingents of sergeants, turcopoles, and other foot soldiers made it imperative they do so. After the Council of Troyes and the Church's endorsement of the Order, donations of cash and properties, and the steady income those generated, started pouring in—something which inevitably led to subsequent widespread rumors about the Order being filthy rich. This turn of events, however, served in prompting Nicodemus and his fellow Templar priests and scribes—the only members of the Order who could read, write, or calculate—to devise elaborate ways to keep track of everything and subsequently put any surplus funds to good use. Also during those formative years, the number of Templar Houses and Preceptories had multiplied to such a degree that very soon there was no major center in Christendom, or Outremer, without one. So, with both those elements in place, one of the first banking services to be offered by the Order was that of safeguarding the money and valuables of pilgrims, while they'd be away from their homes.

However, the idea which gave birth to that particular service wasn't the result of deliberate planning, but in contrast arose out of a chance conversation. One day, Nicodemus was consoling a man who'd had all his money stolen by pickpockets at Jaffa harbor. While lamenting his loss, the pilgrim mumbled that the Order should've been able to offer him protection for such an eventuality as well. This statement plunged the priest into deep thought, and a few moments later the business acumen of his Phoenician heritage generated yet another of his famous ideas. The basic system was this: When a pilgrim would travel from Christendom to the Holy Land, instead of taking his money along, and risk it being stolen, he was supposed to deposit the cash at the nearest Templar House. Then, upon arrival at Outremer, he could visit any local Preceptory to collect it. Obviously, some sort of proof of entitlement was necessary, so each pilgrim was issued a note stating how much he'd deposited and was therefore owed. But over time a few of those plain letters were also stolen, which resulted in non-entitled persons being paid. Hence, the encrypted Credit Note was devised.

Michel stuck out his hand. "May I have the Note our brothers at Pisa gave you, My Lord?"

"Certainly," Gaetani replied. He then took a folded parchment out of his scrip and handed it over to the priest. When Michel opened it up, it looked something like this:

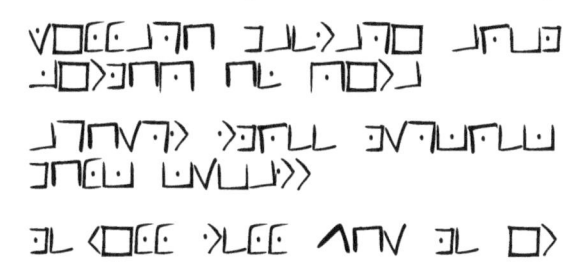

Each symbol in the Note corresponded to a letter located at segments of a hash (**#**) grid pattern and an **X** shape, according to the Templar Encryption Key. The Key was constructed by placing the first two letters of the alphabet in the top left corner of the **#** grid. This was then filled in by putting the remaining alphabet letters sequentially in pairs, in a left-to-right manner, all the way down until Q with R were set into the grid's bottom right corner. Then, S and T were placed in the leftmost quadrant of the **X** figure, while the three remaining pairs were positioned into the empty quadrants, in a clockwise fashion. And in order to differentiate between the two letters in each position, the second identical symbol had a dot in the middle. So, for instance, the letter A was encrypted as ⌐, and B as ⌐. Similarly, Y was encoded as ∧, and Z was ∧.

"Please excuse me," Michel said to the archbishop, and after standing up, he walked into a room adjacent to the chapel. The unusual length of the note had given him an uneasy feeling—which was an additional reason for him not to attempt to decipher the message in front of Gaetani. In the safety of the empty room, the priest then took out the Encryption Key from his cassock's pocket and began writing on a blank piece of parchment. When he'd finished, Michel was startled by what he read:

"Villano Gaetani, Archbishop of Pisa.
"Amount: Three hundred gold ducats.
"He will tell you he's on a pilgrimage. However, the truth is that he has been sent by the pope to investigate rumors of a precious artifact in our possession. Fortunately, they have no idea what the artifact is. His mission is to try to find out exactly what it is and also why we keep it a secret. We advise caution.
"Code word: Pride."

Getting over his initial shock, the priest decided to put on a straight face. He then stepped back into the Chapel, with the deciphered text tucked safely in his pocket.

"Pardon my delay, Your Excellency," Michel said with a smile. And after resuming his seat, he asked the customary next question. "May I also hear the verbal code word my brothers gave you?"

"Yes, of course. It is: *Pride.*"

The inclusion of a code word was the latest improvement to be made to the system. In order to safeguard against the possibility of a thief posing as the rightful owner, a different word was given verbally to each pilgrim at the point of the funds' deposit—but which was also included within the coded message. So even if the encrypted letter got stolen, the impostor couldn't possibly know what the correct code word was.

Many years after Michel's time, the Templars in the future became worried that their ciphering system might have been compromised. As a result, they complicated the procedure considerably by constructing a separate Encryption Key for each Credit Note. And they achieved this by building the code word directly into the Encryption Key.

Each code word given consisted of four or five unique letters. These were then placed in the first positions of the **#** grid pattern, while the remaining letters of the alphabet would fill in the rest, as well as those of the **X** shape. For example, if 'Pride' was the code word, then P, R, I, D, and E would take up the first five grid (**#**) positions in the Key, causing the symbol for the letter A to change from its normal ⌋, to ┗—and all the rest as well. As a result, unless someone knew what the code word was then this new system was virtually impossible to decipher.

Michel smiled again. "Thank you. What amount of your funds would you like to withdraw, My Lord Archbishop?"

"I believe the equivalent of a hundred gold ducats should be sufficient for now."

"Certainly," the priest said. To calculate the correct amount, in the local currency of bezants, he then started moving jettons around the surface of the counting table in front of him. Long before the adoption of Arabic numbers, the Roman numerals still in use at the time complicated calculations considerably. So, it was several moments before Michel could announce, "A hundred gold ducats are equivalent to one hundred and eighty of our bezants, Your Excellency. And after we subtract our five percent expense fees, it means we'll be able to give you one hundred and seventy-one bezants."

Usury was universally condemned by Christianity. So for the Templars to circumvent their charging of interest on loans they extended—or, for this Credit Note service—they simply called it *expense fees* instead. And their profits from this particular service were often not limited to the fees they charged: in the event the customer didn't survive his pilgrimage, the funds and valuables he entrusted to the Order remained in its possession forever.

Michel turned to Stephen and asked, "Brother, would you be so kind as to go fetch His Excellency's money?"

The Templar got up and stepped out of the chapel. Stephen was Michel's first cousin twice removed, and someone from whom the priest expected a great deal in the future. But the fact that Michel already considered Stephen to be the only one capable of succeeding him—even though the thickset young man was barely nineteen years old—was not due to nepotism. Stephen had outshined all his fellow scribes in the mastering of different languages, demonstrating creative thought, as well as in organizational matters. Apparently, the Phoenician homeschooling he'd received during childhood was able to cultivate all those qualities in him. So, Michel's plan was to ordain Stephen as a priest of the Order in a couple of years. Then, in the fullness of time, he would hand over all his duties to him—just as Nicodemus had done, before he passed away fifteen years ago.

"This is a very unusual place for you to be conducting business," Gaetani remarked, after he and Michel were left alone. The archbishop emphasized his comment by blankly looking around the chapel.

"Yes, I see your point. We've found, however, that even if someone is willing to steal another man's Credit Note, he would think twice before lying about it in the House of the Lord. So that's why we require everyone to come here to recover their funds," Michel replied. And while Villano was still nodding on how sensible that policy sounded, the priest seized the opportunity to voice what he'd been considering. "My Lord Archbishop, it would be an honor if you would allow us to offer you accommodation here. That is… if you haven't already made other arrangements," Michel said, with the most welcoming grin he could muster. The priest's decision to offer Gaetani the Order's hospitality was based on one of his favorite ancient Phoenician maxims: *'Keep your friends near, but your enemies nearer.'* And he was counting on Villano not to squander such an opportunity to be in close proximity to those he was sent to investigate.

Predictably, it only took a moment's hesitation for the archbishop to say in a cheerful tone, "That is most generous of you, Father. I would be delighted to stay here, thank you." However, an instant later he frowned. "Shouldn't your Grand Master be the one extending me this invitation though?"

Just as Michel was about to reply, the chapel door opened and Stephen walked in. He placed a pouch filled with coins on the table, and the priest asked Gaetani, "Would you like to count it?"

"I don't think that is necessary," the prelate replied. But after an instant he added, "You haven't answered my question yet."

"I was going to say, just as Stephen stepped in, that I'm certain our Grand Master would welcome the idea of offering hospitality to such a distinguished guest. Still, in keeping with protocol, I should inform him of my initiative—although, I am certain he will have no objections. Please excuse me. Stephen will keep you company while I'm gone."

After saying that, Michel exited the chapel and headed straight for the Grand Master's private chamber. The priest was aware that at this time in the morning, Odo de St. Amand would, as usual, be in a meeting with his second in command, and other Templar knights and officials. The frequent incursions of Nur ad-Din and his Turkish forces against Jerusalem required constant vigilance and planning. When Michel walked into the room, de St. Amand looked up and saw the look on the priest's face. The Grand Master knew him well enough to realize that Michel wouldn't unexpectedly interrupt this strategy meeting unless it was for something very important. So, nothing more needed to be said. Odo immediately asked everyone else in the room to leave; they could resume their discussions after he'd spoken with the priest.

Odo de St. Amand was the eighth consecutive Grand Master. Having joined the Brotherhood barely three years earlier, he rose through the ranks at an accelerated pace—despite his headstrong personality, which provoked either immediate admiration or resentment. On the other hand,

Odo was also a brilliant military tactician, a reputation he'd secured ever since his tenure as Marshal of the Kingdom of Jerusalem. Michel took notice of this and became convinced it was a quality the Order would certainly need in the days to come. So, in 1171 AD, when the previous Grand Master died, the priest used his position as chairman of the Electoral College to sway its decision in favor of de St. Amand. Nonetheless, there was a second reason why Michel chose to back someone ostensibly loyal to the king: for a number of years now, relations between the Order and King Amalric had been strained.

"Villano Gaetani, the archbishop of Pisa, is down in the chapel, and he came to collect the funds he's deposited with our brothers in Italy. So far there's nothing out of the ordinary. However, when he gave me his Credit Note, I found additional information also encrypted in it," Michel said. He then took the decoded text out of his pocket and started to read.

The Grand Master listened attentively while stroking his bushy beard. He continued doing so, evidently lost in thought, even after the priest finished reading the short note. Michel was waiting for his reaction, but a long moment passed before Odo did anything else. Eventually, he unhanded his beard, and sighed. "It appears the pope's problems with the antipope have made him seek other ways to overcome them."

Pope Alexander, the Third of his name, was currently in exile from Rome. Forced to retreat to various locations by the Holy Roman Emperor, Frederic Barbarossa, the pope now lived in the small town of Benevento. The object of their dispute was the emperor's refusal to recognize Alexander as the legitimate pope. As a result, Barbarossa had recognized a series of antipopes, instead of Alexander, with the current one, at that point, being Calixtus.

"Yes, those were my thoughts as well. It seems His Holiness now feels that if he reveals a valuable holy relic to be in our possession, he might gain the upper hand in his predicament. He must believe it would prove *he's* the one favored by God to lead the Church," Michel responded.

"Either that, or perhaps Alexander is hoping to expose some sort of heresy on our part. If he did, it would demonstrate his intolerance for such trespasses—even if it was the Church's favorite sons who were involved and who'd have to pay the price. But, whatever the case may be we mustn't allow it to proceed," Odo said with determination.

Another moment of silence passed between them until de St. Amand's eyes suddenly lit up. He looked excited. "Actually, we could use this development to our advantage."

"What are you thinking, Grand Master?"

"I just remembered what you told me yesterday: about the Assassins' envoy who is currently in negotiations with the king. Perhaps we can use both to cancel each other out. Is Gaetani in the chapel?" Odo asked and stood up. He seemed energized.

The priest frowned. "Yes, he is. But I still don't understand what you mean."

"You will. I'll tell you in a moment. First, let's get going."

Michel paused before following the Grand Master to the door. "Something I haven't told you, until now, Sir Odo, is that I've invited him to stay with us. I am supposed to be taking him your response."

"Excellent. Good thinking, Father, this makes matters even easier. I can give him my reply in person," de St. Amand said with a chuckle, and opened the door.

As they made their way down, the Grand Master briefed Michel on his plan. When they stepped inside the chapel, Gaetani and Stephen were still at the table, just as the priest had left them. Odo walked over to the prelate, bent over and kissed his hand.

"My Lord Archbishop, it is a great joy to have you here," de St. Amand told him, as Gaetani rose to his feet. "Father Michel informed me he has invited you to stay with us, and I thought it only proper to come and also extend this invitation myself. It would be an honor for us to accommodate Your Excellency."

Villano smiled for the first time. "Thank you, Grand Master. It will be my pleasure to stay here."

"I am certain you must be tired from your journey, so allow me and the good Father to escort you to your room," Odo offered.

On the way, de St. Amand informed Gaetani about the rigid daily routine the members of the Order followed. He told him about the many religious services everyone was obliged to attend throughout the day, and also about how the brothers were supposed to eat each meal in total silence, while listening to passages from the Bible. The archbishop was duly impressed by the pious devotion the Templars displayed and said as much.

When they arrived at their destination, the Grand Master showed the prelate in. The room was small, but slightly larger than a normal monastery cell, and was furnished with a simple straw mattress inside, as well as a wooden crucifix on the wall. Nonetheless, Gaetani thanked them, remarking he would be very comfortable.

Just as he and the priest were about to leave, Odo turned and spoke to the prelate, as if in an afterthought. "Father Michel tells me you have come to Outremer on a pilgrimage."

"Yes, as I've told him, I am not getting any—"

"That's funny," de St. Amand cut in, frowning. "When he first informed me of your arrival, my immediate thought was that His Holiness the pope sent you..." Odo said and paused, "... on a mission to convert the Holy Land's infidels." He'd been eyeing Gaetani closely during that brief, mid-sentence pause.

The archbishop's fear of having been exposed was fleeting. Nevertheless, he recovered straight away and responded with a smile, "No, the reasons for my journey are personal. Still, if I were to meet a sincere unbeliever who wished to convert to our true faith, I would never refuse him. It is a sacred duty for every Christian, is it not?"

"Yes, it is," the Grand Master replied, while nodding in

agreement. "But what if those saying they wish to convert are a known group of infidel fanatics? People whose sole purpose in life was to persecute others for not sharing their beliefs? A cabal that considers their leader to be a god... What would you think of then? Could you consider them capable of denying their hard-held convictions and accepting Christ into their lives, even though everything else points in the opposite direction?"

Gaetani was startled by this sudden barrage of questions. He did, however, wish to remain in his hosts' good graces, so he took a moment before replying. "Well, I suppose that if I recognized their desire for conversion to be insincere, then I would be on my guard. They might be trying to trick me, so I would take all necessary precautions."

"Aye, that would be my response as well, Your Excellency," de St. Amand said. "But, we must allow you to rest now. Good day."

After that, the Grand Master and Michel turned around and walked out of the room. Odo had a content smile on his face.

✣ ✣ ✣

North of Tripoli, Outremer
March 22, 1173 CE

WHEN WALTER DE Mesnil and the two younger knights arrived at a narrow patch of land between a pair of low hills, he decided this was a perfect location for them to wait. So they guided their horses up to the hill on the right, and after dismounting they secured their destriers to the branches of an acacia tree there. Then, they took off their helmets, and before sitting in the tree's shade, the Templars placed their white pointed shields—each one adorned with a large red cross—on the ground.

In theory it was still early spring and the weather should have been cooler. But the hot midday sun in the Holy Land, during any season, is always punishing. Especially if someone wears a series of padded undergarments and a long chainmail coat under a white mantle, like these knights did. As a result, every single one of them sweated a great deal. However, it was something which didn't make the least bit of difference to the stench they already gave off: Templars hardly ever bathed.

Walter, the group's leader, wasn't a man who might pass unnoticed. And that was because he wore a distinct black patch over his left eye, having lost it in combat five years earlier. He was a battle-hardened Templar, stationed in Jerusalem, and someone extremely loyal to the present Grand Master. Which was exactly why Odo de St. Amand chose him for this particular mission.

The orders they'd received, before riding out of the Holy City, had been very specific: Abdullah, an envoy of the Old Man of the Mountain—as Rashid ad-Din Sinan, the current leader of the Nizari Assassins was widely known—would also be leaving the capital, under escort. The group's task was to ride ahead and apprehend the envoy en route—before he reached Masyaf. They were to find out what he'd discussed with the king and subsequently dispatch him to meet his Maker. After doing so, de Mesnil had to make sure the Old Man of the Mountain knew it was the Templars who were responsible. Finally, Walter was supposed to seek refuge at the Sidon Preceptory until the situation blew over. Taking him aside, the Grand Master gave assurances that the Order would protect him from whatever repercussions his actions would have.

Shortly after the sun passed its highest point in the sky, Joseph, one of the two younger knights, stood up. "I think I hear horses coming from down there," he said while pointing to the south.

Walter de Mesnil barked an order. "Let's get ready."

They put on their helmets, grabbed their shields, and mounted their destriers. Aligning themselves in the narrow corridor between the twin hills, the Templars unsheathed their broadswords and waited as two mares trotted towards them. The bearded rider on the left was dressed in a yellow, long and loose burnoose robe, while a white piece of cloth was wrapped tight around the top of his head. The clean-shaven one on the right, however, was a king's guard. And when they got to within thirty feet of the knights, he shouted out, "This man is under protection of safe conduct by His Majesty, King Amalric. Move aside, Templars, and let us pass."

Walter addressed him also in French. "My brothers and I have no quarrel with either one of you, good sir. We just need to speak with this Nizari envoy, and then you can continue your journey." Ignoring the guard's ongoing objections, de Mesnil turned to the Assassin next and spoke to him in perfect Arabic. "We mean you no harm. I only want to ask you a few questions before you carry on. Let's go up there and talk in the shade. It's much cooler." Walter pointed to the acacia tree his party had been sitting under, moments earlier. Apparently, de Mesnil's ability to speak the Nizari language fluently was another factor the Grand Master had taken into consideration.

Abdullah's expression betrayed the dilemma he faced: If he didn't do as the Templar asked, he most probably would be cut down on the spot; however, if he did go along as requested, he might be killed after they were done talking. *But if I tell him what he wants, I may be able to survive this,* was his final thought. So, the Assassin nodded to Walter that he agreed.

"Keep him here, while Abdullah and I talk," de Mesnil told his subordinate knights, gesturing to the king's guard. "When we've finished, I'll call out for you to let him pass and they can be on their way." He said this louder than necessary, though, so the guard could hear it and be reassured of their sincere intentions.

Walter sheathed his sword and turned the destrier around. Then, he gestured to Abdullah to come up on his right where the Templar could keep his only good eye on him. After a short trot over to the acacia tree, they both dismounted. But before Abdullah had a chance to sit in the shade, Walter started patting the Assassin down, over his clothes, for any concealed weapons. And when the Templar felt something hard hidden under there, he swiftly stuck his hand into Abdullah's robe and brought out a sharp, pointy dagger. The reproach that registered on de Mesnil's look was as if he was asking, *'What in God's Name are you doing with this?'*

The Nizari threw both his shoulders and hands up. "You didn't expect me to go to Jerusalem completely unarmed, did you?"

"And nobody ever searched you?"

"I suppose they thought it might seem distrustful if they did."

They sat in the shade after this, opposite each other, and Walter placed the dagger on the ground between them.

"So, what does your Old Man of the Mountain want from the king?" de Mesnil asked.

"These discussions were not initiated by Imam Rashid—may Allah bless him always. No, it was your king who first approached our side. He wants us to form an alliance against that devil's spawn, Nur ad-Din, and his forces."

"And you've agreed?"

Abdullah didn't reply straight away. He took a moment considering his options before speaking. "I was authorized to agree, provided a few of our conditions were met."

"What sort of conditions?" Walter asked probingly.

"Our main stipulation was that the annual tributes we pay, to both you and the Hospitallers, must stop."

"But you've never paid us *any* tribute—ever!" de Mesnil exclaimed.

The Nizari cracked a smile. "I know that and you know that, but the king doesn't. Our real problem is the tribute of two thousand bezants we pay annually to the Hospitallers. Twenty years ago, when your Order circulated the rumor we'd agreed to pay you that sum, the knights of the Hospital demanded we pay the same amount to them as well. We tried to explain it wasn't true, that it was just some ruse on your part to cover up your complicity in Count Raymond's slaying, but they didn't believe a word of it. They gave us no choice, so we've been paying them ever since. But, unlike you, we are poor people. We don't produce anything, so we have to rely on other people's donations and handouts in order to survive. To raise and pay such a large sum, every year, is a great burden for us. We couldn't ask for only the Hospitallers' tribute to be cancelled, however, because that would be suspicious. Therefore, the condition we set was for both payments to end."

"From what you're saying then, I assume you did not inform the king, or his officials about our part in the count's murder. Is that so?" Walter asked. This was what he'd been interested in finding out all along.

"No, I did not. Imam Rashid—may Allah shower praises upon him forever—believes it's best to save this valuable information for another, more appropriate, situation."

The knight lowered his head, nodding, which made Abdullah think their conversation was probably at an end, and that he'd be allowed to continue with his journey. Walter, however, lifted his eyes up after a moment and stated, "The day when your Old Man of the Mountain gets to use that information against us will never come." He then grabbed the naked dagger lying in front of him, and with a lightning fast move slit the Nizari's throat. The Muslim never had the chance to even think of protecting himself. Blood spewed out, splattering and staining de Mesnil's white mantle, while Abdullah's eyes remained bulged with disbelief and surprise.

Walter could hear the king's guard shouting in the distance while he stood up and calmly unsheathed his broadsword. He kicked the dead body, for it to fall on its side, and with one mighty chop beheaded the Nizari. Removing the white cloth that was on its top, de Mesnil grabbed the blood-dripping head by the hair and mounted his horse.

The guard was still hurling abuses at him when Walter arrived at the pass where the others were. Ignoring the insults, he threw Abdullah's head over to the astonished guard, and told him, "This is what you will deliver to Masyaf. Tell the Old Man there that the Templars did this, and that we'll do a lot worse if he does not behave himself. After you do so, you are free to return to the capital."

The veteran knight then gave Joseph orders to ride along and make sure the guard did exactly as instructed. After that he took the other young Templar aside and whispered what he was supposed to tell the Grand Master upon arrival in Jerusalem. Walter de Mesnil would also be riding south, but *his* destination was Sidon.

✝ ✝ ✝

Jerusalem
March 24, 1173 CE

ODO DE ST. Amand walked down to the Stables and stepped into Michel's room. The priest was busy scribbling something, but when he saw the Grand Master enter, he looked up and asked, "Are you ready to go?"

"Gaetani hasn't come out of his room yet, so it should be a few more minutes before we leave."

"Are you confident this will work?" Michel inquired once again. He had put the quill down in order to give Odo his full attention.

"I don't think we have much of a choice, do we? The message from the king this morning, saying I appear before him *urgently*, can only mean he's heard what happened. So, I must take our 'alibi' along with me," de St. Amand said.

"Just remember we had no other option. If the king's alliance with the Assassins went through, it would've been simply a matter of time before Amalric found out about our involvement in Raymond's murder, all those years ago.

Something which would have probably forced his hand to cancel the countess's gifts, and our Order would lose Tortosa, along with Arwad. In fact, he might even have gone as far as to take the nearby Chastel Blanc fortress away from us and give it to the Hospitallers. So there are many reasons why you shouldn't be having any qualms about what we had to do."

The Grand Master looked resolute. "I don't have any doubts that crushing the alliance, nor that eliminating the Nizari envoy were necessary, Father. My concern, now, is how Walter de Mesnil heard about Gaetani's advice, in the first place. I hadn't thought this through before, so this is why I've come to speak to you."

"Yes... I see what you mean," the priest said. "It cannot appear de Mesnil was acting under your orders—that would be inexcusable for a Grand Master. On the contrary, everything must look as if he acted of his own accord."

Michel spent a long moment pondering over this problem. But when he next spoke, the solution he came up with sounded so simple it made Odo smile.

"Aye, that should do it," de St. Amand exclaimed cheerfully, after hearing Michel's suggestion. And before getting up to leave, he asked, "Are you certain you don't want to come along with us?"

"I'm positive," the priest replied, as he glanced down at what he'd been writing earlier. Michel never deviated in his implementation of Nicodemus's fundamental axiom: *Every Templar head-cleric—who should preferably be of Phoenician descent—must always keep his pivotal role in the Order's affairs a closely guarded secret and away from the public eye.*

But before de St. Amand left the room, the priest spoke to him again. Odo stopped half-way out of the door and listened to what Michel was saying. "Do you remember I told you that my uncle believed the Ark was our Brotherhood's lucky charm? If it wasn't true, then we wouldn't be able to kill two menacing birds with one stone today. Keep that also in mind, Grand Master."

✠ ✠ ✠

THE RIDE OVER to the king's palace was a short one, and after dismounting, Odo along with Archbishop Gaetani made their way to the throne room. Once inside, they realized the king wasn't alone. With him, among other officials, were also Amaury de Nesle, the Patriarch Archbishop of Jerusalem, and Archdeacon William of Tyre. The latter would eventually become world-famous for chronicling the Kingdom of Jerusalem's history. But, for the time being, he was simply the tutor of Baldwin, the king's only son, and someone who—for unknown reasons—had a very negative disposition toward the Templars.

King Amalric's tall, but chubby frame was pacing up and down, in front of the throne, evidently in a vexed mood. He was dressed in a simple grey robe, with a leather belt tied around his plump waist, and open sandals. When he saw the two men enter, he turned and shot a thunderous glance at Odo de St. Amand. The king said nothing at that point, though, preferring instead to go sit on his throne first. After doing so, Amalric pointed a finger at the Templar and exclaimed in rage, "You are t–t–to b–b–blame for all this, Gr–Grand M–M–Master." The fury the king felt hadn't helped him keep his chronic stutter in check. In fact, it had only served in making it worse.

Both Odo and the Archbishop of Pisa bowed out of respect to the king. But when they resumed their upright positions, and before he could say anything in response, de St. Amand saw, out of the corner of his eye, that Gaetani was smiling. Apparently, the king's speech impediment had amused him. But, Amalric noticed that as well.

"Who the h–h–hell is this?" the king asked, while glaring at Villano with equal rage.

"This is His Excellency Villano Gaetani, the Archbishop of Pisa, sire," Odo replied. "He is visiting the Holy Land on a pilgrimage and is currently staying with our Order here in Jerusalem. I thought it appropriate to bring him along with me today so that I might introduce him to you."

Gaetani bowed again and started to say, "Your Majesty, it is a great pl—"

"Why d–did you d-do this t–to m–m–me?" Amalric cut him off, focusing his angry gaze now on Odo instead.

"Do what, sire?"

"You h–had the Assassins' envoy k–k–killed, that's wh–what!"

"I did no such thing! When did this happen?" Odo asked, feigning indignation and ignorance.

But before the enraged king could reply, Archdeacon William stepped in and suggested, "Allow me, sire." Amalric nodded his consent, and the cleric continued, "What His Majesty is trying to explain, Grand Master, is that the kingdom had reached an agreement with the Assassins to create an alliance between us. But on his way back to Masyaf their representative was ambushed by a group of Templars. The group's leader... one Walter de Mesnil, I believe, then proceeded to decapitate the envoy. And as if that wasn't enough, he also saw to it that the severed head was delivered to the Old Man of the Mountain—in effect ruining what His Majesty is striving to achieve."

Odo's mouth was agape, as he pretended to be shocked. "This is astonishing," he declared. "I know Brother Walter very well, and it's the first time he's done something this foolhardy. I realize how the situation looks, sire, but rest assured I had nothing to do with Brother Walter's actions."

"You d–didn't p–put him up t–to this?" the king asked, in a slightly calmer manner.

"Certainly not," the Grand Master lied.

"Then why d–d–did he d–do it?"

"The only possible reason I can think of now is that he was just following Archbishop Gaetani's advice," Odo replied as innocently as he could. His head leaned a bit to the side to indicate the prelate of Pisa standing next to him.

The king exploded. "What!?" Amalric's plump face had already turned red. He tried to say something, but what came out was so incoherent that William of Tyre was forced to step in again.

"What advice did His Excellency give?" the archdeacon asked with a suspicious frown, clearly not believing this story. Gaetani, on the other hand, was staring at Odo with a very bewildered look. It was as if he was wondering, '*How in God's Name did I get involved in this?*'

"When the archbishop first came to us, a few days ago, he and I spoke at length about how all Christians have a duty in trying to convert unbelievers," the Grand Master started to explain. "But when I informed him there was the possibility of a group of Muslim fanatics wishing to convert, he advised caution. His Excellency suggested such a group might be attempting to trick us, and that we should therefore take precautions. At that evening's Chapter meeting, I repeated this conversation to my brothers—among whom was Walter de Mesnil—as well as the information I'd received about the Assassins agreeing to convert to Christianity. It seems—"

"So you *d–d–did* know about m–my t–t–talks with them!" Amalric interrupted.

"I did, sire. Archbishop de Nesle had been keeping us informed. He told us about the alliance you were determined to forge with the Nizari sect, and that they'd already agreed to accept our true faith. All good outcomes from my point of view," Odo replied. "So good, in fact, that even forgoing their annual tribute would have been worth it."

"But apparently de Mesnil had other thoughts," William added, as if asking.

"Yes. As I was about to say, it seems Brother Walter took Archbishop Gaetani's advice a tad too literally. He must have considered it necessary to investigate just how sincere the Assassins were in their desire for conversion."

At last, the king had someone to fully vent his rage on. "I want you t–t–to leave immediately. You are n–no longer w–welcome in my k–k–kingdom," Amalric shouted at the archbishop of Pisa, pointing to the door.

"But, Your Majesty, I—"

Amaury de Nesle, who had remained silent during this whole time, put his gloved hand up and interrupted Villano's protest. "I think it would be best, Brother. Gather your things and return to Pisa, as soon as possible," the patriarch said in a cold tone of voice.

Gaetani was in a quandary. He did not dare reveal he'd been sent by the pope, or the true reason he was in the Holy Land. On the other hand, he couldn't deny that what Odo said was true because there'd been a witness. And to top it all, the king's intense dislike of him left no room for any further maneuver. As a result, the archbishop had no other choice but to storm out of the throne room with indignation. He did so, however, with a nagging suspicion he'd been tricked into this from the very beginning.

In contrast, Odo de St. Amand was smiling internally. He'd just eliminated the second menacing bird!

"So the annulment of the Assassins' tribute to your Order had nothing to do with de Mesnil's actions? I find that quite hard to believe," William of Tyre said, wanting to get back to the matter at hand.

"I'm certain it did not, because Brother Walter has never taken part in the financial side of the Order. And even though I do condemn his actions, I don't doubt his motives were genuine. I'm sure that whatever he did was because he sincerely felt it would protect fellow Christians from future perils."

"B–But, he's c–c–committed t–treason," Amalric exclaimed.

"And he will be disciplined accordingly, sire, never fear," was de St. Amand's calm response.

"No. I want him arrested imm–immediately and p–put on t–trial in my c–c–courts of law," the king objected.

Odo had been prepared for this as well. After a long pause, and while everyone was looking closely at him, he said, "With the utmost of respect, Your Majesty, I cannot allow that."

Amalric's face had turned crimson with rage and the only word he managed to yell out again was, "What?"

"As I'm sure His Excellency, Patriarch de Nesle, will confirm, sire, our Order is exempt from any secular jurisdiction. In fact, the papal bull *Omne Datum Optimum* is very specific about this matter: no one, aside from His Holiness the pope, can pass judgement on Templar wrongdoings. So, what I *can* promise Your Majesty is that I will hold immediate disciplinary hearings into Brother Walter's transgression. And if need be, I will not hesitate to send him off to Rome for final judgement."

After saying that, Odo de St. Amand bowed to the king with respect and exited the room. Amalric was left speechless.

✦ ✦ ✦

THE OVERALL RESULTS of that day's audience with the king weren't entirely what the Grand Master had hoped for, however. Yes, Villano Gaetani did leave the Holy Land in disgrace, unable to fulfill his secret mission—that was on the positive side; as was also the fact that the alliance with the Assassins was irrevocably in ruins. But as far as Amalric entrusting Walter de Mesnil's fate solely to the Templars was concerned, matters could not have turned out worse. A few days later, the king rode out with a contingent of his guards to Sidon. Entering the Templar Preceptory there, they found and seized the one-eyed knight. Walter was then taken to Tyre where he was imprisoned to await trial.

In his chronicle of the Kingdom's history, William of Tyre, a few years later, cited this incident as a notable example of how the Order's greed had begun to exceed its piety. In his opinion, the Brotherhood no longer demonstrated the admirable qualities it used to in the early days of Hugh de Payns. The only thing his contemporary Templars cared about, he wrote, was amassing property and money. William was therefore convinced that the Order's motive for destroying the Nizari alliance was just so the Brotherhood wouldn't forgo the annual payment of two thousand bezants. As a result, he didn't mention Gaetani's role in these events at all, preferring instead to solely lambast the Templars, for his own, unspecified reasons. And at the same time, William of Tyre kept on poisoning Amalric's mind against the Order with every chance he got.

The king's relationship with the Templars was at an all time low at that point. In the first months of the following year, rumors even started to circulate that since the Order had effectively destroyed his alliance with the Assassins, Amalric was considering asking the pope to dissolve the Brotherhood. But, when Father Michel got wind of this, through his web of spies, he vowed never to give the king a chance to go through with it. So the priest waited for a suitable moment to get rid of him. And Michel had just the thing to do the deed: a particular herb, known since ancient Phoenicia, traditionally used for the treatment of diarrhea. What made this plant very useful in this case, however, was that if ingested in greater quantities than necessary, it had the capacity to generate all the symptoms associated with severe dysentery. Then, after a couple of days, the herb would also cause an intense fever, ultimately leading to the person's death.

In the spring of 1174 AD, the Muslim leader, Nur ad-Din, suddenly died, and Amalric sprang into action to take advantage. His first attempt was to besiege the town and fortress of Banias, north of the kingdom. With the battle-ready Amalric about to leave Jerusalem, Michel realized this was the chance he'd been waiting for. So he gave sufficient quantities of that special herb to a Tyrian cook who'd be accompanying the king's forces. Amalric, however, was forced to abandon the siege early, after confronting fierce resistance. And while the army was returning to the capital, the cook seized the opportunity to prepare a soup for the king—a soup filled with that tasty, but lethal herb. Inevitably, Amalric passed away on July 11.

No one can ever know how the history of Outremer, or the Brotherhood, might have evolved if King Amalric hadn't died just when he did. The immediate outcome, though, was that Walter de Mesnil was freed from his prison cell, never having to face trial. And the matter of disbanding the Templars was forgotten—for the time being. So, in essence, the Order had received a reprieve of about a hundred-forty years.

On the other hand, what Nur ad-Din's death *did* bring about was to bolster someone who'd prove to be a much more formidable adversary: Saladin. This remarkable military leader, of Kurdish descent, took advantage of the resulting power void and was able to unite almost all the splintered, infighting Muslim factions under his command. The days in which the Christians could hold onto the Holy Land, unchallenged, were numbered. After a series of successes, Saladin finally annihilated the unified Christian forces at the Battle of Hattin, in July 1187 AD—a tragic outcome which in effect left Jerusalem defenseless. And when the Muslims recaptured the Holy City, in October of the same year, it sent shockwaves all over Christendom.

The response was to launch a Third Crusade, with the kings of England and France at its forefront. But try as they did, especially King Richard the First—better known as Richard Coeur de Lion—they accomplished little. Other than the retaking of Acre, the Crusade's real objective of reconquering Jerusalem was never realized. Not only that, but bit by bit, over the next century, all Christian territories were lost to subsequent Muslim leaders.

As far as the Templars were concerned, the white and black mantled warriors, proudly displaying the red cross on their chests, actively took part in almost every major campaign. But it's safe to say that after the Battle of Hattin, and the loss of Jerusalem, their standing was in decline as well. So when Acre—the very last of the free Christian cities in the Holy Land—also fell in 1291 AD, they were forced to relocate their headquarters to Cyprus for good.

However, that large Mediterranean island wasn't unfamiliar to the Order. After King Richard the Lionheart had conquered it a century earlier, in 1191 AD, he'd sold it to the Templars. The way with which they started to administer it, though, soon outraged the Greek-speaking natives, causing them to revolt, barely a year later. On Easter Sunday, 1192 AD, a large band of ill-equipped Cypriots decided to storm the Templar headquarters, in Nicosia. But these untrained peasants were no match for the formidable, if few, knights who stormed out of the keep. The Templar charge may have resulted in a bloodbath for the natives, but it made the Order realize it couldn't hold onto the island with the meager forces stationed there. So they returned the island back to King Richard, and he in turn sold it to Guy de Lusignan. And on becoming the first Latin King of Cyprus, Guy allowed the Templars to keep the properties they already owned on the island.

One of those holdings was the tiny, rural village of Khirokitia. A few miles inland from the island's southern underbelly, its strategic location was perfect for stopping invading armies from advancing from the south. So, over the years leading up to 1291 AD, the Order was able to build a formidable manor house there, very near an ancient Byzantine church called *Our Lady of the Field* (or, as it's known in Greek: Παναγιά του Κάμπου). That small, picturesque church still exists today, in excellent condition, while the only remaining evidence of the legendary Templar fortress is a single arched corridor, standing forgotten on the edge of a dirt road.

This general location would be the final resting place for the Templar treasure and... the Ark of the Covenant.

HIRAM

Chapter 11

CLOUD

Jerusalem
959 BCE

SOLOMON HAD FELT uneasy ever since he opened his eyes that day. So, when he made his way up to the Temple Mount and saw Hiram speaking with an assistant, he beckoned him over. The king leaned in and whispered into Hiram's ear, "Are we ready?"

"Yes, sire. I just need to get down there," he replied in an equally low voice.

"Remember. You're to release it only *after* the music starts to play," Solomon cautioned, looking deep into the Master's eyes.

"I know what to do, Your Majesty. Don't worry," Hiram said with conviction. He then bowed his head with respect and walked away. A moment later he disappeared behind the Temple's northern wall.

✟ ✟ ✟

EVER SINCE HIRAM Binne's arrival in Jerusalem more than a year would pass before the first ashlar blocks were ready to be delivered to the building site. Even so, the wait was worth it. The quarry his Phoenician assistants had set up at a faraway mountain—along with thousands of workers and slaves—began producing excellent results. The huge blocks of stone that arrived were expertly cut, perfectly sided, and ready to be placed in the ground. To this end, trenches had already been dug out along the square perimeter Hiram had delineated. So, all that was needed now was for every one of those enormous blocks of stone to be placed halfway inside the ditches, next to each other. Something which the Master and the multitude of men he commanded began to do straight away. It wasn't an easy task though. The sheer size and weight of those monoliths posed great problems in placing them accurately—as well as danger. Many men suffered excruciating injuries, and some were even killed, after getting crushed by them. But, at the end of the project's first two years a tall square of adjacently placed ashlar stones, sticking halfway out of the ground, surrounded Mount Moriah's summit.

The next step was to pour immense amounts of soil into this enclosure so that the preliminary Temple platform could take shape. Fortunately, Hiram and his crew had by then finished all the necessary underground work. They'd already excavated the natural cavity a few feet east of the mount's peak, thus creating the subterranean chamber Solomon requested. And at the same time, the Master had his most trustworthy workers dig a large, almost thirty-foot deep hole near what would later be the Temple's north wall. This was where he'd place the secret crypt King Hiram suggested he should create.

In the months leading up to that, and in order to do so, the Master had received a special permit from Solomon to allow him and his non-Jewish crew to work on the Sabbath. Hiram then devoted every one of those holy days of Jewish inactivity to construct the crypt and necessary tunnels, away from inquisitive eyes, just as his king had recommended. And at the end of each Sabbath, he would cover up the hole with cedar planks, hoping no one would question him about why they were there—which for the most part no one did.

Not until one morning, that is, when Hiram saw Solomon appear on the building site all of a sudden. The Master greeted him cordially, and to direct his attention away from the hole-covering planks he steered the king east to show him the work that'd been done on the underground chamber he'd requested. Solomon emerged from the man-made cave quite satisfied with it, but after he took a few more steps he halted.

"What are those wooden boards doing there, Binne?" the king asked, pointing.

Hiram was quick-witted as always. "As I'm sure you realize, sire, that hole is part of the future Temple's foundation."

Not wanting to reveal he *didn't* know what a foundation was—or looked like—Solomon merely nodded as if he did and continued walking. The Phoenician had been lucky the advisor, Zabud, hadn't accompanied his king that day. Before leaving the site, Solomon expressed his satisfaction about the work being done, and the Master respectfully bent over to kiss the king's hand. The Ring depicting the Star of David was on Solomon's middle finger as usual.

After that isolated incident, Hiram was left virtually unsupervised. So, over the next few Sabbaths he placed the marble slabs, which were to shape his secret crypt, inside the deep hole. A month later, and after all the necessary exits and passageways had been taken care of, he and his trusted crew lowered the vault's roof into the ground. That final, white marble slab, measuring fifteen by six feet, was placed on top of the crypt walls and all together they formed a robust underground box. The only thing left to do after that was to fill the conspicuous hole with earth—an event which took place the very next Sabbath.

When the Mount's initial platform was ready, after pouring massive amounts of soil into the enclosure, Hiram began building the House of the Lord in earnest. By placing more of those perfectly sided ashlar stones on top of the earthen platform, he first created a sturdy surface. Then, over the next five years, he used similar ashlar blocks to construct the eighty-eight foot long Temple, which consisted of three distinct parts:

The first was the elevated, thirty-foot open cube of the Holy of Holies, or Debir. Situated directly above Mount Moriah's summit, this was the special chamber where the Ark of the Covenant would be placed on the day of the Temple's dedication. When this Inner Sanctuary was finished, its walls were overlaid with cedar planks and those, in turn, were painted gold. Also inside there, Hiram's skilled carpenters created two massive Cherub statues, whose touching wings spanned the entire breadth of the room, completely adorned with gold paint as well. The folding doors that concealed the Debir from the rest of the Temple were lavishly decorated with golden figures of cherubim, palm trees, and flowers.

A few steps down from the Sanctum Sanctorum, was the Hekhal, or Holy Place, the Temple's main and largest section. A row of five shewbread-bearing tables would be placed in it, on either side, as well as corresponding rows of tall seven-lamped candlesticks. In the wide corridor separating them there would be nothing else except the Altar of Incense, which was placed three feet away from the foot of the steps.

But the Master's greatest and most notable achievements stood just beyond the richly decorated doors of the Hekhal, to the east. Standing outside, in front of the Porch's facade—the tallest part of the structure, at forty-five feet—were two huge pillars. With each one thirty-five feet high, the towering columns created an impression that their primary function was to safeguard the Temple's entrance. In truth, however, they'd been positioned there because Hiram had decided this was the best way to repay his debt to the Tyrian god Melqart. Built hollow, by placing many brass rings in and above each other, the Master topped the pillars off with large capitals depicting brass lilies and pomegranates, within lattices of chains. But even though they ended up resembling the Tyrian originals considerably, their brass coloring differed from the legendary gold and green of Melqart's columns. Still, Hiram was confident that his pledge to the god had been satisfied.

Solomon had also been pleased with how the pillars turned out. So much so, in fact, that he'd decided to name the southern one *Boaz*, after his great, great grandfather, and the one to the north *Zadok*—after the high priest who'd anointed him king, and who was to officiate at the Temple's dedication. He planned on announcing both names at the very end of the consecration ceremony.

Hiram also supervised the creation of every other necessary object for the Temple. Among many other items, his men had cast ten stands out of bronze, ten brass basins, lots of pots and shovels, the sacrificial altar, and the spectacular Molten Sea as well. This last one, constructed exclusively out of brass, was a huge round basin, measuring fifteen feet from brim to brim, and was capable of holding almost twenty-four thousand gallons of water. It rested on the backs of twelve bronze oxen, which in groups of three faced each of the cardinal points. On the whole, this was the quantity and quality of work that the Master and his workers had produced. However, if one happened to read the chronicles of Solomon's scribes, who were charged with documenting the Temple's construction, one would conclude that the king did all this by himself!

Over the course of those seven years, the Master did not confine his activities only to what was needed for the Temple, though. He'd also been entrusted with expanding the city walls all around Mount Moriah. This was deemed necessary because many Hebrews decided to leave their villages and came to live in Jerusalem after the Temple's construction began. Consequently, the abodes they built outside the existing walls, as well as the dwellings for the thousands of workers and slaves, which surrounded the

Mount with buildings, also needed protection. And since there was no one else who could take on such an important project, Hiram undertook it as well.

The downside of Solomon constantly requiring Hiram's services was that the Master hadn't been allowed to visit his home even once. The only way he kept abreast of family news was with the letters he regularly received from his wife, Mirha. In fact, that was how he learned of his mother's death, four years after he'd arrived in Jerusalem. But, alas, the widow's son had been unable to attend his own mother's funeral.

+ + +

HIRAM HURRIED DOWN the steps into Solomon's hidden chamber. Luckily, the candle he'd lit was still alight, as the manmade cave was otherwise dark. Squatting down, he placed his hand on the large brass box. It felt hot; the flames inside hadn't died out and, other than a slight irritating smell, there was no leakage.

Back when the Temple was nearing completion, Solomon had become increasingly frustrated. He still couldn't think of a credible way to follow through with his scheme—one that wouldn't involve the Master, that is. So, he realized he had no choice but to trust Hiram. Although the king didn't like him very much—as a person he thought the Master was too secretive and too reluctant to share his true feelings and thoughts—nevertheless, Solomon felt certain he'd be discreet. So, when the king revealed the real reason why he needed that hidden chamber all along, Hiram was astonished. Apparently, what Solomon wanted was for a thick black cloud of smoke to appear in the Temple during the dedication ceremony. The king would then use the cloud's appearance to claim that the Lord Himself was present, and that consequently God endorsed his kingship. Solomon looked deep into Hiram's eyes, after this disclosure, as if pleading, *"Help me."* And the Master did.

Inside the artificial cave, he constructed a large brass box, all by himself, which had a tube coupled to its top, leading upward and into the Temple. The tube's end was then fastened behind a small opening on the Hekhal's topmost step—just below the folding doors of the Holy of Holies. Hiram's idea was to burn a large piece of sulfur inside the brass container, generating a considerable amount of black smoke that would for a short time be trapped in the box. At the appropriate moment, he would then release the cloud into the Temple.

Meanwhile, up above, a huge crowd had gathered for the beginning of the ceremony. They gradually filled the entire plateau, and also spilled off onto the road that connected it with the city of Jerusalem, to the south. Dressed in their finest linen robes, the two pillars of the kingdom, King Solomon and High Priest Zadok, stood fittingly beneath the towering columns at the Temple's entrance.

"Let the Ark of the Lord's Covenant be brought forth," Zadok ordered, his loud and commanding tone of voice hushing the excited throng. A few moments later a procession of Levite priests made its way up the road from Jerusalem. Eight of them carried the Ark by its golden rods, while many others followed with the tent it had been housed in, along with other holy implements which used to be in the original Tabernacle.

The crowds reverently parted to allow the procession to pass as did Solomon and the high priest. Once inside the Temple, the priests walked up the steps to the Holy of Holies and placed the Ark under the open wings of the giant Cherubim statues. Zadok followed the procession inside, while the king chose to remain on the Temple's Porch, looking in. Everyone else remained behind him at a distance. The Levites then exited the Temple, leaving the high priest all alone to take up his position in front of the Altar of Incense, facing the Debir in the west. And just as other Levite priests, outside the Temple, began playing a joyful tune with their trumpets and cymbals, and Zadok was reciting supplications to the Lord, a streak of black smoke made its appearance in front of the Holy of Holies. In a matter of seconds, the amount of smoke streaming out formed a thick black cloud which filled the Temple with darkness and a nauseating, pungent stench.

Alarmed, the high priest abandoned his prayers and walked hurriedly toward the doorway. Solomon was waiting for him outside, between the two towering columns.

"Your Majesty, the Temple is on fire," Zadok told him in a frantic tone of voice.

"No, don't be troubled. It is simply the presence of the Lord Himself. God be praised," the king responded calmly, and smiled.

The high priest frowned. "I wish it was, sire, but it definitely smells as if something's burning,"

Sensing a problem between them, two men hurried over. The first was Ahishar, the chief of Solomon's guards, and the other was Jachin, an assistant high priest and one of Zadok's sons. By the time they'd got to where the king and the high priest stood, the black cloud was already spilling out of the Temple's doorway. The crowd gathered farther back started getting restless.

The high priest turned to his son. "Jachin, there is a fire somewhere inside the Temple. We need to put it out."

"My dear Zadok, I've told you: it's only the Lord gracing us with His presence. We should rejoice," Solomon said coolly.

Jachin looked up at the black smoke, which kept billowing out of the Temple, and then down at the king. Solomon's calm, confident expression remained unchanged. *The king must know something we don't*, the cunning young Levite thought. *So, this might be my chance.*

Jachin's relationship with his father had always been difficult. They almost never agreed on anything, which resulted in frequent quarrels. The underlying reason was that Jachin felt his brothers were constantly favored over him. And even though he'd recently been promoted to an assistant high priest, nonetheless he believed this was to be the extent of his career. Until now, that is.

"I think His Majesty might be right, Father," Jachin then said, facing Zadok. "It doesn't smell, or look, like a common fire."

Solomon smiled at the young man. He was pleased to have found an ally.

"No, how can you say that?" the frantic high priest responded, his long white beard trembling as he spoke. "Our Temple could be—"

"You must be overwrought, Zadok," Solomon interrupted him. "Perhaps it's better if you go lie down and let Jachin take over the ceremony. Ahishar will escort you back to your lodgings."

The king looked into the high priest's eyes with a cold, ruthless expression which left no room for contradiction. Zadok sighed with resign and began taking off his Ephod to hand it over to his son. The high priest's Ephod was an elaborate linen garment, resembling an apron; it was woven with blue, gold, scarlet, and purple threads. Jachin removed his simpler one and put on his father's. Then, the chief guard took hold of the high priest's arm and led him away from the Mount.

Sensing that the crowd was getting agitated, Solomon lost no more time. He rushed over to the sacrificial altar and walked up its ramp. Zabud, his trusted advisor, was already there waiting for him. From up there everyone could see and hear the king clearly. He put his hands up and they all quieted down.

"The Lord told me that He would dwell in a thick darkness. And He has come here today to see the house I've built for Him—a house where He can live forever," Solomon said in a loud voice, while extending his open arms in the direction of the Temple and the black cloud still billowing from inside. Then turning around to face the joyous Hebrews gathered there, the king addressed them again. "Blessed be the Lord God of Israel, who has fulfilled everything He promised to my father David. My father had in mind to build a house for the Lord God of Israel, but the Lord said unto my father David, 'Whereas it is in your heart to build a house for Me, and you have good intentions, nonetheless, you shall not be the one to build Me this house. The son of your loins shall do so; he shall be the one to erect My house.' And the Lord has fulfilled His promise. For I have risen up to replace David, my father, and sit on the throne of Israel, just as the Lord spoke. And I have built this house for the Lord God of Israel. And in there I have set the Ark, inside of which is the Covenant that the Lord made with the children of Israel, when He brought them out of the land of Egypt."

By the time Solomon began reciting his dedication prayer, the gathered crowd was ecstatic. They were cheering, and shouting praises to him so loud, that what he said next could barely be heard. Everyone thoroughly believed that God Himself had appeared that day, and that Solomon was His chosen vessel.

The king's deception had been complete.

✝ ✝ ✝

My darling Mirha,

It is my sincerest hope this finds every one of you well and safe.

I was especially happy to read in your letter that Elisa has made us grandparents, yet again. Being our eldest daughter, I never doubted she'd be the first one to make us realize the relentless passage of time by having a family of her own. But, I must admit that three children within the space of barely five years is quite an achievement. Perhaps she and her husband should slow down now?

I was also pleased to hear Ithobal is doing well in his lessons, and that Tanis and Izavel already have suitors pursuing them—a fact, I confess, which didn't make me feel any younger either. When did our little babies become grown women?

All these happy events make it all the more difficult for me to be so far away from you, unable to witness them firsthand. And they also serve to stress my present predicament even more.

A little over a month ago, the Temple's dedication ceremony finally took place. I've already written to you about what Solomon asked me to do for him. Although I'm not proud of the part I played in his deception, I must admit the end result was exactly what he wished for: the Israelites thoroughly believe their God had been present that day, and that Yahweh favors the king. However, the undertaking wasn't without its complications. Zadok, the Hebrew high priest, became convinced that the black cloud in the Temple had been caused by something burning. So, Solomon, facing the possibility of exposure, had to get rid of him. And the king found an unlikely ally in Zadok's own son, Jachin, an assistant high priest up to then. The young man unexpectedly supported Solomon's claim of God's presence, and so the king had Zadok sent away. As expected, the old high priest hasn't been heard of since. Not only that, but at the end of the ceremony, when Solomon was about to reveal the names of the two tall columns gracing the Temple's façade, he surprised everyone by naming one of them Jachin—instead of Zadok, which was his intention all along.

After those events, I had to wait for the frenzy of the weeklong celebrations to die down before I was able to approach Solomon. But when I told him I wanted to return to Tyre, now that my work was finished, the king wouldn't hear of it. He claimed there was much for me to do yet, especially in light of the new palace he wants me to build for him. When I said I hadn't seen my family for many years, and that I could resume work after I returned from making a brief trip home, Solomon's reply was a flat "No." He was probably afraid that if I left, I would not return. So maybe this is why he told me that in a few months a daughter of the Egyptian pharaoh would be coming to Jerusalem. He's planning on marrying her and therefore needs me to build a house for her, as soon as possible. I responded by saying a few months wouldn't be enough to build a house worthy of a princess, but Solomon countered that just by starting it would be enough to show her—and her father—that he was sincere. Now, why in the name of Melqart would someone who already has seven hundred wives and three hundred concubines need to take on another wife is something completely beyond me.

Nevertheless, in view of Solomon's stubborn reluctance to let me go, I had no other choice but to inform King Hiram of this in writing. I delayed telling you about this until his reply came, but I'm sure you already know all about it. I just find it incredibly frustrating that the City Council would once again decide to keep me a hostage here simply because Solomon's armies continue to pose a threat for Tyre. Still, I am a loyal Tyrian and shall abide by my city's wishes, even if this means it will be several more years before we can be reunited.

I live and breathe for the day when I'll be able to see you all again.

With my deepest love and affection,
Hiram

CHAPTER 12

SHEBA

Jerusalem
955 BCE

FOUR WHOLE YEARS had passed since the dedication of the Temple, and Hiram Binne still needed many more to finish everything Solomon required of him. Nonetheless, that year had seen the completion of the small house for the Egyptian princess, as well as the king's legendary throne. This last item, fashioned exclusively out of ivory and gold, was so magnificent that anyone who happened to see it for the first time was rendered speechless. Yet those accomplishments, noteworthy though they were, did not leave even the tiniest of traces on the city's collective memory. What the people of Jerusalem *did* choose to remember, however, was the arrival of the Queen of Sheba.

Leading a trade mission on its way to Tyre, this renowned female ruler of a distant southern kingdom decided to make a stop at Jerusalem. She'd heard of Solomon's wisdom, and of the Temple he'd built, so she was determined to find out for herself if all the stories were true. Her caravan of more than a hundred camels laden with goods, set up camp outside the city walls, and the queen soon sent messengers in requesting an audience with the king. Solomon agreed and the very next morning the gates opened wide to allow the Queen of Sheba and her entourage to enter.

In order to build the king's new palace, Hiram had constructed an additional platform slightly below that of the Temple's. This new surface stood several feet higher from the existing palace of David, and it was from up there that the Master saw the queen's procession begin to make its way into the city. The street, connecting the city's southern gate to David's palace (or, as it was also known, the House of the Forest of Lebanon) was overflowing with people. They'd converged there that morning, bursting with curiosity to see this fabled queen, and they were not disappointed.

She made her entry perched up on the side-saddle of an impressive snow-white camel, while the long purple cape she had fastened around her neck delicately draped the animal's flanks and behind. No doubt produced from the widely sought Tyrian purple dye, this silk cape combined perfectly with the gold-colored robe she wore underneath. With the camel being led forward by one of her men, the Queen of Sheba soon reached a spot which allowed Hiram to get a better look at her. And when he did, the Master realized the stories he'd heard extolling her beauty did her a great injustice. Not only was she beautiful, but she was the most beautiful woman Hiram had ever seen! What caught his attention first was the light olive-colored texture of her skin, as it shined in the morning sun. Yet, when that was coupled with her ruby-colored lips, the high cheekbones, the almond-shaped eyes and her jet-black hair—held back with a gold headdress—the result was breathtaking. Although still in her mid-twenties, the queen projected such an air of authority and deference that everyone on the street that day swiftly moved aside to let her pass. And before long she disappeared behind David's House of the Forest, where she was supposed to meet Solomon, and out of Hiram's view. Only then did the Master begin to notice the rest of her retinue. Coming up behind were two more, ordinary colored camels, burdened with bulging side-satchels—most probably with all the gifts she brought for Solomon. And walking alongside them were about twenty exotically dressed men and women, all even darker-skinned than their queen was.

The mesmerized street crowd lost no time in filling the void left behind by the ongoing procession and started following it towards David's palace. And although Hiram would have also wanted to get another glimpse of the beautiful queen up close, he decided against it. The Master had work to do.

✛ ✛ ✛

Two days later, on the morning following the Sabbath, Hiram was walking up the Temple Mount. A new batch of ashlar stones for Solomon's palace had just arrived from the mountain quarry, and his men would need instructions on how to proceed. Since there were about five thousand of them assigned to this particular task, the only place he could gather everyone, in order to address them all, was the easternmost edge of the Temple's plateau.

Strangely enough, for those times, the Master tried to maintain a good relationship with as many of the men who worked for him. Whether a laborer was a free man or a slave, this distinction never made any difference to Hiram. He and his assistants treated each one with respect, and on occasion even strived to solve personal problems they faced. Therefore, it wouldn't be an exaggeration to say that the workers respected their Master so much that they worshiped him to some extent.

The thousands of laborers were already there, standing randomly around the platform's eastern side. Hiram was still busy heading up the sacrificial altar's ramp when, to his left, Solomon and the Queen of Sheba appeared from inside the Temple.

The queen smiled as she turned to face Solomon. "What's this? Have you planned another spectacle for me?"

The Jewish king had been startled to see this massive throng of people in front of him all of a sudden. Nevertheless, he recovered quickly and said in a dismissive tone, "It's only Hiram with his workers. Come along, my dear, I still have to show you what's been done for my new palace up to now."

He and the queen started to step away from the Temple, on a southern direction, when Hiram, high on the altar, raised a clenched fist straight up, causing the workers' hubbub to die down at once. The queen, noticing the abrupt silence, stopped walking and looked over to the altar. Solomon, Jachin—who was by then the new High Priest—and the rest of their party halted as well. The Master unclenched his fist and with the palm leveled sliced the air in a left-to-right manner. From the center of that imaginary line he then brought his open hand down in a hacking vertical motion—as if he wanted to carve the letter T on the air. The men, most of them with a smile, responded to this by shouting a thunderous, "Yes, Master." After that, they began moving in an orderly fashion to form the rows and columns of their three separate classes: the metalworkers, the carpenters, and the stone craftsmen. That was how they were supposed to stand in order to receive their work instructions.

Only when his men started stepping into their groups did Hiram sense that someone's gaze was fixed upon him. Turning his head to the right, he realized the queen had been standing there all along. The Master's eyes locked onto hers for the first time. And as far as he could detect from the look in her stunning green eyes it was one of wonder and admiration. In contrast, though, Solomon's expression, as he stood next to her, was one of anger and resentment.

✝ ✝ ✝

THAT NIGHT, HIRAM was in his room getting ready for bed.

The day's work had been especially demanding, and he felt tired. At one point, as he was washing up, the Master heard a faint knock on the door. Not expecting anyone at that hour, he opened it with unease and looked out. A young, dark-skinned girl stood there, dressed in a long, cream-colored linen tunic, her black hair fashioned into a bun on the top of her head.

"Please forgive the lateness of the hour, Master. But my queen would very much like to speak with you," she said, struggling with the Hebrew words, while looking down bashfully. Hiram recognized her from being in the queen's party that morning.

"Now?" he asked in a slightly irritated manner.

"If you would be so kind, sir, yes," the girl persisted.

Hiram sighed with resignation, told her he needed to become presentable, and shut the door to do so. *This is most unusual*, he thought. *I wonder what she wants to speak to me about.*

With his curiosity peaked, but also feeling strangely excited by the prospect of seeing that beautiful creature up close, he changed his clothes as fast as he could. In a matter of minutes, the Master put on his finest linen robe, tied a black leathery cord around his waist, fixed his untidy hair, and exited the room.

Solomon had provided a few private chambers at David's Palace for the queen and her retinue to use, so the walk over didn't take long. The handmaiden held the door open, allowing Hiram to step in. She followed. The room's plentiful illumination, in addition to seeing the queen so suddenly in front of him, as she reclined sideways on a chaise longue, caused the Master to stop in his tracks. Even though she wore a sleeveless blue silk robe, which covered her well-proportioned figure entirely, a few of her small olive-hued toes *did* peek out just beyond the robe's hem.

Sensing the agitated and flustered state he was in, the queen broke the silence by saying in fluent Hebrew, "Thank you for coming at such a late hour, Master Binne. I am Nikaula, the Queen of Sheba."

"Yes, I know, Your Grace," Hiram said and bowed with respect.

"There is no need for such formalities. Come, sit by my side," she said with a radiant smile, while gesturing to a seat next to her divan.

The Master sat, as rigidly upright as he could, and glanced around. Aside from him, the queen, and the handmaiden who'd invited him over, there were two other, older women sitting across the room. Apparently, it wouldn't be proper for an unmarried queen to be left all alone with a man—especially at night.

"When I saw you this morning, I asked the king who you are, and he informed me you're his architect from Tyre," Nikaula said, breaking the silence once again. Her overpowering green eyes were looking deep into his.

"Yes, I am, Your Grace."

"I was on my way to Tyre, you know, before I decided to make a stop at Jerusalem. And the reason I've invited you here tonight is that I want to hear more about it. What's your city like, Master Binne?"

It was Hiram's turn to smile now, as images of his native land began flooding his mind. "Oh, it is without a doubt the most beautiful city in the world, Your Grace. It's situated on a large island a few miles off the coast, surrounded by the bluest waters you'll ever see. And the palm trees, along with the plethora of gardens everywhere, provide every other color one can dream of. There are two seaports, at either end of the realm, and in between them are some of the most impressive buildings that—"

"You paint quite the picture," Nikaula interrupted. "But your eyes betray that it's also a rather nostalgic one. How long has it been since you were there?"

"From the time I first arrived in Jerusalem. It has been eleven years now, ma'am," the Master replied. He sorrowfully bowed his head. "The king hasn't given me permission to visit my family even once since then. There has always been so much to do."

"Your family...?" the queen asked, her voice trailing off so that he'd supply the details.

"Yes, my wife, son, three daughters... and now my grandchildren," he answered with a cheerless grin. He brought his face up to look at her.

A glint in her eye revealed this wasn't something she'd wanted to hear. Nonetheless, an instant later she flashed a smile and exclaimed, "But where are my manners! I haven't offered you anything to drink yet." Nikaula then turned and said something in her native tongue to the young handmaiden.

But before the girl could get up to carry out the order, Hiram said, "No wine for me, Your Grace. I find it doesn't agree with me at night anymore. A cup of water would be fine, thank you."

Nikaula's beautiful green eyes opened wide with surprise. "You speak our language?" she asked.

"Not as such. I just know a few expressions. An old uncle of mine used to be a mariner trader, and over the years he had travelled to your southern land many times. He taught me a few of your words when I was a child, so when you mentioned your word for wine, I remembered it."

The look of admiration she'd given him earlier in the day appeared once again. "You never cease to amaze me, Master Binne," Nikaula remarked. Then, turning to her handmaiden she gave additional instructions and the young girl stepped out to bring the refreshments.

The queen looked at Hiram persistently for a long moment. So persistently, in fact, that he was forced to avert his eyes. "Are you also good with riddles, Master Binne?" she asked after a while, her gaze never leaving him.

He frowned, puzzled by this unexpected question, but managed to reply, "I'm passable, I guess. Why?"

"It's simply because I posed some of these riddles to the king the other day and... Well, let's just say his performance didn't live up to his reputation as the wisest man alive."

"I'm sure he did the best he could... under the circumstances," Hiram said, refraining to add that Solomon was perhaps distracted by her intense beauty.

She chuckled. "Oh, he did. That is, up to the point when his advisor, Zabud, was beside him. When I finally realized the old man was feeding Solomon the answers, I asked the king to send him away. After that, he couldn't figure out a single one," the queen stated, with a mischievous smile. "Shall we begin?"

"Yes, by all means," the Master replied, still puzzled where all of this was leading.

"There is an enclosure with ten doors. When one door is open nine are shut, and when nine are open one is shut. What is it?"

Hiram looked down. He didn't want to be distracted by her and started to think hard. At that moment, the young girl returned and handed him a cup of water. He took a sip, and then his face lit up.

"The enclosure is the womb," the Master exclaimed. "And the ten doors are the ten orifices of man, that is to say: his eyes, ears, mouth, nostrils, the openings for the discharge of feces and urine, and the navel. When the child is still in its mother's womb, the navel is open, but all other openings are shut. On the other hand, when the baby emerges from the womb the navel closes and the other orifices open up, becoming functional."

"Very good, Master Binne!" the queen congratulated him, while displaying her pearly-white teeth in a wide smile. "Let us proceed. What does not move while alive, but does so when its head is cut off?"

Hiram was relieved because he knew this riddle from childhood. Being in proximity to Mount Lebanon, and with his city's livelihood depending so much upon the mighty cedar trees that grow there, this was one of the very first riddles every Tyrian child learned. Still, he took a moment, as if he was thinking, before he said, "The timber that's used to build a ship."

"Excellent!" Nikaula stated, looking quite happy with his outstanding performance. "Now, for the last and most difficult one: It goes ahead of all in a storm at sea. It's a cause of praise by the wealthy, and of shame to the poor. It honors the dead, but saddens the living. It's a source of joy to birds and of grief to the fish. What is it?"

The Master had not heard this riddle before, so he asked the queen to repeat it—there were too many details. When she did, he started to ponder about what goes ahead of everything else on a ship when it's caught up in a storm. There were only two possible answers for that: the ship's prow, or its sails. The wood, out of which a prow is constructed, didn't satisfy the rest of the riddle's clues, but on the other hand...

"Flax!" he blurted out excitedly. "When woven into cloth it makes a ship's sails, fine clothes for the rich, rags for the poor, and shrouds for the dead. The birds enjoy its seed, yet the fish get caught up in the nets it creates."

Nikaula was looking at him intently when he turned to gauge her reaction. After taking a moment, she said in a tone overflowing with admiration, "You are as impressive tonight as you were this morning, Master Binne. No wonder your men love you so much."

Sitting so near to the queen, and even though the many lamps perched up on the walls illuminated the room a great deal, Hiram was able to witness the pupils in her eyes beginning to dilate. And from his experience this could only suggest one thing: Nikaula was attracted to him.

Although the Master hadn't been intimate with his wife, for the past eleven years, this didn't mean he'd refrained from enjoying the company of other females. In fact, Phoenician society did not frown upon this. With much of its male population consisting of tradesmen, mariners, or builders—who travelled off to distant lands for great periods of time—it was considered inevitable they would seek comfort in women other than their wives. In essence, what was important to Phoenicians was that the love a couple felt for each other remained true, not the physical action lasting a few minutes. So, after many such dalliances, and already in his forty-eighth year, Hiram was by now capable of recognizing the telltale signs of female attraction. Initially flattered, of course, he cast that aside at once, as he started to think: *But, she's probably even younger than Elisa, my eldest daughter!*

Troubled by where this was going, since he loved his wife without reservation, he inquired, "Why are you asking me all this, Your Grace?"

"I just want to see if there is a man insightful enough to be worthy of me," the queen replied, in a matter-of-fact manner.

This response worried him even more, so Hiram decided to veer the conversation in a different direction. "Is that why you put these riddles to King Solomon?"

The question made her smile. "Actually, I wasn't planning to, but he provoked me. He kept on boasting throughout dinner about how much his God favors him, about how wise He has made him, etc, etc, so I decided to put Solomon to the test. But, he was measured and was found wanting," Nikaula stated with a chuckle. Then, she added in a more serious manner, "Besides, I could never marry a man who already has a thousand women, and become just another number. It would be an insult to my own kingdom. Oh, he tried to woo me, for sure, except he failed miserably at that as well. Do you know what he compared me with?"

"No."

"With a company of mares in the Pharaoh's chariots," the queen said in a raised voice, and burst out laughing. "Can you believe that? I suppose the compliment was hidden in the fact that I was compared to several horses instead of only one."

Nikaula's loud, intense laughter that followed soon spread contagiously to all the other women present in the room. It took them a few moments to get ahold of themselves again.

This is becoming extremely dangerous, Hiram thought—all the while also smiling, as if he enjoyed the humor. And while the women were still chuckling over the queen's words, he saw his chance. Standing up, the Master bowed and said, "If there is nothing else, ma'am, I must take my leave. It has been a long day, and tomorrow looks like it might be even longer."

Caught off guard, the queen looked disappointed at first. An instant later, though, she reassumed her normal, regal demeanor. "Yes, of course. But, you still have a lot to tell me about Tyre. We must do this again in a few days. Rest well, Master Binne."

Hiram thanked her, took a deep bow, and stepped out of the door. While he did, though, he was so preoccupied with his own thoughts that he failed to notice someone lurking in the shadows nearby.

✣ ✣ ✣

It was midmorning the next day when a messenger was seen running up to the new palace's platform. Approaching Hiram, he told him, "Master, the king would have a word with you."

The Phoenician instinctively did not like this—whenever royalty wanted to speak with him it had usually been to his detriment—nonetheless, he replied that he would be there presently. So, after giving instructions to his principal assistants, Madal and Mattan, about how to carry on with the work in his absence, he took the downward winding path toward the House of the Forest of Lebanon.

Solomon was in the great hall, as the Master walked in, sitting upon his magnificent gold and ivory royal throne. A sight which made Hiram think about how the king never missed a chance to impress—even for an audience of one. And that was because, surprisingly enough, there was no one else in the room. Except for Zabud at Solomon's side, as always, there were no courtiers, or any of the king's wives present.

The Master approached the golden platform, bowed and waited for Solomon to address him. It did not take long. The king arched his left eyebrow and said, as if asking, "I understand you visited the chambers of the Queen of Sheba last night, Binne."

Getting over his initial surprise, Hiram replied in a cool tone, "Yes, I did, sire. She summoned me."

The king inspected his fingernails, feigning indifference. "And what was the reason for that summons?"

"She wanted me to inform her about Tyre."

Undoubtedly, this caught Solomon's attention because he looked up and started to ask a stream of questions in rapid succession. "Why? Is she planning to continue her journey to Tyre? Did she mention anything about King Hiram being a widower now?"

"Neither subject came up, sire."

At that point, Zabud bent over and whispered in Solomon's ear. It must have served to remind him of something, because in the next instant the king exclaimed, "Ah, yes! Quite a bit of laughter was heard coming from the room. What happened? Were you telling them one of your Phoenician jokes?"

"No. It was perhaps after a comment the queen made."

"And what was that?"

"I honestly don't remember," Hiram lied, looking down.

By the time the Master brought his eyes back up, Solomon was looking at him through narrowed, furious slits.

"Let me tell you something, Binne, so listen closely," the king began to say in a severe tone. "By marrying the Queen of Sheba, I can create the largest kingdom this world has ever seen. I plan on doing so, and I'll suffer no one to stop me. I've seen how she looks at you, and if you think you can win her over to yourself think again."

Hiram was trying to squeeze in a few words to reject those charges when Solomon imperiously raised his hand and went on. "What's more, if I'm successful this will also be beneficial to your home city of Tyre, in terms of trade," he said in a softer tone, as if that could offer the Master an incentive. However, Solomon's face soon clouded over again, and he stated, harshly, "Stay away from her! I'm warning you. If you spoil this for me, I shall have your head, Hiram Binne."

PART TWO

DEATH

GEORGE

Chapter 13

TUBAL-CAIN

Larnaca, Cyprus
December 2013 CE

GEORGE MAKRIDES UNLOCKED the door and walked into his apartment. Joanna, who'd been watching the evening news on the sofa, turned and looked over, somewhat surprised; she hadn't expected him back so soon. Nevertheless, she squealed happily, jumped up and darted across the living room. Arching her bare feet up, she wrapped her arms around his neck and kissed him on the lips.

"You look so handsome in this suit... and your little black tie! If nothing else, you Masons certainly know how to dress," Joanna said with pride, after they'd exchanged a few kisses. "But, you're early. Didn't you go to eat with the others?" she asked with concern, still holding on to him.

"I didn't feel like it," he replied dejectedly. He kept his right arm around her waist and twiddled her long golden locks in his other hand.

"Why? What happened?"

"I'll tell you all about it after I change," he promised. They let go of each other, and as she was reclaiming her usual spot on the sofa he walked into their bedroom.

George and Joanna had been living together for the better part of the past six months. After getting engaged, they decided that, given the circumstances, staying in the small, one-bedroom apartment he rented was the most sensible thing to do. The times could be very treacherous if they attempted anything else. Normally, when young couples got engaged in Cyprus, they would start thinking about building a house, or buying a bigger apartment—to be ready for when they got married and would start having children. But the country's economy, at that point, was in ruins. Following several disastrous (some would say criminal) economic blunders by the former government, the European Union had been forced to step in. So, by March of that year, aside from imposing a series of austerity measures on the newly elected administration, it imposed the closure of the island's second-largest bank as well. Then, it applied—for the first time ever in world history—a bail-in of the biggest bank by giving it 48% of all its deposits, over a certain amount, as a capital injection. Thousands of people, depositors of both institutions, lost the bulk of their savings almost overnight, primarily because of unchecked governmental incompetence and bankers' greed. Interestingly enough, one of those affected was also Joanna's father, who might have been able to help them with their future housing needs. However, he lost more than two hundred thousand Euros and was therefore no longer in a position to do so. Experiencing all this turmoil around them, and with the rapidly rising level of unemployment, the young couple felt lucky to at least be able to hold on to their jobs. As a result, any decisions concerning better living conditions would have to be dealt with at a later date—*if* the climate changed.

Joanna saw him step out of the bedroom. "Shall I fix you something to eat?"

"No, I'm not hungry. I had a couple of drinks and some nuts at the bar before the meeting started."

He plumped down beside her while Joanna turned the TV's volume off and adjusted her position to face him. She knew he'd tell her what was bothering him, in his own time; there was no need for pressure. From early on, George had decided he would keep nothing from her. Consequently, aside from past details of his personal life, he'd also told her about everything which went on in the Lodge. He wanted no shadows hanging over their relationship, and therefore couldn't care less if he wasn't supposed to reveal any of the so-called Masonic 'secrets.'

"One of the items on tonight's agenda was to vote for someone who'd been proposed to join the Lodge," he began. "I know this guy. He's a decent enough chap, so I voted in favor of his entry. But..."

"So, what happened?" Joanna asked, after George trailed off for a moment and seemed lost in thought.

"He was blackballed," Makrides blurted out, after snapping out of his trance.

Joanna started chuckling nervously. "He was... what?" She was a bit concerned this had sexual connotations.

George recognized the look on her face and smiled. "Take your dirty little mind out of the gutter, it's nothing like that. When we have a vote in the Lodge, we're each given two small, marble-sized balls: a white and a black one. If you want to vote in favor of a candidate, you place the white ball into the ballot box, but if you're against him you put the black one in. This guy, Jack, got three black balls—literally denying him entry once and for all, and with no questions asked."

"But, why?"

"Apparently, Jack is now dating Luke's ex-girlfriend, and it seems the reason she dumped him a few months ago was because she wanted to hook up with Jack. So, Luke got together with a couple of his cronies in the Lodge, and they all agreed to block Jack's entry. It was an act of pure jealousy and spite. That's why I'm upset, and that's why I didn't want to go eat with them after the meeting ended tonight. I couldn't stand to watch the smug expression Luke had on his face anymore."

"Oh, honey, it's all right," Joanna said tenderly, as she came closer and started stroking his hair. "I thought you said you like Jack."

"I do!" he replied, puzzled as to where she was going with this.

"Then why are you so upset he isn't going to be a member? You should be glad," she added, with a cheeky grin. Joanna knew perfectly well that Freemasonry had proven to be a huge disappointment for George, and that the only thing still keeping him in was to figure out how and why it all started.

He looked into her big, blue eyes and chuckled. "You're absolutely right. I *should* be happy he's going to be spared all the expense and aggravation," George stated. But then he took on a more somber expression. "The thing is, for me, it was the meeting's *second* example of how this institution doesn't mold its members into better people at the end of the day. Obviously, deep down I knew that it couldn't, but I guess I'm so naïve I just hoped it *might*—at some point."

"What was the other?" she asked.

"Before I tell you, I'll have to fill you in on something that slipped my mind at the time. Remember, about a month ago, when I went to the installation of the Greek Lodge's new Worshipful Master?" After Joanna nodded she did, he continued. "Well, during a point in the ceremony, where the new Lodge Master was to be sworn in, the presiding Worshipful Master asked everyone to stand, as a sign of courtesy. But, the Grand Master and other members of the Grand Lodge who were there, for reasons of their own, didn't—even though they'd always done so in the past. Now, being one of the most influential Cypriot Masons, this outgoing Worshipful Master probably thought he could boss everyone around—including the Grand Master, who's his superior in a way. So, he interrupted the ceremony, for a moment, to aggressively *order* the Grand Master and the others to stand. Which they did. Nevertheless, as soon as the new Lodge Master was installed in his chair, the Grand

Master stormed out, looking very angry and upset. Well, tonight an official circular from the Grand Lodge was read, informing us that this Past Master has been permanently expelled from the Brotherhood for insulting the Grand Master."

"They can do this? I thought that once you're a Mason, you're always a Mason," Joanna wondered.

"I thought so too, but apparently it *is* possible. It just goes to show that not only Freemasonry *doesn't* improve its members' thoughts and deeds, it actually corrupts them. Especially if they feel their joke of an authority and power is being threatened. Oh, you should have seen them that night, darling. Even though he and the Grand Master had been Masons for many years, they were grandstanding, just like a pair of giant egos locked in combat, vying for who was the biggest. It was sad. And the saddest part is they used to like each other... they were friends." He shook his head. "No, I'm beginning to suspect that the only reason Masonry got started was just to satisfy men's self-importance. And that it's been perpetuated by others who need to believe they belong to something greater than themselves, all the while feeling as if they're serving a greater good."

"But what about the money they give to charity? Surely that's all right, isn't it?"

"Yes, it is. Although you don't have to belong to a secretive organization if all you want to do is assist the less fortunate. Besides, a large amount of what's raised just goes to fund all that pomp and circumstance they put on. No, trust me, love, if Freemasonry ceased to exist no one could tell the difference."

George was still shaking his head, so Joanna didn't press the issue. And she was right because after taking a moment he had more to add. "I'm sure most Masons are good men, with the best of intentions, but whatever it claims Freemasonry *cannot* change human nature. It certainly can't eliminate arrogance, or ambitious greed, or even keep vanity in check. I've seen all these vices, and more, in many of the members. Now that I think of it… Do you know how they address a member of the Grand Lodge in Greek?" he asked. When Joanna shook her head, he told her, with a chuckle, "They call him a *Glorious Brother*. And the Grand Master is addressed as *Most Glorious Brother*. Can you believe that? I mean, if that's not the purest way of boosting someone's ego and vanity, I don't know what is."

"Then why don't you just quit?" she asked.

"Because, the only good thing to happen tonight was that they voted to make me a Master Mason at the next meeting. I've stuck with this thing for two years now, so I don't think waiting another month for that would do me much harm."

"But you already know what happens from everything you've read on the Internet. Why go through with it?"

"All the rituals I've seen are about what goes on in American Lodges. This could be different—just like it was in the previous Degrees. Anyway, I feel it's best if I experience it firsthand. Whatever the case may be, though, come January, I'll either solve this puzzle about Freemasonry's origin, or give it up altogether," George said with conviction. "With its worldwide membership deteriorating for a long time now, I don't imagine my quitting would make much of a difference anyhow."

A mischievous little grin then appeared on Joanna's face. She moved closer. "In the meantime… what do you suppose we should do? I mean, now that you're back home so early?"

✝ ✝ ✝

Larnaca, Cyprus
January 13, 2014 CE

THE LODGE'S MEETING, that winter evening, had only one thing on its agenda: George's Raising Ceremony. Accordingly, the invitations sent out to members advised all Entered

Apprentices and Fellow Crafts—except for the candidate—not to show up, because even if they did they'd be asked to leave. None of them could take part in what happened in the Third Degree.

So, with only Master Masons—and George—present, the Worshipful Master and his Officers began with the Opening Ritual to the Fellow Craft Degree. After that was adequately taken care of—by making sure the Lodge was properly Tyled, by having every relevant question answered, and by executing all the appropriate Signs and Steps—the Master nodded to the Senior Deacon. He, in turn, walked over to George and invited him to stand.

While doing so though, Makrides looked across the room to where his best friend was sitting. Alex smiled, when he noticed George's fleeting glance, and made a small thumbs-up gesture to wish him good luck. George was thankful Alex was there for his sake. Ever since Maria chose to end their relationship, eight months ago, Alex had blamed her decision on the fact he was a Mason. So, from that day he'd missed many more meetings than those attended.

The Senior Deacon took the candidate's right hand in his and led him north of the Senior Warden's pedestal, both turning to face east. That proved to be the Worshipful Master's cue to announce, always by heart, "Brethren, the Candidate to be raised to the Third Degree this evening is Brother George Makrides. But it is still necessary for him to give proof he is well versed in the Second. Therefore, I shall proceed to submit the required questions." He then asked Makrides, "In what manner were you prepared for the passage into the Second Degree?"

The Senior Deacon whispered the reply into George's ear, and he repeated. "In a similar way to the First, except that in this Degree I was not hoodwinked, and it was my left heel that was slipshod."

Following a few more questions, to which George gave sufficient answers, always with the Senior Deacon's assistance, the Master enquired once more, "What were the names of the two great columns which stood outside, at the entrance of King Solomon's Temple?"

"The left pillar was called *Boaz*, and the one on the right *Jachin*."

After that, the Senior Deacon placed George's hand in his, led him up the four steps to the elevated platform in the east, and to the left of the Master's pedestal. They both turned, facing south.

The Worshipful Master swiveled in his seat, looked at George, and asked, "Do you give your word of honor that you will stay the course throughout the ceremony of being raised to the Master Mason's Degree? And do you also pledge you will safeguard all which shall be revealed to you as you have already done for every other secret of Masonry?"

George was about to roll his eyes when he heard about safeguarding the so-called 'secrets' of Freemasonry. Nevertheless, he decided against it and replied to both questions with a simple, "I do," instead.

"Then, I will inform you of the pass grip and pass word necessary for admission into the Degree that you seek." The Master of the Lodge stood up, and after coming near took George's right hand into his. "The pass grip is performed by pressing your thumb in-between the second and third knuckles of the other's hand," he revealed, while demonstrating. "This demands a pass word, which is: *Tubal-Cain*. Tubal-Cain became the world's first metal craftsman, by casting his work in brass and iron. You must be careful to remember this word because you will need it in order to gain admittance into a Lodge of a superior Degree."

The Worshipful Master then released George's hand into that of the Senior Deacon and resumed his seat, while the Officer led Makrides towards the Temple's entrance. On arriving between the two tall, bronze-colored columns there—which alluded to those of Solomon's Temple—they did an about-turn to face the Master in the east. George saluted him with the Sign of the Fellow Craft Degree and was ushered out of the room.

Once outside, George was greeted by the Tyler, who proceeded to give him instructions on what to do. Whispering, so he wouldn't disturb those within, the Officer told Makrides to take off his coat and tie, as well as his undershirt. On top he was supposed to be wearing only his shirt, but unbuttoned, so his chest would be fully exposed. After that, both trouser legs had to be rolled up, in order to bare the knees, and his shoes replaced with slippers. Having done as instructed, George then put on his Fellow Craft apron again—which was also white, as that of the First Degree, except for the two blue rosettes in the bottom corners—and waited.

When he felt sufficient time had elapsed, the Tyler knocked on the Temple door. A few seconds later, the Inner Guard opened it and asked the Tyler, "Who goes there?"

"Brother George Makrides, who has been regularly initiated into Freemasonry, passed to the Fellow Craft Degree, and has made such progress that he hopes it will entitle him to be raised to the Degree of a Master Mason."

"How does he hope to obtain the privileges of the Third Degree?"

"By the help of God, the united aid of the Square and Compass, and the benefit of a pass word," the Tyler replied, once more by heart.

George then performed the pass grip with the Inner Guard, and gave him the pass word, *Tubal-Cain.* An event which prompted the Officer to say, "Halt, while I report to the Worshipful Master," and shut the door.

After another brief interval, both entrance doors opened wide, and the Tyler told Makrides, in a whisper, to step inside. He did, up to the point where he stood in-between the twin bronze columns once again. Makrides stopped there because directly in front of him stood the Inner Guard, flanked by the Senior and Junior Deacons, as if to obstruct him from going any further. When both doors closed behind him, George realized that the Temple was now shrouded in near total darkness, save for a single floodlight that shone above the Worshipful Master's pedestal. The Inner Guard then took a step closer and placed the open legs of a compass on George's bare chest. He raised the instrument up high next, as if to show he'd done so, and resumed his seat. The Senior Deacon now took hold of Makrides's hand and led him to a stool, three steps to the east.

The Lodge Master's voice rang out in the semi-darkness. "Let the Candidate kneel while the blessing of Heaven is invoked on our proceedings."

The Senior Deacon instructed George to kneel on the stool, and to place his right hand over his left breast. After the three main Officers of the Lodge struck their gavels, and everyone stood, the Worshipful Master began to recite the prayer. "Almighty and Eternal God, Architect and Ruler of the Universe, at Whose creative fiat all things were first made..."

As always, George's mind started to wander after hearing those opening few words. And with good cause. In the faint lighting of the room he'd been able to detect two objects more worthy of his attention: The first item was the altar. Normally situated in front of the Master's desk, that tall, upright piece of furniture was now at the foot of the steps leading to the east, with an open book (probably the Bible) resting upon it. However, the second object—in between him and the altar—was even more interesting, and one he'd never seen before. It was a long, open box made up of vertical black planks, less than a foot high, which enclosed it on all sides. And with a dark mattress placed inside, it looked very similar to a burial casket. As this item was completely black, Makrides might have missed noticing it altogether had it not contrasted with some of the white floor tiles beneath. But, as usual, George's thoughts were interrupted by the end of the prayer and everyone chanting, "So mote it be."

When the Worshipful Master ordered, "Let the Candidate rise," Makrides was guided around Lodge a couple of times by the Senior Deacon. In these perambulations he performed the Signs and handshakes of the first two Degrees and gave the relevant pass words of *'Boaz'* and *'Jachin'* to both Wardens. At some point, after all that, George was led to the Senior Warden once more and instructed to communicate the pass grip and pass word he'd been taught prior to exiting the Temple. And when Makrides replied the pass word was *Tubal-Cain,* and that Tubal-Cain was the first artificer in metals (brass and iron), the Senior Warden lifted George's right hand all the way up. "Worshipful Master, I present to you Brother George Makrides, a Candidate properly prepared to be raised to the Third Degree."

The Deacons were then told to inform the Candidate on how to advance to the east by using the proper steps. So, the Senior Deacon took hold of George's hand and guided him to where the casket began. Leaving Makrides to stand there, the Officer walked over to the other side in the east, faced him, and said, "The method of advancing from West to East in this degree is by seven steps, the first three as if stepping over a grave. To assist you, I shall first perform them, and you will copy me afterwards."

The Senior Deacon went back to the head of the casket, next to George, and straddling over it three times, ended up at its eastern end. The Officer then took four short paces, due east, bringing him directly in front of the altar, at the foot of the stairs. Having shown George what he was supposed to do, the Senior Deacon walked back to where Makrides stood and helped him through the whole process. Once he was standing in front of the altar, George heard the Worshipful Master say, "It is only fair to inform you that a very serious trial of your fortitude and fidelity, and a more solemn Obligation await you. Are you prepared to go through with them?"

"I am," George replied, with both Deacons now on either side of him.

"Then you will kneel on both knees and place your hands on the Volume of Sacred Law."

Makrides did as instructed, taking care not to disturb

the Square and Compass which were placed on the Bible. Everyone stood, and he repeated the oath that the Lodge Master started reciting. And, after a few minutes, when it was finally over—by him repeating, '*So help me God, and keep me steadfast in this my solemn Obligation of a Master Mason*'—George could not help but wonder that the actual ordeal to his fortitude was for him to have survived that longwinded and tedious oath.

Descending from his pedestal, the Worshipful Master made his way down the steps until he stood directly above Makrides. "Let me once more call your attention to the position of the Square and Compass. When you were made an Entered Apprentice, both Compass points were hid. In the Second Degree one was revealed. And in this, the whole is exhibited implying that you are now at liberty to work with both of its points in order to render the circle of your Masonic duties complete," the Master said, and took hold of George's right hand. Lifting it up, off the Bible, as if hinting that George should stand, the Worshipful Master commanded, "Rise newly obligated Master Mason." Makrides did so, while the Lodge Master and everyone else resumed their seats. Still facing east, George was then led a few paces back, by both Deacons, until they reached the foot of the casket and stopped.

The Worshipful Master spoke. "Having entered upon the Solemn Obligation of a Master Mason, it is my duty to call your attention to a review of those degrees in Freemasonry through which you have already passed. Your admission among Masons in a state of helpless poverty was emblematic of the entrance of all men in this, their mortal existence. Proceeding onwards, you were led toward the Second Degree to contemplate the secrets of Nature, and the principles of the Seven Liberal Arts and Sciences. Nature, however, presents one more great and useful lesson. She prepares you for the closing hour of your existence. And when she has conducted you through the intricate windings of this mortal life, she finally instructs you on how to die.

"Such, my Brother, are the peculiar objects of the Third Degree in Masonry: They invite you to reflect on this awful subject; and teach you to understand that, to the just and virtuous man, death has no terrors equal to the stains of falsehood and dishonor. Of this great truth the annals of Masonry afford a glorious example in the unshaken fidelity and noble death of our Master *Hiram Abiff.* He was slain slightly before the completion of King Solomon's Temple, at the construction of which he was, as no doubt you are well aware, the principal Architect. The manner of his death was as follows. Brother Wardens..."

A soft, but eerie melody started to play over the Temple's sound system, just as both Wardens abandoned their pedestals and made their way to where Makrides stood. The Deacons took a step back and returned to their seats while the Junior Warden positioned himself on George's right and the Senior Warden on his left. The Junior Warden then whispered to Makrides to cross his right foot over his left and having done as instructed both Wardens took hold of his arms to steady him.

When he realized everyone was in place, the Worshipful Master began his narration of the Hiramic Legend: "Fifteen Fellow Crafts, finding the work was nearly completed, and that they were not yet in possession of the secrets of the Third Degree, conspired to obtain them with any means, even by resorting to violence. At the moment, however, of carrying their conspiracy forward, twelve of the fifteen recanted. Yet three, of a more determined nature than the rest, persisted in their impious intentions. To execute this atrocious plan, they placed themselves respectively at the East, West, and South entrances of the Temple, where our Master had retired to pay his adoration to the Most High, as was his usual practice at the hour of noon.

"Having finished his devotions, he attempted to exit by the South door where he was opposed by the first of those ruffians. Armed with a heavy Plumb Rule, and in a threatening manner, this vile Fellow Craft demanded the secrets of a Master Mason, warning Hiram that death would be the consequence of a refusal. Our Master, true to his obligation though, answered that those secrets were known to just three in the world and that without the consent and co-operation of the other two he neither could nor would divulge them. He intimated, however, that patience and industry could, in due time, entitle a worthy Mason to a disclosure of them. Yet, for his own part, he would rather suffer death than betray the secrets entrusted to him. This answer not proving satisfactory, the ruffian aimed a violent blow at the head of our Master. However, being startled by the firmness of his demeanor, it missed the forehead and was deflected to his right temple..."

At that point, the Junior Warden touched George's right temple with a plumb rule, allowing the Worshipful Master to add, "...but with such force as to cause him to reel and sink to his left knee."

The Senior Warden whispered to Makrides to kneel, for a moment, on his left knee, and to stand and cross his right foot over the left once again. While he was going through those motions, George wondered: *Why hasn't he mentioned the thug's name?*

The Worshipful Master went on with the story. "Recovering from his shock, our Master made for the West entrance where he was accosted by the second of those ruffians, to whom he gave a similar answer with undiminished firmness. Then, that ruffian, who was armed with a Level, struck him a violent blow on the other temple..."

To illustrate that part of the tale, the Senior Warden touched George's left temple gently with a level, and the Lodge Master added, "... which brought him to the ground on his right knee."

The Senior Warden whispered to George to sink to his knee once more—the right one, this time—then to stand up and re-cross his legs. And again, Makrides was thinking: *Why isn't he saying the ruffians' names?*

"Finding his retreat cut off at both those points," the

Worshipful Master continued, "he staggered, faint and bleeding, to the East entrance where the third ruffian was waiting. The scoundrel received a similar answer to his insolent demands—for even at this trying moment our Master's resolve remained unshaken. And when the villain who was armed with a heavy setting Maul, struck him a violent blow on the forehead, it laid him lifeless on the ground."

The last thing George saw, before being grabbed by the Wardens, was the Lodge Master, up high on his pedestal, pretending to strike him with a maul in his hand. The Wardens brought Makrides back to lie, face up, on the casket's mattress. They made sure his hands were at his sides and his feet crossed before taking up their positions on either side of the coffin-like box.

"The Brethren will take notice that in the recent ceremony our Brother has been made to represent one of the brightest characters recorded in the annals of Masonry, namely Hiram Abiff," the Worshipful Master remarked. "He lost his life as a result of his unshaken fidelity to the sacred trust assigned to him. Brother Junior Warden, you will now endeavor to raise our Master's representative by the First Degree's Grip."

The Junior Warden straddled the coffin, and after taking George's right hand, he deliberately let it slide from his grasp. Resuming his position, he reported, "Worshipful Master, it proves a slip."

"Brother Senior Warden, you will try the Second Degree's," the Lodge Master ordered.

Likewise, the Senior Warden also straddled the box and allowed George's hand to slide from his own. Consequently, his report was the same.

"Brother Wardens, having both failed in your attempts, there remains a third method: taking a firmer hold of the sinews of the hand and raising him by the Five Points of Fellowship. These are: hand to hand, foot to foot, knee to knee, breast to breast and hand over back. With your assistance, I shall attempt exactly that."

With the eerie music being switched off all of a sudden, George could now make out the distinct sounds of the Worshipful Master abandoning his seat and walking down the steps. Then, he felt the Master separate his feet and grab onto his right hand with a powerful grip. And with both Wardens assisting on either side, Makrides was brought up to stand.

"It is thus how all Master Masons are raised from a figurative grave to a reunion with their former companions," the Lodge Master stated, still holding onto George's hand.

The Worshipful Master then proceeded to instruct Makrides on the 'secrets' of the Third Degree, which as always were just another Grip and a Word. And having done that, he allowed George to exit the Temple in order to fully dress.

On George's re-entry, with the lights having been restored, he was first invested with the Master Mason's apron. After that, he was led up to the east, in front of the Worshipful Master's pedestal, where he was informed of the events which followed Hiram's murder.

"A loss as important as that of the principal architect could not fail to be severely felt," the Lodge Master began. "The prefects deputed a few of their number to make King Solomon aware of the utter confusion into which the absence of Hiram and the lack of his designs had plunged them. But also to express their fear that some catastrophe must have been responsible for his sudden and mysterious disappearance. King Solomon ordered an immediate assembly of all workmen, upon which three of them were nowhere to be found. On the same day, the twelve Craftsmen, who were originally involved in the conspiracy, came to the King and made a voluntary confession of everything they knew up to the time they withdrew from the plot. This naturally increased King Solomon's fears for the safety of his foremost artist. He therefore selected fifteen trusty Fellow Crafts and ordered them to make a diligent search for our Master, in order to discover if he was still alive, or if he had suffered death while protecting the secrets of his exalted Degree.

"And so, they formed themselves into three groups and departed from the three entrances of the Temple. Many days were spent in a fruitless search. Indeed, one party returned without having made any discovery whatsoever. A second, however, was more fortunate, when a brother caught hold of a shrub that was near where he sat and to his surprise it came all too easily out of the soil. On closer examination, he found the earth had recently been disturbed. He and his companions, therefore, reopened the ground and discovered the body of our Master indecently interred. They covered it up again with all respect and reverence, and to distinguish the spot stuck a sprig of acacia at the head of the grave.

"Then, they hastened to Jerusalem to convey the terrible news to King Solomon. He, when the first emotions of his grief had subsided, ordered them to return and raise our Master, while informing them that by Hiram's untimely death the Third Degree's secrets had been lost. The king also charged them to be very careful in observing whatever grip or word might occur whilst paying this last, yet sad, tribute of respect.

"They performed their task with the utmost fidelity. And on reopening the ground, two of the brethren descended into the grave and endeavored to raise him by the Entered Apprentice's Grip which proved a slip. Then, they tried the Fellow Craft's, which proved a slip likewise. Having both failed in their attempts, a zealous and expert brother took a more firm hold on the sinews of the hand, and raised him with the Five Points of Fellowship. At the same time, others, more animated, exclaimed *'Machaben'* or *'Machbinna.'* Both words have similar meanings, one signifying the death of the builder, the other that the builder has been struck down. King Solomon, therefore, ordered that those Words and that Grip should define all Master Masons from then on, until such a time when the genuine secrets could be restored.

"It only remains to account for the third group which had pursued its search in the direction of Joppa. They were debating their return to Jerusalem when they accidentally passed a cave and heard sounds of deep lamentation and regret coming from inside. On entering the cave, they found three men answering the description of those missing, who, on being charged with the murder and finding all chance of escape cut off, made a full confession of their guilt. They were bound and taken to Jerusalem where King Solomon sentenced them to be executed in ways their heinous crime so aptly merited."

The Worshipful Master paused briefly before going on. "Our Master was ordered to be re-interred as close to the Sanctum Sanctorum as the law of Israel would permit. He was not buried in the Holy of Holies, because nothing common or unclean could ever be allowed to rest there, but in a grave near the Temple."

✝ ✝ ✝

AFTER THE MEETING was over, almost everyone in attendance went to a local fish & chips restaurant to eat. As usual, Alex sat next to George.

"I hope you found this ceremony more interesting than the other two," Alex said, as if asking.

"Well, it certainly has given me a great deal to think about."

"Think about what, exactly?"

"The story's inconsistencies, for starters," George replied. But when he saw Alex's puzzled look, he lowered his voice and proceeded to elaborate. "The legend tells us that the Temple hadn't been finished yet. So why would Hiram want to go pray in an unfinished, unconsecrated Temple? And then again, did he, a Phoenician, believe in the God of the Jews? I find that a bit hard to accept."

"Perhaps he did, and just went off somewhere inside the Temple to worship," Alex offered.

"Maybe so, but history informs us the Temple *was* completed, even though the story implies the workers didn't know what to do next—because of Hiram's murder. If what this legend says had actually happened, then they wouldn't have been able to finish it, since he was no longer around and all of his so-called *'secrets'* vanished with him... right?" George reasoned. "Which brings me to an even greater inconsistency: Hiram was killed because he refused to reveal those secrets. And the reason he gave his attackers was that, before doing so, he first needed permission from the other two who also knew them: Solomon, and the King of Tyre. So why on earth did King Solomon tell everyone the secrets were lost? Who was lying, Hiram or the Jewish king? If Hiram was, it wouldn't bode so well for the image of the pious and honorable Master the rest of the story tries to paint. And what's up with them using a grip to raise a decomposing dead body, or applying whichever word they notice as a replacement? That's like telling someone who's lost his house keys that it's okay to use any other key he finds lying around. It simply won't work! Not only does this whole story appear silly and childish, but it sounds a lot as if they were practicing necromancy, if you ask me," George added heatedly.

Alex was still processing everything his friend said, unable to provide a response, when Makrides continued. Apparently, he still had a lot to say on the matter. "Whoever came up with this story didn't think it through very much. Either a separate Third Degree, which included commoner Master Masons, never existed—and Hiram lied again when he promised his assailants they could join one day—or it was highly exclusive, consisting of just himself and the two kings." George shook his head. "No, now that I think about it, I'm inclined to believe there *were* no other Third Degree Masons because if they existed there wouldn't be so much despair over Hiram's death. And furthermore, it makes me suspect that whatever was lost after his murder wasn't simply a meaningless word, or a grip. It must have been something else, much more substantial, and much more relevant. Even so, what puzzled me the most, during the ceremony, were the names of the murderers."

"But, the ritual never mentions any names," Alex objected, frowning.

"And that's exactly my point! The Worshipful Master didn't say the first attacker was called *Jubéla*, the second, *Jubélo*, or that the third—the one who delivered the fatal blow—was *Jubélum*. The American Lodges name them, and I find it strange the British ceremony doesn't."

"Maybe the Americans came up with those names. Or, perhaps the United Grand Lodge of England decided to leave them out because of how silly they sound," Alex suggested, with a chuckle.

"Possibly, but it certainly looks as if someone went to considerable trouble for those names not to be mentioned," George responded.

As he was saying that the waiter brought them their food, interrupting the conversation. And since one thing led to another, afterwards, they never had a chance to pick it up again.

On Thursday, three days later, Alex got a call from George asking him what his plans were for Saturday morning. "I plan on sleeping," was his reply.

George chuckled and persisted, "But, when you wake up, would you fancy a ride with me?"

"Where to?"

"I'll tell you then. Does half past ten sound okay?"

✝ ✝ ✝

Cyprus
January 18, 2014 CE

TRUE TO FORM, whereby the latter half of January usually provides the island with days of much milder weather, that Saturday was brilliant. With a brisk eighteen degrees Celsius, a light south-easterly breeze blowing, and without a cloud in the sky, it felt more like an early spring morning, rather than one deep in the heart of winter.

Alex's mood, however, was in direct contrast to the cheerful sunshine. When he stepped into the car, instead of a greeting, he merely grumbled, "This had better be worth it!"

George smiled. "Yes, good morning to you too," he said, and started driving. He'd been certain that with Maria out of his friend's life now, Alex would've stayed out late the previous evening, trolling the bars in search of female company. So, Makrides took the precaution of calling him up at ten, to wake him and make sure he got ready. Alex had not taken kindly to the disturbance.

But, after several minutes of silence, and a few generous swigs of coffee, from the thermos he'd brought along, Alex's grouchiness apparently started to fade away. Curiosity got the better of him, so he asked, "Where are we going, by the way?"

"To Khirokitia," George replied. He was glad to see his friend in better spirits.

"Why? What's in Khirokitia?"

"The only surviving structure from the time of the Knights Templar in Cyprus," Makrides said.

Alex frowned. The hangover, from the previous night's drinking binge, wasn't helping him concentrate. "Hold on! The Templars were in Cyprus?" he asked, bewildered.

"Yes, they were. In spite of what you hear in most documentaries, they *didn't* return to Europe en masse after the Holy Land was lost. They came *here* to set up their new headquarters. And one of their properties on the island was a fortified manor in Khirokitia. It was so prominent at the time, that the Templars were even detained there, when they all got arrested in 1308. That's where we're going."

"Don't tell me it still exists," Alex said enthusiastically.

"No, I'm sorry to say it doesn't. The only thing left of it is a solitary stone archway standing in a remote field."

"Then why go there?"

George looked over, saw the perplexed look on Alex's face, and realized he had to explain his reasons in full. "Okay, let me start from the beginning. When I first joined Freemasonry, I was very puzzled by its use of secret handshakes and passwords. So, I asked myself: *Why does an institution like this need such complicated ways of recognition?* And the only answers I could come up with were that either the Masons needed them for protection, or they'd been plotting something. Now, contrary to what many conspiracy theorists would have us believe, I'm sure a plot can be ruled out. Not only is the Brotherhood completely law-abiding—it's even written in the Constitutions that all Masons must respect the laws of every land—not only has something like this never been implied in the Lodge, but I very much doubt any of the members I know could ever plan, or execute, a fiendish conspiracy. And besides, over the three hundred years of its existence why hasn't anything happened yet? So, I became convinced a plot couldn't be the reason, leaving the need for protection as the only possible explanation…"

"And that's exactly what the official position is," Alex cut in suddenly. "The stonemasons needed those handshakes and passwords to protect them from impostors, when they went around Britain, and from project to project, in search of work."

"Ah… but, you see, I never bought that fairytale," George countered. "Soon after I became a Freemason, I found out that at no time did medieval England have a central stonemasons' guild. One, that is, which controlled all the workers. The guilds in existence were strictly local affairs, and they often disbanded after a project was finished. So how did the stonemasons come up with, and enforce, all the handshakes and passwords every one of them—miles apart from each other—was supposed to know by heart? It just doesn't make sense."

The car had already passed through the western outskirts of Larnaca and was now on the highway heading towards Limassol. To their left, high on a flat hill, were several giant wind turbines, their massive white blades tirelessly rotating to convert the soft breeze into electricity.

"However, when I started thinking that the Templars could have created Freemasonry," Makrides continued, "the use of handshakes and passwords, as a means for protection, began to make perfect sense. At first, of course, they would've needed them to protect themselves—they were outlaws, as you know, on the run. But, after all the original Templars eventually died out, those who followed—and who in time went on to become the Freemasons—probably had an extra, equally important, reason for continuing their use: they would now be protecting *something*, instead of also *some ones* anymore. And this object, or objects—whatever they are—must have been extremely worthwhile for them to take the time and effort to carry on. Maybe it even involved that fabled Templar treasure nobody's ever found. Therefore, the question now became: *Where did they hide it?* One thing which made me—"

"I realize this might be my hangover talking, but that's very flimsy reasoning, mate," Alex interrupted. "And besides, we've all heard the story claiming the Templar treasure was spirited out of France, in the nick of time, and shipped off to Scotland. It was in that movie, about a famous painter's code... what's his name?"

"Yes, yes, I know the one you mean, although that one had a different premise. However, there are other books, movies and documentaries which do claim it'd been transported to Robert the Bruce's Scotland, ended up in Rosslyn Chapel, etc, etc—the classic crap scenario," George scoffed. He took a moment to gather his thoughts. "Look, Alex, I'm aware my reasoning may be a bit weak. But, how else could you explain an ancient organization like this still hanging onto such strange handshakes and passwords in today's world—all the while insisting they're its only secrets—if it wasn't trying to protect something valuable?"

Alex shrugged his shoulders.

George had an energized expression on his face now. He kept alternating glances between the road and his friend. "And I'm not saying anyone knows what it is anymore. Over time, that knowledge must've drifted away from collective memory, leaving only the superficial explanations given today. Even modern Masons obviously don't understand why they have to apply those handshakes any longer. They, like so many generations of Freemasons before them, simply repeated everything verbatim. If they were aware of the reasons, they'd all be out treasure hunting by now. But those who followed in the Templars' footsteps, back then, most certainly had important incentives for keeping them in use. And as for the Knights Templar spiriting their valuables away from France, now *that's* a scenario I don't find plausible. As you know, their last Grand Master, Jacques de Molay, left *Cyprus* before he travelled to France, and was eventually arrested."

"I actually didn't know that," Alex replied with a grin.

"Well, he did. And he took nothing of significance with him. So what do you think is more likely: The Templars leaving all that was precious to them in France—where it might be at the mercy of the king and the pope, at any given moment? Or, secure it at their headquarters, where the bulk of their forces was stationed to keep an eye on it?"

"So you believe the Templar treasure may be in Cyprus?"

"Yes, I do. Just for the sake of argument, let's agree the Masonic rituals do contain clues about this treasure's hiding place. Okay?" George asked and looked over at Alex. He nodded. "Now, in all three Degrees there's no mention of any other location, except Jerusalem and nearby towns in the Holy Land. But, history tells us the Templars didn't abandon Jerusalem, or the Holy Land, all of a sudden. They were gradually forced out by the Muslims, over many years, and for sure they would've taken all their valuables away with them as they went. So this secret hiding place is certainly not in present-day Israel. One could then suggest that the next possible candidate for a site might be

Cyprus where their last headquarters was. On the other hand, someone else could challenge that, by saying such a suggestion has no basis. Fortunately, though, the Master Mason's ritual lends that notion considerable support with the Degree's Pass Word."

Alex frowned. "What... do you mean *Machaben* or *Machbinna*?" He turned to look at George.

"No, of course not—those are nonsensical words, which nobody even knows what they mean. To tell you the truth, the fact that the Third Degree requires *two* Words to define it just goes to show how irrelevant both of them are. No, I'm talking about the *Pass Word*. The one a candidate needs so he can gain entry into his Raising Ceremony. I mean: *Tubal-Cain*."

"He was supposed to be the world's first artificer in metals, so what?" Alex remarked, puzzled. "What's so revealing about his name?"

"Not so much his name as the first thing you just mentioned: about him being the earliest craftsman of metals. Which—and this is important—the Ritual claims in passing were brass and iron. But, if you remember what we were taught in school, it's a known fact the first metal mankind ever dabbled with was neither brass, nor iron: it was copper—which is *the* major component of brass, by the way. And do you know from where the ancient world got most of its copper?" George asked.

"I do," Alex exclaimed, excitedly. "It was from Cyprus. And it was so famous for this metal ore the island got named after it." He felt happy to finally be able to contribute.

"Very good," George congratulated him, but not in a condescending way. "Yes, it did come from Cyprus! And you probably also remember that the major Phoenician colony on the island was Kition—as Larnaca was known back then. Hiram's fellow Phoenicians must've shipped him a great deal of copper from here, so he could build those two famous pillars of his. That's why I believe *Tubal-Cain* supports the idea of Cyprus being the location where the treasure is hidden."

Alex chuckled. "And *I believe* you're grasping at straws."

"All right, let me defend my position," George said with a grin. He was feeling excited to be able to hammer out his deductions with someone. "Don't you find it strange that the Pass Word for entry into Freemasonry's most important ceremony is the name of a metalworker who had nothing to do with masonry? I mean, here we have an institution, which prides itself on originating from the stonemasons of old, and they just go and give up their top Pass Word to some other skill's founder? Doesn't that strike you as odd and yet revealing at the same time? They could have found some other name, or word, to choose from, but instead—"

"Okay, okay, you win!" Alex cut in, once more, but impatiently this time. "Say you've convinced me it does sound odd for them to do so. And let's also say *all* your theories hold water: that there *is* a treasure and that it's located in Cyprus. Just tell me already, do you know where the bloody thing is?"

"I'm glad you asked me that, because this is where it gets really interesting," George replied. He had a wide smile on his face now. "Remember when you suggested the names of the murderers—*Jubéla, Jubélo,* and *Jubélum*—which they still mention in American Lodges, could've been invented by the Americans?"

Alex rolled his eyes. *Here he goes again*, he thought, but eventually nodded.

"Well, they couldn't! Not those particular names, anyhow, because the common element in all three of them, *Jubé*, is an Old French word. And whereas the Templars had everything to do with Old French—it being their mother tongue and all—the Americans never had ties with that language. No, if our American brothers had come up with any names, I think it would've been something like, *Humpty, Dumpty,* and... *Stumpty...* or other equally ridiculous combinations," George said with a chuckle. "And do you know what *Jubé* means?"

"No, of course I don't," Alex sighed. He then added sarcastically, "But, I have a sneaking suspicion you're about to tell me."

"It means *rood screen*: the partition which separates a church's sanctuary in the east from its nave. You know the one I mean... It's the tall, wooden panel that has all the images of saints and Jesus in our Greek Orthodox churches. Don't you see?"

"All I see is that the straws you're trying to hold onto keep getting thinner and thinner."

"And I'd agree with you, if I hadn't been able to find supporting evidence," George stated in triumph. "Grab that printout from the back seat for me, will you?"

Alex turned around and picked up a solitary folded page that was lying there.

"Go ahead and read the lines I've highlighted—out loud," George asked him.

Complying with his friend's request, Alex started reading: *"Now I pray you take good heed... For this you must need to know... Then to church when you go... Upon the rood you look up then... In holy church left little words..."* He turned to face George, and asked, "What is this?" The expression on his face was bewilderment itself.

"These are excerpts from the Regius Poem, the oldest of all Freemason landmark documents. It was written at the end of the fourteenth century. And what's interesting is that no such document has ever been found to date prior to the Templars' destruction. That alone should make us take their involvement with the Masons more seriously. Anyway, I'm getting sidetracked... This Poem was written in Old English, but luckily I found a modern translation. Each line you've read is the first of a new paragraph, just after the Poem has finished going over the Seven Liberal Arts and Sciences..." Makrides paused and looked deep into his friend's eyes. "Remember those from the Fellow Craft Degree?"

"I do..." Alex replied, as if preoccupied, and remained

lost in thought for a long moment. When he next spoke, it was evident that all his skepticism had faded away. "This certainly throws a different light on your ideas. So, you think the treasure's in a church somewhere?"

"No, I don't believe the Templars would desecrate holy ground by burying anything inside one. Nonetheless, the rood of whichever church they chose could very well hold the next vital clue. It might tell us where to go from there," George said, with a hopeful smile.

"Yes, but which one? There must be hundreds, maybe thousands, of churches in Cyprus."

"I know. However, if we only consider those around at the time of the Templars the ones remaining are very few. And, fortunately—and not by coincidence—the place we're heading to has a great candidate. In fact, it's the main reason we are making this trip to Khirokitia after all," he finally revealed. "Not far from the manor's remains, is an ancient, Byzantine church called, *Panayia tou Kambou*, in Greek, or *Our Lady of the Field*. It's dedicated to the Virgin Mary and was probably built around the seventh century AD. So, this church was definitely there during the time the Templars used their manor. And as luck would have it, once again, it's in excellent condition."

Soon after, the car exited the highway and passed underneath it, through a tunnel, to the other side. The road now started to climb upward. Moments later the two friends saw a sign pointing toward Khirokitia's main attraction: its archaeological site. What modern Khirokitia is world-famous for isn't its links to Templar history, but rather for the discovery of a nearby Neolithic settlement. At about nine thousand years old, this prehistoric settlement—already a UNESCO World Heritage Site—is considered one of the earliest and best preserved in the world. But, neither of them was interested in archaeology at that point, so they passed it by.

The upwardly winding road, which hugged the village on the right, after a mile or so, brought them to another, albeit left-pointing, sign, which said: *'Panayia tou Kambou.'* Following it, they turned onto a narrow, downsloping side street, and soon arrived at a junction. George stopped the car. In front of them was a signpost with information on two opposing destinations. By taking the dirt road to the right they could reach the *'Royal House,'* or, by going left, the church. Makrides aimed the car right. And while he drove, George informed his friend about why the Templar ruins were now called *'Royal House.'*

"When the Templars were dissolved," he said, "all of their properties passed to the Hospitaller Order. This one did too. But, many years later the Hospitallers gifted the manor to a King of Cyprus and it became a royal piece of property—hence, the name. It remained in that capacity until the end of the sixteenth century when the Turks conquered Cyprus and finally demolished it."

As soon as he'd finished speaking, as if on cue, the remains of the manor appeared in front of them. George parked the car, and they both got out for a better look. When they did, though, a pair of mongrel dogs behind a tall metal gate ran up to it, bared their teeth and barked at them viciously. Being guardians of the fenced-in olive grove, just across the ruins, it seems they didn't take kindly to strangers. However, with a fence separating them from the mutts, the two friends ignored them and stepped closer. Even if they'd hoped to see more, though, it was evident that the only thing left of the once imposing manor was only a tall arch-shaped passageway, with remnants of thick walls on either side. Open at both ends, and about twenty feet deep, layers of ancient blocks had been expertly piled on top of each other in order to create the arched corridor. And right above the keystone where the inwardly curved walls met, a coating of white concrete was visible—probably set there in recent times, to protect the whole construction from collapse. But, the surrounding area was nothing but farmland, filled with just orange and olive trees, so other than that there wasn't much else to see. As a result, after

Makrides took a few pictures, they retraced their route and drove on to the church of *'Our Lady of the Field.'*

When they parked and got out, George exclaimed, "My goodness, they've fixed it all up! The photos I've seen were of it surrounded by gravel and overgrown weeds everywhere. I mean, I knew it was in good condition, but now, there's a stone pavement, courtyards on all sides, and even short, stylish walls here and there. It's as if this isn't the same church anymore. Somebody really took great care of it!"

Nonetheless, they could see that it was small. Constructed out of thick blocks of sandstone masonry and with a total length of only fifty feet it was more similar in size to that of a countryside chapel. George intuitively realized that the side they faced was its southern one, because to the right it ended up in a shorter semi dome, typical of where the sanctuary is always placed in the east. And at just about the middle of the structure, it was crowned with a circular, five-foot domed mound.

"Let's go in," Alex suggested, after they'd looked for a while.

Although there was a door on the south wall, it appeared shut from inside, so they made their way over to the west. The double doors there, under a prominent sandstone arch, were also closed, but fortunately the securing bolt had no padlock attached. George slid it back and pushed the door open. When they stepped in, the first thing that struck them was how even smaller that church's interior seemed. They were now standing in the narthex which served as a kind of entry hall. It was also small, barely twelve feet in depth, and opened into the nave via a wide stone arch. The two friends passed through and now stood at the nave's westernmost point. On either side of them, placed up against the walls, and facing east, were two pairs of standing pews: the special, tall-backed chairs, with folding seats and high armrests, found in all Greek Orthodox churches.

George took a couple of short steps forward and stopped in the center of the nave. At that moment he was overwhelmed by how incredibly calm and peaceful he felt; maybe more so than at any other time of his life. Perhaps it was the total silence, or the slight traces of sacramental incense he could smell, or possibly even the fact that the only light in there was what filtered through the western door—he wasn't quite sure. Nevertheless, after savoring that feeling for a second, Makrides decided to concentrate on what they'd come for, and which was right in front of him.

The iconostasis, in the east, was much smaller, and shorter, than any of the other rood screens he'd seen before, displaying only two large, byzantine-style images. The one on the left showed the Virgin Mary holding the Baby Jesus, and the one to the right portrayed an adult Christ, gesturing His blessing. In between them was a red velvet curtain, with a gold cross embroidered on it, purposefully drawn to conceal the sanctuary. On the very top, a single, horizontal beam connected two structural columns on the north and south walls. This timeworn piece of wood, which held the entire rood screen together, had barely visible carvings on it, of various shapes, all but faded by the relentless passage of time. However, the item to stimulate George's interest was the one just below that connecting beam, and directly above the entranceway to the sanctuary. It was a piece of old wood, almost a foot high and three feet wide, which still had tracings of the *fleur-de-lis* and other flowery designs that'd been carved on it.

That's a very odd and irregular piece to set above a sanctuary's entrance! Makrides wondered. So, when he stepped closer to get a better look, he saw it was an ancient-looking plank, with the original gold paint almost completely peeled off its carvings. But what he did next was something he would never, in future, be able to explain why: George began tapping on it. His fingers tapped lightly all over its surface, with no part sounding unusual, until he reached the bottom right corner. Then, it began to sound hollow.

Wait, a minute! Maybe there's... he started to think, but never got to complete the thought.

"Hey, come take a look at this!" Alex had cried out to him.

With everything that he'd been sensing, seeing, and thinking, Makrides had forgotten all about his friend. So, he turned around to see Alex over by the standing pews, next to the southern door, eagerly pointing at one of the armrests. He took the two steps necessary to get there, and bent over to see what the fuss was about. On the vertical edge of the wooden armrest was a crude, handmade engraving of a single eye and an eyebrow above it. George was astonished, and his expression expressed exactly that as he straightened up.

"All the armrests have them, front and back—I checked," Alex continued excitedly. "They're just like that 'All Seeing Eye' symbol we have in the Lodge!"

Makrides looked deep into his friend's eyes. "It's as if someone is trying to tell us we're in the correct place."

"I know, right?" Alex agreed, still appearing very excited.

They remained in that amazed state for a moment longer until George decided to speak. "Although this might be a happy coincidence, I think I've found something much more relevant. Come give me a hand."

They walked over to the rood screen, and Makrides told Alex about the hollow sound the *fleur-de-lis* board made at its bottom-right corner. "There could be something hidden inside. So, step into the sanctuary and push the plank out towards me."

"But it's probably screwed down," Alex objected, frowning.

"No, it isn't. It's just wedged in between that beam on the top and the curtain's wooden frame. Go ahead. See if you can loosen it out a bit. You're much stronger than me, anyway," George then told him, with an encouraging smile.

Alex rolled his eyes at that transparent attempt at flattery, nevertheless did as he was asked. He pulled back the velvet curtain and stepped into the sanctuary. At the moment he was about to place his hands on the back of *fleur-*

de-lis board to start pushing, though, they both heard the distinct sound of a car door closing outside.

"Quick, get out of there!" George whispered.

Alex rushed out and slid the curtain back into place. Then, they took a few swift steps, to an arch on the north side, and stood around casually, as if studying a faded wall painting of the Crucifixion there.

A few seconds later, an old man, with snowy-white hair and a matching, bushy mustache, walked into the church. In all probability a farmer by the way he was dressed, he bid them good morning in Greek and proceeded to light a candle in the narthex. After that, he stepped through to the nave, crossed himself twice, and headed over to the images of Jesus and the Virgin Mary to express his adoration by kissing them. With his religious duties properly taken care of, the old man then smiled and politely asked the two friends where they were from. George told him from Larnaca, and, to pre-empt any questions about what they were doing there, went on to remark that the church was in excellent condition now.

"Yes, it is," the man replied. "The Antiquities Department did some excavating here, a few years back, and fixed it all up when they finished." After saying that, he glanced around, as if to make sure nobody else could overhear, leaned in, and added in a conspiratorial whisper, "Some even say they found an old tunnel connecting the church to the ruins of the knights, over there." He was pointing north, to where the Templar manor used to be.

George could hardly contain his astonishment on hearing this, so he responded with, "Really?"

"Yes, indeed," the old man replied, while both sides of his bushy mustache lifted up in a wide smile. He seemed particularly happy to be able to share such privileged information.

"What else did they find?" Alex then asked.

"Oh... I don't know... the usual stuff, I guess," he said, putting an abrupt end to their questions. He started to look restless after that, so he told them, "Well, my cows won't milk themselves… I'd better be off. It was nice meeting you boys."

He wished them a good day and left in a hurry.

"It's just one thing after another today!" George stated in an amazed tone, expressing his thoughts out loud.

Alex looked at him closely. "Do you suppose what he said is true?"

"No, I don't think so," Makrides replied with conviction, after a brief pause. "A discovery like that would be huge. It would've definitely made the news, and we'd have heard about it by now. He was probably just trying to sound important. Or maybe this was something his granddads told him as a boy. You know how people in villages are. They're always making up stories."

They stood around, as if in a daze, for a few more seconds, before George snapped out of it and said, "Anyway, let's get back to it."

Walking over, Alex took up his position inside the sanctuary and began pushing the *fleur-de-lis* plank out, from behind, while Makrides grabbed onto its right edge and pulled towards himself. After a few strenuous moments of pulling and shoving, centuries-old dust flew about as the board's side started to emerge. And just when George thought he could see a gap on the plank's bottom surface, something fell down. He caught it in midair.

Alex stopped pushing and came alongside his friend. "What is that?" he asked.

George had turned west, so the light drifting in through the entrance could help him see. The object in his hands was a slender bronze-colored tube, about nine inches in length, and less than an inch in diameter. Both ends were sealed with wax.

"You were right! There was something here after all!" Alex exclaimed excitedly.

Makrides didn't respond. He calmly took out his car key and used it to start removing the wax from one end of the tube. The ancient, brittle substance fell to the church floor, and very soon the opening was clear. George peeked in the thin-walled container and saw there was something inside. Then, pointing the tube's open end down, a rolled up parchment started to appear. He pinched it carefully between thumb and forefinger and brought it out.

"Is that paper?" Alex asked.

"No, by the feel of it, I think it must be vellum. It's a much older, animal-skin material they used for writing in the Middle Ages," George replied. He then placed the brass tube on a nearby standing pew, kneeled, and unrolled the single-page parchment on the floor. It was about eight inches wide and more than a foot long. Alex also got down on his knees, to help keep the document open.

The top line on the page had this written on it:

Aes erectum spiritum gelidum sentit

The next two lines after that looked like this:

⌑⋅⌐ ⊐⟩∨ ⊔⊓⊓⌐⌐ ⌐⋅⌐⌐⊓⊓ ⊓⌐⊓⊐⟩⊂⊓⌐
∨⟩⊐⌐⊓⋅∇⊐⟩⊂⊓⌐ ⌐⌐∨⋅⌐⊏⊐⟩⊂⊓⌐ ⌐∨⌐

And everything else on that page—and about halfway through the other side—had the same incomprehensible symbols.

Alex's mouth was agape with astonishment. "What *is* that?" he asked, while staring into his friend's eyes.

"I guess the first line must be something in Latin," George replied, looking back down on it.

"No, I mean that gibberish script filling the rest of the page."

"I don't know, but I think I've seen these symbols before. Let me check," Makrides said, while taking his smartphone out of a side pocket.

"And I'll find out if that line is really Latin," Alex stated, also retrieving his mobile.

Fortunately, the reception in there was excellent, so the two of them spent the next few minutes surfing the Internet.

"You were right—again! It *is* Latin," Alex exclaimed, being the first to break the silence.

"Have you found out what it means?" George asked, looking up from his phone.

"The online translator says, and I quote, *'Bronze erected wind chill it feels.'*"

"What? That makes no sense." Makrides was thoroughly confused.

"How about you? Have you discovered what those strange shapes are?"

"Give me a minute," George replied, and once again began tapping and swiping on his phone's screen. It took him more than a minute, but eventually he looked up. "It's a substitution cipher, one which uses a symbol of a corresponding grid fragment instead of a letter. This particular cipher is called a Pigpen, also known as..." and he paused a second, for dramatic effect, smiling with excitement, "believe it or not, the *Masonic Cipher*. Apparently, the early Masons used something similar to send coded messages to each other. This website even has a diagram of the encryption key they used. See?" George turned the phone around so that his friend could look at the diagram.

A	B	C		J·	K	·L
D	E	F		M·	N	·O
G	H	I		P·	Q	·R

```
  \ S /     \ W /
   \ /       \ /
  T X U     X ⋇ Y
   / \       / \
  / V \     / Z \
```

"The site also says the Knights Templar used a variation of this," he added.

"Well, try it," Alex suggested. "Let's find out what those first two lines say."

Makrides nodded and took out a notepad and pen that

were always handy in his jacket. He passed them over to Alex to write. Then, he looked at each symbol on the parchment and called out its corresponding letter, according to the website's encryption key diagram.

"Now, that's just sad!" Alex stated, after a while, when all the letters had been jotted down.

"Why? What does it say?" George asked impatiently and turned around to look.

What Alex had written was this:

Njc dxs bqqj jhfqf hfppdxfhj stcdqsdxfhj jcsjedxfhj lwj

When Makrides saw it his jaw dropped, and when he looked into his friend's eyes they both started to laugh. "That's total gibberish... in any language!" George exclaimed between guffaws. "I mean... it's not even Chinese. What were these people thinking?"

It took them almost a minute to compose themselves.

"Obviously this isn't the right encryption key," Alex said after they'd stopped laughing and stood up.

"You think?" George responded, with no small trace of sarcasm. "Well, we can't stand around here to find the correct one," he continued. "Someone could step through that door at any moment and see us."

He'd already rolled up the parchment and was now about to put it back into the tube. Moving the container to and fro, to fit the scroll through the narrow opening, Makrides heard a slight but unmistakable sound: the clink metal makes when hitting upon metal. *Something else must also be in there,* he thought. So, George set the vellum document down and aimed the tube's open end to the floor, over his cupped hand. He wiggled the brass cylinder back and forth again, and a couple of seconds later something rattled inside before a ring fell into George's palm.

Alex witnessed the entire incident amazed. "Will wonders never cease today?" he asked. "What is that?"

George turned the object around, bringing it close to his friend. "It appears to be an ancient silver ring with a Star of David engraved on the top."

"I don't believe it. We *have* found treasure. Who do you think it belonged to?" Alex was still very much excited.

"I know as much as you do, my friend," Makrides replied. "And unless we crack this code, we won't find out any more." He slipped the ring into the container and fitted the vellum parchment in as well. Then, he placed the tube into his jacket pocket.

Makrides stepped over to the sanctuary entrance. Before pushing the *fleur-de-lis* board back into place, he looked up at the cavity on its base to make sure there was nothing else inside he hadn't noticed. There wasn't—the gap's carved shape matched that of the brass tube perfectly. And when Alex also helped with returning the wooden plank to its previous position, it was as if it had never been disturbed.

"We've probably broken a bunch of laws by coming in here and finding this," George said, while tapping the side of his coat where the tube was tucked in. "So, we'll have to agree to tell no one."

"None except Joanna, you mean."

"No, this time not even she should know. This must be *our* secret. Okay?"

Although Alex seemed a bit reluctant he nodded. They were walking toward the open door in the west, when he remarked, "I'm still disappointed about the encryption key not working. But what I find totally puzzling is that first phrase written in Latin."

"Yes, it is baffling," George agreed. They had just stepped out of the church, and he was busy pulling the door shut and sliding its bolt back into place. "I suspect it must be very important, though. Someone put in considerable effort, and took a lot of time, to write that document in code—not to mention carving that cavity under the *fleur-de-lis* board. So, what the Latin phrase is trying to say just might be the key which will allow us to read the rest of the parchment. In addition, that is, to also finding out whom the ring belonged to, and what its role is in all of this."

Nevertheless, before unlocking the car doors, to get in and drive off, Makrides had one last thought to share. "And I have another sneaking suspicion that the answer, like so many others, is in the Masonic rituals… somewhere."

Alex was feeling excited. "Even if we can't crack this code, we can still sell the ring and the parchment. We're going to be rich!"

MASONS

Chapter 14

GUNPOWDER

London, England
March 1604 CE

Henry tapped on the door twice before entering the study room. He was well aware his master disliked being disturbed while working, and the lateness of the hour would certainly not help. Still, he had a duty to perform.

"There is a gentleman wishing to see you, Sir Francis," the valet announced.

Sir Francis Bacon looked up from what he'd been writing. "At this time of night?" he exclaimed, visibly vexed. But, after letting out a sigh, he enquired in a calmer tone, "Has he at least stated his business, or his name?"

"Neither. He claims the reason for his visit is of a private nature, Sir Francis, to be disclosed only to you."

Bacon sighed again, resigning himself to the fact that he would not be able to continue his work. "You had best show the gentleman in, then."

Henry bowed to his employer before leaving while Francis stood up from the desk and stepped over to the blazing fireplace. On arrival, he turned around to greet his unexpected visitor from there.

At forty-three years of age, Sir Francis Bacon was not what one might call an impressive man. The sum of his facial features, which in youth may have been pleasing, if not handsome, had a rather blubbery quality about them now. He had high, rosy and fleshy cheeks, a bulbous nose, a double chin concealed beneath a thick ruff, plus a fashionable, auburn moustache with a matching pointed beard. Nor was his height anything exceptional either; at five feet four, he was a man of average stature. His sole redeeming feature, however, was the singular sparkle his eyes emitted: although dark in hue they had an unusual brilliance.

But when Henry next opened the door, the one who followed him in was a man who truly *did* impress. Standing at six feet tall, thanks to a powerful, athletic frame, he was also strikingly handsome, bearing a well-trimmed moustache and pointy beard to good effect. His dress was what one would expect from a gentleman of those times, as well, consisting of a dark-colored silk doublet, a large trunk-hose swelling out at the hips, and high brown boots. In addition, he had a starched ruff around his throat, and a short cloak of red fabric thrown over his doublet.

This gentleman was not bashful either. For as soon as he was admitted into the room, instead of bowing to his host, he walked over, extending a hand. "Your servant, Sir Francis. The name is Robert Catesby. I do apologize for the lateness of the hour."

Bacon took Catesby's hand into his own, and at once felt a familiar pressure being applied to his first knuckle by the visitor's thumb. Instinctively, he returned the pressure, and nodded to Henry that he was excused. When the valet closed the door behind him, Francis invited Catesby with a gesture to take an armchair by the fire. He sat in the one across from him.

"Once again, I am truly sorry for troubling you so late, Sir Francis," Catesby said. And after leaning in, he added with meaning, "Or, should I rather say... Grand Master."

Bacon had correctly deduced his visitor's identity from

their handshake, but resolved not to show he'd been surprised by that last comment. "How long have you been a member of our Society, Brother Robert?" he asked in a calm tone.

"I was initiated nine months ago. However, I was informed you are our Grand Master only tonight."

"May I inquire as to who made this information available to you?"

"My cousin, and fellow Society member, Francis Tresham," Catesby replied with a smile. "He has been a Fellow Craft for two years now."

Bacon's external features betrayed no emotion. But, in reality he was quite unsettled. The fact that an Entered Apprentice could so easily find out he was the Secret Society's Grand Master was a serious breach in security. Still, he decided to delay chastising anyone for the time being; Catesby had yet to reveal his intentions. "And now you know I am the Grand Master, what is it you require from me?" he asked.

Catesby took a deep breath. "Would you not agree, Sir Francis, that a man's faith constitutes one of the most important elements in his life?"

"I would," Bacon replied with a nod. "In fact, I find it equals in importance to serving one's country, as well as in seeking the truth."

"Then, would you not also agree that all men should be freely allowed to worship the Almighty as their particular faith prescribes?"

"I would... in a perfect world," he responded, but with less resolve now. He frowned. "What are you trying to tell me, Brother Robert?"

"I am a Catholic, Sir Francis!" Catesby blurted out. "And for the past seventy years, the people of my faith have been hunted down, persecuted and discriminated against relentlessly." The emotion which registered on his face was intense. Bacon did not respond, though, allowing his guest to continue. "When King James was to ascend the throne, we had high hopes that he at least would treat us with tolerance—him being the son of a Catholic martyr queen, that is. He even gave assurances, early on, that those were his intentions. But, he has deceived us, Sir Francis! Not only has he ordered every Catholic priest to abandon this land, not only has he reintroduced the heavy fines all unyielding Catholics must pay, but a few days ago, in Parliament, he spoke of peace being secured only if everyone subscribes to the true religion—*his*... *Reformed* religion."

Bacon's immediate thought was to be thankful his guest hadn't also been made aware of two additional snippets of information about him; or else the visit would have probably never happened. The first was that Bacon was an ardent Protestant, with a deep dislike of Catholics. And the second was that twenty years earlier he had openly urged, as a Member of Parliament, for King James's mother, Mary, Queen of Scots, to be executed.

"You make a passionate case, Master Catesby," Francis said, his expression and voice revealing no emotion yet again. "But what does the plight of Catholics have to do with me, or our Society?"

"Is not one of the Society's principle aims to provide aid to the downtrodden?"

"Yes it is, but only on an individual basis. Never on—"

"But if a Catholic uprising was to take place... for example in the Midlands, would our Society not rally to its aid?" Catesby cut in.

"No, it would not! That would constitute a violation. And, more importantly, it might risk revealing our existence—which is something we have strived so hard and for so long to keep a secret."

"Then, allow me to ask you this, Grand Master. How is it that the Society got involved, and even provided leadership, when the peasants revolted more than two hundred years ago? Were they in greater need of our support?"

It took whatever inner reserves Bacon had not to show he was taken aback by those questions. "The times were much different, as was also the situation which provoked that revolt. And in any case, it was decided upon reflection that our involvement was a mistake, never to be repeated," he replied calmly. But he could not prevent a frown from clouding his brow. "Are you contemplating something similar, sir? Because if you are, I must stress the perils you may be placing our Society in. Not to mention the sacred oaths you have taken to preserve the secrecy of its existence at all costs."

It took him a few seconds, but Catesby eventually flashed a brilliant smile. "Do not alarm yourself, Sir Francis. Although the nature of a disease often requires a sharp remedy, it was purely a hypothetical question. What I do mean to ask of you, however, is whether you might use your influence with the king to make him view the religious needs of Catholics in a more tolerant light."

Bacon had not been deceived by the sudden change in course. Still, he wasn't going to allow any lingering misapprehensions about this new direction as well. "His Majesty may have knighted me last year, but we are not friends, or even have any other sort of relationship to speak of. And I hardly think I'd be able to influence him on any issue, let alone on such important matters of state. So, I'm afraid I cannot be of any assistance to you on this front either."

While saying that Bacon stood up, indicating to his guest that their interview was over, and rang the bell to summon Henry. When the valet appeared both gentlemen bowed courteously to each other, and Catesby started walking toward the door. Before he stepped out, though, Francis added in a strict manner, "Remember what we talked about, sir. No rash actions." Catesby turned, bowed again, and walked out without saying a word.

When the study room door closed, Bacon went over to sit at his desk. The conversation had unnerved him. He spent a few minutes in deep contemplation and then began scribbling something. He rang the bell, and when Henry reappeared, he gave him a note. "Take this to Lord Monteagle's manor in Hoxton. See to it that it's delivered to His Lordship's hand alone."

✢ ✢ ✢

London, England
October 24, 1605 CE

"Are you certain you want to do this, Francis?" Dr Richard Foster asked. "It will not be straightforward, you know. Many will object and just go on using them all the same."

"I realize that," Bacon replied with a sigh. "Yet, I feel we must. I've never agreed with the notion of having clues in our ceremony's wording. If the names of the murderers remain in the ritual as they are, someone might eventually put two and two together. And if the crypt is discovered one day and its most precious item is handed over to the pope, then his claim of being Christianity's only true spokesman may be strengthened considerably. Neither of us would want such an outcome."

They were sitting in Bacon's study room, after supper, discussing changes he was thinking of making to the Society's rituals. In those times it was still the prerogative of whomever the Grand Master was to personally decide on such issues; no collective decision by the Grand Council was necessary.

Before responding, Foster took a long drag on his pipe, and turning his head upward he blew out a steady stream of smoke. "Yes, of course. But even *we* are not aware of where it is exactly. All we know is that it's in Ottoman occupied Cyprus… somewhere. So, I do not believe somebody would be able to retrieve it anytime soon."

"That is as may be—for now," Francis said, after taking a sip of sherry from his glass. "But any clues left guiding the way to its hiding place might unravel everything in future. If someone were to discern that a rood in some church on the island contains directions, then that person could very well find them."

"Do you not think the transposing of the two columns will be enough to confuse this future would-be sleuth?"

"One can only hope. It is odd, yet when the last Templars founded our Society they set the Lodge's endpoint in the *east*. As you know, they were still preoccupied with returning to the east back then; with recapturing Jerusalem. They therefore placed the entrance of the Lodge in the west, and the Holy of Holies, along with the Master's seat, in the east, in order to give that cardinal point added importance. However, it is the exact opposite orientation from that of the actual Temple of Solomon—the very Temple they were supposedly recreating."

"You are correct. I *do* know all this," the doctor responded with a chuckle. He knitted his brow after that. "Are you suggesting the Lodges should switch the positions of the columns then?"

"No, it would create too much confusion at the moment, on top of everything else. I was merely reflecting upon what the Templars did aloud." He took another drop of wine, and Bacon's eyes lit up, in a flash of inspiration. "What might do the trick, though, now that I think of it, could be this: to refer to the columns according to the position of each, as one looked at Solomon's Temple from outside—exactly as it is described in the Bible." Bacon paused for a few seconds, allowing it to sink in. He smiled. "Yes, that should muddle the final clue sufficiently enough. Perhaps, in time, it might even cause so much uncertainty that the pillars' positioning, or size, won't remain as standardized as they are today."

Foster was still nodding his agreement, when Bacon added lightheartedly, yet decisively, "Grand Secretary of mine, it is my wish that you inform our Lodge Masters, and all Past Masters, on two decisions I have just reached. The first is that they should remove those ridiculous names from the Master's Installation Ritual. Henceforth, Hiram's murderers shall be referred to only by way of numerals; for example, ruffian number one, or villain number two.

Second, when they refer to the Temple's columns no cardinal points will be mentioned anymore, but rather by which was on the left and which on the right. Consequently, *Boaz* shall in future be referred to as the *left* column and *Jachin* as the one on the *right*."

The doctor, who was also the Grand Council's Secretary, was now grinning. "I shall, Grand Master. You will have no quarrel from me."

Bacon smiled contently. "I am so glad we are in agreement. Our ancestors would feel very happy if they could see us now, cooperating in such harmony."

This last comment was based on the fact that both men *did* share a common ancestry. Back in the end of the fourteenth century, the Grand Master at the time, Anthony Norridge, had made a historic decision: someone as irresponsible as Wat Tyler would never again be allowed to determine the Society's fate. To that end, he needed men who shared his knowledge and values, and who could steer the Society into the future as he would have himself. In short, he needed men of Phoenician origins. So, after getting in touch with a number of such families in Tyre, most of which were his relatives, he chartered a ship to bring them all to England. The ship's captain—who was a member of the Brotherhood—in addition to saving those people from a life of deprivation under a ruthless Ottoman rule, also performed another valuable service for Norridge during that voyage. A task few knew about, at the time, but which was at the center of what the two Free-Masons were discussing.

Those Tyrian families, armed with the qualities which had proved so successful for their ancient ancestors, began to thrive in the freer and more fertile environment England provided. Though they kept in touch with each other, they inevitably intermarried with the local population. But this, in turn, only served to strengthen the duty each parent of Phoenician descent felt about secretly educating the next generation on its unique heritage. Sir Francis Bacon, on his mother's side, and Dr Richard Foster were descended from two of those families. So, they were both well aware of all these facts when they were elected for their respective fifteen-year terms at the Society's Grand Council elections of 1602 AD. In truth, they and a handful of other Phoenician descendants were the only ones left who knew anything about the Society's Templar origins.

Foster took another puff from his pipe. "Now that you mention the last Templars, perhaps we should also discuss eliminating the part of the First Degree initiation which alludes to them."

"What part do you mean?"

"That which the candidate is asked how much he can contribute to his new Brotherhood, only to remember he has left all his money behind in the Chamber of Reflection. One could easily connect it with the vows of individual poverty the original Templars took."

"Someone perceptive enough could indeed," Bacon agreed. "However, the way it is worded does not make direct reference to them, but rather serves in introducing the candidate to the solidarity members should display to one another. Then, in turn, it provides an opening for the Lodge Master to list all the ways our Society offers aid to the downtrodden. No, I do not think—"

His words were interrupted by a knock on the door, and by the valet entering the room. "Pardon me, Sir Francis, but Lord Monteagle is here to see you. He says it is urgent."

"Show him in, Henry."

They both rose from their seats, but when Monteagle walked through the door, he stopped in his tracks as soon as he noticed Foster. "I do beg your pardon, Sir Francis. I expected you to be alone at such an hour."

"That is quite all right, My Lord. Pray come in," Bacon encouraged him. He then made the introductions. "Dr Richard Foster, former President of the College of Physicians, may I present His Lordship William Parker, 13th Baron Morley and 4th Baron Monteagle."

The two gentlemen bowed courteously to each other,

after which Francis asked his new guest, "May I offer you some refreshment? We are having sherry if you would care to join us."

The baron nodded as did Bacon to Henry for an extra glass. When the valet produced it and left, Francis poured the wine, eyeing the young nobleman closely as he sat down. Not yet thirty years of age, Monteagle's attire was fashionable, with a thin ruff surrounding his throat, upon which a pointy ginger beard rested. But his large owlish eyes betrayed he was in a state of agitation.

"My man informs me Your Lordship's reason for calling is urgent?" Bacon asked in a calm tone, handing him the glass.

"Yes. It has to do with something you requested from me about a year and a half ago," Monteagle said before proceeding to gulp down the entire contents of his glass. Then, after a fleeting glance at Foster, he added, "Perhaps it would be best if we talked privately on the morrow though."

A few seconds passed before Bacon was able to remember. And after smiling with realization, he reassured his guest, "You may speak freely in front of the good doctor, My Lord. He is one of us. In fact, he is our Grand Secretary. I have no secrets from him."

Monteagle turned to face Foster. "I do beg your pardon, Brother Richard. I had no idea."

The doctor shook his head as if to say it was an honest mistake. But, Bacon was becoming impatient. "What is it about this affair that makes your visit so urgent, My Lord?"

The baron eyed his glass. It was empty. So, in order to fortify him to start talking, Francis refilled it.

"Last year, when you informed me of your conversation with Robert Catesby," Monteagle began, "I thought nothing of it. Nevertheless, I did keep an eye out on his cousin, as per your instructions. And nothing occurred—nothing, until today, that is. This afternoon, that said cousin, Francis Tresham, who also happens to be my brother-in-law, paid me a visit in Hoxton. And what he revealed was very—"

"A thousand apologies, My Lord," Foster cut in, "but did you say Francis Tresham?"

"Yes, I did. Do you know him?"

"I do. He is a patient of mine, and also a member of my Lodge. As is this man, Catesby, you mention, as well." The doctor frowned and looked inquiringly over at Bacon.

"I neglected to inform you on purpose, Richard, because, as Brother William has just stated, I also thought nothing much of it at the time. Catesby might have been letting out steam by what he told me. Nonetheless, in view of the fact that His Lordship here is Tresham's brother-in-law as well, I decided to let him know so he could monitor the situation. Apparently, I was correct. Pray continue, My Lord."

Foster nodded, seemingly satisfied by the explanation, and they both turned to face Monteagle.

The nobleman took a deep breath. "The purpose of Tresham's visit was to caution me not to attend the upcoming opening of Parliament on the 5th of November. When I asked him why I should do so, he was evasive and simply proceeded to list all the ways with which I could excuse myself from attendance. I persisted, however, only for him to blurt out that if I did, I would die. Though stunned, my next obvious question was to enquire as to why anyone would want to kill *me*, specifically, for attending the House of Lords. His reply was that I would not be the only one. The king, the queen, their children, all the bishops and lords... everyone would perish that day. Even you, Sir Francis, I daresay."

His audience was so stunned that both their mouths were agape. It took Bacon a few seconds to regain his composure. Finally, he was able to ask, "And how will this be achieved?"

"It seems Catesby has not been idle since meeting you, Grand Master. He has enlisted eleven other, likeminded Catholic fanatics, who are ruthless enough to do anything for their beliefs. One of those, a former mercenary by the name of Guy Fawkes, is an explosives expert. Together with

Catesby they hatched a plan to blow up the House of Lords, by placing kegs full of gunpowder in a cellar beneath it. After leasing that undercroft, thirty-six barrels have been stockpiled there so far. When the session of Parliament begins, the plan is for the fuse to be lit, blowing everyone up to kingdom come."

Monteagle needed a fortifying sip of sherry before continuing. "Tresham is the last conspirator to be recruited, so far. Apparently, Catesby feared that if his cousin were implicated you might find out, Sir Francis, and he wanted to avoid that at all costs. However, the group was by then in desperate need of funds, in order to fulfill their plan, so Catesby was forced to consider bringing Tresham into the fold. But when he was apprised of the entire scheme, he was appalled. Francis Tresham is a Catholic, as am I, but neither of us would ever condone such despicable actions. He spent the next ten days racked by guilt. Nevertheless, after much reflection, he decided he could not suffer such a fate for me, hence he told me everything."

Bacon was shaking his head in disbelief. "But the realm would be left leaderless after that, plunged into anarchy. What does Catesby ultimately want to achieve by committing such a heinous act?"

"It seems his fundamental aim is to reinstate Catholicism as the premier religion in England. If everything goes according to plan in London—and the king, with all his lords, are dead—they will then orchestrate a Catholic uprising in the Midlands. The plotters will use this unrest to kidnap Princess Elizabeth, from Coombe Abbey, and as she is third in line to the throne, she will be installed as their puppet queen. I am certain the princess is ignorant of these intentions, but they will use her all the same." Monteagle looked deep into Bacon's eyes after saying this, and asked, "What do you suppose we should do now, Sir Francis? Shall we notify the authorities?"

Bacon looked down. "Something must be done, that is for sure. I just do not know exactly what... yet. I need some time to think." Then, as if newly energized, he looked up and told Monteagle, "I thank you for bringing this to my attention, Brother William. You must go back home now, and I shall inform you on the morrow about what is to be done. In the meantime, speak of this with no one!"

The baron rose from his seat, as did Bacon with Foster, and after bowing politely to them he left.

"This almost defies belief!" the doctor exclaimed, after they resumed their seats.

"Yes, it does," Bacon agreed. Then in a sudden fit of rage, he slammed his palm down on the chair's armrest. "But, I will be damned if those papist bastards are allowed to take over the realm again!" After a moment, he was able to calm himself and added in a cooler, yet more sinister, tone, "They still have not paid for what they did to the Templars."

"What are you thinking?"

"As I have said, I do not know. But for sure, we must help crush this Catholic plot—just like our predecessors did for the Lincolnshire Rising and the Pilgrimage of Grace, seventy years ago."

+ + +

London, England
October 26, 1605 CE

LORD MONTEAGLE WAS supping alone that evening, since his wife, Elizabeth, was away visiting her mother in Northampton. He had just swallowed the last of the almond cake, washing it down with raspberry wine, when his servant, Thomas Ward, hurriedly entered the dining room.

"My Lord, I was on my way back, after purchasing that ale you sent me for, when a stranger approached me on the street. He handed me this letter and brazenly demanded I give it to you. But, before I could ask him how he knew me, or anything else, he disappeared into the shadows."

Thomas was breathless, holding up a folded piece of paper in his hand.

Monteagle said nothing, merely extended his own so that Ward would give him the letter. He broke the unmarked seal and surveyed its contents.

"It is unsigned," the baron remarked. Then, looking down at it again, he started shaking his head. "I cannot make out this scribble, Thomas. You do it for me. Read it aloud, would you?"

He handed the piece of paper back to his servant, and Ward began reading the letter's contents, albeit with some difficulty:

"My Lord, out of the love I bear to some of your friends, I have a care of your preservation. Therefore, I would advise you, as you value your life, to devise some excuse to shift of your attendance at this Parliament; for God and man hath concurred to punish the wickedness of this time. And think not slightly of this warning, but retire yourself into your county where you may expect the event in safety. For though there be no appearance of any stir, yet I say they shall receive a terrible blow this Parliament; and yet they shall not see who hurts them. This counsel is not to be condemned because it may do you good and can do you no harm; for the danger is passed as soon as you have burnt this letter. And I hope God will give you the grace to make good use of it, to whose holy protection I commend you."

"What is this?" Monteagle exclaimed, after Thomas finished reading. "Some sort of foolery to stop me from attending parliament, as is my duty?"

Ward offered no reply though appeared to be visibly shaken by what he had just read. His master was lost in thought, and after a long moment passed he looked up, deep into Thomas's eyes. "It might be a threat, however. And if so, I must act without delay."

Monteagle stood up from the table and ordered his

servant, "Make sure my carriage is readied, Thomas. I shall ride to Whitehall immediately to warn the Earl of Salisbury. The hour may be late, but as Secretary of State, His Lordship, Robert Cecil, will know what to do."

Ward bowed and rushed off to carry out his master's command. Monteagle smiled. *This is going exactly as planned.*

The previous day he had met with Bacon.

"I've given a lot of thought to this quandary we find ourselves in," Sir Francis had said, "and believe to have found the solution."

The baron nodded in anticipation, and Bacon began to unfold his plan. "Tomorrow evening, before supper, send a servant of yours out on some errand. Before he returns, I shall have someone unfamiliar intercept and give him a letter for you. When he delivers it, pretend you cannot make out the handwriting and ask him to read it out loud. This last part is very important since you will need someone to corroborate it was not you who wrote the note in the first place."

Monteagle frowned. "What will this letter contain?"

"I do not want to spoil the authenticity of your reaction by revealing its contents now, My Lord. However, suffice it to say it will be a vague warning, cautioning you not to attend the opening session of Parliament. I shall arrange for my valet, Henry, to write it. That way no one can recognize the handwriting."

"Do you trust him?"

"I do, explicitly."

A frown appeared on the baron's brow once again. "The problem is that my only manservant who can read properly is Thomas Ward."

"I know him. Why is that a problem?"

"His family has strong ties with John and Christopher Wright, both of whom are involved in the conspiracy. He might inform them I've received a warning."

"So much the better," Bacon remarked with a smile.

"This might make them give up their dreadful plan altogether. Yet, the letter will be so vaguely written that I feel it will not be enough to deter them—given their level of fanaticism. In any case, as of tomorrow, the undercroft shall be under surveillance."

Monteagle nodded, encouraging Francis to continue. "After Ward has read you the letter, you must ride to Whitehall at once and hand it over to my cousin, Robert Cecil, the Earl of Salisbury. Now, knowing Cecil, he will try to discredit its importance, as it did not come to him from one of his spies. But you must put the fear of God in him, Brother William. Describe what would happen if a conspiracy *was* to be uncovered, and the king found out he knew about it and said nothing. That should rattle him up nicely. Tell him, as well, that this might provide a nice opportunity for His Majesty to demonstrate his intellect by solving the puzzle the letter will pose, *after* he returns to London from his hunt. Imply, also, that having the king do so would be to Cecil's advantage. However, until His Majesty returns, caution Cecil to do nothing—except from allowing the plot to ripen, so to speak. It is always best to catch a culprit in the act rather than to have him abandon it beforehand."

"But how will they find the explosives?"

"His Majesty's own father was murdered after an explosion rocked his house in Scotland. So, the king will be quite sensitive to certain words in the text alluding to a detonation, and it should not take long before he realizes what the threat really is. If, however, they are not able to find their way to the undercroft, *you* can guide them there by taking part in the search parties they set up. Insist to Cecil that he includes you."

"Pardon me for questioning your plan, Sir Francis, but why send the letter to me? Would it not be better if *you* were involved? I mean, the earl is your cousin after all. If you were to deliver it to him, would that not lend the matter more credence?"

Bacon had been prepared for that question. Nevertheless, he looked down. "I fear the fact that I am Cecil's cousin will not make me appear as a reliable source in his eyes. For reasons I shall not go into now, the truth is he does not like me very much—nor I him, for that matter. Which is all the better, since I dare not get involved directly in such a high profile case, as this might turn out to be. Especially not now that I am Grand Master; it could create all sorts of undesirable repercussions." He then looked up and added, "If, however, this information were to originate from someone who is a Catholic himself it would seem far more reliable. Do you not agree?"

The baron nodded, albeit a bit reluctantly, and Bacon added, "Many events will be put into motion after tomorrow, which makes me think we should avoid meeting again until all the dust has settled." But sensing Monteagle's continued unease, his expression mellowed somewhat. "A great deal depends on you, My Lord. In fact, I would even go as far to say that our very realm, as we know it, relies on you to play your part correctly. So, be extremely careful."

That evening of October 26, 1605, Lord Monteagle's carriage rode out into the dark streets of London. He was on his way to meet with Robert Cecil… and history.

✝ ✝ ✝

BELIEVING THE PLOT was still intact, even after hearing about Monteagle's letter, Catesby and two of his co-conspirators left the capital on November 4. Their task was to set the Midlands' uprising into motion, after all the heads of state would be blown away by the explosion. But, around midnight of that same day, Guy Fawkes was discovered in the undercroft beneath Parliament, guarding 36 barrels of gunpowder.

On the morning of the 5th of November, London was abuzz with rumors of the failed conspiracy. So, fearing for their lives, most of the other plotters abandoned the city in a hurry.

After many attempts to get support for an uprising resulted in failure, Catesby and his men made a last stand at Holbeche House, in Staffordshire, on November 8. In the battle with the local sheriff and militia which ensued, four of the conspirators were killed, including the ringleader himself.

The next day, Guy Fawkes finally yielded to the excruciating torture he'd been subjected to on the rack up to then. He made a full confession, revealing all the plot's details, as well as the identities of everyone involved.

By the end of the following week, Tresham and the seven other surviving members of the Gunpowder Plot were arrested and taken to the Tower of London. They were to await torture, trial, and certain execution.

✚ ✚ ✚

London, England
December 23, 1605 CE

IT WAS MID-AFTERNOON when the valet announced, "Dr Foster to see you, Sir Francis." He held the door open for the doctor to step in.

Bacon looked up from his desk. "Thank you, Henry. Would you be so kind as to warm up some mulled wine for us?"

Anticipating the return of Bacon's servant, Foster did not address the issue he had come to discuss. Instead, he walked over to the armchair by the fire, sat down, and remarked, "I finished reading your book, *The Proficiency and Advancement of Learning*."

"What did you think of it?"

"I believe it is a solid treatise. And one which will help bolster natural philosophy in the years to come. But, I must say I was quite surprised to find so many positive references to Solomon in it."

"Yes." Bacon smiled. "Well, contrary to us, who know what his nature was truly like, he *is* considered the embodiment of wisdom by the Bible. Therefore, I had no choice but to include him." He rose from his desk and made his way over to sit in the armchair opposite the doctor. "I even plan on using his name, albeit slightly changed to Salomon, in a new book I began dabbling with not long ago. A work of fiction, this time."

"What will you call this new book?"

"I still have a long way to go, but I've thought of naming it *New Atlantis*. I doubt though if I will publish it while still alive. It would probably be best if this appeared posthumously."

"How so?"

"Because I plan to elaborate on a few of the issues our Society strives for. Issues such as, the worldwide abolition of slavery, the separation of church and state, freedom of expression... subjects which are still very contentious. So, I would not want to bring any unwanted attention to myself, or the Society, during my lifetime."

As he was saying that, Henry opened the door. He was carrying a tray with two beakers of mulled wine on it. After placing them on a table next to his master he left. Bacon handed one over to the doctor. And while he blew softly on the contents of his own, steaming, beaker, he looked over at Foster and asked, "Is it done?"

"Yes. Tresham died at noon." The doctor's head hung low.

"Thank you, Richard. I know how hard it must have been for you."

Foster sighed. "It is not easy taking someone's life when you have dedicated your own to keeping your patients alive and healthy. Still, I understand the necessity. If Tresham had been subjected to the rack, there is no telling what he might have revealed about the Brotherhood."

"How did you leave matters?"

"My diagnosis was that he died of strangury, an inflammation of the urinary tract—something I had been treating him for quite some time. But with Tresham being a traitor, I very much doubt the crown will put any effort into trying to uncover I'd actually poisoned him. So there should be no problems with that. However, this morning, right before he passed away, we had a moment alone together. In a rare flash of lucidity, Tresham told me that Catesby's sole motive for joining the Society was to gain support for his plot. He also expressed how sorry he was he had ever proposed him for membership."

"I never doubted his motive was other than that—something which, unfortunately, reflects poorly on our recruiting methods. We shall have to look into those."

Foster frowned. "Now that you mention Catesby, how was *his* death arranged? You never told me."

Bacon took a sip of mulled wine from his beaker. "When I heard the Sheriff of Worcestershire was in hot pursuit of the plotters, I sent an urgent, coded message to John Streete. He is a member of ours up in Worcester and also an excellent marksman. I urged him to join the posse as an interested party and stressed how important it was for the Brotherhood Robert Catesby should *not* be taken into custody. And Streete did his duty admirably. It is rumored he brought down Catesby, plus another conspirator, at Holbeche House, with a single bullet."

The doctor's eyebrows shot straight up. "Unbelievable," he remarked, while shaking his head. However, Foster then remembered the final part of his conversation with Tresham and turned to face Bacon. "He was near the end, beginning to speak incoherently, when Francis mumbled—as if to himself—about how baffled he still was that Monteagle had received a letter of warning. This reminded me of something I've been meaning to ask you all along. Did you not fear Catesby might confront Tresham about the letter, and that Tresham might reveal he'd already warned Monteagle in person?"

"No. Tresham would be too afraid to confess he had betrayed the plot, just so he could save a relative of his—in any form or manner. Indeed, I was relying on his genuine look of surprise when Catesby inevitably confronted him about the letter's existence. And given it would seem so incomprehensible to him, Tresham would have no problem convincing Catesby he was not the author; which, as it appears, he did. So there was never any danger in my mind of anyone realizing that Monteagle knew of the plot *before* he also received a letter warning him of it. Anyone other than Tresham that is. And this is another reason why it was necessary to silence him forever."

Both refrained from speaking, for a long moment, sipping their beverages in silent reflection. After a while Bacon looked up. "I feel our Society has had a narrow escape with this whole business. If Catesby and Tresham were tortured—especially Catesby—there is no telling what they might have revealed. And all my efforts of keeping the Brotherhood away from Cecil's attention would have been for naught."

The doctor glanced at his friend with fondness. "You handled this difficult situation admirably, Francis. In fact, I would even go on to say that what you did has saved the entire realm. Yet, no one will ever thank you for it."

"I was not fishing for compliments, Richard, merely speculating on how dangerous it would've been if Catesby and Tresham had talked. We should have taken precautions beforehand."

"What sort of precautions?"

Bacon did not reply. Instead, he seemed to be lost in thought for a while. Then, as if an epiphany struck him, he exclaimed, "I think we must also consider using the various stonemasons' guilds as Lodges, from now on."

Foster knit his brow, indicating he did not follow, so Sir Francis elaborated. "I shall propose to the Grand Council that all members of the Brotherhood, especially the high profile ones, must join the stonemasons as well. By doing so, if anyone of us is arrested in future, he can confess to *that* membership instead of the Society's."

"I think it is a capital idea." The doctor looked pleased. "With the stonemason guilds being in such decline now, they will for certain welcome gentlemen as members and patrons. I shall second the motion."

✛ ✛ ✛

LATE IN JANUARY 1606 AD, the trial of Guy Fawkes and the seven other surviving conspirators began, on charges of high treason. And since there was never any doubt as to what the final result would be, they were found guilty as charged. A few days later, they were all hanged, drawn and quartered.

Fawkes may have failed to blow up Parliament, as he so desperately desired, nonetheless his name and fame—or rather, infamy—lived on. The first lasting outcome he would bequeath to popular culture was his very own name. Today, when someone refers to any adult man the colloquial idiom of *'guy'* is widely used; while in a similar vein all those in a modern group of people (irrespective of gender) are collectively referred to as... *'guys.'* And the second enduring result Fawkes left behind arose the same month as his death, when the English Parliament passed the *'Observance of 5th November 1605'* Act. Also known as the *'Thanksgiving Act,'* it established an annual celebration for the deliverance of king and country from evil. Still commemorated to this day across Britain, Bonfire Night is popular for burning effigies of Guy Fawkes—and in some instances, the pope. This inevitably gave rise to well-known folk ditties, such as this, to appear:

Remember, remember the Fifth of November
The Gunpowder Treason and Plot
I know of no reason
Why the Gunpowder Treason
Should ever be forgot!

At the same time, the Secret Society, which had been so instrumental in the Plot's failure, was undergoing, yet another, transformation. Following Bacon's suggestion, the Grand Council ratified the dual membership Free-Masons must have. And from that day onward, brothers of the Society started to join stonemason guilds, something which they could now be more open about. This turn of events transformed the way some of the guilds operated since their rituals gradually adopted those of the Society.

The earliest surviving record of such an entry was that of Elias Ashmole—founder of Oxford's Ashmolean Museum. In October 1646 AD, he was accepted by a stonemasons' lodge in Warrington, Lancashire. Ashmole later wrote in his diary that on that day he had become a *'Free Mason.'*

Chapter 15

FORMATION

London, England
February 1717 CE

JOHN THEOPHILUS DESAGULIERS was down on all fours, drawing. At first, he'd used a piece of chalk to outline a large rectangle on the wooden floor. Then, within that shape, John drew depictions of the *Boaz* and *Jachin* pillars on either side. Having completed them to his liking, he was now putting the finishing touches to another important Masonic symbol: the *All Seeing Eye*. Working slowly but surely, he wanted everything to be perfect for that night's initiation.

Desaguliers had his back to the door, and was so absorbed in his task, that he did not notice Paul Foster step in. They were both in the large hall situated above the Rummer & Grapes Tavern, in Westminster's Channel Row: their Lodge's usual meeting place. Not wanting to alarm his engrossed fellow Mason, Foster first made an attempt to clear his throat a bit. But there was no reaction. So, Paul smiled and decided he had to make his presence known. "I knew I would find you here."

John had been so startled to hear someone's voice all of a sudden, that he jumped up a little. Instantly turning his plump figure around, Desaguliers started to glare at the person behind him. But realizing who it was, after a split second, he rapidly changed his expression to that of a relieved smile. He had too much respect for Paul, as well as being twenty years his junior, to keep looking at him in anger.

They exchanged courteous greetings as the older man stepped closer. Even at fifty-four, Foster still retained his slender figure. He wore silk stockings almost up to the knee, dark-colored breeches, and a white ruffled shirt, covered by a long collarless black coat: a prerequisite for Masonic meetings. Offering his hand, he helped the similarly attired Desaguliers to stand—both men sporting fashionable light gray wigs on their heads as well. In fact, they were dressed in such an identical way that only the preaching bands attached to John's shirt collar made a difference: two white, stubby pieces of cloth, resting side by side on his upper chest to signify that he was also a priest.

While John Theophilus was busy patting the chalk dust off his coat and breeches, Foster gazed at the floor drawings and sighed. "It is such a pity they will not be seen tonight, Father."

Desaguliers looked up surprised. "What do you mean, Brother Paul?"

"I mean that this evening's initiation has been postponed."

"Postponed? And by whom, may I ask?"

"By order of the Worshipful Master," Paul replied in a matter-of-fact manner. When he saw that a disappointed expression started to appear on John's face, however, he decided to explain in full. "Apparently, Brother Payne met with Anthony Sayer, the Master of the Apple-Tree Tavern Lodge, today and they agreed to hold a joint meeting there tonight. To lend the occasion added significance they've even invited four more Lodges to take part."

Desaguliers was more puzzled by this. "But to what end?"

"I really cannot say. All I know is that Worshipful Master Payne asked me to find and notify you. Apparently, the Tyler had been unable to locate you at home, but knowing how you always like to draw the floor symbols before an initiation, I was certain you'd be here."

John was lost in thought. Snapping out of it, he almost asked whether Sir Christopher knew about all this. However, he remembered just in time that Paul was not part of the Society's Grand Council anymore. So, instead, he wondered, "How on earth will the Apple-Tree hall be able to accommodate all the members from six Lodges?"

"No, no. The Apprentices and Fellow-Crafts won't be attending," Foster pointed out, shaking his head. "Only the Worshipful Masters, Wardens and Past Masters, such as you and I, have been invited."

That sounds even more suspicious, Desaguliers thought. However, he chose not to express that sentiment aloud. Alternatively, he nodded and asked, "What time is this meeting scheduled to start?"

"Six o'clock."

John took out his pocket watch and looked at the time. "This leaves us barely half an hour to get there. We had better get a move on."

Left with no alternative, he stepped over to where a pail and mop were always placed against a wall. Dipping the mop into water he reluctantly started to wash away all of his drawings from the floor. This was standard practice at the time since the symbols exhibited by Masons on their meeting room floorboards were for no one's eyes other than theirs.

Foster looked on with sympathy as Desaguliers mopped off his designs. "It would be so nice if we could have these figures permanently imprinted... perhaps on a tapestry, or a painting, of some sort. Then, it would be unnecessary to draw and erase them every time we had a meeting."

"Where would the fun be in that?" John asked with a smile while passing the wet mop over the last line. "I enjoy drawing them, even if I do know they are destined to be deleted."

After the symbols had been successfully expunged, they hurried down to the bustling street and hailed a hackney carriage. Before getting in, Foster shouted out directions to the driver, "Apple-Tree tavern, in Charles Street, Covent Garden, please."

Once inside, they settled themselves onto the hard wooden seats. But, John's mind was racing. "Which are the other four Lodges that were invited to this meeting, Brother Paul?"

"Well, let me see... Aside from ours and the Apple-Tree, there is the Masons Livery Lodge, the Crown Ale-House Lodge, in Parker's Lane, as well as the London Tavern Lodge at Bishopsgate... And... oh yes, the Goose & Gridiron Ale-House Lodge in St. Paul's Church yard." Foster then paused for a moment, still in thought. "So, all in all there will be four operative Lodges and two speculative ones present."

Desaguliers nodded, as if thanking Paul, but what he'd just heard hadn't appeased his concerns. *The Goose & Gridiron, Sir Christopher's mother Lodge is one of them*, he thought. *I shall definitely have to discuss this with him after I find out more.*

Sir Christopher Wren was currently the Secret Society's Grand Master, having originally been elected to the post thirty-two years earlier.

✠ ✠ ✠

THE TWO ADJECTIVES of 'operative' and 'speculative,' Foster had mentioned, were used by Secret Society brothers to distinguish the membership composition of each public Lodge: the members of *operative* Lodges were predominantly professional stonemasons, whereas those in *speculative* ones consisted mainly of gentlemen.

Ever since Sir Francis Bacon's idea had been approved,

many brothers began joining stonemason guilds—in parallel to their Society Lodge memberships—particularly in the London area. And as expected, the stonemasons welcomed those men of higher status into their midst. Holding their publicized gatherings at well-known taverns and halls, instead of undisclosed locations, those newly emerging entities started to adopt Society structure and rituals as their own. And by doing so gradually transformed their guilds into Lodges—albeit, not covert ones in their case. The reality was that the stonemasons had nothing to lose. By the beginning of the 1600s, work became so scarce that most guilds faced dissolution. As a result, this was a most serendipitous turn of events for them. The *masons* got to rub shoulders with patrons from the gentry, so to transform themselves into *Free-Masons* as well, was a small price to pay. However, the downside for the Society was that over the next few decades the membership numbers of its own, ever secret, Lodges began to wane.

The Great Fire, which devastated London in 1666 AD, did not help matters much in this regard either. Stonemasons from all around Britain surged to the capital to find work, and predictably flooded the—what were now—public Lodges, once again. (It is necessary to keep in mind that these were *public* not in the sense that anyone could drop in on their proceedings at random, but rather in that their existence wasn't kept a secret any longer.) In turn, this set of circumstances allowed the stonemason Lodges to add members from the upper and professional classes more easily than the always covert Society Lodges were able to. So, in essence, what had been a plan for its survival eventually backfired on the Secret Society. And the irony was that the Grand Council could not share its predicament with the public Lodges, nor seek their support: the new institutions were completely oblivious to the Society's existence.

By the 1680s, the situation had become desperate. So, in order to reverse this continuous downward spiral, the Grand Mastership was offered to Sir Christopher Wren.

'*Who better to help us than London's rebuilding champion?*' the Council members had thought at the time. As a result, in 1685 AD, Wren was lured from his Goose & Gridiron public Lodge to be elected the Society's Grand Master, unopposed. As his first fifteen-year term was considered successful—in that membership numbers began to improve somewhat—he was reelected in 1700 AD, again unopposed. But, his second period in office proved to be the exact opposite of the first. Sir Christopher had lost the vigor of his youth by then and neglected his duties as head of the Secret Society. Nonetheless, out of sheer ambition, he so wished for a third term in 1715 AD, that the few Society members still active allowed him to have it—even though he was already at the advanced age of eighty-three. The sad fact of the matter was that none had dared take on that key position in his stead.

✝ ✝ ✝

WHEN THEY ARRIVED at their destination, Desaguliers and Foster entered the Apple-Tree Tavern, and headed toward the back stairs leading up to the hall above. Navigating their way around was not difficult since they'd attended meetings at this Lodge many times in the past.

The resident Tyler, who sat with a drawn sword at the top of the stairwell and just outside the hall's doorway, knew both men well. So, after extending his greetings, he allowed them to pass without any of the necessary formalities. Once inside, Desaguliers looked around the assembly room. There were about forty other Masons there, everyone dressed like him and Foster—wigs and all. Some were standing near the large oak table in the center, talking, while others sat in chairs scattered throughout the hall, most of them puffing on their pipes. The meeting had not yet begun.

Much to his surprise, the very next instant, a few of those standing by the table raised their voices above the rest and started shouting teasing compliments in his direction. Taken aback by this, Desaguliers had to spin around to see who the actual target of their banter was: Hannah, a handsome tavern maid had followed them up the stairs holding an oversized tray filled with rummers of foaming ale. Pleased by the all sudden attention, the wench grinned, deposited the drinks on the table, and hastily ran back down again—smiling still.

Locating George Payne, his Worshipful Master, in conversation with someone across the room, Desaguliers left Foster by the door and walked toward them. As he got near, John heard the other man say, "Perhaps this would also be a good opportunity to finally settle on the Noachian legend for the Master's ceremony?"

The legend just mentioned was one rivaling that of Hiram Abiff, and one which had started gaining popularity with several Lodges. In essence, it required a Lodge's incoming Worshipful Master to portray Noah, instead of Hiram, as part of his installation ritual. Given that no murder had taken place, since Noah was already dead from natural causes, this ceremony focused on three Past Masters acting out the roles of Noah's sons, and on their attempts to bring him back to life. By using the Five Points of Fellowship, they needed to raise their Biblical 'father' from the dead so that he'd reveal his long lost secret to them. After successfully resurrecting him they not only managed to learn what that 'secret' word was, but also to secure a worthy successor in the person of the new Worshipful Master.

Alarmed though he was by hearing this suggestion, Desaguliers never got a chance to comment on it. Payne noticed him come near, and asked, "Where have you been? We looked all over for you."

John did not reply, merely posed a question of his own. "What *is* all this, Worshipful Master?"

While the other Mason was excusing himself, Payne took note of the priest's reproaching look. So, he realized he had to explain in full.

"Very well," Payne began. "I met with Anthony Sayer this morning at a coffee shop. One thing led to another, but our main topic of conversation centered on our Lodges, and how Free-Masonry should proceed in the future. After much discussion, we finally agreed that perhaps having a central governing body—one which will oversee every Lodge in London, that is—might be beneficial for them all. We therefore decided to bring this idea forward and invited the most senior brothers from six Lodges to a meeting."

Desaguliers mouth was agape with disbelief. "And Sayer agreed?"

Payne chuckled. "Agreed? It was actually his suggestion!"

John did not know how to respond to that, so he asked to be excused and walked away. The situation was even more serious than he had feared. Spotting Anthony Sayer over by the fireplace, he headed over there to speak with him. Sayer was leaning back in a chair, smoking his pipe, but when he saw Desaguliers coming in his direction a sly smirk appeared on his face.

John stopped in front of him. "Brother Anthony, we need to talk."

"We do indeed," Sayer responded, as he rose to his feet. And after leading Desaguliers over to a corner where they could speak more privately, he asked in a complacent tone, "What can I do for you, Father?"

"I was racking my brain, throughout the journey here, as to the object of this meeting. But never in my wildest dreams did I expect anything like this. Do you realize the damage it will do to the Society?" John's large, owlish eyes were looking at him accusingly.

Even so, Sayer's cavalier attitude did not waver. "By *Society*, I gather you are not referring to the Royal one, correct?"

This sarcastic comment referred to the fact that Desaguliers was also a Fellow of the Royal Society, alongside—or rather, under—Sir Isaac Newton. Disregarding it though,

John then asked with agony, "Why are you doing this?" But, he did not give Sayer a chance to reply. He lowered his voice to a whisper and added, "As a current member of the Grand Council surely you understand that if this follows through, it would spell death for the Society."

Sayer grinned on hearing that. "Your belief it is still alive is most refreshing. But, as a fellow Council member answer me this then: When was the last time Sir Christopher convened a formal meeting of the Council? Or better yet, when was the last time we, as a Society, provided aid to someone oppressed, or in dire straits? I wager you will find it challenging to answer either question."

Given that Desaguliers was momentarily struggling to come up with a response, Sayer grasped the opportunity to press on. "In that case, allow me to assist. Ever since I was first elected to the Grand Council, seventeen years ago, Sir Christopher has convened Council meetings only twice. And as I am sure you know, from the day of *your* election, two years ago, has yet to do so. But more to the point, throughout my entire time in the Council, no downtrodden has ever been provided with aid. Whenever a proposal to do just that was brought to his attention, Sir Christopher would always insist it did not satisfy his criteria—whatever they are. So, I ask you, Father: What is the point of remaining in the shadows if no good comes of it? What does the Society even stand for anymore?"

Desaguliers scoffed. "And what you propose will help fix the Society's problems?"

Sayer had assumed a more somber expression now. "No. What Payne and I are proposing is the creation of an entirely new body. One that shall preserve the Society's salient features, of course, but one which will be more in touch with the times. The Society has outgrown its usefulness, Brother John; it is an entity of a bygone era. There is no need for clandestine institutions anymore. In fact, there are many reasons to believe that maintaining this level of secrecy could prove to be extremely dangerous." After saying that, Anthony Sayer frowned. "But, I still do not understand why this idea upsets you so."

Desaguliers had his reasons—private reasons. However, he chose not to reveal them. So, instead, he countered with another question. "And who will be leading this new entity? You? I could not help but notice Sir Christopher is not among those present."

"I managed to convince Brother Payne that there is bad blood between me and Wren, so Payne agreed not to extend him an invitation. In any case, Sir Christopher's presence here would serve no purpose. Especially not since our objective is to abandon the inefficient ways with which he currently manages the Society."

"So, it *will* be you!"

Sayer glanced down. "Yes, but not just me. Brother Payne and I shall both be providing the necessary leadership to all these brothers—the vast majority of whom are not aware the Society even exists, including George Payne." Then, suddenly, as if an epiphany had struck him, Anthony Sayer looked up and into John's eyes. "You could be the third one, you know."

Desaguliers was briefly taken aback by this, so Sayer carried on. "What we are trying to create here is a flexible vehicle to carry Free-Masonry into the future, Brother John. Therefore, it would be pointless to continue holding elections once every fifteen years. That is much too long a period for someone to occupy *any* position of power. So, Payne and I decided there should be a new Grand Master annually, in the same way as every Lodge has a new Worshipful Master. I shall go first, followed next year by George Payne... and you could be the third."

Seeing as Desaguliers was silently considering this, Sayer sought to convince him even further. "If you think of it, Brother John, you'd be an ideal candidate for the Grand Mastership. You are well read, intelligent, young and energetic, dedicated, a member of the Royal Society and the clergy... you possess all the necessary qualities. I would much prefer having you on our side rather than against us. What say you?"

In fact, Sayer's proposal had touched a nerve. Desaguliers had always secretly believed he was destined for greatness. But, whatever he got involved with, he was overshadowed by sacred cows: Sir Christopher Wren in the Secret Society, Sir Isaac Newton in the Royal Society—men so awe-inspiring that no room for personal distinction would ever be available. This might be my chance, he thought eagerly.

It took a few seconds before Desaguliers looked up. "You make a compelling case, Brother Anthony. Though I would be reluctant to witness the Society's demise, maybe the time *is* ripe for something new. However, my final agreement will depend on having a few conditions satisfied. I'd like—"

"Worshipful Master, perhaps we should begin?" someone asked Anthony Sayer, interrupting John.

"Yes, Brother Charles, you are right. We have kept everyone waiting far too long," Sayer said to the Mason who had spoken. Then turning to Desaguliers, he smiled. "It makes me happy that you agree. And I am certain all your concerns can be addressed. But if you will excuse me, we must get this meeting under way."

Sayer nodded to John Cordwell, the Worshipful Master of the Crown Ale-House Lodge, who clapped his hands to get everyone's attention. When all conversations died down, Cordwell walked over to the fireplace, turned about-face and began addressing the assembled Masons.

"Brethren, I welcome you. As the eldest of the Worshipful Masters here, I have been asked to preside over this meeting. There shall be no rituals taking place tonight as I am sure most of you already know our business here is of an entirely different nature. I therefore expect it to be briefer than usual, so we can all go downstairs to dine after we finish. But, to acquaint us with the matter we shall be dealing with first, I now call upon Worshipful Brother Antony Sayer to do so."

Stepping next to Cordwell, Sayer began. "Brethren, I would also like to welcome you all to this unusual meeting. Unusual not in the sense that no rituals will take place, but rather in that of what its final outcome shall be. An outcome I believe posterity will not refrain from recognizing as historically significant."

He took a deep breath. "Our primary function, as Free-Masons, is to erect inner temples for virtue and dungeons for vice. But, unless our allegiances are explicitly stated, the meetings we hold, in order to fulfill these vital personal objectives, may be deemed suspect. Ever since the Battle of Preston, last year, the reign of our beloved King George is now considered safe from the Pretender, James Stuart. However, there are some within crown circles who may feel that our Lodges, by holding their meetings behind closed doors, are just wasp nests of Jacobite sympathizers. And if that belief is strengthened, the state could very well take measures against us, by shutting us down. The only way to counter such a potentially disastrous development is for all Lodges to unite under a central governing body. By having a *Grand Lodge* in place, one that shall declare our undying allegiance to His Majesty and to those who lawfully succeed him, I believe such a dreadful occurrence can be avoided. It will not—"

"The king would never have such a problem with *us*," someone said all of a sudden, cutting into Sayer's speech. Everybody turned their heads to the back of the hall, only to realize it had been Edward Strong, the Master of the Masons Livery Lodge, who had spoken. Seeing as he had everyone's attention now, he proceeded to explain his interruption. "The fact that our Royal Charter has never been revoked is the first reason why His Majesty would not. But, the other, and more important one, is that we have never adopted your so called '*Free-Mason*' rituals or philosophy, nor do we ever hold our meetings behind guarded doors. We are a *Company* of stonemasons, Master Sayer, not a Lodge, as you always incorrectly refer to us." He paused for a moment and looked around. "To be honest, I do not understand why we were even invited this evening, other than to lend credibility to your attempts to pass your Lodges off as having something to do with stonemasonry—which they most certainly do not. Nevertheless, I decided to accept your invitation, because declining to do so would be viewed as bad manners on my behalf. And I thank you for it, but we cannot be a part of what you are trying to create here, Master Sayer. So, if you will excuse me, I bid you all a good night."

As Strong walked toward the exit, a stunned silence hung over the hall. Sayer looked confused. "Well..." he said, uneasily. "Is there anyone else who—"

He did not get to complete the question. This time it was Jason Barrett, the Worshipful Master of the London Tavern Lodge, who cut in. "The brethren of my Lodge have also decided not to take part in this. Albeit for different reasons," Barrett stated.

Sayer shot him a thunderous look from across the room. "And may I enquire as to what *your* reasons are?"

"Certainly," Barrett replied, his eyes unwaveringly fixed on Sayer's as well. He stepped closer, accompanied by his two Wardens. "To be brief, we feel that our Lodge is in no need of supervision. It has been silently fulfilling its mission for many years, without a higher authority over it dictating what it can or cannot do. And it will continue to do so for many more. In fact, listening to you just now, trying to frighten the brethren into accepting your plan only strengthens my belief that our decision is correct."

"Perhaps it is because you are all secretly Jacobites," Sayer countered with anger.

Barrett looked down, smiled and shook his head. "I shall not even dignify that with a response, Brother Anthony." Then, looking up and into Sayer's eyes, once again, he continued. "What I do see happening here, though, is your desire to create positions and subsequently gain power, only to feed your own ambitions. Well, our Lodge will have nothing to do with this abomination you are trying to fashion. But, allow me to be even more frank with you. If this... *'Grand Lodge'* of yours ever tries to disturb the sovereignty of *our* Lodge, by requesting old documents, or our books of Minutes, let me tell you this: We would rather see them burn than hand them over to you."

While Barrett and his Wardens were storming out the hall, Sayer scoffed. "Having such Jacobite traitors amongst us only goes to prove the dangers I just warned you about, my brothers." Everyone looked back at him in silence. "Is there anyone else who disagrees with this proposal?" He glanced around the room for a moment. No one seemed eager to say anything, so he added, "Very well, I take it we are all in agreement." Then turning to John Cordwell, he nodded for him to carry on.

Cordwell cleared his throat and announced, "We shall hold the formal formation of the *Grand Lodge of London and Westminster* in four months. On St. John's day, June 24, we shall meet again, this time at the Goose & Gridiron Ale-House Lodge in St. Paul's Church yard, to elect the Grand Lodge's first officials. This meeting is adjourned. I think it is time for us all to go down to dinner now. I am famished!"

✟ ✟ ✟

THERE WERE TWO main reasons why the Secret Society deteriorated like it did. One was that those who succeeded Sir Francis Bacon into its Grand Mastership were not of the same high caliber he used to be. Aside from other factors, his successors lacked the vision, determination and resourcefulness he'd brought to the position. And the second reason—albeit, in direct relation to the first—was that the pool of available Phoenician male descendants had decreased significantly over time. The long centuries, ever since Anthony Norridge *'imported'* those Tyrian families to England, in 1382 AD, had inevitably taken their toll. After too many generations of intermarrying with the English population very few of them were now aware of their ancient heritage anymore. Some lived up north, mostly in Yorkshire, but in the south, and especially in London, only three remained: John Theophilus Desaguliers, Paul Foster and Roger Carter.

John's Tyrian ancestors were on the same boat bound to England as the rest. But when their ship docked at La Rochelle for supplies, his paternal forefather decided he did not want to live out his life in a stuffy city such as London. He would much rather continue being a fisherman, and La Rochelle seemed like the ideal location to carry on with his profession. Consequently, he and his wife abandoned ship, and started living and raising their family at that French port. However, destiny always has a way of correcting random events and setting them back on course. Three hundred years later, just a few months after John Theophilus was born, the French government exiled his father from La Rochelle for being a Protestant. So, those two Phoenician descendants, along with John's mother, were left with no other option than to end up in the British capital after all.

On the contrary, Paul Foster was a Londoner by birth. He was the great grandson of Richard Foster, Bacon's friend and fellow Grand Council member. And like his great grandfather he also took an interest in the Secret Society and got elected to its Council, twice. Unfortunately, though, following a quarrel with Sir Christopher Wren, he had no choice but to resign. In fact, he'd been so dispirited by the whole affair that when elections were held a year later, in 1715 AD, Paul was not interested in putting himself forward again.

Roger Carter may have been the youngest of the three with Tyrian ancestry, but he did show a lot of promise, nonetheless. Having been born in Scotland, he lost both parents at a young age—an event which forced his maternal grandmother in Edinburgh to step in and take over his Phoenician upbringing. Years later, after graduating from the local university, and his grandmother's death, Roger's ambition led him south to London where he started making a living as a tutor to children of the gentry. Roger finally came across the other two men sharing his lineage when he joined the Crown Ale-House Lodge. And when they met, he knew of his connection to them, from everything his grandmother told him. At twenty-eight years of age now, he was already the Junior Warden of his Lodge. But, aside from Roger's rapid rise in the Masonic hierarchy, he was also starting to make a name for himself as a novelist: the two short stories he had recently published were very well received.

The three Phoenician descendants were still sitting around a table at the Apple-Tree Tavern, after everyone else had finished their dinner and gone home. Foster took a swig of ale while looking at Desaguliers. "I felt certain you'd object to Sayer's proposal and say something—like the others did."

"Why is that?"

"I noticed the two of you speaking, just before the meeting began. Your conversation appeared to be so intense at times, that..." Although Foster's voice trailed off, to lure the priest into providing an account of what had been said, Desaguliers chose to remain silent. So, after a moment, Foster went ahead and asked, anyway. "Did he manage to convince you?"

John Theophilus sighed. "Yes, he did." But before Foster could ask him how, he preemptively continued. "As much as I hate to admit it, Sayer made me realize that the Secret Society is indeed a thing of the past. Especially with Sir Christopher in charge, and the way he has been handling its affairs for over three decades..." Then, eyeing Foster, he added, "I don't think it is necessary to persuade *you* of that."

"No, you do not," Paul Foster said, looking down. Then after a moment he glanced up at Carter and told him, "You are so lucky you've had nothing to do with that old goat."

"And as matters stand, as of tonight, he probably never will," Desaguliers added with a chuckle. Although, after glancing around for anyone who might overhear them, John Theophilus leaned in, and when the other two did so as well, he began to whisper. "Look, I am not insensitive when it comes to tearing down something our ancestors built, but in this instance it is true the Society has run its course. There are no religious wars anymore, serfdom has been abolished, and the rule of law prevails in the realm. Essentially, there is not much for a Secret Society to do any longer. This is why I feel that what Sayer told me, about the Society being a relic of the past, is regrettably accurate. So, forming a Grand Lodge to replace it just might be the right thing to do. Instead of having an entirely secret organization, which no one outside it even knows it exists, we shall now have a visible one—but with secrets. I don't think that is too much of a sacrifice at the moment." He sat back. "However, this does not mean I would abandon everything our ancestors had a hand in."

Foster frowned, for a moment. Then, his eyes lit up as he understood. "You have set conditions to Sayer."

"Not yet, but I shall," Desaguliers responded with a mischievous smile. And when the others looked at him inquiringly, he began to elaborate. "My first of two conditions will be that since the Society will not be around any longer to provide aid to the downtrodden, then this ought to be replaced by Charity. I shall demand the virtue of Charity forms one of the Grand Lodge's cardinal objectives."

The others nodded in agreement. "What is the second?" Foster asked.

"That it is time for a Third Degree to be created—a Master's Degree, which every Fellow Craft brother can be raised to. And that this new Degree's raising ritual should be about Hiram Abiff, our fellow Phoenician, not the one with all the Noah nonsense. It must—"

"You do realize there are a couple of problems with this, Brother John," Foster interjected. "The first is that either of them is already used whenever a new Worshipful Master is installed. And the other is that the Noah ritual has gained quite a following among Lodges in recent years. They might not be willing to give it up so easily."

Desaguliers frowned. "Yes... but, we can always come up with a new ceremony for installing a Worshipful Master. It does not need to be an initiating ritual as such." And after pondering Foster's second point, for a moment, he added, "Perhaps, we can incorporate some element from the Noah ritual into that of Hiram's, so there'll be less resistance. Perhaps... Yes! Maybe we could use the Five Points of Fellowship from Noah's ceremony while raising Hiram. There is not much else in it of real substance, anyway." He was happy with himself for coming up with a good solution.

"Aye, that might do it," Foster said, nodding.

Carter had remained silent all this time, drinking his ale, while the others were talking. Without warning, he smiled and surprised them both by saying, "Perhaps a Fourth Degree should be added as well."

Desaguliers turned to face him. "What do you mean?"

"I'm still a Fellow Craft, not a Worshipful Master yet, so I obviously do not know what the Hiram and Noah rituals are about in detail. I am aware, however, that Hiram's real story had to do with him being killed in the Temple of Solomon. And I recently remembered something my grandmother mentioned to me as a young boy, about a group of people finding the Ark of the Covenant. She was too old and could not remember who they were, but she did tell me the fact it was hidden had to do with how and why Hiram was murdered."

Foster and Desaguliers glanced at each other briefly. So, as the eldest, Foster took it upon himself to ask the question. "What are you proposing?"

"I just thought it might make sense to supplement Hiram's murder ritual with yet a higher Degree about finding the Ark, which was buried... possibly under the Temple. And that this may be helpful in getting rid of the Noah story once and for all." The other two remained silent, but Roger felt so excited that he impulsively went on. "If this is agreed to, perhaps we could even persuade those who will get elected to the Grand Council to depict the Ark of the Covenant on the Grand Lodge's coat of arms. That would certainly afford it more solemnity, don't you think?" He was smiling, expecting them to congratulate him.

Desaguliers shook his head. "That is not such a good idea."

Carter's smile turned into a frown. "Why?"

"There is much you do not yet know," Foster replied.

"Then, enlighten me. Please!" Carter said, looking at them both, beseechingly. "By the time I reached an age I could understand, my grandmother was getting old and starting to lose her mind. She told me bits and pieces of what she remembered; for instance, names of others with Phoenician origins—such as yourselves—and a few stories, but these were in no way complete. So, I never got to hear the whole account of what our ancestors accomplished, or had a hand in."

Desaguliers and Foster looked at each other once again. Then, giving into Carter's imploring look, they began to educate him—he was one of their own, after all: They told him about how those of Phoenician origins, at the time, had helped the Knights Templar find the Ark of the Covenant, and Hiram's remains, up on Temple Mount; about the fact they took the Ark with them to Cyprus and hid it there; about how and why the remaining fugitive Templars in England created the Secret Society; and, finally, about the Society's struggles, throughout the centuries, to secretly provide aid and justice to all those in need.

Both men took turns narrating those events in hushed tones, and in answering the questions Carter posed along the way, that it was almost midnight before they finished. In fact, it was so late that they were the only ones still around. As everyone else in the tavern had already left, the innkeeper had been eyeing them closely, from afar, for quite some time. He was apparently eager for them to leave as well, so that he could close up, and return home.

Carter's smile was overflowing with wonder. "This is all so incredible! I had no idea our history was as rich as this." But, after pausing for a moment, in an effort to collect his thoughts, he added, "Maybe we should go get it, then."

Desaguliers looked at him, with a puzzled frown. "Go get what?"

Carter leaned in and whispered, "The Ark of the Covenant, what else?"

Before Desaguliers could utter a reply, Forster intervened. "No, no, Roger. Whatever you have heard from us tonight is for your ears only. And it is not to be acted upon—ever."

"Yes, I understand. But, why abandon the Ark on that island? If we went to recover it, we'd make the find of an era. Our names would be so famous everyone would recognize them for centuries to come." Carter was still excited, glancing at both of them in turn.

"Because we do not know where the Ark is," Desaguliers told him dejectedly, lowering his eyes. "We only know it's on the island of Cyprus. Yet, the exact location is a mystery. There were rumors that our rituals contain clues as to its whereabouts, except no one alive knows what those clues are any longer." He then raised his eyes and focused them on Carter's. "But that is beside the point. Even if we did possess the Ark's location, it must never be retrieved. The decision to hide it permanently from the world was a deliberate one. And that is because, if revealed, this may create all sorts of unwanted repercussions: It might strengthen the Roman Catholic claim that it's the only true Christian creed; or it might clear a way for the papacy to slander the Templars, yet again. So, you see, Brother Roger, allowing the Ark to rest in peace, wherever it lies, is the only viable option. You do see that, do you not?"

Carter was nodding.

"So, you must never mention anything about it to anyone. This is very important," Foster told him.

Carter nodded again.

"Or about whatever else you have heard tonight," Desaguliers added.

Roger Carter was still nodding when he said, "Certainly. Now, if you will excuse me, it appears I had too much ale to drink." He grinned. "I need to go relieve myself."

Standing up, he then went out the tavern's back door. There were no indoor toilets at the time, so he stepped out into the alley to do his business.

Foster watched him closely as he walked away. Then, turning to face Desaguliers, he said in a grave tone, "I think I had better keep an eye on our young brother."

✝ ✝ ✝

London, England
June 24, 1717 CE

FOUR MONTHS LATER, on St. John's day, everybody was present. The Worshipful Masters, Wardens and Past Masters of the four Lodges were all gathered up on the first-floor hall of the Goose & Gridiron Ale-House. And the reason they were there was none other than the public formation of the Grand Lodge of London & Westminster—or, as it would later be called, the Premier Grand Lodge of England.

Before dinner, John Cordwell, the Worshipful Master of the Crown Ale-House Lodge, as the eldest Master there, rose from his seat to address those present. "Brethren, I would once again like to welcome you to our gathering tonight. Its purpose, as I'm sure you are aware, is for our Lodges to officially establish a Grand Lodge—a Grand Lodge which will unite and watch over them all. This is indeed a joyous occasion, but it is marred by the fact that one of our own is forever unable to attend. Brother Roger Carter, the Junior Warden of my Lodge, was brutally murdered just two days ago. And while we wait for the authorities to determine who the vile perpetrators were and bring them to justice, I think it only proper to begin our assembly by observing a moment's silence in his memory. Brethren, please be upstanding."

Desaguliers had gasped when he heard about the murder. Now, as he rose to his feet, he whispered to Paul Foster, who was next to him, "Did you have anything to do with this?"

Foster bowed his head and whispered back, "I will tell you later. Be quiet."

After the moment of silence was over—with everyone chanting thrice, "May his memory live on forever"—Cordwell asked them all to resume their seats. Subsequently, he invited whomever wished to declare his candidacy for the office of Grand Master, that of either Grand Warden, or for any other of the ten-member Grand Council, to do so. And quite a few did. For the Grand Mastership there were three candidates, including Anthony Sayer, as well as several more for each of the other positions. Then, a disagreement broke out about which voting method should be used. Some maintained that using paper ballots to vote in secret was more preferable while others argued that a show of hands would be more in the spirit of the occasion.

While that discussion was in progress, Foster took Desaguliers by the arm and led him to the other side of the hall where they could talk without being overheard. John Theophilus's expression was grave. "What have you done?" he asked, before Foster had a chance to say anything.

"What needed doing," Foster said matter-of-factly and crossed his arms.

Desaguliers gasped with disbelief. "You know I cannot condone murder. It is a—"

"Not even if it's necessary?" Foster interjected.

That aroused John's curiosity. He whispered roughly, "How was *this* necessary?"

"Four months back, I promised you I would keep an

eye on Carter," Foster began. "And I did. On frequent occasions, I saw him speaking with Jason Barrett, the Master of the London Tavern Lodge—at that very tavern—in especially hushed tones. Not knowing what they were saying though, I gave Carter the benefit of the doubt. So, I convinced myself he wasn't betraying any of our secrets. But, a few days ago I intercepted this letter addressed to him." Taking a folded piece of paper out of his pocket, he showed it to Desaguliers.

"Is it from Barrett?"

"Before I answer that, I think you should listen to what it says." Unfolding the page, Foster began reading its contents: "Dearest Roger, I was very happy to hear from you the other week. As always, your letter reminded me of all the interesting conversations we had, during our years at the University of Edinburgh together. But you have surpassed yourself this time, my friend. What you revealed, about the Knights Templar being responsible for creating Free-Masonry, I must admit has kept me awake many a night. Do they still exist? How have they managed to go undetected for four centuries? I eagerly await your replies, as well as the next nugget of revelations you've promised, concerning the Ark of the Covenant. I remain your eternal friend, Andrew Michael Ramsay."

John's mouth was practically agape with astonishment. "Incredible. Who is this Andrew Ramsay, anyway?"

Foster folded the letter and put it back into his waistcoat pocket. Then, his expression turned into one of disgust. "He's a Scot troublemaker, currently living in France."

"Then how do you know so much about him?"

"About seven years ago, somebody proposed him for Society membership. The one making the recommendation claimed Ramsay was a bright, gallant young fellow who would be a welcome addition for us up in Scotland. But, Ramsay went abroad shortly after that, and his invitation to join was put on hold. After two years passed, I learned that not only had he converted to Catholicism by then, but that he was also a Jacobite sympathizer. So, as you would expect, we wanted nothing to do with him anymore."

"Yet this never stopped our late Brother Carter from keeping in touch with his university chum. Or, from telling him things we revealed in confidence," Desaguliers said, with more than a hint of contempt in his voice.

"Surely, you realize, Father, that taking this particular course of action was necessary. I wasn't aware of everything Carter had already divulged to Ramsay—or possibly to Barrett—but for certain I was not going to stand idly by while he told him, or anyone else, more. And most of all if it concerned the Ark."

Desaguliers sighed. "Yes. I see it now. You had no alternative other than to silence him."

Foster lowered his eyes. "I did not soil my hands with Carter's blood, yet paying others to do it for me doesn't diminish my complicity. And being forced to end the life of one of our own lineage—whatever that even means anymore—was not an easy choice, believe me. I will be—"

"Brethren, if you would all please return to your seats," Cordwell said in a commanding voice, interrupting Foster. "We shall now proceed to vote by a show of hands, as has just been agreed."

Everybody sat down and the voting began. When it was all over, the first Grand Council to result from it was composed of: Anthony Sayer, as Grand Master—a foregone conclusion for many; Captain Joseph Elliot and Mr. Jacob Lamball, as Grand Wardens; and seven more in the other, lesser, positions. Then, so much cheering erupted in the hall that Cordwell was forced to raise his voice above everyone else's. "I would like to congratulate our first Grand Master and also invite him to say a few words."

With a beaming smile on his face, Sayer walked over to the center of the fireplace. He shook Cordwell's extended hand and cleared his throat. Everyone stopped talking.

"Brethren, I wish to thank you all for the foresight and

vision you have shown in allowing this unprecedented endeavor of ours to reach fruition. And I would especially like to thank Brother Cordwell for the excellent manner in which he presided over these two meetings. Last, but not least, my thanks go to everyone who voted that I should be the first to lead this new institution of ours into the future.

"This is indeed a historic day, my Brothers. It is the day our Lodges have decided to unite under a common banner. And with good reason: The Grand Lodge we've formed today will be able to rise above the obscurity that four humble, albeit autonomous Lodges can offer. Eventually becoming greater than the sum of its parts, it shall be the proud gatekeeper of great symbols and of truths that never die. Truths which I believe can be better served when a few adjustments are made. The first of these is that it is time for a Third Degree to be added to the existing two: a Master's Degree."

Sayer paused long enough so he could seek out Desaguliers's face in the back and subtly wink at him. It was as if he was saying: *Thank you for your support, John. I shall keep my end of the bargain.*

The new Grand Master continued. "You are all well aware that it is currently forbidden to have any religious discussions in our Lodges—a very sensible precaution, I must admit, given the many persuasions in existence today. But, bearing in mind the events of our previous meeting, in February, I feel another prohibition must also be applied: that of any political discussions as well. Only by having such a ban in place, shall we ever stand a chance of convincing His Majesty we are truly loyal to him. And with his royal favor secure, I am certain it will pave the way to another change I have been thinking of: new members must be made through application, not by invitation, anymore. It is…"

Anthony Sayer was still speaking when Desaguliers turned his head slightly to the right. Sitting next to him was the Junior Warden of his Lodge, James Anderson, who was also a Presbyterian Minister. "I have read a few of the sermons you've published," John Theophilus whispered. "They are quite good. You write well, Brother."

Although Anderson was surprised by the sudden compliment, he managed to whisper back, "Thank you, Brother John, that is most k—"

"When you write of these events later on, I want you to bear in mind two things," Desaguliers cut in. "First, that this was a *revival* of Free-Masonry. And second, you must make no mention of the two Lodges walking out in February, or their reasons for doing so."

Anderson looked back at him, astonished. Why on earth Desaguliers was telling him this?

John Theophilus smiled at Anderson, and patted his shoulder twice, reassuringly. "We shall speak more of this later," he whispered.

TEMPLARS

Chapter 16

WELL

Khirokitia, Cyprus
June 2, 1308 CE

THE GUARD'S HAND moved toward the hilt of his sword. At the same time, he took two steps, positioning himself between the priest and the gate. "I am sorry, but you cannot leave the compound, Father. None of you can."

Stephen de Safed stopped in his tracks. While he'd expected *some* degree of resistance, the knight's apparent readiness to use force was surprising. Nevertheless, with a pretext already prepared, Stephen smiled and addressed him, in the sweetest possible manner. "I was only going to Our Lady's chapel, across the field there, to pray, my good sir knight. I'm not running away, I assure you."

The chain-mail-clad knight scowled. Even though it was still early in the morning, beads of sweat were trickling down his bearded face. The punishing heat and humidity, which summers in Cyprus inflict, were in full swing. "Why would you want to go to that *Greek* Church to pray, Father?" he asked in a disapproving tone. "Perhaps you Templars truly *are* a group of heretics and blasphemers, just like the rumors say."

The priest shook his head. "No. The Greeks may be heretics, but everyone in our Order is a devout Roman Catholic, sir." Then, smiling sweetly once again, he added, "And that chapel is still a House of God is it not?"

The knight's scowling expression turned into a puzzled one for a moment. "I suppose so..." he said with hesitation. But then his resolve resurfaced. "In any case, the governor's orders are explicit: none of you must leave the manor compound—for whatever reason. So, I'm afraid you will have to carry out your devotions at our own chapel here, Father."

Stephen nodded, as he realized the knight was determined not to let him pass. So, stepping back into the center of the courtyard, he scanned the familiar surroundings. On the northeast, southeast and southwest corners of the structure were three high siege towers, upon which other knights stood watch. To the northwest there was the large manor house, next to the stables. And enclosing everything on all sides were the twenty-foot-deep walls. It was a well-fortified stronghold, ready to withstand any prolonged siege, yet regrettably, short of climbing over the ramparts, there was only one way out: The long, stone passageway, to the south, with heavy gates at both ends; the one from which he had stepped away, moments ago.

This guard is clearly prejudiced against our Order, de Safed thought. *Maybe that explains why he didn't attend mass with us at dawn. But, there is nothing for it. I'll just have to think of a way to gain his trust. And after I've got it, he won't stop me again.*

✦ ✦ ✦

"Ah, Brother Marshal, welcome," Stephen said, when he saw Aymon d'Oiselay step into the kitchen before noon. "I would shake your hand, if my own was not covered in so much flour."

Aymon lost no time in realizing that, aside from the priest, there wasn't anyone else in there. And it was puzzling—especially at that time of day. So, not being one to beat about the bush, or exchange pleasantries, he asked, "Where is all the kitchen staff?"

"I sent them away for a while."

The marshal was about to ask why as he came closer. But then he noticed that the priest was busy kneading dough on the table. This aroused his curiosity even more. "What are you doing, Father? Since when have *you* prepared the bread?"

"It's not bread I'm trying to..." de Safed started to say. Then, he smiled. "In any case, I will explain later. But first, tell me everything. You and I haven't had the chance to speak since they brought you in last night."

The highest ranking Templar of Cyprus sighed, an unhappy expression etched on his face. "As you know, on Tuesday, I led a delegation to Nicosia to convince Governor Amaury, and everybody else, of our Order's innocence. Two days later, though, and while we were still having talks, Amaury de Lusignan had our Nicosia preceptory searched, apparently looking for treasure. When I heard of it, I ordered everyone to ride out with me to Limassol. I was so enraged by Amaury's deceit that I was determined to fight him to the end. However, after his forces surrounded our headquarters the next day, I found myself facing two equally bleak outcomes. Either we would all stay the course and starve to death, or, we'd charge out and kill as many fellow Christians as we could in the process. So, I decided to surrender, under the condition that our brothers and I were to be brought here."

But the memory of those events only served in bringing d'Oiselay's rage to the surface once again. He pounded his hand on the table. "That bastard! After everything we did to help him banish his brother, the king, he rewards us like this?" Aymon then plumped himself onto a chair, looking particularly miserable. "I should've anticipated something like this would happen and taken more precautions."

"Don't be too hard on yourself, Marshal. None of this is your fault," de Safed said in a soothing tone. "I'm certain Amaury was under a lot of pressure. Receiving an edict from the pope, ordering our arrest and confiscation of our properties is not an easy matter to ignore for long. Nevertheless, he did give us time to prepare."

The marshal looked into Stephen's eyes. "What are you talking about, Father? If Pierre de Bologna's coded message hadn't arrived last December, we'd have no idea the arrests were taking place in France. And we certainly wouldn't have been able to construct the crypt, or hide the Ark and the rest of the treasure. So, it's Brother Pierre we must thank, not that bastard Amaury."

"Of course we owe it all to Pierre de Bologna," Stephen agreed. "What I was referring to was the *extra* time the governor gave us after receiving the papal orders, early in May. It enabled us to fill in the hole and bring flocks of goats to trample all over the grounds. Now there's no visible sign of where the Ark is buried. So, he helped us with that at least, did he not?"

Aymon was nodding, reluctantly, as he looked over to the priest again. "You still haven't told me what you're doing, though."

"This morning, the knight posted at the gate wouldn't allow me to pass," Stephen said, as he continued pressing his knuckles into the dough. "He seemed quite ill-disposed toward our Order. So much so that—"

"I know the one you mean," d'Oiselay cut in. "His name is Raymond de Bentho. And yesterday he was extremely hostile to all of us on the way from Limassol. He kept gloating that with him being captain of the guards here no Templar would ever see the outside world." The marshal then slid a curious glance at the priest. "But, where were you going when de Bentho blocked your exit?"

"The only thing we haven't done, until now, was to leave instructions on how to locate the crypt. I was—"

The marshal interrupted him again. "You know I disagree with that, Father. Leaving directions to the crypt's location might be very dangerous. Anyone could find them and unearth what we hid. If that happened, and given our

Order's current situation, there's no way we'd ever convince His Holiness the pope we're not the heretics everyone thinks we are."

Stephen smiled. "I share your concerns, Brother Aymon. And that is why I wrote everything down in our very own code. None, except members of our brotherhood, will ever be able to decipher the parchment." The priest stopped what he was doing for a moment and looked at Aymon. "But it is necessary we do so. As I've explained to you before, there is no guarantee we will survive this. Bizarre stories about torture and burnings at the stake are coming out of France. Who can say if that won't be our fate as well? If it is, then following Pierre de Bologna's suggestions is the only way to safeguard our legacy. He proposed we should bury the Ark and everything else in the vicinity of Our Lady's chapel. We've already done that. However, we have yet to leave directions as to the crypt's whereabouts." Stephen's expression softened. "I believe we owe it to him, Marshal. What if we don't survive, but de Bologna does and comes looking for the crypt? What then? Or, better yet, what if the Grand Master himself does?"

Aymon d'Oiselay still had doubts. "But why trust an isolated chapel, in the middle of nowhere? Wouldn't it be more prudent to hide the directions somewhere here, within the Manor?"

Stephen shook his head in disagreement. "The guards could search the compound at any time, and if a parchment with coded text were to be found it would not look too good for us. They'd demand we tell them what it says—maybe even torture us to do so. No, that remote chapel is the safest solution. And, seeing as de Bologna has been able to elude arrest, he'll most probably try to contact us again. I shall then write back to him so he knows we followed his instructions to the letter."

Aymon nodded, accepting this was most likely the best course of action. "Do you know where to put the parchment inside the chapel?"

"Yes. I have a good idea of where to hide it without desecrating that holy place in any way. And the parchment won't be exposed because I'll be placing it in a container. But everything must be done soon. There is talk the governor isn't too happy with having every Templar in one location. He may order some of us to be transferred somewhere else—perhaps to our stronghold up at Lefkara village."

Then, all of a sudden, Stephen's eyes lit up. He cleaned his hands with a rag, reached into his cassock, and produced a slender brass cylinder.

"Mentioning the Grand Master made me remember something," Stephen said. "If he's the one who'll be retrieving this cylinder, I am certain he'd also want to find an additional item inside: his Ring."

This took the marshal by surprise. "But, Brother Jacques de Molay gave it to *me* for safekeeping," Aymon mumbled, uneasily. "If you hide the tube in the chapel... then, anyone could stumble onto it."

"While that is a possibility, think of what would ensue if they search you and find a ring with the Star of David tied around your neck. Just because this has yet to happen does not mean it won't. How will you be able to explain that? Will you tell them who it truly belongs to? Or, will you tell them *how* it came to be in the Grand Master's possession?"

Once again, Aymon saw the truth in Stephen's words. So, he reluctantly untied the cord around his neck and handed the Ring over. While Stephen was busy sliding the Ring into the brass tube, the marshal remembered what he meant to ask. "You haven't told me how you expect to get past Raymond de Bentho. Or, why you've been kneading that dough."

"I don't know if Sir Raymond will ever come to hear mass with us. But when he does, he's going to witness a miracle." The priest was still chuckling when he started unfolding his plan to Aymon. And after all was explained, Stephen added, "That's why I sent everyone away from the kitchen.

I didn't want them to see what I was about to prepare."

"What can I do to help?" the marshal asked.

"Warn the brothers who'll be coming to mass tonight not to comment on anything that may seem out of the ordinary. Or, to look as if they've seen something which is."

☩ ☩ ☩

WHEN DUSK FELL later that day, the Manor's chapel bell chimed. It was a call to everyone that Sunday's Evening Prayer Mass was about to begin. Soon after, the Templars, each one clad in his individual white or black mantle with the blood-red cross, dutifully made their way into the chapel.

But the bell wasn't chiming for the Templars alone. It was also a summons to worship for all the off-duty knights guarding them. Peter Ysan, and his captain, Raymond de Bentho, were two of those. As they made their way over to the chapel, de Bentho shared his concerns with his fellow knight. "Before the Holy Land was lost, I was able to witness how the Templars fought the Saracens, on multiple occasions. And I was in awe of their bravery and dedication. But ever since the papal letters arrived, revealing their secret heretical ways, I've wanted nothing to do with them anymore. The problem is, though, short of travelling to Limassol every time I want to hear mass, there's no priest other than theirs nearby. So, we will attend mass with them this evening, but other than that we shall neither speak nor fraternize with them. They are our prisoners and our sole task is to guard them closely. Is that understood?"

Ysan nodded as they stepped into the chapel. Making their way through the throng of standing Templars, the two knights arrived at the front row pews. They sat down—next to Aymon d'Oiselay—just as Stephen de Safed was kissing the cross at the midpoint of his stole. He then placed the liturgical vestment's center on the back of his neck, allowing the two long ends to dangle in front of his cassock.

After de Safed blessed the congregation and the appropriate passages of Scripture were read, he turned to face the altar. With his back to everyone, he picked up the Host wafer, symbolizing Jesus's Body, from a silver dish. Holding it up with both hands, high above his head, he proclaimed, "Behold the Lamb of God. Behold Him who takes away the sins of the world."

Raymond de Bentho nudged Ysan and whispered, "Did you see that?"

Ysan looked up. "See what?" the knight whispered back, somewhat startled.

"The Host! It's three times larger than normal and white as snow!"

"No, I'm sorry. I was looking down just now," Ysan said, whispering still.

Anxiously, Raymond swiveled in his seat and glanced at the Templars behind him. He needed to determine if anyone of them had also seen something unusual. They all had blank expressions on their faces.

Having heard the whispered exchange, Stephen cracked a smile as he brought the Host wafer down. Then, with a deft, pre-rehearsed move he slipped the extra large Host into his cassock's sleeve. He lifted the chalice of wine, symbolizing Christ's Blood, and started reciting the Secreta prayer. While doing so, his other hand picked up a second, normal-sized Host, which was in the silver dish all the time. Turning to face the congregation, he was mindful to avoid looking directly at de Bentho. Nevertheless, out of the corner of his eye, he did sense Raymond's surprise on seeing the ordinary wafer now. After Stephen finished the prayer, he received Communion by placing the Host in his mouth and washing it down with a sip of wine from the chalice. Only at that moment did he risk throwing a fleeting glance at de Bentho. The knight's eyes were wide open with bewilderment.

When everyone else had also received the Eucharist, the final blessing was given. That signaled the end of the service, and all the Templars began filing out of the chapel. In the commotion they created, Stephen seized the opportunity to swiftly remove the large wafer from his sleeve and place it under the silver dish, unseen. He then took off his stole and was about to kiss its midpoint cross, before putting it away, when de Bentho came near. Taking the priest's hand, Raymond bent over and kissed it.

"I'm afraid we have not been formally introduced, Father," the knight said. "My name is Raymond de Bentho."

"And I am Stephen de Safed. Did you enjoy the service, Sir Raymond?"

"I did..." the knight replied, his voice trailing off a bit with hesitation. "It's just that... there seemed to be something strange about the Host you consecrated."

Stephen stood there with a doe-eyed expression on his face, feigning bafflement. "Did the one you received not agree with you? They were all freshly baked this afternoon."

"No, it's not that," de Bentho said, with a slight touch of irritation. Then, he asked. "May I see the communion wafers you used tonight?"

"Certainly. There they are." The priest pointed to a second silver dish on the altar where his supply of Hosts was stacked. They were all the regular, off-white, round wafers—about an inch in diameter—which were always used for communion.

"No. The first Host you consecrated tonight was three times larger than these, and extremely white."

"I fear you must be mistaken, Sir Raymond. These are the only wafers I have."

The knight looked down and began shaking his head in disbelief. Stephen said nothing else, allowing it to sink in.

When de Bentho looked up after a moment, he had a completely different expression. It was as if he'd seen light at the end of a long, dark tunnel. "Father, I came to mass tonight believing that everyone in your Order is a heretic and mortal sinner. But, the Good Lord found a way for me to realize my error by allowing me to witness a miracle. I cannot find any other explanation for what I've witnessed."

Stephen began to nod. "The Lord does indeed work in mysterious ways."

Raymond bent over to kiss the priest's hand once again. And before stepping out of the chapel, he added, "I would like to apologize for the way I spoke to you this morning, Father. If there is anything I can do for you, please do not hesitate to ask. I bid you a goodnight."

The priest was feeling elated. All his efforts in preparing that oversized, brightly white Host had paid off. But now that he was left alone there was one more thing he needed to do: destroy the evidence. So, he picked it up, from under the silver dish, and proceeded to eat it. The wafer was delicious.

✛ ✛ ✛

AROUND MID-MORNING THE next day, Stephen peeked out the window. He was in luck: the guard posted at the gate was Raymond de Bentho. *This is it*, he thought, and took a deep breath. Stepping out into the courtyard, he began walking toward the gate, as casually as possible.

"Good morning, Father," de Bentho called out in greeting. And when the priest got near, the knight added, "I apologize for not attending mass at dawn. I was stuck on duty here."

"That's quite all right, Sir Raymond. We all have our duties to fulfill."

"Would you like to go to Our Lady's Chapel, out there, to pray?" de Bentho asked him, unexpectedly.

It's going to be easier than I thought. Then, Stephen said aloud, "I would indeed! That is, unless it would cause you to frown upon me."

Raymond smiled. "You have been touched by the Hand of God, Father. This much is clear to me. I could never frown upon something you do."

"Well, that is most kind of you. Thank you, Sir Raymond," the priest said, after feigning a bashful grin.

The knight then opened the first gate and escorted Stephen through the long, arched passageway to the outer gate. Unlocking its heavy doors, he pushed one out and said, "When you return pound on it so I can let you in. But, please don't take too long, Father. I wouldn't want word reaching the governor that I've been doing favors. You understand."

"Of course. I shall only be a short while."

Stephen had just taken a few steps forward when he heard the knight call out to him, "Father, stop!" Initially he froze. Then, whirling around, the priest saw de Bentho holding the brass cylinder. Tendrils of terror began ransacking the insides of his stomach. Rummaging his pocket, where the tube *should* have been, he discovered a hole in one of the corners.

How could I have been so careless? Stephen chided himself.

But, de Bentho was smiling. "This fell out of your cassock." And after taking a few steps forward, the knight handed it over.

The priest was sweating, and it wasn't altogether because of the heat. He grinned nervously. "Thank you once again, Sir Raymond." He held up the cylinder. "This is... an offering I wanted to take—"

"There's no need to explain, Father," Raymond cut in. "I trust you completely. Enjoy your visit to the chapel."

After saying that, the knight turned around, walked through the gate and closed it behind him. Several seconds passed before Stephen's heart could stop pounding. And when it did, with the cylinder tucked away in another pocket, he headed on to fulfill his mission.

Aside from being a loyal Templar, Stephen had an additional, personal motive for wanting to keep the crypt's contents safely hidden: just like Pierre de Bologna, his distant Phoenician lineage from Tyre also included Hiram Binne.

And with Hiram's embalmed head being one of the items inside the crypt, he'd do anything to prevent the Church from getting its hands on it. The reason was simple. If that were to happen, Pope Clement would secure the vital evidence he lacked at the moment. He would, at long last, have the head the Templars were accused of 'worshiping' in their initiation rituals; and he'd use it to tarnish the Order's reputation for all time. That was something the priest could never allow.

The distance to the chapel was about five hundred feet, so it only took Stephen a couple of minutes to reach it. When he arrived, however, he was surprised to see a flock of sheep grazing outside. With the surrounding area not providing good grassland, due to an abundance of olive trees, this didn't happen often. But, he had a vague idea why the sheep were out there. So, ignoring the flock's watchdog, which started barking at him, the priest stepped into the church.

The contrast to the intense sunlight was so overwhelming that it took Stephen a few seconds to adjust to the ill-lit interior of the chapel. All the while he thought: *Will today's surprises never cease?* As expected, the flock's shepherd was in there, sitting at a pew across the rood screen.

When the elderly man noticed the priest enter, he got to his feet and bowed with respect. Stephen then exhausted his knowledge of Greek by greeting the Cypriot shepherd and wishing him a good morning. The native reciprocated and went on to add something else. Stephen didn't understand what the shepherd said, so he just nodded and smiled. He lit a candle and stood reverently in front of the Virgin's icon, all the while waiting for the old man to get up and leave. But, the shepherd returned to his seat in silence. Apparently, his devotions were not over.

He's taking too long, the priest thought. *And this cylinder is burning another hole in my pocket.*

When a few minutes passed, and the native showed no signs of getting ready to go, Stephen decided he couldn't waste any more time. He nodded to the old man and stepped out of the chapel. He was wondering about what to do next, when, about fifty feet from the door, and a little to the right, he saw something interesting: the stone wall of a water well he knew was dried up.

Perhaps Aymon was correct about not placing the cylinder in the chapel. It attracts a lot of shepherds and villagers, who come here to worship all the time, Stephen thought. *This might be even better. With the well being dry no one will bother with it.*

Navigating his way around the grazing sheep, and ignoring the barking dog once again, the priest stepped over to the well. Its circular stone wall stood at almost two feet above the ground, yet the well's barren depth extended to several more. Stephen reached inside and actively began searching for loose stones, below ground level. When he found one large enough, he pried it out. But, before taking the cylinder out of his pocket he glanced at the chapel door. There was no sign of the shepherd coming out. He turned around and then looked in the direction of the Manor. Fortunately, the trees in the way hid him from the siege towers. No one could see him. So, he grabbed the cylinder and fitted it inside the hole. It was a perfect fit. Then, taking the loose stone he set it back into place.

As Stephen retraced his steps to the Manor, he was sweating again. Nevertheless, he did feel confident his mission had been a success.

✦ ✦ ✦

EVEN IF THE priest did have second thoughts about hiding the cylinder in the well, he wouldn't be able to do anything about it. Two days later, an order came from the governor: the Templar leaders were to be taken to the inland stronghold of Lefkara. It seems that Amaury de Lusignan had received information the Templars were planning to escape by hiring a Genoese ship.

As a result, Aymon d'Oiselay, Stephen de Safed, along with several others were moved to Lefkara. They never returned to Khirokitia.

HIRAM

Chapter 17

THEFT

Jerusalem
955 BCE

HIS KING'S LETTER had arrived the day before last. Hiram put off reading it, however, for two reasons: The first was that since this wasn't in reply to anything *he'd* written, it could only mean King Hiram wanted something—again. And royal wishes hadn't served the Master well for the past eleven years. All they had done was to keep him hostage in Jerusalem, and apart from his family. But, when Hiram woke up that day, and saw the scroll lying there, he realized he was just delaying the inevitable. So, he unrolled the parchment and began to read:

My dearest friend,

It is my sincere hope this finds you well.

I know the last thing you need at present is to hear from me. With the way your life has been, this past decade, you must dislike me a great deal by now. In my defense, though, everything I've asked you to do was simply to ensure Tyre's welfare and survival. Which I'm certain you acknowledge, or else you'd never have agreed to any of it. In fact, I am relying on your love for our city-state, once more, to help me in my latest predicament.

As you may remember, before leaving Tyre, I mentioned Solomon had suggested handing over a number of cities to us as extra payment, when the Temple would finish. It's been four years since it has, but he's been stalling the whole time. And as if this wasn't enough, my most recent intelligence suggests the cities he plans to give us are worthless. Therefore, after much reflection, I've reached the conclusion that Solomon won't reconsider unless we hold some sort of leverage over him.

This is why I need your help, my dear friend, yet again. You are the best suited for this particular task, so I'll come straight to the point. There is nothing the Israelites treasure more than their Ark of the Covenant. If you can remove it from the Temple, and transport it to Tyre, then we'll have all the leverage we require.

I realize what I'm asking is dangerous, but I have every confidence in your resourcefulness. And if you succeed, it will mean you'll be able to return home at once and be permanently reunited with your family. So there's a considerable incentive for you to go through with it. I just hope you decide to do this as soon as possible.

As always, I remain your trusting friend,
Hiram, King of Tyre.

The Master had to read it twice more if only to make sure he understood correctly. How could the king ask this of him? He was a builder, not a burglar. And what about the danger Solomon's armies posed? Was that no longer a factor? If stealing the Ark wouldn't provoke a Hebrew attack, Hiram didn't know what could. Then again, if he was successful, it would mean he'd finally be able to go home. And that was something Hiram never took lightly.

Nonetheless, there'd been a second reason why the Master put off reading his namesake's letter. Ever since he met with the Queen of Sheba, three nights back, Hiram was troubled. And that wasn't because he had feelings for her. On the contrary, it was because Solomon had threatened him to stay away from her—or else. The problem was that the queen wasn't aware of this fact. So, for two nights in a row, she'd sent her handmaiden over to his room, requesting his company. He respectfully declined both times, alleging fatigue, but Hiram was certain she'd persist. Therefore, in the midst of all this turmoil, the last thing he needed was to read yet another of his king's requests.

Now, though, after he'd plucked up the courage to read the parchment, Hiram started thinking: *This may be the solution to all my problems. Solomon's palace might take another decade to finish, which means I won't be able to see Tyre, or my family, until then. And that's assuming he doesn't come up with another project for me to start. No, I've been stranded here far too long. I have to do this and get out of Jerusalem.*

✝ ✝ ✝

THE MASTER DID not give any more thought to the matter—the day's work had been difficult and tiring as usual. Returning to his room at night, he'd just finished splashing water on his face, when he heard the sound of three faint knocks. Hiram wiped himself dry with a cloth and sighed. *She doesn't give up, does she?*

He walked over to the door and opened it, only to discover the queen had changed tactics. Instead of the handmaiden, Nikaula herself was standing there.

Hiram took a hesitant step back. "Your Grace!" he exclaimed, looking very surprised.

"You have been avoiding me, Master Binne," the queen said with a slight frown, as if scolding him. Then she flashed one of her brilliant smiles. "May I come in? Or is that too much to ask?"

She might as well. If nothing else, no one will spot her at my doorstep if she does, he reasoned. Aloud, though, he said, "Certainly, ma'am, do come inside."

As the queen stepped into the room, Hiram stuck his

head out. It was dark, but fortunately there was no sign of anyone lurking. He shut the door.

The Master offered Nikaula a chair and sat in the one across her. As always, she was dressed in a way which enhanced her beauty. She was wearing an ivory-colored satin robe with a gold belt around her waist—a perfect combination for her light olive-hued skin. And her hair was pulled up into a bun while long silver earrings hung down, highlighting her slender neck. Hiram had been caught so unawares that an awkward moment of silence passed between them. The queen decided to break it.

"I chose to come myself tonight, fearing that if I sent my girl over you'd only decline again," she said, looking at him intently. "Is King Solomon making you work too hard?"

Hiram was forced to look down. Her stunning green eyes were like fiery emeralds blazing their way through him. "No, it's the actual project that is demanding, ma'am. The faster I finish the king's palace, the sooner I can get back home to my wife and family."

Slowly raising his eyes, he realized that, once again, this wasn't something the queen wanted to hear. This time, though, it was she who looked down. "You must love your family very much."

"Yes, I do. It's what is most precious to me. And I would do nothing to risk my chances of being reunited with them."

The Queen of Sheba understood. Hiram's veiled warning that *she* might jeopardize that possibility for him made her realize he'd never be interested.

Nikaula sighed. "I see," she said, and rose to her feet. Hiram stood up as well. In an instant, though, her cheerless frown transformed into a gracious, regal smile. "While I'd love to ask you a few further questions about Tyre, I just realized how late it is. So, I shouldn't keep you from resting. Sleep well, Master Binne."

She headed toward the door. Before reaching it, however, the queen added, "Tomorrow evening King Solomon is hosting a state feast in my honor. I do hope I'll see you there."

Hiram cracked a grin as he opened the door for her. "I highly doubt it, Your Grace. The king may value my ability to build things for him, but he has yet to invite me to any state function."

The queen nodded, but before stepping out she lingered on the threshold. Turning around to face him a tear appeared in her eye, poised for release. "When you are reunited with your wife, please tell her from me that she's an extremely lucky woman." Nikaula then touched Hiram's arm for a second and walked away.

✚ ✚ ✚

THE NEXT DAY, much to his surprise, an invitation for that evening's state feast *did* arrive. Around mid-morning, a messenger ran up the new palace's building site to deliver it. When the Master read the note, the messenger asked him what his reply would be. It only took a few seconds for Hiram to say he would attend. He was curious as to why he'd been invited this time.

At dusk, with the workday finished, Hiram headed down to his room. He bathed, trimmed his beard, and shaved off the stubble above his upper lip. Then, after donning his finest Tyrian robe, Hiram made his way over to the Throne Room. When he stepped inside, the Master saw the normally empty hall filled with long tables and chairs. By his reckoning, there were enough to accommodate two thousand people—which was handy, since nearly half of them would be just Solomon's wives and concubines.

Hiram wanted to avoid sitting at one of the front tables where the queen could spot him. He was therefore in the process of searching for a suitable place at the back when a young slave boy came near. "Master Binne, the king requires your presence at his table," the boy said. He then pointed toward the golden platform at the end of the long hall. "Up there."

Even though this was also highly unexpected, there was no getting out of it. So, Hiram nodded to the boy, and started following him through the throng of people who'd gathered in the chamber. As they approached the dais, he noticed that the king's gold and ivory throne had been pulled back to accommodate a table on the platform. The lavish royal seat had then been placed at the table's center, with Solomon already sitting on it, facing the crowd. To his right were the Queen of Sheba and the kingdom's high priest, Jachin. Solomon's aid, Zabud, sat on his left, next to the commander of the armies. At the far left-hand edge of the table was Ahishar, the chief guard, while the chair on the opposite side was empty. Since all the other seats were occupied, Hiram correctly deduced it was intended for him.

Solomon saw him approaching and shouted, "Hurry up, Binne! You are keeping everyone waiting."

Hiram hastily ran up the platform's steps and bowed. "A thousand apologies, Your Majesty. I didn't know I was supposed to sit here."

"Well, you are. So, sit down," the king said, and with an annoyed flick of the wrist indicated the empty chair to his left.

After the Master sat, Solomon clapped his hands and servants started bringing food to their table, as well as to every other one in the hall. This made Hiram wonder: *That's strange... Was he waiting for me to begin the feast?* Nonetheless, it was one which truly lived up to its name. Among various other delicacies, there were roasted legs of lamb, platters of freshly baked bread, and a wide selection of marinated vegetables, all to be washed down with plentiful, sweet red wine. The Master noted to himself that the last time he ate so well was before he'd left Tyre.

While eating his meal, Hiram took extra care not to look in the queen's direction. Yet, out of the corner of his eye, he couldn't help but notice all the attention Solomon gave her: The king kept placing the choicest morsels of meat on her plate; whenever she took a sip, he immediately filled the queen's silver cup with more wine; and to top it all off, he constantly flattered her on how beautiful she looked that evening. The queen, in contrast, didn't respond. She would eat and drink whatever he served her, but other than that she said nothing to Solomon. *He's having a really hard time winning her over to himself,* Hiram thought. A brief, satisfied smirk made an appearance on his lips.

A few minutes later, Solomon clapped his hands again and a troupe of musicians appeared. After taking up positions in the vacant space in front of the dais, they began playing their instruments. And when the melody was in full swing, several scantily clad, barefoot girls ran in and started to dance. Swaying and spinning their nimble young bodies they soon had everyone's attention. So much so that people near the back of the hall stood up for a better view.

Hiram welcomed the distraction. At least now, he had something else to concentrate on aside from avoiding eye contact with the queen. But, when the music and dancing stopped, and the applause died down, he heard her speak to the king for the first time.

"Were these teenage dancers a few of your wives?" the queen asked, her tone oozing with reproach.

Solomon hesitated. "Why, yes... Did you not enjoy their dance?"

"I did. It's just that I believe a wife shouldn't be forced to put on such shameful displays. A wife ought to be treated with respect. She must be cherished," Nikaula said with conviction.

It was at that moment when Hiram's concentration failed him. Glancing briefly at her, for the first time that evening, Hiram realized she was staring back at him with an expression of wistful sadness. Solomon, though, intercepting her gaze whirled his head around to see who she was looking at with such intensity. The king's features hardened when he realized it was Hiram. Nonetheless, he glanced down at his plate, popped a morsel of meat into his mouth and chewed on it for a while. When he'd swallowed, Solomon looked into Hiram's eyes.

"Do you know why I keep the Temple unguarded, Binne?" the king asked.

All other conversations around the table stopped. Hiram shook his head, not knowing where Solomon was going with this. "No, my liege, I do not."

"Aside from the Ark of the Lord's Covenant, there's a great store of gold and precious gems in the Temple's Holy of Holies. Now, why would I leave all my kingdom's treasures there without someone to guard them?"

"I really can't say."

"Because the Ark will protect whatever's inside. Everybody in Jerusalem knows this. And that's what makes me confident no one would dare steal from the Temple," Solomon said. He smiled.

Hiram opened his mouth, but then chose not to speak.

"Let me tell you a true story," the king went on. Looking out of the corner of his eye, he wanted to make sure the queen followed the conversation. She was. "Long ago, when our Philistine enemies dared to take the Ark away from us, it wreaked so much havoc upon them that they were forced to return it. As a result, they delivered it to a village of ours, near the border. Those villagers, however, did not treat the Ark with respect. Instead, they opened it up to see what was inside. An action which naturally made God angry, and He did not take long to express His wrath: fifty thousand of them were struck down dead in an instant."

The Master's expression was skeptical.

"I see you don't believe me," Solomon said. "Well, then, let me give you another example. Many years later, my father was moving the Ark to Jerusalem. When one of the oxen pulling the cart stumbled, the Ark was in danger of falling off. A young man, Uzzah, who walked beside the cart, put his hands up to protect it; except he had no business touching the Ark, so the Lord killed him on the spot."

"But if God kills anyone who touches it, how were the

priests able to take the Ark into the Temple four years ago?" Hiram wondered.

Solomon was about to reply when the high priest spoke up. "Allow me to answer that, sire." The king gestured his permission, so Jachin went on. "First of all, the priests used the golden poles at its sides to carry it in. And secondly, even if they hadn't, the Ark would never have harmed them. By divine providence, it can sense who's allowed to touch, or move it, and who isn't. Is that not so, Your Majesty?"

"It certainly is, kohen. I couldn't have explained it better myself," Solomon said, nodding.

Hiram frowned. *This is very suspicious.* "Why are you telling me this, sire?"

"Oh, I just thought it might be an interesting fact for you to know," the king said, in a rather nonchalant manner. Then, turning to Nikaula—who had stayed silent all this time—he asked, "More wine, my dear?"

The next hour or so was uneventful. That is, until the Queen of Sheba thanked the king for his hospitality and excused herself: she was feeling tired. When Nikaula passed briefly in front of Hiram, neither he nor she risked glancing at each other again. He watched her, though, as she made her way to the exit. Escorted by Solomon, the crowds respectfully parted in silence to let them pass. Although her posture was upright and regal, as always, Hiram could not help but sense the queen was exceptionally sad. He felt sorry for her, but there was nothing he could do; his priorities were with his wife and family.

After Solomon saw Nikaula out, he returned to the dais. He remained silent until a few minutes later when he coughed a few times. And in what seemed like a pre-planned move, the very next instant, his chief of guards, the army general, and Jachin, all stood up in concert. The three men bowed to Solomon, bid him a good night and left.

Thinking it might be an opportunity for him to return to his room, Hiram also made to stand. But, as he was getting onto his feet, the king spoke. "Sit down, Binne. There's something we still need to discuss." Solomon's tone left no room for contradiction.

Hiram sat back down and looked over at Solomon and Zabud—the only ones remaining at the table. He wondered what the king wanted to talk about at such a late hour, but what Solomon uttered next was totally unexpected. "I want you to steal the Ark of the Covenant."

The king didn't even try lowering his voice as he said this. The commotion made by everyone in the hall was so loud that none of them could've overheard him.

Still, it took Hiram a few seconds to make certain he'd heard correctly. *Now both kings want me to steal the Ark? This is too much of a coincidence*, Hiram thought. "Why would you want me to do that?" he then asked aloud.

At that moment, Zabud attempted to whisper something into the king's ear, but Solomon shrugged him off. "No. This needs to be done, Zabud." Then, looking back at Hiram, the king replied, "You clearly didn't believe that the Ark can protect itself, as well as everything else in the Temple. This is your chance to prove me wrong."

"And if I refuse?"

The king had a sinister sneer on his face. "In that case, I shall have you executed."

Hiram's mouth was agape with astonishment. "What have I ever done to deserve this?" he asked, after taking a moment to collect himself.

"You disrespected me, and my nation's beliefs, in front of the Queen of Sheba."

"I merely expressed an opinion... a thought. There was no lack of respect intended, sire."

"Nevertheless, you will do this to prove your point," the king insisted.

Hiram knitted his brow. "But if what you believe is true, sire, then I shall die trying to steal the Ark. And if I refuse to do so, you will have me killed, anyway. You're not giving me much of a choice."

"Well, it's the only one available at the moment," Solomon said harshly. After saying that, though, his expression mellowed. "And just so I don't appear too heartless, I'll even give you an incentive. If you succeed in taking the Ark, I shall allow you to go home for a month. But, you must do this before the end of Sabbath, two nights from now."

Hiram's head was spinning. *Everything is happening too fast*, he thought.

The king spoke again. "And to guarantee that no man will stop you from going through with it, I'll even give you this." He took off his Ring and tossed it over to the Master. The silver Ring bounced off the table a couple of times before stopping in front of Hiram's hand. Solomon looked on as Hiram picked it up and scrutinized the six-pointed star engraving. "It was my father's, so take good care of it."

He continued, "The best time to do the deed will be tomorrow, just before dusk. If the Temple priests haven't left to start their observance of the Sabbath, by the moment you arrive, show them the Ring. Seeing it should convince them you have my permission to be there. And after everyone's gone, take the Ark somewhere safe... your room, perhaps. Then, if you're still alive after it's all over, send someone to bring me an acacia sprig. That way, I'll know you were successful, and we can put this entire business behind us."

The Master took a long moment considering everything. When he had, to the extent that he could, Hiram still remained puzzled about one issue. "I don't understand... Why should I dispatch a sprig of acacia?"

"Because it's symbolic. As you are probably aware, the Ark was constructed from acacia wood," Solomon replied with a satisfied smile. Hiram's question meant he'd agreed to do his bidding. "Go and rest now, Binne. You have a big day ahead of you tomorrow."

Hiram actually *didn't* know the Ark had been built with acacia wood. Nevertheless, he put Solomon's Ring into his pocket, bowed to the king and walked down the dais without saying another word. Solomon and Zabud watched him as he made his way out of the Throne Room.

The king turned to his aid. "This went better than I expected. Do you recognize the necessity of intercepting King Hiram's letter now?"

Zabud had a grave expression on his face. "I still feel this might be dangerous."

Solomon's eyes opened wide. "What are you saying, Zabud? Didn't you see the way the queen looks at him? Evidently, she has a bizarre fascination with this low-born Phoenician." The king shook his head. "No, unless Binne is discredited in her eyes, I'll have no chance of winning her over and persuading her to marry me. But when she finds out he attempted to steal the Ark of the Covenant—our nation's most prized possession—it will do just that. She was sitting right here when he heard everything inside the Temple is unguarded. So, it'd be no great leap for her to work out he decided to take advantage of that information." Solomon put a nut in his mouth and chewed. Looking closely at Zabud, he added, "Listen, the Phoenician was going to try to steal the Ark for his king, anyway. At least now, we'll know *when* he will be doing it, stop him from going ahead, *and* be able to take advantage."

"But what if something goes wrong?" Zabud persisted. "What if something happens to him? He still hasn't finished building the palace for you."

"Then, you must make sure those goons you've hired don't harm Hiram, or allow him to even touch the Ark. What instructions have you given them?"

Zabud took a deep breath. "It wasn't easy finding someone who'd be willing to ignore the inactivity of the Sabbath. More would've been preferable, but at least I found three. I told them that as of noon tomorrow they must keep a continuous watch outside the Temple. If at any time, before dusk, they spot Hiram and his men go in, they have to silently follow them inside. And before he and his crew get near the Ark, they are supposed to apprehend everyone and bring the Phoenician to you. Even though my men will be armed, I've warned them not to harm Hiram in any way."

Solomon nodded. "Good. I can take my Ring back from him when he's brought to me. Maybe I'll even add an extra charge that he stole that too. What happens, though, if Binne and his team decide to enter the Temple after dark, and your goons can't see them go in? Have you considered this?"

"Yes, of course. If no one enters before nightfall, their orders are to hide inside the Temple and wait for the Phoenician to arrive."

"Excellent." The king's smile widened. "You've done an outstanding job, Zabud. With a single operation, not one but two vexing problems will simultaneously be eliminated: King Hiram's plan of holding the Ark as leverage against me will be foiled; and, most importantly, Binne will be branded a thief in Nikaula's eyes, thus giving her no choice but to marry me."

"I still think we shouldn't underestimate his—."

"Stop worrying, old man," Solomon cut in, with a quick flick of the wrist. "Our plan is perfect. There's nothing Binne can do to upset it. Now, let's get ready."

✦ ✦ ✦

WHAT THE HEBREW king hadn't accounted for, though, was the existence of a secret crypt under the Temple.

The next morning, the Master rounded up his trusted assistants, Madal and Mattan. After revealing the contents of their king's letter, he also told them about Solomon's ultimatum.

Madal looked into Hiram's eyes. "If we go through with this, Master, it will mean we'll have to leave Jerusalem and abandon the palace project."

"I don't know about you, but I've had enough of this city. I am ready to go home," Hiram said, looking closely at them both.

Mattan nodded. "Whatever you decide, Master. We'll be with you, as always."

After Madal also nodded his agreement, Hiram smiled and thanked them. The Master then proceeded to unfold his plan. Finally, he revealed that a cart and horses would be waiting for them, well beyond the city walls, to transport them—and the precious cargo—to Tyre.

At high noon, the Master and his assistants made their way through the city's northern gate. Walking past the guard, Hiram told him they were going to inspect some of the ashlar stones that'd been delivered and stacked out there. It was the hottest hour of the day, so the guard indifferently waved them by. The three Phoenicians stepped over to the blocks and started patting on them, as if to check their suitability, while also keeping a close eye on the guard. When Hiram noticed him go into his little guardhouse, he gestured to the other two, and they all dashed to the foot of a nearby hill, unnoticed. On arrival, the Master sighed with relief when he realized the large boulder he'd put there was undisturbed. Moving it to one side, they crept into the space behind it. Hiram then produced a lamp from his satchel and lit it, just as the others were pushing the boulder back to seal the entrance. With the lamp being held against the darkness ahead, they saw the underground passageway the Master's men had carved many years earlier. It was an upsloping tunnel, with staves to support its roof, every few feet, while breasting boards blocked the soil from falling in, on all sides. Hiram was happy everything was intact.

"It's such a pity all of this hard work will have to be destroyed," he moaned after a moment. "Nonetheless, when we leave tonight, we'll have to collapse the staves and bring down all the boards behind us. Accessing the crypt through here must no longer be an option."

Both his assistants nodded as they started their trek up the tunnel. At about four feet wide and almost five at its highest points, this meant they had to walk hunched over most of the way. It was an arduous climb, taking them the better part of an hour to complete. Eventually, though, they saw the crypt's northern wall up ahead. Three feet from the ground there was a large square marble, which sealed a window-type opening on the wall. Hiram put his fingers through the hole at its center while the others pushed the marble slab in. When it gave way at last, he lowered it down gently and they all climbed into the crypt.

"Make yourselves comfortable. We'll be here for a few hours," the Master informed his men.

While Mattan and Madal were busy setting their satchels down, and lighting extra lamps, Hiram walked across to the other wall. It too had a window-like opening, with a marble slab to seal it shut. Tugging on the slab's handles, he brought it down and held out his lamp. He wanted to check everything was still in place. The narrow space outside the opening was shaped like a water well's shaft, extending all the way up to the Temple. Hiram stuck out his head and looked up as far as he could see. He was pleased: The shaft's walls, reinforced with a coat of gypsum mortar, had allowed very little soil to fall down into the pit, despite all the years; the wooden rungs nailed to the rock face across were undamaged; and the rope was exactly where he'd left it hanging.

Hiram sat down and grinned. He was feeling rather proud of himself. When King Hiram suggested he should construct an additional crypt, his namesake had never told him where to place it. But in the Master's mind it stood to reason that a secret crypt could only be useful if it were near the Temple. And from there it wasn't too much of a stretch to decide it should be connected to the part of the Temple which the Hebrews valued most: the Holy of Holies. Now, obviously, Hiram could never have foreseen his current predicament. And yet, it had made perfect sense to him, at the time, that there ought to be some way of accessing the crypt—preferably from beyond the city walls. So, thanks to his ability to plan ahead everything was now in place; even for an unexpected situation such as this. His smile widened.

✝ ✝ ✝

Time in the buried chamber passed slowly. After they ate from provisions they'd brought along, Hiram advised his assistants to get some sleep. The night would be long and tiring, and they would need the rest.

The Master, on the other hand, was too wound up for a nap. He was constantly thinking that in a few days—if all went well—he'd at last be reunited with his beloved wife and daughters. Not only that, but he would also get to meet his son and grandchildren for the first time. Images of Mirha, and everyone else, looking surprised as they'd see him in front of them all of a sudden, kept flooding his mind. He'd yearned for that moment for so long, that tears began to sting his eyes.

Hiram shook his head to fight back the tears. For those happy moments to materialize, everything had to go as planned. He needed to concentrate. In that subterranean crypt, there was no way by which to tell when the sun would set. So, he sat listening for any sounds coming from the Temple priests up above. Only when those stopped trickling down would it mean nightfall was approaching, and the priests had gone home.

After a long period passed without hearing anything, Hiram felt it was safe to go up. He shook his assistants' arms, and they groggily opened their eyes.

"It's time," he whispered. "We have to be very quiet, though. I think they've left, but someone might still be up there."

Clambering out of the crypt's opening, they stepped onto the wooden rungs and began their ascent. Hiram went first, holding a lamp to light the way. After he'd climbed about twenty feet, he glanced up and saw the brass bar and the large panel near it. Both were exactly as he'd left them. The bar kept a sizeable flagstone in the Holy of Holies' floor in place; and the board covered the base of a huge, seemingly structural, yet hollow column. This column contained enough loose earth to fill the shaft, and it was supposed to do just that whenever the rope attached to the panel's locks was pulled.

The Master listened intently for signs of the priests' presence before going up any further. He did so, however, not because there was any chance of someone being in the Holy of Holies. In truth, no person was allowed inside there: that privilege was reserved exclusively for the high priest, and only once a year at that. What did concern him, though, was whether anybody in the adjacent Holy Place of the Temple might hear noises coming from the Debir and raise an alarm.

After he felt confident no priest remained in any part of the Temple, Hiram passed his lamp down to Madal. He then moved the brass bar to one side, and lifted the hefty flagstone up, setting it against the wall. He emerged into the Holy of Holies, through that large gap in its northeastern corner, and offered a helping hand to Madal. When Mattan also climbed through, they all looked around the golden chamber, in wonder. They hadn't been in there since the Temple had been completed four years earlier. Still, it was a sight to behold. The walls, the ceiling, the floor—everything—was covered with gilded gold. Towering above Hiram and his assistants were the two cherubim statues, whose massive wings spanned the entire width of the Debir. And under them, the golden coffer so many venerated and desired: the Ark of the Covenant.

For a moment, Hiram became distracted by a few chests he'd noticed stacked up against the rear wall. When he turned his gaze back, though, he saw that Madal was about to place his hand on the Ark.

"No, stop!" he whispered roughly.

Madal's hand froze in mid-air, while his face registered a puzzled look.

The Master felt angry with himself for allowing Solomon's stories to affect him. Still, the excuse he gave for his outburst did sound rather weak. "I wanted to be the first to touch it."

Madal shrugged and walked away. He so blindingly trusted Hiram that the only thought to cross his mind was that for sure there was a good reason.

Hiram stepped over to the Ark of the Covenant. He then cautiously placed his hand on its Mercy Seat: the space on the Ark's lid between the two kneeling, winged cherubs. At first, he felt nothing. After a second or two, though, he sensed a slight vibration, and an eerie humming sound. The Master swiftly withdrew his hand. Both sensations stopped.

"Did you hear that?" he whispered.

Mattan and Madal looked at each other. "Hear what, Master?" Mattan whispered back.

"Never mind," he replied. Encouraged by the fact that at least no bolt of lightning had struck him down yet, Hiram touched the Ark again. He left his hand there longer this time, but nothing happened. He was relieved. *My imagination's probably playing tricks on me.*

Realizing valuable time had been wasted, he snapped out of his reverie and decided what to do next. After he and Madal tested the Ark's weight, Hiram confirmed it was too heavy for any one of them to carry alone. So, the only solution available was to tie the Ark and lower it down through the floor hole. While Madal went to fetch the ropes, Hiram and Mattan removed the poles from the Ark's sides. They'd need them later to transport it through the tunnel.

Once the Ark and the poles were safely lowered down, and placed inside the crypt, the Master glanced back at the chests he'd noticed earlier. All five were overflowing with gold and gems. When both of his assistants climbed back up into the Holy of Holies, Hiram looked at them with a mischievous little smile. "I think we should take our king an extra prize. Tie these chests up so that we can lower them down too." He chuckled. "I wish I could see Solomon's face when he finds out his treasure has also disappeared."

They were all in the crypt after the last chest had been lowered and brought in. And while Madal and Mattan were busy placing the poles on the Ark's sides, Hiram suddenly remembered there was something he still needed to do. After lighting a candle, he rushed over to his satchel and grabbed an item from inside. "You finish up," he told them. "I forgot to leave this up there."

He was halfway out the crypt's window-like opening, when Madal looked up and asked, "What is that, Master?"

Hiram smiled. "It's a sprig of acacia. When Solomon sees it, he'll know who took everything. In any case, I'll explain later. I won't be long." And in an afterthought, he added, "When I return, we'll pull on the rope to fill the shaft and seal this window. So get ready."

After saying that, the Master climbed up into the Holy of Holies again. He set the candle down and walked over to where the Ark used to be. After placing the acacia sprig on the floor, between the massive cherubim statues, he stood there for a few seconds. Thinking about the expression of disbelief King Solomon would have made him chuckle.

Then, Hiram heard the noise.

Complete silence had prevailed in the Temple up to that point. So, to hear something crash onto the Holy Place's floor all of a sudden, a few feet beyond the partition, startled him. He swiftly turned his gaze to the hole in the northeastern corner—the one he'd climbed through only a moment ago. *Maybe I should just go down and ignore this*, he thought at first. But that wasn't who Hiram was. His innate curiosity demanded he should find out the cause of the disturbance. The Master, therefore, had no choice but to step over to the corner, and instead of going through the gap and down to safety, he pulled the bar back into place and used the flagstone to seal the opening shut—just in case.

He then reached into his pocket, retrieved Solomon's Ring, and placed it onto his finger. Hiram had neglected to tell his assistants about the Ring because he was certain he'd never need it. Now, though, it might come in handy.

Taking a deep breath to fortify himself, Hiram cautiously opened the inwardly folding doors—which separated the Holy of Holies from the rest of the Temple—just a little...

Chapter 18

PAPYRUS

Tyre
954 BCE

KING HIRAM WAS seated at his usual spot around the center table when an aid stepped into the Council Room. Walking over, the man held out a papyrus scroll. "This just came from Jerusalem, sire. It's addressed to you."

The king took it, broke the seal, and unrolled the sheet. After throwing a quick glance at its contents, he looked up at his aid and said, "Thank you. You may go." Hiram had expected that some sort of reaction would arrive—sooner or later—and it was not one he'd been looking forward to. So, he wanted to be alone while reading what the papyrus had to say:

To Hiram, King of Tyre,
Greetings.
I must begin this note, my brother, by confessing how much your response to the twenty cities I handed over has saddened me. Clearly you do not feel they constitute adequate repayment, but insisting they are worthless, and calling them the 'Land of Cabul' is a bit excessive don't you

think? Not that I would have done anything different, mind you, had I known of your reaction beforehand. And the reason is simple: you owe me a great deal more than I do you at the moment.

But allow me to be more specific. Your little stunt with Binne has cost me the loss of my kingdom's entire treasury in gold and precious gems, the Ark of the Covenant, as well as—and perhaps more importantly—the Queen of Sheba. Her infatuation with him was so great that when she heard of Binne's disappearance, not only did she not stop to even consider my marriage proposal, she and her entourage headed back to their kingdom the very same day. Apparently, the news distressed the queen so much she did not wish to carry on with the original plan of continuing their journey to your city.

Do not get the wrong impression though. The notion of using the Ark as leverage against my giving you inferior cities is understandable; in your position, I probably would've done the same. However, I regret to inform you that the result of your ill-conceived plan is contrary to the one you'd hoped for: I no longer care the Ark of the Covenant is in your possession.

I'm sure you and Binne are having a good laugh at my expense right now, as you read this, but it is important I make a few things clear. I may have tricked my people into believing the cloud of smoke, during the Temple's dedication, was Yahweh himself, but that was merely an act of political expediency on my part: I needed them to accept I was his chosen vessel. At the time, there was never any doubt in my mind he existed, or that he's as powerful as everyone believes. And I was certain Yahweh would know I meant no disrespect by demonstrating in such a fashion that he favored me. After all, it was a state of affairs he himself is supposed to have decreed. Nevertheless, the fact that Hiram was able to steal the Ark of the Covenant so easily, and get away with it, threw my entire belief system out of the window. If I'd accepted the gods many of my wives have been urging me to place my faith in, Binne wouldn't have escaped unpunished. Even your own gods, Astarte and Moloch, would probably have handled the situation better than this nonexistent Yahweh.

On the other hand, the men my aid hired to make sure nothing bad happened never stopped insisting that Hiram was dead. Upon discovering the Ark was gone, they claimed one of them killed him—in the heat of the moment, by accident—but alas before he revealed the secret of the Ark's location. And I was convinced Binne had taken it, not them, because of the sprig of acacia which was on the floor of the Holy of Holies; no one else could've possibly known the connection. Then, as the three ruffians, fearing for their lives, fled and went into hiding after that Sabbath, it took my guards almost a week to find them. And when they did and were brought before me, the fools had the audacity to repeat those lies to my face. After finding no body, though, or any traces of blood inside the Temple, their story was a bit hard to swallow. I therefore had them executed in such horrific ways, so as to set an example to anyone who might even think of not carrying out his duty to me: The first I had his throat cut open; the second his heart pulled out; and the third one disemboweled. Up to their dying breaths all three persisted in their deceit—and complicity in Binne's escape—crying out that he was truly dead.

So, as you can see, brother, the fact you possess the Ark is of no consequence to me anymore. Actually, I ask neither for its return, nor Hiram's. He has taught my own builders so much over the years that they should be able to complete my palace in a satisfactory manner. Therefore, I have no need of him any longer. What I do need from you, however, is sixscore talents of gold, to be delivered by the next full moon. That should be an amount sufficient enough to cover all my losses. And if you do not, you will realize how strong and capable my armies and chariots still are. They have not plundered, pillaged or raped in quite a while now, so it would be a pity for you to allow them to commit such atrocities upon your city.

Although it is true that my personal faith in Yahweh has been shattered, my people continue to believe in him. Consequently, I shall consider using some of your gold to construct a replica of the Ark. If I do, the Commandment Tablets and other items I took from the original will be placed in there. My aid, Zabud, feared something might go wrong and urged me to remove them, as a precaution. To be honest with you, this has been his only solid piece of advice in quite a long time.

And in case you are wondering, I do not worry I've disclosed all this information. Knowing the penchant you Phoenicians have for secrecy, I feel confident none of it will ever leave Tyre.

In closing, I shall be expecting your gold to be delivered by the next full moon. And after we have put this unfortunate business behind us, perhaps we can form a partnership for future commercial ventures together. I am certain both of our kingdoms would benefit from such a relationship.

I remain, as always,
Solomon, King of all Israelites.

The Tyrian king looked up from the papyrus, amazed. *Incredible! He actually believes Hiram is still alive.* A moment later, however, a tear streaked down his cheek. He really missed his friend. *And I am to blame for his doom. I'm the one who delivered him into that madman's hands.*

King Hiram began to weep.

Although Solomon was convinced nothing would ever be heard outside Tyre, much of what the papyrus contained did. Transmitted through oral stories Phoenician parents educated their children with, throughout the eons, a couple of its points even reached our modern era, ultimately finding their way into Freemasonry. The first consisted of the ways with which Hiram's murderers were executed: they gave inspiration for the Penal Sign each Masonic Degree uses. And the other is included in the Master Mason raising ritual, with the widespread mention (and in some jurisdictions, the actual use) of an acacia sprig at Hiram Abiff's initial, makeshift grave.

GEORGE

CHAPTER 19

NORTH

Larnaca, Cyprus
February 11, 2014 CE

GEORGE MAKRIDES TURNED the silver ring again around in his palm. He'd spent the last half hour scrutinizing and thinking about it. With thick band walls and a broad bezel, it was a sturdy piece of jewelry. And just by a simple inspection, anyone could appreciate how ancient it was: the ring's multiple scratches and markings bore witness to that. What made it stand out, though, was the Star of David engraving which protruded from its top. George grinned. *So, that's why the Templars chose the Square and Compass as their main Masonic symbol. One has only to add two horizontal lines for a crude Star-of-David shape to appear. This design must've been very important to them.*

When he and Alex returned from Khirokitia they googled the term, *Star of David*, only to find it yielded millions of results. However, the very first entry had a link to yet another webpage which piqued their interest. It spoke about the *Seal of Solomon*: a signet ring allegedly belonging to none other than the Biblical Jewish king. And that was not all. Apparently, it was also an item steeped in bizarre medieval stories and occult traditions. Alex was deliriously happy after reading that. He loved everything to do with the arcane.

I always suspected the Knights Templar were behind Freemasonry's creation. And everyone knows how central Solomon's Temple is for the Masons. But for this to go all the way back to the time of Solomon himself, now that's something I never expected, George marveled. *How did the Templars get their hands on it? And what's this ring's connection to the parchment and the Templar treasure?*

His train of thought was interrupted by the sound of keys on the door outside. Losing no time, he slipped the ring into his pocket. Joanna was about to step into the apartment, and he didn't want her to see it. In fact, George had yet to tell her anything about what he and Alex discovered. And he wasn't planning to, either. From everything he'd read, there was a looming possibility of danger involved for anyone trying to find that hidden treasure. So, Makrides felt he must shield her from harm.

George put on his most innocent, welcoming smile as she stepped in. "You're home early!"

Joanna sighed as she set her keys down. "Stella is sick. So, the doctor asked me to cover her night shift tomorrow, and let me leave ahead of time." But when she came closer and noticed the TV wasn't turned on, she frowned. "What are you doing?"

"Just thinking."

"You've been doing a lot of that lately," she said in a concerned tone. "Are you still worried about Alex?"

Relieved not to be grilled about his actual thoughts, George nodded. "Yes. But I'm sure he'll be okay. He has another job interview tomorrow."

After Alex's bank decided to cut costs, it had to let many of its employees go. Unfortunately, one of those who found himself unemployed all of a sudden was Alex. Ever since that day, two weeks back, he was extremely worried and depressed over the bleak financial situation in which he'd soon find himself. The severance pay they gave him wasn't a great deal. It was just enough to tide him over for a couple of months.

"He's a smart fellow, he'll find something else, for sure," Joanna said in a confident tone. But Makrides looked distracted again, so she asked, "Is that all that's bothering you?"

"Nothing a juicy kiss of yours won't fix," George said with a smile. He then opened his arms wide, and she fell into them.

✝ ✝ ✝

Larnaca, Cyprus
February 12, 2014 CE

THE FOLLOWING AFTERNOON the two friends met at a coffee shop. And with Alex being fussy about spending money, George promised it would be his treat.

"How'd your meeting go?" he asked.

"Not very well, I'm afraid," Alex said after a sorrowful sigh, looking down. "I can't say I blame them, though—I was the one who asked for the interview in the first place. It seems the economy is still in such a lousy state nobody is hiring." He then brought his eyes up and chuckled in a self-mocking manner. "If anyone told me, two months ago, that the only way to fix my financial situation was to find ancient treasure, I'd call him crazy."

"We'll get there, I'm sure," Makrides said, trying to cheer his friend up.

Alex shook his head vigorously. "But it's been almost a month now, George, and we're nowhere near to cracking that bloody code. There are just too many variables. It's like trying to play Mastermind without being given any clues whatsoever."

Alex's frustration wasn't groundless. Early on, they'd discovered that setting up the right Decryption Key—which would help them assign the correct letter to each symbol—wasn't as straightforward as they thought it would be. Many factors were involved: A Key might consist of a single hash sign (**#**), and one **X** figure, whereby the entire alphabet would fit into their partitions in pairs. Or, it might be composed of two hash signs and two **X**s, with a solitary letter being set into each of the compartments (just like the one they found on the website). In both cases, though, the second identical symbol would have a dot in the middle to differentiate it. But where things really got haywire, was *how* to place the letters into the **#** and **X** segments, to begin with. In the hash's case, they might be placed in a left-to-right manner, or up to down. And as for filling in the **X** quadrants—after choosing the correct starting point, out of four available—that could be done in a clockwise, an anticlockwise, or any number of other ways.

George took a sip of coffee. "I've been telling you. It's not the tons of combinations which are to blame. The software you wrote took care of that."

"Then why are we only getting gibberish? We haven't found a single identifiable word—in *any* language!" He shook his head again in frustration. "No, there must be something we've overlooked."

"I still feel the answer is in the improvement the Templars introduced to their encryption system. You know, the one I read about where they gave their customers a codeword, consisting of unique letters, and built it into the—"

"But I've taken this into consideration and included a relevant option in the app and... and nothing!" Alex cut in, irritated.

"That's because we haven't found the right word yet," Makrides said in a soothing tone. He looked down at his phone where an image of the ancient parchment was displayed. "It's as if someone is calling out to us from centuries past to solve this puzzle," he mumbled, concentrating his gaze on the photo. Then, Makrides recited the first line's translation from memory, "*'Bronze erected wind chill it feels.'*

This Latin phrase has been bugging me from the beginning. There's no way whoever wrote the parchment would've included it—and on the top line at that—if it didn't serve a purpose. And as I've told you time and time again, what it points at *must* be in the Masonic rituals somewhere."

Alex knit his brow in reflection. "Well, our Lodge doesn't meet again this month. But the Greek one has a meeting tonight... if you want to go."

George nodded. "Yeah, that might be a good idea. The Greeks have slightly different ceremonies than ours, so it might be helpful."

They both took sips of coffee and remained silent for a while, lost in their own thoughts. Then, Alex's eyes lit up. "What do you think the Templars hid? The Holy Grail perhaps?"

"No, that's just Hollywood, sensationalist talk. Frankly, I don't believe it ever existed," Makrides said, shaking his head. "No, whatever they found must've been something to do with the First Temple: *Solomon's* Temple. And *it* had nothing to do with Christ's era—that Temple had been destroyed and replaced by then. The only truly valuable item at its time was the Ark of the Covenant." Then it dawned on him. "Come to think of it..." George said as his voice trailed off. "This has always puzzled me. Did you know the United Grand Lodge of England has the Ark on its coat of arms?" Not waiting for his friend to reply he continued, energized by the thought. "I mean, here's an item which isn't mentioned in *any* of the three Degree rituals. Yet, it's on the Grand Lodge's seal? What's it doing there?"

"That's probably due to the Royal Arch Degrees of the York Rite," Alex replied matter-of-factly. "They're all under its jurisdiction."

When George looked back at him with a baffled expression, Alex felt pleased to be familiar with something his know-it-all friend wasn't. "One of our Lodge brothers even told me, after a few too many drinks one night, that during his initiation into the York Rite's top Degree he supposedly 'found' the Ark of the Covenant in some ruins."

"This is brilliant!" George exclaimed. "Why haven't you told me any of this before?"

Shrugging his shoulders, Alex replied, "I guess because it never came up." He then frowned, picked up his phone and started to tap and swipe.

Makrides watched him, puzzled. "What are you doing?"

Alex didn't reply, but continued to stare at the screen as he swiped and typed. A few moments later, though, after waves of disappointment washed over his face, Alex responded. "I thought the word 'Ark' might be our answer. So, I ran the app and entered the letters A, R and K into the Key's first three positions."

"And?"

"And nothing. It's still gibberish. I even tried A, R, C and H—just like the Grand Lodge spells it—but nothing meaningful comes out either."

"I could've told you 'Ark' isn't our word," George said.

"Why not?"

"Because it satisfies none of the clues in the Latin phrase: the Ark of the Covenant wasn't made of bronze, and it had nothing to do with feeling cold."

After nodding a few times, Alex then looked into his friend's eyes and smiled. "Although it'd be perfect if that's what the Templars hid. It would bring in a pretty penny for sure."

What's this now? George thought, frowning. "How do you mean?"

"Just think of it: if we found the Ark, we could start a bidding war. *Everyone* would want to own it. I'm sure the Israelis wouldn't mind paying top dollar to get their hands on it again. We'd be rich!"

Makrides took a deep breath. "No, Alex... we would either be in jail or dead." And taking advantage of the brief silence Alex's stunned gaze provided, he explained. "To dig up ancient relics and sell them, without handing them over to the proper authorities, is a crime. Not to mention a relic such as this: the Ark of the Covenant is potential dynamite. Revealing it will probably spark religious and political turmoil of gigantic proportions. Even real wars, not just bidding ones, might break out because of it. If we're still alive by the time they do, that is."

"Then why are we doing all this, if not for the money?" Alex asked. He had a strange look on his face.

"I sympathize with your current tight spot, man, but to be honest with you, I'm just doing this out of curiosity. Ever since I was initiated, I've always wanted to find out what Freemasonry was all about. Remember?"

All of a sudden, Alex exploded. "Well, I am *not!*" he shouted, and banged his fist on the table. He looked furious.

A couple sitting nearby, having heard the commotion, turned around to see what the fuss was about. Although also startled by Alex's violent reaction, Makrides glanced at them and grinned innocently as if to reassure everything was okay.

But, Alex ranted on, in an equally harsh tone. "I'm not doing this out of curiosity, George. And I certainly don't have your luxury for intellectual pursuits at the moment. So, if we do find something, we're selling—period. My survival depends on it. Don't mess this up for me, I'm warning you!"

"Okay, okay, relax," George told him. "Before we get there, though, a lot has to happen. First, we have to break the code. Then, we have to find *where* they stashed it—that is, *if* the parchment points to anything hidden. And if it does, we don't know for certain what the Templars stashed away, do we? It could be something else entirely and not a treasure trove... *or* the Ark. For instance, it might be the Templar Archives everyone thinks are lost. So, let's take this one step at a time. We'll go to the meeting tonight and see what happens from there. Okay?"

Alex seemed to be calming down. "Yeah, you're right. Look, I'm sorry for yelling at you. It's just that—"

"I know," Makrides cut in, patting him on the shoulder. "You have too much on your mind right now. I understand."

After George paid the bill, they got up to leave. All the

while, however, he was thinking: *I've never seen Alex in such a state before. He must be really stressed out to shout at me like that. And if we do find anything, he might get us into a lot of trouble. So maybe it's best if I don't discuss this with him—for the time being, at least.*

✝ ✝ ✝

THE GREEK LODGE'S meeting that evening had more Masons present than usual. The main item on their agenda was a First Degree initiation, and apparently the candidate's father, who was a longstanding member, convinced a few others to attend as well, in order to honor him and his son.

George and Alex, after donning their Master Mason aprons, stepped into the Temple and sat in the appropriate rows of seats to the south before the meeting began. Earlier, to allow him to detect if something important would be mentioned during the ceremony, Makrides had bought a booklet containing the entire ritual. And he followed it all the way through, but didn't notice anything significant. Aside from a few unfamiliar, archaic Greek words, nothing else triggered his curiosity, or fit what the parchment's Latin phrase described.

The initiation was now at the point where the new Mason had just reaffirmed his oath. And after the Worshipful Master 'dubbed' him with a sword, he gave instructions for the neophyte to be led to stand between the two bronze-colored columns at the western entrance. Then, the presiding Lodge Master asked a Past Master sitting nearby to deliver the Degree's lecture. Dutifully acknowledging the request, the Past Master walked down the steps of the East and soon arrived in front of his new brother.

Since this part of the ceremony wasn't transcribed in the booklet, George stuck his finger into the pages and closed it. There was no choice now but to listen carefully to what would be said.

The Past Master first explained to the neophyte that the

purpose of the lecture was to show how a Lodge must be properly *'tyled'*—which means, making sure only Masons are present at meetings. Towards this, he added, "With certain actions and words you shall learn tonight, you'll be able to convince any Lodge you may happen to visit in the future, that you are a true Freemason."

He then proceeded to instruct the new member on how to execute and cut the Sign of the Degree. Next, he taught him how to perform the secret handshake and the proper way to utter the Sacred Word, *Boaz*. And after they'd practiced the handshake, the Past Master pointed to one of the tall columns, which was to the novice's left: it had a large silver 'B' on it. He said, "The first letter of the Sacred Word is carved on the *North* Pillar of the Temple. And it was the name of one of the two bronze columns which graced the entrance to King Solomon's Temple, where..."

George's eyes widened. *That's it!* In fact, he was so startled by what he'd just heard that three things happened simultaneously: He gasped; released his hold on the booklet, causing it to fall to the floor; and stopped listening to what the Past Master went on with.

Alex, who sat next to him, noticed his friend's unexpected reactions and whispered, "Are you okay?"

"I'm fine," Makrides whispered back. "It's just... a sudden itch. There must be a mosquito in here." He bent over, picked up the booklet and pretended to scratch his itching leg.

Frowning for a second, Alex then focused his attention back on the Past Master and what he was saying.

After the meeting was over, Pavlos, their mutual friend, invited them both to stay for the Festive Board which was to follow. Alex accepted, but George declined, claiming he was too tired and that he had an equally difficult schedule the following day. Wishing them a good night, he got into his car and headed home.

Two hours later, he was driving to Khirokitia.

☩ ☩ ☩

GEORGE HAD BEEN digging for quite some time. And even though the night was chilly—with three degrees Celsius and a mild northern wind blowing—he was sweating from all the exertion. After he'd already dug four feet down, he abruptly stood up and looked around: he thought he sensed something. The almost full moon that night did cast some light on the surrounding grounds, but George couldn't see or hear anything out of the ordinary. *It must've been my imagination*, he decided. So, he shrugged, bent over and continued to dig.

But the very next moment, when he heard Alex's voice all of a sudden, it made him jump. "I was sure I'd find you here. By the way, you're trespassing in someone's private property you know!"

Makrides straightened up and watched as Alex stepped through the gap he'd cut in the wire fence a couple of hours earlier—the fence separating the grove of olive trees they were in from the church of *'Our Lady of the Field.'*

"My, my, you have been busy tonight: Cutting fences... digging... a regular commando. You told me you had a difficult day tomorrow, but I didn't realize it started *this* early," Alex said, with no small trace of sarcasm. He stopped walking about ten feet from the hole in the ground, his right side turned slightly back.

"Listen, Alex, I can expl—" George began to say.

"*It's a sudden itch*," Alex cut in, making air quotes with his fingers. "That little performance of yours kept bothering me all the way through dinner. And it wouldn't let me go to sleep when I got home either. Then it dawned on me you must've spotted something important during the ceremony. When I called your apartment and there was no answer, and your mobile was switched off as well, I felt sure you'd be here. Just for the sake of curiosity, what was it?"

Even by the faint light the moon gave off, George could

tell that Alex looked furious. So, he hopped out of the hole, sat on the ground, and began explaining. "After the Past Master said that 'Boaz' was the name of their Temple's *North* pillar, everything made sense. And when I checked the Lodge's orientation next—Worshipful Master in the east, entrance at west—I confirmed that *Boaz* is indeed the northern one of those two columns. However, that's not how we, in the English Lodge, know it. We were just told that Boaz stood outside on the *left-hand* side of King Solomon's Temple. When I got home, I looked this up in the Old Testament and sure enough Boaz *is* described as being on the left side of the Temple's façade. Which means it was originally positioned to the *south*."

Alex still appeared livid, but when his brow creased for an instant, about to form a puzzled frown, George went on. He felt glad to bring his friend up to speed, even under such circumstances. "Okay, let me make things simpler for you. The way Solomon's Temple was oriented back in its day, was the exact opposite from a Lodge's orientation now. The Biblical Temple had its entrance in the east, while the reverse is true of a modern Lodge. The only possible explanation for this must be that when the fugitive Templars set up the first Lodges, they were still so obsessed with the Holy Land in the east they made that cardinal point all important. Now in no way is this standardized around the world, but if one enters certain French, Greek, or other European Lodges today—as if stepping into the Temple of Solomon itself, except from the west—one finds the Boaz pillar on the left, as it should be, only it's to the North. I've even seen a French website describe this layout as the 'Antient,' or 'Ancient' one. But, apparently someone saw fit to muddle this in British Lodges, just like they omitted the names of Hiram's killers. Still, they weren't able to stop it all from finding its way to Continental Europe and America. Leaving that aside, though, the important question is this: what does everyone living in the Northern Hemisphere associate the north with?"

Alex hesitated a little before replying. "With... feeling cold?"

"Exactly."

"So the Latin phrase, *'Bronze erected wind chill it feels,'* pointed to the word *Boaz*?"

"Yes, it did. By several Masonic standards, the most famous northern, bronze column," George said with a proud smile. "So, I opened the app, adjusted it for a single grid-and-X Key, inserted B, O, A, and Z into its first four positions and the text just flowed. Mind you, it was written in Latin, not English. I guess the assumption must've been that Latin was a safer bet to use, if you're going to address someone in the future. Anyway, with the help of an online translator and a few educated guesses I managed to translate the parchment's entire contents. It took me almost two hours to do so."

"And what does it say?"

George stuck a hand inside the front pocket of his quilted jacket. And after producing a couple of folded pages, an instant later, he held them out in Alex's direction. "Here, take it."

Not making a move to step closer, though, Alex suggested, "You'd better read that to me. Your flashlight is right there."

Puzzled a bit by this, but going along with the request all the same, Makrides lit the pages and began reading:

"This is the year of our Lord thirteen eighty two.

"Dear Brother, and I address you as such because none other than a dedicated member of our Brotherhood would have been capable of getting this far. Congratulations. Your Lodge must be truly blessed to have a scholar such as yourself in its ranks. The fact you were able to deduce the Word necessary to read this is no small feat. And beforehand, you had correctly detected the hiding place of the copper tube containing this page; which, for your information, was not the location of the original directions left behind. Initially, that was the water well across from the Chapel's entrance.

But even at the time it was feared to be a risky choice, due to the dilapidated state the well was in. I therefore instructed a ship captain, also a Brother of ours, to substitute the first parchment with this, and relocate the tube inside, to the rood of the Church. That you are now reading these lines must mean he will be successful. Once again, please accept my sincerest compliments on all your intellectual achievements..."

"I imagine you must've felt quite proud of yourself after reading that," Alex interrupted, with a sneer.

"Yes, I did." George smiled, deciding to bypass Alex's scornful remark. He continued to read:

"Obviously, I am not aware of the era this finds you in, or the particular circumstances of it. But be wary. Everything our founding Brothers entrusted to the crypt's safety, they did so consciously and with a great deal of forethought. Especially as concerns their most prized item, which I am certain you will recognize as soon as you come upon it.

"The underground crypt has a doorway facing south. Its location is thirty normal paces north, upon exiting the Chapel's western entrance, and about five feet down.

"In closing, I would once again urge you to exercise extreme caution on revealing the crypt's contents. If there are forces still powerful in your world, which might harm our Brotherhood because of them, then my advice would be to keep everything hidden. Still, you have proven your mettle, my Brother, therefore I feel confident in entrusting this matter to you and your sound judgement.

"Kissing you thrice on the cheeks in spirit, I remain yours in Brotherhood, Anthony Norridge."

As soon as Alex had heard all that, he turned his head back and looked at the church. "Umm... I don't know if you've noticed this, *mate*, but if you draw a straight line from here, through the opening in the fence, and to the 'Panayia tou Kambou' chapel, your starting point is a bit off."

"Yeah, as a matter of fact, I do know," George replied. "I read somewhere that the church was expanded about 15 feet to the west at the beginning of the 16th century. So, the original entrance this guy Norridge talks about—whoever *he* was—must've been at the point where the lower part of the roof starts in the middle there." He pointed towards it.

Alex glanced at the chapel behind him. "I hope you're right."

"Indeed, I believe I am," Makrides said as he hopped back into the hole. And after making a relevant gesture, he added, "Come on. There's an extra shovel here you can use."

But when Alex made no move to step forward, George straightened up after a second and looked at him questioningly.

"I'm not here to help you dig."

"Then why are you here?"

"I came to make sure you didn't take off with all the loot and leave me in the lurch," Alex replied. His expression turned sinister before he added, "As no doubt your intention was all along. You weren't going to tell me anything, if I didn't happen to *'pass by'* here tonight, were you?"

"Listen, man, we've talked about this," George said. "The only thing I want—"

"Yes, we *have* talked about it," Alex interrupted, in an angry tone. "And obviously you don't understand how desperate I am now." After saying that—as if to emphasize his point—Alex's hands reached back and produced a G3 assault rifle. It had been hanging on a sling, behind his right shoulder all the time. He pointed the firearm menacingly in George's direction.

Makrides gasped. *This is getting dangerous.* Then, chuckling nervously, he asked, "What are you doing, Alex? The National Guard issued those weapons to us reserves for safekeeping, and to keep them close by in case of war. They weren't meant to hold people at gunpoint for personal reasons. If you shoot me with it, I don't know on how many counts they'll send you to jail for."

"I'll just have to take my chances, won't I?" he replied

in an icy tone, the rifle firmly trained on George. "Now, get on with it: dig! And don't even *think* of shoveling dirt at my face. I've seen that movie."

Not wanting to aggravate the situation, Makrides said nothing. He reluctantly bent over and resumed digging.

A half an hour later, the pit was down by another foot: the grove's soil was soft, so it wasn't too much of a challenge. At some point, Alex had stepped closer. Still keeping the weapon pointed at George, he magnanimously agreed to assist him by lighting the hole in the ground with his own flashlight.

"What happened to the dogs?" Alex asked all of a sudden.

"Hmm?"

"This is the same olive grove across the way from the Templar Manor ruins, isn't it? There were two dogs barking and snarling at us when we came here the last time. What happened to them?"

He wants to be chatty now? George wondered. "I took care of them," he replied, almost in a grunt.

"How?"

Makrides straightened up and rubbed his aching back muscles. "We had a bunch of leftover meatballs in the fridge. So, I slipped a couple of sleeping pills into each. When I arrived here, and was about to cut the wire fence, the mutts ran over and growled at me. But when I threw a few meatball treats inside, and the dogs ate them, they started getting woozy. They're over there," he said, pointing in the distance. "Should stay sound asleep till noon, I reckon."

"You're *so* clever!" Alex sneered again, with a great deal of sarcasm.

"Not as clever as you are, it seems. I'm the one still digging," George countered. He then picked up his shovel and thrust it angrily into the ground, at the northernmost location of the pit. But it had only gone down a few inches when he heard a grinding sound: the sort metal makes when scraping against stone. After throwing the meager amount of soil in his spade out of the hole, he poked the ground with his tool. It clinked. There was something solid underneath. Makrides let go of the shovel, knelt, and cleared a spot. The underlying surface felt like marble to his touch.

Having heard the noise, Alex now stood at the edge of the pit above. He shone his flashlight in. "Did you find something?"

Still groping around, Makrides replied, "I think I've reached the crypt's roof."

A few minutes later, after the area was cleared, they could see the southern edge of a marble surface almost dissecting the hole's round base. "The way into the crypt is probably six to seven feet down there," George said, standing on the marble top. He was pointing to the other half of the pit's bottom part still filled with soil.

"So?" Alex asked indifferently, shrugging his shoulders.

"So, I'm not going to be able to do it on my own. I am dead tired now as it is. Unless you pitch in, we're going to have to give up."

Alex went over his options for a moment. Not wanting to abandon the project, or to have the pit still open come morning, he agreed. "Okay. We can each take half hour shifts to dig. But don't get any ideas—the G3 stays by my side all the time."

They stuck to that schedule. And as the pit, on its southern side, dropped to lower and lower levels, the crypt's doorway was eventually revealed. Between two thick marble walls there was another slab, about three feet wide, positioned inside the structure. But being unable to push or slide it in, they continued digging.

It was around 5 a.m., two-and-a-half hours later, and on George's shift, when his spade hit upon something on the otherwise smooth entranceway. After clearing the soil, he saw a flat piece of metal, about four inches long, sticking out on the slab's right side. It was parallel to the ground.

Oh, they're good! he thought. *In positioning a handle about a foot above the crypt's base, they probably expected those digging would've given up by now.*

Noticing the lack of activity, Alex looked down, rifle in hand. "What's going on? Have you found a way in?"

"There seems to be a knob here."

"Well, try it. What are you waiting for?"

George looked up. "Don't you want to be the first to go through? I mean, you're the one obsessed with finding treasure."

"And have myself buried in there by you? I think not." Alex shook his head. "No, you go and describe what's inside."

"You've become completely deranged," George scoffed. He then knelt, grabbed onto the lever with both hands and said, "Okay, here goes." But even though he pulled it to one side, then the other, and tried pushing it in, with whatever strength he had left, the entryway slab wouldn't budge. While going through those motions, however, he noticed that the handle felt loose on its right side. So, Makrides decided to turn it. And during the process of turning the lever all the way up, until it stopped at a right angle to the ground, he heard sounds of metal objects disengaging inside. It was as if something had been released. Encouraged by this, Makrides then used the now upright handle again to slide the doorway to the left. It rumbled and began moving.

When the marble slab slid all the way behind the adjacent wall, it exposed the pitch-black darkness of the crypt's interior. And with George being crouched right outside, the rank and stale air trapped within for hundreds of years drifted out. But not even those unpleasant smells—or the fact his lifelong friend had transformed into a dangerous psychopath all of a sudden—were able to diminish the euphoria he felt just then. He'd been able to solve a centuries-old riddle, almost singlehandedly. Deciding to take a few seconds to relish that sense of triumph, Makrides made no move to step inside.

At the same time, Alex was already sitting on the pit's rim, facing north, his legs dangling down, with the riffle on his lap. "Come on, man, get in there. What are you doing?"

George stood up and switched on his flashlight. Inside the crypt, he noticed outlines of objects on both sides of a narrow corridor in the middle. Making his way through the doorway, he first had to step down an artificial ledge about a foot high: it was the distance the pit still needed to be dug out so as to level with the vault's floor. When he pointed his flashlight to the left, Makrides saw stacks of deep, open shelves lining the entire length of that side. And as those compartments rose all the way up to the crypt's ceiling, he saw they were crammed with so many scrolls, vellum pages and bound parchment books that the shelves sagged under their weight. George was now halfway in the almost ten-foot wide, ten-foot long and seven-foot high chamber.

"I think we've found the lost Templar Archives," he shouted, barely able to contain his enthusiasm.

Alex's voice drifted in. "What makes you so sure?"

"Most of the pages here have a red cross stamped on them. They *must've* belonged to the Templars."

"Okay, what else is in there?"

As he turned his flashlight to the right, George saw more objects stacked up against the back wall, though not all the way to the top. These, however, were hidden from sight beneath canvas tarpaulins. Deciding to check them out later, he continued his rightward rotation. But when the flashlight beamed on another item there, it made him jump.

"Whoa!" he exclaimed and took a quick step back, slamming into the shelves behind him.

"What's happened?" Alex shouted down.

The sudden shock, combined with the stale air inside the vault was making it difficult for George to breathe. So after rushing to the doorway, he took several rapid gulps of much-needed fresh air. Looking up at Alex, after a moment, he said, in rapid gasps, "There seems to be a dead guy's head in there."

"What? Just the head? Whose is it?"

"How the hell should I know?" Makrides yelled. "Identifying ancient embalmed heads, and especially if they're enclosed in silver casings, is not exactly my area of expertise."

"Okay, okay, take it easy," Alex said in a calming voice. "So besides the head, and the Templar Archives, what else is inside?"

After taking a few more deep breaths, George glanced up again. "There's a lot of stuff concealed under canvasses. So, I don't know what they contain."

"Well, don't you think we should uncover them?" Alex's tone was dripping with sarcasm.

George nodded and headed back into the crypt. Spotting a large, also covered, object next to the doorway on the right, he decided to start with that. If it concealed any unpleasant surprises as well, at least the exit was near. As he shone his flashlight on the item, though, to get a better look, he noticed the material covering it wasn't the rough, dark-colored canvasses the others had. On the contrary, it looked more akin to light-gray lace. This piqued his interest, so he started to remove it. And when the object was fully uncovered, George's eyes opened wide.

To be told that a wooden chest was discovered inside a secret, underground crypt wouldn't be much of a surprise to anybody. Finding one, though, covered in gold throughout, at those exact dimensions, and with two kneeling, opened-winged, golden angel statuettes on its lid, was just short of miraculous. This was indeed the long-lost Ark of the Covenant.

"We were right," George announced.

"About what?"

"The Ark is in here, after all."

"Really? Are you sure?"

"Pretty sure, yes."

"So it's true…" Alex said, his voice trailing off with wonder. "This must be what the Templars used to blackmail the Catholic Church with, back when they started, leaving the pope no choice but to make them rich and powerful. Just like that... whatchamacallit painter's Code movie said."

"No," George snapped. *Boy, he's so messed-up, he can't even think straight anymore.* Stepping to the doorway, he looked up and said, "The reason the Knights Templar hid the Ark down here must've been they never wanted anyone to know they had it—precisely as the parchment implies. And the fact the Church eventually colluded in destroying them, and gave all their property away, can only suggest the Templars never had anything against it in the first place. Moreover, the Church's relentless attacks on Freemasonry, later on, just prove all those conspiracy theories are utter bollocks."

This caused Alex to glance down in reflection for a moment. "Okay, whatever. Try lifting the Ark to see how heavy it is."

Makrides frowned. "We've discussed this, man. It's dangerous. We could get into a lot of trouble if we try to sell it. Listen, the Archives alone could fetch us a lot of money. If we sold them off, piece by piece, to history buffs and museums, I'm sure we'd make a bundle."

But Alex didn't seem to be listening. He merely lifted the rifle off his lap, put his finger on the trigger and pointed the weapon down on George. "Indulge me, would you?"

After glaring at him for a couple of seconds, Makrides sighed and stepped back into the crypt. He positioned himself in front of the four-foot-long Ark, bent over and opened his arms wide, getting ready to grab onto its sides.

Do not touch that!

George stood up and poked his head out of the doorway. "I wish you'd make up your mind. Do you want me to pick up the Ark to see how heavy it is, or not?"

"What are you talking about?" Alex shouted down. "I never said another word. Now, stop messing around and lift it up already!"

Extremely puzzled, and frowning, Makrides turned back to stare at the Ark.

You understood correctly, George. But what you thought you heard did not reach your brain via sound waves.

"This is it! I'm going nuts," Makrides whispered to himself. "I'm hearing voices in my head now."

You are not going insane, George Makrides, believe Me. This was the best way to reveal My Will to you. I know what your friend plans to do, nonetheless the Ark of the Covenant must never leave this crypt. The world is in a precarious state as is, without subjecting it to the added discord the Ark's discovery would bring about. Even without the Tablets of My Commandments inside, this coffer is a potent enough symbol in and of itself. Therefore, you have to choose: Do as I say and live, or try to move it and the both of you shall die. I always provide a choice.

Becoming impatient Alex yelled down, "Well? Is it too heavy?"

George staggered to the doorway. He stepped out of the crypt and chuckled nervously. "You're not going to believe this," he said, looking up. "But a voice in my head is telling me that if we try to move the Ark, we're going to die."

"That's it!" Alex howled. "I've had enough of this." And as he scrambled to his feet, he started struggling with the rifle's cocking handle. Desperately trying to pull it back, he wanted to force a cartridge into the firing chamber. George braced himself.

But Alex couldn't. The handle appeared to be stuck. Then, out of nowhere, a sudden, violent gust of air blew, sweeping him off his feet and landing him on his back. The weapon fell a few yards away.

In his mind, George knew he shouldn't be concerned, but he couldn't help it. "Are you okay?"

Alex groaned. "I can move my arms and legs, but for some reason, I'm not able to get up."

Tell him he is to stay there for a short while, the Voice said.

After shouting that out, George stepped down into the crypt and glanced at the Ark, as if awaiting further instructions.

Before you go away, you and your friend will rebury this chamber, making sure no signs of it are left behind. And until the day you die, neither of you shall mention its existence, or this evening's events, to anyone.

George nodded his agreement. But encouraged by the reprieve they'd been granted, he dared to whisper a question. "Is it possible for us to take a few of these Templar documents to sell at least? I mean, Alex is in a financial pickle at the moment, so if he got something to show for tonight's efforts, I'm sure it would help guarantee his longterm silence."

No, that would only lead to questions about where you found them, and therefore compromise the crypt's location, the Voice replied. About a second later, though, another string of remarks filtered into George's brain. *You have a gentle heart, George Makrides. With everything your friend has put you through tonight, you not only seem to have forgiven him already, but you also care about his welfare. That is good. Forgiveness is good. So, in light of this you may each take a few of the items in the back.*

And when Makrides looked questioningly toward the covered objects on the rear wall, the Voice said: *Yes, there. They do no one any good by staying in here unused. You may take all you can carry on your persons. I would even suggest removing your coat, and help your friend take off his also, so you may use them as carriers.*

Still unsure about what this proposal entailed, nevertheless George removed his jacket. And while he was in the process of looking for a place to set it down—before going up to get Alex's overcoat—his eyes fell on the severed, mummified head. *I wonder who that belonged to,* he thought.

This is all that remains of my faithful servant, Hiram Binne. Or, as you know him, Hiram Abiff, the Voice revealed, in a rather sad tone. *He was the one who unwittingly did my bidding to wrest the Ark from Solomon's possession. I wished to test his faith with this, but Solomon failed. Alas, Hiram lost his life in the process.*

Startled though he was on hearing those revelations, George refrained from thinking or whispering anything else. Instead, he stepped through the crypt's entryway and clambered up, out of the pit.

Alex, lying flat on his back on the ground, lifted his head and stared at his friend as he emerged. "What's going on, George? What's happened to me? Why can't I budge from this spot?"

Setting his flashlight down, Makrides told him, "Calm down, Alex. If I said I can explain all this to you, I'd be lying. I have a feeling, though, that everything will be okay. Trust me. Now, take off your jacket."

"Why? What do you need it for?" But as he realized George had a determined look on his face, he voiced a different concern. "I can't move. How am I supposed to take it off?"

Yes, he can. Tell him to sit up.

"Just sit up," Makrides repeated.

And as Alex rose to an upright sitting position and started to remove his jacket, he smiled. "Well, look at that! I can move."

But as soon as he'd taken off his jacket and handed it to George, he attempted to stand up. Not only did he not succeed, but within the next two seconds his back was pinned to the ground again. It was as if a giant foot had stepped on Alex's chest, forcing him down. He coughed and groaned.

"Don't go anywhere," George shouted back as he scurried down into the pit.

"Couldn't if I tried," Alex said in a self-mocking tone.

Makrides entered the vault, with Alex's jacket in hand, and headed toward the rear wall. Halfway in, though, he stopped, turned and glanced at the Ark. "Thank you for sparing his life," he whispered. "I know he can be a pain at times, but he's my dearest friend and I love him." But when no reply came, he added, "And I promise that neither of us will say anything, to anyone, about the Ark, the crypt, or whatever happened tonight."

Amused chuckles echoed around in George's mind. *I know.*

✢ ✢ ✢

AFTER GEORGE SEALED the crypt's entrance, he hauled the two jackets onto the surface. And when he also brought the two shovels up, he noticed that Alex was no longer 'glued' to the ground. They each took a spade, and without exchanging a word started to shovel the mounds of earth back into the pit together.

An hour and a half later, the hole in the ground had disappeared, and they were both stomping the soil, trying to make the area look as inconspicuous as possible. Strangely enough, even though they'd spent many hours doing strenuous manual labor—especially George—neither of them felt tired. In fact, an unexplainable energy had fortified them to refill the pit, in record time.

Satisfied no one would be able to detect that a secret crypt remained underground they made their way toward the breach in the fence. Stepping through, onto the *'Panayia tou Kambou'* chapel's side, Makrides cut a piece of wire, brought the two fence parts together and began mending it. The sun had risen for quite some time now, and even though the new day was cloudy, there was no need for flashlights anymore.

Deciding to break their long, awkward silence, George said, "At least, now we know what was lost when Hiram was killed, don't we? And it certainly wasn't something trivial as a Masonic *Word*."

As he stood nearby, Alex replied with a simple, "Hmm?" His mind was apparently miles away. "What did you say?"

George repeated it, but after Alex's expression remained baffled, he realized: *Alex doesn't know what I heard, or that the severed, mummified head used to be Hiram's.* So, once he filled him in on everything the Voice said, including the part about Hiram and Solomon, he added, "Turns out what was really 'lost' was none other than the Ark of the Covenant itself."

Alex nodded several times, while hearing all that, but it was clear his thoughts remained elsewhere. "Listen, George," he said, looking deep into his friend's eyes, "I'm really sorry I was such a jerk. I don't know what came over me. And pointing a gun at you... Ugh, what was I thinking?" He sighed.

Makrides had just clasped the final part of the fence back together, and before Alex could add anything else, he patted his shoulder twice. "You were under a lot of stress these past few weeks. Granted, that wasn't the best way to handle the situation, but it all turned out all right."

"Thanks to you it did! If I'd had my way, we'd probably be lying dead right now—killed by a thunderbolt, or something."

"Just remember to never mention anything about all this, or that may still happen," George said and chuckled. "Now, let's get into our cars and finally warm up a bit. We'll speak again later."

They both lifted their jackets carefully off the ground, and made their way across the Church's courtyard, over to where their vehicles were parked. His car's electronic door lock beeped, but before stepping inside, Makrides extended a hand toward Alex, in a no-hard-feelings gesture. He didn't take it though. Instead, he let go of his jacket, reached forward and hugged George.

"You saved me, man. In more ways than one," Alex said, his voice breaking up a little, and squeezed tighter. "Thank you."

George also let his jacket fall down and used both hands to pat his friend on the back. "You're welcome."

After they got into their cars, the subsequent revving of the engines provided the only indication someone had been in the area, on that peaceful, chilly morning.

✝ ✝ ✝

IT WAS HALF past seven when George opened the door to his apartment. He picked up the jacket off the floor, placed the crook of his other arm beneath it—to make sure its contents wouldn't rip through—and walked in. But as soon as he'd taken a couple of steps he noticed that Joanna was asleep on the couch. She was still in her nurse's uniform.

Having heard the commotion, she groggily opened her eyes. "What time is it?"

When he told her, Joanna bolted up to a sitting position. "Where were you all night?"

Without replying, Makrides stepped over to the kitchen table and set the bulging jacket down. It clunked, but its contents remained concealed.

"When I finished my shift at five, and got home, you weren't here. And I couldn't reach you on your mobile either," she went on. "I was worried sick."

"Unfortunately, I can't tell you where I was."

Joanna got to her feet and moved toward him. "What do you mean you can't tell me? You were going to go to that Greek Lodge's meeting last night, weren't you? Is this another one of their Masonic cloak-and-dagger stunts?"

He was still shaking his head when she came near. "Wait a minute! This isn't the outfit you usually wear to the Lodge. And why are you so filthy? You're covered in dirt," Joanna exclaimed. She sniffed at him. "And you smell!"

George chuckled. "I wasn't with another woman, if that's what you're afraid of."

"Clearly," Joanna said, starting to sound angry. "I don't think you'd find many bimbos willing to roll around in the dirt with you. So, explain yourself, Mr. Makrides. Does this have something to do with the Lodge?"

"No," he replied. But after a second, he reconsidered. "Well... not entirely. In any case, I'm done with them. I know I told you I'd quit in January, but I'm only a month late. Freemasonry has given me all it could." He chuckled. "Literally. I won't be going there again, any time soon."

"And why are you so happy all of a sudden? You still haven't told me where you were all night... Well?"

He could think of only one way to put an end to those ceaseless questions. So, George reached over and peeled away the parts of his jacket covering what it contained. And when she saw, Joanna put both hands over her mouth to stifle a scream. Her eyes opened wide.

Inside the jacket were numerous small gold bars, and a large assortment of sizeable diamonds, rubies and emeralds. Along with an abundance of gold and silver coins, there were so many precious objects lying there, that all together they created a mound almost a foot high.

"I reckon there must be enough here for us to build two houses—*each.* Maybe more," George said. "And don't worry. Alex has about the same amount as well. He's set for life."

Joanna's eyes moved over to stare at him now with the same dumbfounded expression, her hands still firmly pressed over her mouth. A whisper drifted out from between her fingers, "Oh, my God!"

"I can never tell you where I was last night, or from where I got this, but I promise you we did nothing wrong or illegal."

She must have been satisfied with that explanation because Joanna sprang into action and threw her arms around him. "I've never been so happy for you to smell as awful as you do right now," she said in between short bursts of kisses.

"But I'm filthy... How can you stand kissing me?"

"I don't care," Joanna said and kept on smooching.

But when her emotional eruption subsided, she remained in his arms and asked in a small voice, "You swear you didn't steal this?"

"I do. We did not steal anything." And after he chuckled a few times, George added, "In fact... we actually had Permission."

THE END

APPENDIX

CHRONOLOGY OF EVENTS

c. 2750 BCE (BEFORE CURRENT ERA):
    The Phoenician city of Tyre is founded, according to Greek historian Herodotus.

966 BCE:
    Construction begins on the Temple of Solomon.

    [Author's Note: Although no empirical or archeological evidence exists about the Temple, other than what is written in the Old Testament, the conventional date for the start of Solomon's reign is circa 970 BCE. And given that the Old Testament (1 Kings 6:1) states that construction began four years after he assumed power, then 966 BCE is considered the most likely year for the Temple's beginning. This book treats these dates, as well as the existence of King Solomon and his builder, Hiram of Tyre, as historically true.]

959 BCE:
    Seven years later *(1 Kings 6:38)*, Solomon's Temple is completed and dedicated.

1095 CE (CURRENT ERA):
    Pope Urban II preaches the regaining of the Holy Land from the Seljuk Turks during the Council of Clermont. His sermon launches the era of the Crusades.

1099 CE:
    July 15: Those who participated in the First Crusade conquer Jerusalem. The result is a bloodbath for all Jews and Muslims still in the city.

1119 CE:
    During this year, the Order of the Knights Templar was founded. However, the exact date, reason, or how many men it originally consisted of are matters still widely debated.

Easter Sunday: Seven hundred Christian pilgrims, en route to the River Jordan, are attacked by bandits. Three hundred of them are massacred and a further sixty taken as slaves.

1129 CE:

January 13: The Papal Council of Troyes endorses the *Poor Fellow-Soldiers of Christ and of the Temple of Solomon,* under the active influence of Bernard, Abbot of Clairvaux (later canonized as Saint Bernard). The first articles of the Order's Latin Rule are drawn.

1139 CE:

The Papal Bull, *Omne Datum Optimum,* issued by Pope Innocent II, makes the Templar Order officially answerable only to the papacy and permits them to have their own class of priests and clerics.

1142 CE:

The Crac de l'Ospital castle is gifted to the Knights Hospitaller by Raymond II, Count of Tripoli.

1144 CE:

The Papal Bull, *Milites Templi,* issued by Pope Celestine II, confers further privileges upon the Templars.

1152 CE:

Raymond II, Count of Tripoli, is murdered by a Muslim sect called the Assassins. The reason for this unprecedented action has never been unraveled. However, after pursuing the culprits, the Knights Templar coerce the sect into paying their Order an annual tribute of two thousand bezants. It was an exorbitant amount for those times.

1173 CE:

An Assassin envoy is murdered by a group of Templars. Their reason for doing so remains a matter of speculation.

1174 CE:
>Amalric, King of Jerusalem, dies of dysentery—barely two months after the death of his arch Saracen enemy, Nur ad-Din.

1187 CE:
>Saladin defeats the Christian army at the Battle of Hattin and a few months later goes on to conquer Jerusalem.

1191 CE:
>Both Templar and Hospitaller Orders move their headquarters to Acre.
>
>The Templars buy the island of Cyprus from King Richard I, the Lionheart.

1192 CE:
>The Templars return the island to King Richard after an unsuccessful rebellion by the Cypriot natives. He then sells it to Guy de Lusignan, who becomes the first Latin King of Cyprus.

1285 CE:
>Philip IV, the Fair, is crowned King of France.

1291 CE:
>Acre, the last Christian stronghold in the Holy Land, is seized by the Sultan of Egypt.
>
>The Templars relocate their headquarters to Cyprus.

1307 CE:
>*October 13:* Templars throughout France are arrested on King Philip's orders—including the Grand Master, Jacques de Molay.

1308 CE:
>*May 6:* The Pope's orders to arrest the Templars reach Cyprus. The island's governor, Amaury de Lusignan, however, does not act on them until May 12.
>
>*June 1:* The Templars surrender to Amaury's forces in Limassol and most of them are taken to their Order's fortified manor at Khirokitia.

1309 CE:
Pope Clement V relocates the Holy See to the town of Avignon.

1310 CE:
May 12: Fifty-four Templars are burned at the stake as relapsed heretics.

Sometime between May and December: Pierre de Bologna, one of the principal defenders of the Order, disappears. He is never to be seen or heard of again.

1312 CE:
March 22: The Papal Bull, *Vox in Excelso*, issued by Pope Clement V, after the Council of Vienne, permanently dissolves the Order of the Knights Templar.

May: The next Papal Bull, *Ad Providam*, transfers all the Order's properties to the Order of the Hospitallers.

1314 CE:
March 18: Jacques de Molay, the last Templar Grand Master is burned at the stake in Paris.

1348 CE, June, to 1349 CE, December:
The Black Death, a bubonic plague pandemic, devastates Europe and the British Isles. Modern estimates on the number of deaths range from 40% to 60% of the entire population.

1381 CE:
May 30: The Peasant's Revolt begins in England.

June 4: The rebels gather at Bocking.

June 7: Wat Tyler (someone completely unknown up to then) is acknowledged as the rebel leader at Maidstone.

June 12: The insurgents arrive outside of London. John Ball gives a legendary sermon.

June 13: The rebels enter the city, unobstructed, and proceed to sack and pillage.

June 14: An insurgent force leisurely walks into the Tower of London (the drawbridge was down and the gate open) and proceeds to behead Archbishop Sudbury, along with Treasurer Robert Hales. Meanwhile, King Richard II meets the revolt leaders and agrees to the abolition of serfdom, along with other reforms.

June 15: Wat Tyler is murdered and beheaded, bringing the revolt to an end. The king revokes all concessions made.

c. 1390 CE:
The Regius Poem, the oldest of Freemasonry's Landmark documents, appears in England.

1571 CE:
The Templar Archives are believed to be destroyed by the Ottoman Turks when they conquer Cyprus.

1604 CE:
February: Alleged first meeting between Robert Catesby, Thomas Wintour and John Wright in Lambeth, London. They discussed Catesby's plan to blow up the king and all the lords of England at the next opening session of Parliament.

May 20: Catesby, Thomas Wintour, John Wright, Guy Fawkes and Thomas Percy meet at the Duck and Drake Inn, in London. They swear an oath of secrecy.

October: Robert Keyes is admitted to the group.

1605 CE:
March 25: By then, Robert Wintour, John Grant, and Christopher Wright were also involved in the Gunpowder Plot.

October 14: The last of the thirteen conspirators, Francis Tresham—a cousin of Robert Catesby—is recruited.

October 26: William Parker, 4th Baron Monteagle,

and Tresham's brother-in-law, receives an anonymous letter warning him to stay away from the opening session of Parliament on November 5. The letter's author is still a matter of conjecture.

November 4: Near midnight, Guy Fawkes is discovered and arrested in the undercroft beneath the House of Lords, alongside the 36 barrels of gunpowder he was guarding.

November 8: Catesby and three of the conspirators are killed by the local sheriff and his men at Holbeche House, in Staffordshire. They had fled there after the Plot was uncovered.

December 23: While a prisoner in the Tower of London, Francis Tresham dies, following a sudden deterioration of his health.

1606 CE:

January 30-31: All surviving plotters are hanged, drawn and quartered.

1717 CE:

February: Four London Lodges meet and decide to form the Grand Lodge of London and Westminster in June. In many accounts this meeting is stated to have taken place in 1716, but that is due to the fact that under the Julian calendar—still used in England at the time—New Year's Day was March 25.

June 24: The Premier Grand Lodge of England is formed under the initial name of *Grand Lodge of London & Westminster*.

1737 CE:

March 21: Chevalier Andrew Ramsay makes a famous oration at a Lodge in Paris, which in a vague way links Freemasonry to the Templars.

1738 CE:

April 28: The Papal Bull, *In Eminenti,* issued by Pope Clement XII, becomes the first in a long series of papal edicts to attack and condemn Freemasonry.

1751 CE:
>The Antient Grand Lodge of England, a rival Grand Lodge is formed in London. Its seal featured the Ark of the Covenant.

1813 CE:
>The two rival Grand Lodges amalgamate to constitute the United Grand Lodge of England. It remains Freemasonry's principal governing body in the U.K. to this day, and it too has the Ark of the Covenant on its Coat of Arms.

HISTORICAL PERSONS

(Taking part or mentioned—in chronological Order)

King Hiram: King of Phoenician Tyre, reigning from 980 to 947 BCE.

Hugh de Payns: Co-founder and First Grand Master of the Templar Order.

Godfrey de St. Omer: One of the original Knights Templar, as were also **Payns de Montdidier**, **Archambaud de St. Agnan** and **Geoffrey Bison**.

Bernard de Tramelay: Fourth Templar Grand Master (1151-53 CE).

Andre de Montbard: Fifth Templar Grand Master (1153-56 CE).

Warmund de Picquigny: Patriarch Archbishop of Jerusalem (1118-1128 CE).

Stephen de La Ferté: Patriarch Archbishop of Jerusalem (1128-1130 CE).

Odo de St Amand: Eighth Templar Grand Master (1171-1179 CE)

Villano Gaetani: Archbishop of Pisa (1146 - 1175 CE).

Amalric I: King of Jerusalem (1163 - 1174 CE).

Amaury de Nesle: Patriarch Archbishop of Jerusalem (1158-1180 CE).

William de Tyre: Bishop of Tyre, and historical chronicler of the Kingdom of Jerusalem.

Abdullah: An Assassin envoy.

Walter de Mesnil: Templar knight and murderer of Abdullah.

Rashid ad-Din Sinan: The Old Man of the Mountain and leader of the Assassins.

Peter (Pierre) de Bologna: Templar Ambassador to the Holy See, and one of its principal defenders after the arrests.

William de Grafton: Preceptor of Ribston and Yorkshire, England.

Jacques de Molay: Last Templar Grand Master.
Aymon d'Oiselay: Last Templar Marshall of Cyprus.
Stephen de Safed: Templar priest in Cyprus.
Amaury de Lusignan: The younger brother of King Henry II of Cyprus. Amaury forced his brother into exile, declaring himself the island's governor.
Raymond de Bentho: A knight charged with guarding the Templars at Khirokitia, Cyprus. Although initially hostile toward them, a miracle he believed took place, during mass one day, completely changed his point of view.
Peter Ysan: Another of the knights deputed to guard the Templars at Khirokitia.
Reynaud de Provins: Templar Preceptor of Orléans.
John Wycliffe: English philosopher and theologian. Those supporting his views on how the Catholic Church should be reformed were called the *Lollards*.
Wat Tyler: Leader of the Peasants' Revolt in 1381 CE. Other than his involvement in the Revolt nothing else is known about his life.
John Geoffrey: A bailiff of Brentwood.
Jack Straw: Wat Tyler's lieutenant.
John Wrawe: Chaplain and Revolt conspirator.
Sir Francis Bacon: English philosopher, statesman, scientist, and author.
Robert Catesby: Leader and mastermind of the infamous Gunpowder Plot.
Francis Tresham: Last of the Plot's thirteen conspirators.
Dr. Richard Foster: Physician of Francis Tresham.
William Parker: 13th Baron Morley and 4th Baron Monteagle, Francis Tresham's brother-in-law. His involvement was crucial in foiling the Gunpowder Plot.
Robert Cecil: 1st Earl of Salisbury, King James's Secretary of State and chief minister. He was Francis Bacon's cousin.
John Streete: The man who killed Robert Catesby and Thomas Percy, allegedly with a single shot.

- ***John Theophilus Desaguliers:*** A French-born member of the Royal Society and philosopher, who was also the Premier Grand Lodge of England's third Grand Master.
- ***Sir Christopher Wren:*** Noted astronomer, physicist, and member of the Royal Society. As an architect he was entrusted with rebuilding most of London's churches after the Great Fire of 1666 CE. St. Paul's Cathedral is considered his masterpiece.
- ***George Payne:*** The second Grand Master of the Premier Grand Lodge of England.
- ***Anthony Sayer:*** The first Grand Master of the Premier Grand Lodge of England.
- ***John Cordwell:*** City carpenter, and second Grand Senior Warden of the Premier Grand Lodge of England.
- ***Edward Strong:*** Master of the Worshipful Company of Masons.
- ***Andrew Michael Ramsay:*** Also known as Chevalier Ramsay, he was a Scot Freemason, who gave a famous oration at a French Lodge in March 1737.
- ***James Anderson:*** The author of the first Masonic book to be published, titled, *'The Constitutions of the Free-Masons.'*

ABOUT THE AUTHOR

Andreas Economou is a retired banker and a resident of Larnaca, Cyprus. After almost 30 years of 'slaving' in a bank, he now happily spends his days writing.

The more than two decades he used to be a Freemason gave him all the necessary inspiration to write **Templar Secrets**. And yes, in case you haven't already guessed it, he *is* the expelled Past Master of *Chapter 13*.

Feel free to contact him by email:
aeconomu@cytanet.com.cy.

Or, via his website at:
www.AEconomouAuthor.com.

If you've enjoyed this please leave a review.
Thank you.

Lightning Source UK Ltd.
Milton Keynes UK
UKHW041815210219
337795UK00001B/207/P